THE MIRACULOUS M... OF CLARA MARTINELLI

PETER HOWARD

Cover design by tatlin.net

Other books by Peter Howard

Other books include *The Certain Guilt of an Innocent Man*, a political thriller set in West Africa and London, and *The Best Guitarist in the World and Other Tales of the Unexpected*, a short story collection.

Dedicated to the Kogi of Columbia

There is no life without thought

*Our ancient experience confirms at every point that
everything is linked together, everything is inseparable.*

The Dalai Lama

PART ONE

THE DREAM OF CLARA MARTINELLI

I work solely because it is impossible for me to do anything else.

Alberto Giacometti, *Giacometti: A Biography* by James Lord

2013

1

Nepal

For the third day in a row the Samudran brother Rinzen was assigned the task of overseeing the cremation of an elder. Soon there would be no elders left, as those still alive were afflicted with the dreadful wasting disease and the treatments applied so far had failed even to alleviate the symptoms, let alone tackle the disease itself.

Rinzen paused at the monastery gates, thankful for the cool northerly breeze that brought hints of winter amid the flutter of maple leaves. He gazed out across the valley, a view of Nepal's mountains and forests that usually lifted his spirits and reinforced his commitment to his life's task. Today, the sight brought a sigh to his chest. Although he did not doubt his calling, the plague that had wiped out so many elders raised questions that were not the business of a mere brother; but still he failed to silence them. Questions like what would happen when there were no elders left, and who would ensure that Sarmand continued its work?

The male of a mating pair of black eagles called across the ravine; its voice, plaintive as a chanting elder, quivered on the gathering wind. No, Rinzen shouldn't think about these things, he should trust that his mentor, Elder Kwato, would guide him and his fellow brothers.

He shivered as he carried the pot containing the ashes of Elder Torma. What was he doing, dawdling to watch the birds and the change of seasons? He needed to relieve Amdong; the boy had already been in meditation for over eight hours, far longer than was expected of someone his age.

Without ceremony, Rinzen emptied the ashes into the Well of Life at the centre of the cloisters and hurried into the outer lobby of the temple. He opened the door to the inner temple and stood for a moment to let his eyes adjust to the dim light cast by ten oil lamps arranged in a circle on the floor around a wide, shallow bowl of water in the centre of the ten meditating brothers. Every Samudran ritual was performed in the presence of a bowl of water; the water represented the origin of all life, and the honouring and conservation of water in all its manifestations was at the heart of their philosophy.

Rinzen shivered again: any heat generated by the brothers' bodies rose the five or six metres into the polished plaster dome and out through air vents. The sound of his own breath pierced the silence; his heart boomed loud as a temple drum and yet no one stirred. Rinzen knew he had to make his interruption, had to relieve the boy, but this was not the way it was meant to be done: all ten should be relieved at once, that was the ritual. But there were barely enough seniors to maintain the trance and only one elder well enough to take the lead. Everyone knew this was too much of a strain and that something would have to be done.

Rinzen began the ritual he had performed two thousand times during the eight years he'd been a senior. He stood behind Amdong and tapped his index finger three times on the youngster's right shoulder. Amdong exhaled a long breath and slowly unwound from his cross-legged position until he stood in front of Rinzen. They bowed to each other and Rinzen lowered himself onto the meditation mat.

As he gazed at the water bowl his heartbeat slowed and all he could hear was the faint echo of his blood as it pulsed through his arteries. His mind, freed from the sounds of the outside world, turned its awareness to his toes, foot arches, heels, shins, knees and lifted away from his body as it reached his thighs. Bodyless, he observed the turning planet and joined the others as they massaged its bruises, eased its exhausted muscles, stretched its ligaments so the water readily flowed through its arteries and veins – cleaning, lubricating, repairing.

~

A week later, it was Rinzen whose meditation was broken, called to attend Elder Kwato, who had been afflicted during the session and had crawled from the temple like an injured dog.

The elder's eyes were closed, his breaths low and even, his brow relaxed. Tiny beads of perspiration gathered along his hairline, and Rinzen noticed, for the first time, several grey hairs. Elder Kwato had slept in this small room for over forty years, and yet there were few signs of his presence: two notebooks and the stub of a pencil lay next to a half-burned candle in the stone niche next to the bed. On the plain wooden desk by the window a handful of books, mostly on the subject of arboriculture, stood between bookends carved by Rinzen from offcuts of the chinar tree. Rinzen recalled how, when he'd first chiselled into the wood, he'd felt as though there were prisoners trapped inside waiting to be liberated. Sure enough, some weeks later, two golden eagles had magically emerged.

'Rinzen?'

'Yes, Master, I am here.'

'There is very little time.' Elder Kwato clasped Rinzen's hand. His grip was limp, his palm cold and damp.

'You must go to the monasteries at Qo and Barnang and ask them to send elders here to maintain the everlasting vigil, warn them about the wasting disease, but tell them that they will now be safe.' His eyelids opened to reveal dull pupils deep in watery sockets. 'Tell them that when Kwato, the last of the elders of Sarmand, has exhaled his final breath, there will no longer be a risk of infection. Tell them that if they do not come, the corner of the triangle that is Sarmand will cease to be and the earth will be endangered.'

'You want me to … leave Sarmand? And go so far – all the way to Qo, and then Barnang? But I am just a senior, Master, and I have never—'

Kwato turned his head to look at Rinzen. 'All is not well with the world. There is drought when there should be rain, heat when there should be cold, fruit when there should be flowers. Even the strongest trees groan in the night, bending and twisting under the weight of their own branches. The rivers of the world do not run free, their waters – the essence of life on earth, the life force of we Samudrans – are stagnant and polluted. Our meditations are fragmented and I fear that the axis of the earth has shifted.'

'The axis has shifted?' Rinzen's eyes widened as he tried to imagine what that meant.

'Rinzen, you will remember from your studies in astronomy and geography what is at stake here.'

Rinzen wracked his brain, recalled discussing a seemingly far-fetched hypothesis on the consequences of the polar ice caps melting; that eventually the weight of ice would be insufficient to stabilise the planet in its near upright position and the earth would tip onto its side, causing massive tidal waves, cataclysmic earthquakes, rendering entire continents uninhabitable. Was that what Elder Kwato was anticipating?

Rinzen gently squeezed the old man's hand, hoped for some response, willed him to show his former strength.

'Going out into the world might alarm you, Rinzen, but I would not ask you to do this if I did not think you were ready. You are as skilled as any elder, and although you will need all your strength, you will endure. You have mastered your spirit, trained your mind and body, and have grown into a man of good judgement and careful observation – skills you will need on your journey.' The old man's eyelids flickered, but he kept them open. 'Do not despair. From this parting we will take the same road, as ever. Take the volume of Ryōkan's poetry that is on my desk. In the library, in the wooden chest under the window, you will find a map of the way to Qo and Barnang.'

Rinzen knelt beside the bed, his face near his mentor's. The old man's lips were pale, his eyelids now closed and still, his breathing reduced to a whisper of air that barely stirred his fine nasal hair.

'I will do as you ask.' Rinzen clasped the cool, flaccid hand between both of his. 'And I promise you that although we are only seniors and juniors, we will maintain the vigil whatever the hardships.'

Rinzen fought back the tears. He could not imagine life at Sarmand without his mentor. For many years he had been tutored in the art of emotional control, and had learned to channel any tendency to self-indulgence into the life of duty to which he was committed. To weep, even over the loss of his mentor, would be a betrayal of Kwato's trust, a sign that he was not ready to assume the responsibilities entrusted to him. He leaned over the old man and kissed his forehead.

Rinzen sat on the stool beside Kwato's bed. With eyes closed, Kwato continued, his voice stronger, more urgent. 'On the far side of the world there is a tall mountain that rises from the seashore and disappears into the clouds. Those who live on the mountain have been there for countless generations: they have resisted invasions, rejected modernisation and remained true to their one task. They have always tended to the rivers that flow down their mountain. They care for the plants and animals, the birds and insects. And, like us, Rinzen, they see the interconnectedness of nature.'

Rinzen's hand jolted. 'These … mountain people, they enter the trance as we do? They work within the spirit of the earth as we do?' He had never imagined anyone but the Samudrans could do such a thing.

Kwato nodded. 'Few in our modern world have the mental focus to do as we do: to enter the spirit world and nurture it as a living reality, to support the planet and keep the world in balance.' He smiled faintly. 'So, you see, we are not alone in our work. Take comfort from knowing that these brothers exist, that the burden is not ours alone.'

'What are they called, these brothers across the world?'

Kwato's eyes opened. His last words were: 'They are called the Kogi.'

Rinzen read Ryōkan aloud. The light in the cell dimmed with each stanza, but the words shone on the page, his sole focus the spirit of Elder Kwato. He read in English, taught to him by Kwato so he could enjoy poetry and scholarly works from around the world. He read many poems, of wandering and loss, and of the importance of finding one's true nature.

If your heart is pure, then all things in your world are pure.
Abandon this fleeting world, abandon yourself,
Then the moon and flowers will guide you along the way.

In total darkness he read without seeing. He knew that Kwato was no longer breathing, that his heart had stopped, but Rinzen recited every poem in the book.

At dawn he covered the elder's face with the blanket, left the cell and was not surprised to see his friend Keung perched cross-legged on a stool outside the door. A short distance away, four seniors waited. They nodded to Rinzen, walked past him into the cell, and began the chant that would last another two days and nights until the spirit of Kwato had departed his body.

'Let's run,' Keung said.

'And jump,' Rinzen said.

Keung led the way along a track that followed the contours of the hill: his stride lengthened as the stiffness from a night of sitting unravelled. They branched onto the path towards the waterfall and overtook a herd of musk deer in full flight, darting amongst them, spurring them on; they leapt the waterfall pool and carried on up the hillside until the trees thinned to scrub, the scrub to bare rock, rust-coloured and textured like pumice, warm on the soles of their bare feet. They ran on, accelerating as the incline steepened, choosing their path by instinct and barely touching the ground. They leapt deep, wide ravines carved by ancient rivers, bounded from boulder to boulder across last winter's avalanche, and arrived at the summit calling Kwato's name.

The echo ricocheted around the valley.

2

London

Clara Martinelli awoke from a dream convinced that the only way to prevent the imminent death of her beloved mother was for her to play the harp without stopping. She needed to play her harp twenty-four hours a day, otherwise her mother would expire in the gruesome manner foretold in the dream.

She jolted upright and snapped open her eyes, heart pounding, sweat pouring from her scalp.

It wasn't just a dream; it was an omen.

She was so certain of this interpretation, it was as though she had already consulted a wise oracle, or an eminent psychoanalyst or the *Oxford Dictionary of Dreams* – if such a book existed.

As Clara shook her head to dislodge the image of her mother's distended, gaping mouth she saw her Lyon & Healy, the favourite of the five harps she owned, in its usual place next to the bedroom window of her London flat. She scrambled out of bed, sat on the stool and tilted the harp towards her. She loved the lustre of its elegant, fluted column, revelled in its bright, loud sound. It was the Lyon & Healy that had featured in her dream, and it was the Lyon & Healy that would save her mother.

She played softly so as not to disturb her lover Henry, splayed out on his back, unshaven and coated with pungent sweat from his late-night drinking session. She pressed her ear against the harp's soundbox and stroked the strings to the slow rhythm of Henry's soft snoring: an unusual duet, essentially soporific.

She closed her eyes to let the music vibrate unhindered through her naked body. The sounds entered her bloodstream, her nervous system; it was as though the harp were one of her limbs or vital organs. She had no inclination to play familiar pieces; instead, she plucked notes and chords that harmonised with her heartbeat and flowed with the blood pumping round her body; she played sequences that massaged her muscles and warmed her belly, and glissandos that made her ears smile.

Minutes or hours later she was jolted from her reverie.

'You rude woman!' Henry said, to which she retorted, as if rehearsed, 'As nature intended.' This stumped him for a second or two, but she could see only too clearly that he was aroused.

'I had this dream, a vision,' she said, to distract him. 'I was playing at the Wigmore Hall while my mother lay critically ill in a hospital bed. I finished the piece, stood to take a bow, and walked off stage. At that moment, Mother's mouth gaped open and out came a terrible gurgling sound.' She frowned at Henry. 'Her death rattle.'

'Sounds like one of your guilt trips.' Henry slumped back against the pillows. 'Yet another example of you seeking your mother's approval, intent on pleasing her with your six hours of practice a day, your balanced fresh fruit and veg diet, your eight hours of beauty sleep.'

Clara stared at him, said nothing. The cool wood of the harp's soundbox against her chest vibrated as she plucked the strings. She sought a melody that suited this mood, a tempo to prolong her sensuality, to keep her from slipping back into thinking, to stay in her body and out of her head. To experience the music was all she wanted, all she ever wanted. She let the vibrations course through her, improvised with her fingers, resisted the resonance of bass notes, prolonged the ascent to crescendo, built on the refrain until chord blended into chord, her fingers chasing the dance. She closed her eyes to shut out all but the music, and when she awoke, Henry was no longer in bed.

'Henry,' Clara called, 'are you still here?'

She glanced around the bedroom, checking if his clothes were still there, immediately noticed the alarm clock's digits – 9.10 – and lurched to her feet, staggered into the bathroom and turned on the shower.

Monday morning. Rehearsals at 10. What was she thinking, playing for so long? And why hadn't she heard the alarm?

She flipped the shower control to full cold and gasped as it smashed through her hair to her scalp and made her ears tingle. The distinctive opening notes of *Toccata and Fugue in D Minor*, the piece from her dream, blared in her brain and jolted her head from the flow of water; she slipped, but held her footing and saw again the ghoulish sight of her mother's head tilted backwards, her mouth stretched obscenely into a painful gape, the roaring rattle drowning out the water pounding on the glass screen. She shouted 'No! No! No!' to dispel the sight and sound of her dying mother, stuck her face under the gushing water and pressed her hands against the black and white tiles.

Why this dreadful nightmare of her two loves – mother and harp – entwined in a hellish dependency? It couldn't really be an omen, could it?

She forced herself to get dressed and rushed from the flat without breakfast.

Her hair was damp when she boarded the Tube train at Old Street, still damp as she marched along Kensington High Street at 10.05. As she entered the rehearsal room, the conductor of the Delphian Chamber Orchestra, Roland Peach, was finishing a sentence with the words '... concert at the Wigmore Hall.'

Of course, that's the connection … Silly damn dream.

'Ah, Ms Martinelli. Good of you to join us.'

Not a good sign, the 'Ms Martinelli'. 'Sorry I'm late, Roland.'

~

Remnants of the dream lingered through the morning rehearsal, but thankfully they were less distinct, less terrifying; a general feeling of unease and nervousness replaced the violent imagery and flashes of sound. It made her think though, made her realise how much she loved her mother, still needed her, still wanted her mother's daily input into her routine – even though she was now twenty-six years old and what they called a virtuoso. She was principal harpist with the orchestra, in demand for solo concerts, had her own flat in Shoreditch, even had a lover, but she still needed, still wanted, her mother.

During the afternoon session, as she looked away from Roland's baton and glimpsed his red socks, the dream crashed into reality and she was back at the Wigmore Hall: she saw the conductor's sweaty forehead, his shoes so highly polished they reflected the lights, his red socks …

She heard her name being called, far away, perhaps from another room or from outside the building – 'Clara? What's the matter?' – then a hand on her shoulder and Roland leaning over her, frowning.

'Yes,' she said, wondering why he'd walked into her dream.

'Why did you stop playing? Are you ill?'

~

Later, flat on her back on the living room floor, she replayed the events in the dream frame by frame and banished each in turn. Finally, she was able to convince herself that it was only a dream, a nasty, lucid dream; just a tangle of fears that had bubbled to the surface.

~

When her mother rang the doorbell at 9 the next morning, Clara had already showered, completed her stretch routine, breakfasted on granola and hot lemon with ginger, and was well into her warm-up schedule on the harp. She buzzed her in, left the flat door ajar, and resumed playing.

'Good morning, Clara,' Grace said. 'Careful not to slump.'

'Morning, Mother.' Clara pushed back her shoulders. Willingly. For once not the least bit irked by her mother's immediate criticism of her posture.

'You'll get backache if you sit like that, then before you know it, you'll have those migraines again.'

Clara looked away from her hands and disguised her close inspection of her mother's face with a smile. She certainly didn't look like someone who was about to rattle and die in a hospital bed. No sign of the dream-mother's deathly pallor, the stretched jaw, the wrinkled eye sockets. She looked so fit and well, more energetic and enthusiastic than she'd been in years, certainly not a woman for whom death was imminent. This might, in fact almost certainly did, have something to do with Grace's growing intimacy with Lawrence Greene, a relationship that had taken her mother ages to recognise for what it was – a love affair. During the past year or so Grace had mentioned going to the theatre with Lawrence, or out to dinner, and once on a day trip to Oxford, but when Clara teased her about her finally having found a man that could measure up to Clara's father, Grace had said she was talking nonsense. Recently, though, Grace's vehement denials had been replaced with a simple smile and a change of subject.

'You look radiant today, Mum.' Grace liked it when Clara called her Mum.

Her mother could boss her around all day today if she liked, and Clara wouldn't rise to it. She was fit and well, that was all that mattered. There were days when the neverending instructions and reminders – to do her exercises, to get those eight hours of sleep, above all to continue striving for perfection – made Clara snappy and tetchy, but today was different. Today Clara was full of appreciation for all the wonderful things about her loving, caring mum. Today she was all too aware that her professional success as a virtuoso harpist was in large part down to her mother. Grace had sacrificed a lot when Clara's father had died, taking over from him, the famous Sicilian baritone Ettorre Martinelli, responsibility for Clara's musical education. She remembered herself at seven years old, just days after her father had died: Grace was standing over her, making her redo a particularly difficult exercise on the harp, and they were both sobbing. But Grace wouldn't let up: 'We are both very sad, Clara, but your father wouldn't want that to stop you playing. We shall carry on as if he was still here. I will be tough on you now, like he used to be, even though it's hard for both of us. When it comes to the harp, we won't pussyfoot around, we won't worry about politeness. As your father used to say, we have one aim – perfection – and all the rest is nonsense.' Her mother had stayed true to her word and in the subsequent nineteen years hadn't stinted in her devotion.

Clara played on now, moved onto the cycle of fifths, while Grace went through to the open-plan living room/kitchen, no doubt to clean its already sparkling surfaces, tidy any wayward magazines into piles and sweep the oiled wood floor. All done silently, so as not to disturb the harpist's concentration.

Clara played the first of the concert pieces, *Asturias* by Albeniz. It sounded different on the Lyon & Healy, brighter

25

and louder than the Salvi she'd left at the rehearsal room. She loved both harps but went through phases of preferring one or the other, and right now the Lyon & Healy was her favourite. At the end of the piece, she shook out her arms, splayed her fingers and played it once more.

After she'd played it the third time, her mother glided into the bedroom with a cup of coffee. 'It sounds a bit flat in the middle. You are focusing on the piece, aren't you? Not daydreaming?'

Here we go, Clara thought. Nothing is ever quite good enough, is it. Don't rise to it. Smile, nod, sip the coffee.

'Perhaps the coffee will help liven it up.'

She stepped away from the harp. Maybe Mum is right, maybe I am playing badly. And I know why. 'I'm just going to walk around the flat, loosen up.'

As soon as she left the bedroom, an invisible weight lifted off her shoulders. Damn dream – she had to get some perspective. Maybe she should tell her mum about it, then she would talk her out of it. But it was so horrible. No, no point in worrying her with it. Pity she couldn't move the Salvi back and forth to rehearsals, at least until she'd forgotten that damned dream and the Lyon & Healy in it.

Clara stopped playing at noon, pulled on her trainers and, with Grace, went for a brisk walk. She resisted the temptation to go via Curtain Road and drop in on Henry at his furniture showroom. They'd agreed not to see each other during the week so that Clara could keep to her practice and rehearsal routine and get to bed early, but sometimes the gaps between weekends seemed to go on forever and she longed for Saturday nights, to be extracted from her insular world and lose herself in his swaggering presence.

As they walked through Mark Street Gardens, Grace said, 'What a lovely spring day. Isn't the cherry blossom gorgeous?'

'Wonderful.'

'If only the air was cleaner down here in Shoreditch. It can't be good for your health.'

'But I love it here, Mum and besides, Henry is just around the corner.'

'Well, it's your life, I suppose.'

'I'm sorry you have to come so far to see me, but we agreed that I needed a change from Crouch End.'

'Talking of travel, I know I promised I'd come over on Tuesdays, Thursdays and Saturdays while you're rehearsing on the other days, but I'm afraid I can't come next Tuesday.'

'Oh?' Clara said, but then immediately thought she sounded like a spoilt brat denied some treat. 'No problem, Mum. Are you doing something nice?' That sounded better; no hint of disappointment.

'Lawrence booked it ages ago. It's a special riverboat tour along the Thames – a lot of history, I expect, but he promised it wouldn't be too dry.'

'You mean washed down with champagne cocktails!'

'I didn't mean that! But who knows?' As she smiled, tiny lines appeared around the outer edges of her mouth and eyes, the only signs of ageing as far as Clara could tell. In fact, at fifty-two, Grace's figure was as slender as it was in the photos of her on her wedding day, aged twenty-four. She was stylish and neat, favouring tailored dresses with high necklines, usually in autumn tones to suit her short auburn hair, and she took good care of her fair complexion. No wonder Lawrence had stuck around.

'Well, have fun.' She didn't resent her mother's relationship with Lawrence, she deserved to be happy, but Clara did need her those three days a week. 'Think of me toiling away in my garret.'

'Your lovely flat is hardly a garret.'

They marched on to Bunhill Fields, then down to Finsbury Circus before zigzagging through the side streets to arrive in Phipp Street exactly half an hour after setting out.

Grace had prepared an avocado and rocket salad, and she opened a tub of her homemade hummus to go with the rye bread. When they'd finished eating, Grace looked at the clock and nodded at Clara – her cue to lie on her back for half an hour with an eyemask to rest her eyes. Then there were hand exercises and warm-up scales. Whether it was these familiar routines or simply the passage of time since the dream, Clara didn't know, but for the whole two hours of practice on the concert pieces she was immersed in the music and played at performance level. Even Grace was satisfied enough to nod and smile at her.

The afternoon ended with the usual hour of yoga, where Grace made sure Clara's postures were exactly as the teacher had instructed. She pushed and pulled her into position, counted through the holds, egged her on to feel the stretch, to breathe into her muscles, lubricate those joints and focus, focus, focus.

Afterwards, while Clara rested on the yoga mat, Grace put on her coat. 'I've left you a nice thick minestrone on the stove, darling. Don't go to bed too late, will you? See you on Thursday.'

Clara mumbled her goodbyes and kept her eyes closed, enjoying the warmth of the early evening sun on her eyelids. After a while, she got up and opened the wide patio door. As soon as she walked onto the balcony, she saw her neighbour, Gareth Fulbright, staring at her through his open door.

One of the negative aspects of living in a U-shaped building was the ease with which neighbours could look right into her bedroom and living room. Fulbright made no attempt to disguise his fascination with his neighbour, even though he'd confessed to Henry that harp music got on his nerves, so much so that he kept the windows closed when Clara practised. Fulbright smiled – or rather, he leered – and nodded his head. He was tall and thin, his back bent into a stoop, his elongated head twisted up from his neck so that he appeared to grovel, and Clara half expected to see him wring his grimy hands. As he ran his purple tongue across his thin lips, she shuddered at the image of a reptile in a man's clothing. Her instinct was to stick her tongue out at him, an impulse she resisted; she settled instead for a flick of her head and a rapid retreat.

Fulbright's prying eyes disturbed her, but she couldn't possibly close the curtains on such a beautiful blue April evening. Perhaps if she played a loud classical piece he would go out, or at least retreat from his living room. Until he did, she would have to stay near the wall, in the blind spot where he couldn't see her.

She left the door wide open and plucked the strings randomly, discordantly, but that soon proved unsustainable and she found herself lost amid the memories and melodies of 'My Way', with images of Fulbright's head bobbing tortoise-like on his scrawny neck giving way to visions of herself and Henry, fit and healthy, skiing through pristine pine forests at breakneck speed.

3

Nepal

Rinzen stood on top of the inner wall and looked down into the courtyard where the novices sat cross-legged, balanced on stone discs the size of his hand, some of the younger ones wobbling as they tried to stay steady. He and the other seniors could maintain that position – unwavering – for many hours, even when sitting on a thin wire stretched between temple poles, and one day the novices would be capable of similar feats. They had so much to learn, so many years of training, before they could take their place in the inner temple.

He turned away and walked along the wall as far as the gate tower; here the juniors, aged from twelve to nineteen, were jumping up the eighty steps that led from the outer to the inner gates. To graduate from novices to juniors, these boys had to reach mental and physical milestones, one of which was the ability to leap up the steps ten at a time. Novices started by jumping up two steps and remained on five for about a year. Juniors learned techniques to leap eleven, twelve, thirteen steps and so on until they could easily make twenty. Seniors overcame mental restrictions and learned to bound up forty steps in one leap and, without pausing, to make the second leap to the top of the eightieth step. At the point when they were admitted as elders, they had to be able to jump eighty steps with ease.

To reach each point on the leaping scale required absolute belief, an unlocking of the mind, a freeing of the imagination to allow the body to perform extraordinary deeds. This athletic prowess further tuned the brother's mind, and mental leaps soon took over from their physical manifestation.

Rinzen waited until it was Amdong's turn. He could tell by the grace with which the seventeen-year-old reached the top step in four bounds that he could easily manage greater leaps, but the youngster did not presume to exceed the target set by his instructor. Others in his age group took five or six leaps, on target to achieve jumps of twenty steps during their twentieth year.

Perhaps, Rinzen thought, Amdong could be made a senior two years early.

He jumped from the wall, walked around the temple to the cloisters, and sat on a wooden bench in the deep shadows, thankful to be alone. Kwato's words spiked in his mind: 'In the wooden chest under the window, you will find a map of the way to Qo and Barnang.' Could he do this? Just pass through the gates and walk for days in the unknown world? Apart from three visits in over twenty years to his parents' village less than a day's walk away, Rinzen had never ventured far from the monastery and the mountain above. He sprang to his feet and strode around the cloisters.

There were no more elders left.

He grabbed hold of the bar above his head with his right hand and lifted his body so that his arm was fully extended horizontally, in the position called 'Standing in the Sky'. He remembered the first time he'd seen Elder Kwato do this: back then, as a seven-year-old, he thought he must be dreaming. Even at that age he knew such a thing was impossible, but it wasn't long before he realised that the elders, and even the seniors, were capable of many impossible things. And soon he took his first steps along the path that led him to this moment, when Standing in the Sky seemed easy compared with the task he now faced. The training of his body and his mind had been incremental, a matter of concentration, of discipline, ultimately an act of faith in the wisdom of the elders. Now that there were no more elders, was it up to him to assume that role, to ensure that the training of novices and juniors proceeded correctly, to hold the company of seniors together, to make the right decisions to secure the future of Sarmand?

Rinzen dropped to the ground, lay on his back and gazed at the cloudless sky. Two hawks circled high above him. Elder Kwato said he had detected a shift in the axis of the earth. What did that mean? Did they need to intensify their meditation to reverse the shift? He should have asked him that one last question, but perhaps in his illness the great master himself had been unsure.

Rinzen found Keung in the seniors' garden, starting to practise Standing Still – probably the most demanding of all the exercises – and watched him from the gateway. Where Rinzen was lithe and slender, Keung was short and solid, with heavy, muscular limbs and the rugged facial features of a mountain man. But despite his tough-man physique, boxer's nose and prominent forehead, Keung was much more easygoing than the melancholic Rinzen; he was sanguine, with a quick, playful wit and an incisive mind.

Keung was capable of performing Standing Still for many hours, easily from dawn to dusk, but he no longer had time for long sessions. Standing Still sounded simple – and some of the juniors joked about how easy the seniors had it compared with the physical labours they endured – but required supreme concentration, or rather the absence of concentration. The practitioner had to empty his mind and train his body to soak up the fragrances all around him – from the earth, the plants, the air – so that even the most sensitive hunting dog would walk straight past him as though he were invisible. Which of course was one of the purposes of the training, to become invisible, to no longer be burdened by a physical body, to be present only as a spirit, a mindless, bodyless soul.

'You're waiting for me?' Keung said.

'It is the fourth day,' Rinzen said. 'We need to perform the funeral rites. And decide what to do now there are no elders left.'

Keung nodded. 'I know, I've thought about that. What do you think about making all of the older juniors into seniors? And maybe move up some novices? And you and I, perhaps Amal and Dachen, should assume the role of elders until help comes from Qo. We need —'

'Wait,' said Rinzen. 'Let's take one thing at a time. I agree we should advance the novices and juniors, but do we have the right to become elders? If Kwato thought so, he would have said.'

'I'm not saying that we would become elders, just perform their essential functions – teach the novices and juniors, lead the meditation – as Amal is right now.'

'Let's talk to all the seniors about it later.' Rinzen dropped his eyes. 'Keung, I'm afraid.'

'What, the fearless Rinzen? Never.' Keung put his hands on Rinzen's shoulders. 'I know how you feel about fear. As though your training has failed you, that fear is self-indulgent and therefore unacceptable. But this feeling you have is not fear, it is apprehension. The unknown lies before you, the gates to the world – closed for all these years – are about to open, and you have no choice but to pass through. All I know is that your mentor, the wise Elder Kwato, thought you were ready, so you need to trust in that.'

Rinzen placed his hands over Keung's arms and gripped them. He knew that Keung wanted to embolden him, but his friend's encouraging words did little to alleviate the overwhelming feeling that he was certainly not ready to venture out into the world, whatever Kwato might have said.

~

33

At noon, meditation was suspended and all the brothers – novices, juniors and seniors – assembled in the courtyard beside the outer temple. No one spoke, no one moved. Rinzen, Keung, Amal and Dachen carried the litter from Elder Kwato's cell into the courtyard, and led the procession out through the inner gates, down the eighty steps to the outer gates, and on into the forest. Many of the people from the nearest village – Sunkhani, about twenty kilometres away – had walked for many hours to pay their last respects to Elder Kwato, even though they knew they were not permitted to approach the pyre. The brothers heard them sing a song for those about to embark on a long journey, full of heartfelt wishes.

The bearers placed the litter on the ring of stones and joined the circle around the pyre. Rinzen focused on Kwato's body and spoke some farewell words. 'Death is the only certainty; it comes when it will and we welcome it ... Elder Kwato's spirit has flown above the mountain and shines down upon us.'

The sixteen seniors lit their torches, approached the pyre together and set it alight. Without further ceremony, without a tear shed, Keung led the procession back to the monastery, leaving Rinzen to watch over the cremation until the last ember lost its heat.

He sat on the ground upwind of the pyre, stared into the fire and recalled aspects of Kwato's life. This silent contemplation of an elder's time on earth was usually undertaken by a fellow elder, but now that there were no more elders, the task fell to him, the oldest of Kwato's pupils.

He pulled the blanket over his head. His eyes penetrated the hot centre of the fire, and he drifted into a reverie. He recalled Kwato's intellectual prowess, his brilliant ability to leave his opponents' arguments in a tangled mass of contradictions. As Rinzen knew from personal experience, he was motivated not by malice but by a fervent desire to help his fellow Samudrans achieve their potential. He had the highest expectations of those under his mentorship, the same standards he imposed on himself. He pulled you up after him – always encouraging, he set the bar higher and higher, higher than you ever thought possible until you found you had reached it.

Rinzen closed his eyes and travelled back to his first one to one lesson with Kwato. He had been so nervous it was all he could do to sit still, but the elder knew the best way to put a novice at ease was to tell him a story – *the* story – about the original Samudrans. As with all great stories, this one started with 'Once upon a time ...

During a long hard winter over a thousand years ago, six men were stranded in a hut in the high mountains. Night after night a storm raged, snowdrifts all but burying the hut, and soon they ran out of food and they were in danger of starving to death. One night, huddled around the dying embers of their small fire, the men took it in turns to describe the meal they would eat if they survived the winter. When it came to the turn of the leader, Jamyang, he placed a bowl of melted ice next to the fire and invited the others to focus on it, to together imagine a dish of rice and vegetables reflected in the water's surface. The group survived until the spring thaw, sustained only by the jointly imagined food. Realising the power of meditation, they swore allegiance to each other and called themselves the Samudrans, named after *Samudra*: the 'gathering together of the waters'. '

Rinzen remembered that Elder Kwato had paused at this point in the story, laughed his high laugh, and said, 'Be careful, Rinzen, if you keep your mouth wide open the flies will lay their eggs in your throat!'

Rinzen had been so obviously delighted with Kwato's story that when he became a senior, his mentor asked him to tell the story to some of the novices. He would always start the story as Kwato had, then go on to tell them that as the years passed the Samudrans experimented with the power of meditation in all spheres of life, developing a rigid physical and intellectual regime to accompany their practice. They found they could influence the ecology of the region, the country, the whole world.

They discovered they could harness the combined power of their minds to travel into the core of the earth, that they could remove obstructions, massage bruises and stretch ligaments to allow cleansing water to flow readily through arteries and veins. As the centuries passed, many more were inducted into the order, and the Samudrans realised their work had become essential to the health of the planet and its rotation in a steady state.

The novices never questioned whether Rinzen's story of the first Samudrans was a myth or historical fact, but none doubted that their work was essential. By the time they became seniors, Rinzen and Keung knew every detail of the annual winter celebration – the Origin – when all brothers from junior to elder trekked into the mountains and re-enacted the meditation on a bowl of melted ice, visualising a steaming bowl of rice and vegetables. It was tough going for some of the juniors, and Rinzen recalled his own difficulty focusing on the bowl while his body shook in the piercing icy wind.

An image of Elder Kwato at last year's celebration flashed through his mind: hatless and gloveless in the harshest winter for many years, the old man smiled as he focused on the melted ice and recited Jamyang's invitation to imagine food in its place. And sure enough, the water boiled, and when the steam cleared there was the sacred meal, almost impossible to resist.

No one had expected that to be Kwato's last Origin, or indeed the last Origin for every one of the elders; the devastating wasting disease had not yet come to Sarmand.

Rinzen stood up and used the metal rake to push the ashes into the centre of the pyre. He knew he should look upon Kwato's death as just part of the cycle of life, but how would he manage without him? How would Sarmand, indeed all the Samudrans manage? Kwato had been elected to the Samudran Supreme Council as soon as he became an elder. They rotated their meetings between the three monasteries – Sarmand, Barnang and Qo – and Rinzen had heard that Kwato's fellow councillors regarded him as the wisest and deferred to him on many occasions. His death was bound to be a great loss to the council, especially now that one of the three remaining monasteries had no elders.

Before the great disaster of 1934, when Marming, the largest and most eminent of the monasteries, had been destroyed in the earthquake, there had been five Samudran centres, all in Nepal. The brotherhood survived that devastation, but ever since the landslide of 1995 had destroyed Khare, it had been a struggle for Sarmand, Barnang and Qo to properly fulfil their task of keeping the planet stable, healthy and rotating on its axis.

In the darkest hour of the night Rinzen lay on his back and gazed at the stars. He let his eyes lose their focus, and pictured himself sailing weightlessly through the Milky Way, swept along by faint music – like the first waterfall after the spring thaw – from an instrument he'd never heard before. Or was it simply the wind whispering through the trees?

What will I do without you, Master? You have gone too soon; I am not ready …

At dawn, he carefully scooped Kwato's ashes into the clay urn and then shovelled earth over the remains of the fire. The sight of Keung waiting in the cloisters brought the first tears to his eyes. Such a good friend.

'Elder Kwato will be welcomed in the Well of Life.' Keung circled Rinzen's shoulders with his right arm. 'Imagine the wisdom down that bottomless fissure in the earth! They'll continue to help us, you know, keep the engine going, all those generations of loving souls with warm hearts and trained minds down there, meditating tirelessly for all eternity.'

Rinzen placed the urn on the wide stone surround and peered into the darkness below. 'I'll pour them in, shall I?'

'Shall we do it together?'

They gripped the urn and slowly tipped its contents over the edge.

'So long, Elder Kwato,' Rinzen said.

'We'll be joining you later,' Keung said. 'Much later, hopefully.'

4

London

On her way to Old Street station on Wednesday morning, Clara thought she felt Henry's presence close by and scanned the busy pavements for him. She was still looking around as she descended into the station. Funny how non-musicians were astounded by the work involved in being a professional musician. Henry thought musicians just turned up at concerts, did a bit of tuning, then started playing.

'As if.' She'd laughed as she said it, so he got her to describe a typical day, then thought she was kidding when she told him about her six-day week – the five or six hours of practice, the two hours of exercise, the early nights and the controlled diet. 'And I'm not unusual. We all do it, some even more.'

And here she was on a typical rehearsal day. She'd already done an hour's exercise (she'd do another hour plus an hour of yoga later) and was on her way to the studio for a seven-hour session with half an hour for lunch. She'd be hard at it until she sat down to eat some vegetarian concoction at around 7pm, then she'd read, listen to some non-harp music and be in bed by 9pm.

Her whole life had been like this, and she really couldn't remember a time when it hadn't been. Her father bought her first small-scale Celtic harp when she was four years old. Even at that age, he'd encouraged her to practise for several hours every day. He taught her to read music and how to play the piano, but he never tired of telling her that when he heard her play the harp for the first time, he knew she was a born harpist. Now, twenty years later, she could still see his sparkling bright blue eyes, still hear him tell her in his thick Italian accent that when someone was blessed with such a talent it was their duty as a human being to make the most of it. She hadn't really understood what he meant at the time, but she loved to play the harp and loved to please her papa, so she practised more and more until it seemed, looking back, that there was nothing else to remember – just her seated on a stool playing the harp and her father, wide-eyed, encouraging her. He bought her a twenty-two-string lever harp for her sixth birthday and reluctantly allowed her to go to school, but her mother was under strict instructions to bring her home straightaway so she could get in a few hours' practice before supper.

With only four rehearsal days to go until the concert, Roland, dressed in his customary black suit and black polo-neck, put on his serious face and said, 'The fun and games are over. We are going to play all the pieces, in order, this morning. Then a very short lunchbreak before we do it all again this afternoon. Any questions?' He didn't wait for any. 'Good. Positions, please, and no chatting.'

Clara heard Marco, the principal cellist, suck in a breath. Clara held onto her smile and bit her lip.

Roland didn't look happy at lunchtime. But she knew Roland, knew he was perfectly capable of acting disappointed because he thought it would make everyone try harder, practise more, bleed for the work. Maybe he was right. But most, if not all, of the orchestra needed no encouragement – they'd give it their all whatever Roland did or said.

When the orchestra finished the final piece in the afternoon session – *Toccata and Fugue in D Minor* – Clara didn't stand up when the others did. She stared at her hands resting on the strings: would her mother rattle and die when she let go?

'Come on, Clara,' Roland said. 'They want to lock up.'

'You go, Roland. I just want to practise that bit from "Le Carnaval de Venise". I lost the fingering and need to get it right or I won't sleep.'

'Sounded fine to me.' He arched his left eyebrow. A master of facial expressions, Roland could move each feature independently, and after a time you knew exactly what each one meant. It was part of his genius. The arched eyebrow meant he could tell you were hiding something.

'All the same, could you ask if I can have another ten minutes?'

Roland laughed. 'All right, perfectionist!'

When the caretaker appeared at the door ten minutes later, Clara was no nearer to deciding what to do. He swung his keys and smiled at her. She played on, nodded at him, then suddenly stopped, stood up, grabbed her bag from behind the harp stool and strode from the studio.

With each step the blood pumped up her neck and filled her head, but she made it outside, leaned against the wall and closed her eyes in a failed attempt to staunch the tears flowing down her cheeks. What's wrong with me? This is madness. OK, it was a horrible dream, and yes, it would be the end of her world if Mum died, but—

Wait! All I have to do is ring her.

She wiped her face and dashed back inside. There were times she really regretted not having a mobile phone.

'Are you OK, Clara?' Fiona, the receptionist, said.

'Could I use the phone? Just a local call.'

'Of course.'

Clara closed her eyes, willed her mother to pick up. It went to voice message, but what could she say: just checking you aren't dead?

She dialled Grace's mobile.

'Hello.'

'Mum!' Did she scream that? Calm down. 'Hi, Mum.' Better. 'Just checking you're well enough to come over tomorrow.' Stupid thing to say.

'Of course, darling. Why wouldn't I be? Lawrence and I are just—'

'Great. Bye.'

Of course she wasn't dead. How ridiculous.

She made her way home, wishing her friend Julia wasn't on tour. Julia would snap her out of these morbid feelings; she was always so definite; you couldn't help taking her opinions as absolute truths. If she were here, she'd help her get some perspective on this damned dream. Not only was Julia the only person she confided in – about men, her mother, career choices – she was also her only real friend. Maybe it was her strange upbringing with its exclusive focus on the harp, or maybe she just wasn't very good at making friends, but Clara hadn't bonded with the other harpists at the Royal College of Music; it was always Julia she sought out, even though Julia's specialism was the violin.

Ah well, Julia wouldn't be back from Hong Kong for another two weeks; she'd just have to wait.

~

After lunch the next day, Grace opened an A3 portfolio on the table, spread out the photographs of her late husband and sighed. 'I don't know what to think about this book any more, Clara.'

'But it's an honour, isn't it, to have Papa featured in a book about the great baritones? Especially one written by Guiseppe Fantoni?'

'I suppose so, but you know how your father detested fame, thought it undermined the art.' Grace frowned, shuffled the photographs without really looking at them, and sighed again.

'Is there something else, Mum?'

Grace looked up and Clara saw what she thought were tears in her eyes. 'Memories,' she said. 'So many memories, buried for so long. I haven't enjoyed the interminable interviews, have you?'

The truth was that Clara had enjoyed the interviews. She loved talking about her papa, even though her own memories were mixed up with what her mother and other people had said about him, so she couldn't tell what the real memories were. 'Oh, Mum, it must be so hard for you.' She reached across and put her hand on Grace's.

'It's not that I want to forget him, not that at all, but the man kept on about what Ettorre was working on when he had the stroke – and that was such an awful time.'

'God, how insensitive!' Clara squeezed Grace's hand. 'But this book will mean that Papa is never forgotten. It's going to be a historical record, nothing to do with being famous. And ...'

'What?'

'Well, maybe all the pain will have been worth it for that. Maybe if you focus on that, the rest will seem less painful? I don't know, sorry, I can't imagine what it's like for you.'

'Thank you, Clara. You're such a good daughter.' She smiled, kept her tears from falling. 'Right, let's look through these photos, find some that show him at his best, his most handsome.'

Clara sifted through a few. 'I've always loved this one. He looks so sophisticated, standing under that ancient street lamp, like an actor in an old black and white movie.'

'That was behind La Scala. 1987. I was four months pregnant.' Grace took the photo and gazed at it. 'Funny, I can't remember who took it. But you're right, I'll put it in the "definite" pile. What about this one?'

Grace grinned and handed Clara one that showed her papa sitting on a stool, wearing a bright white shirt but without a jacket or tie. He was leaning forward, his face

43

creased in concentration. At the right side of the picture was part of a harp with a small hand plucking at the strings.

The room seemed to darken; the image zoomed in and out of focus and then stayed sharply defined. 'His face ...' Clara said. 'I can still see that look. It's what keeps me going.' She jolted, looked at Grace. 'I've never seen this one before. All those times when we got out the photos, how could I have missed it?'

'Because I only just came across it. It was in amongst his sheet music and I found it when Señor Fantoni asked to look at the scores. I can see it's shaken you, darling. Water?'

'No. No, thanks. It captures him, don't you think? Or at least it captures him for me. It's as though he was willing me on, lending me the full force of his own talent and concentration. You know ...'

'Go on.'

'It sounds silly, but when I have an off-day, can't get up the enthusiasm to practise or exercise or play even my favourite pieces, I often get the sense he's looking at me. Looking at me just like that. And then I know I can do it. Silly, I know.'

'It's not silly. I ... I also call on your dear papa. Not so much in recent years, but when you were younger and your musical life was such a whirl, with a million decisions to make all at once, well then, I did actually talk to your father after you'd gone to bed at night. He helped me then as he still helps you now.'

'Let's not put this in the book. It's ours, isn't it. Only ours.'

'You're absolutely right. This is ours. Yours now – I'll have it framed for you.'

Clara leapt up, rushed round the table, threw her arms around Grace and held on tight, letting the tears flow onto her mother's shirt. She felt her melt in her arms.

~

With only a week to go until the concert, Roland had insisted on an extra Saturday rehearsal. When she left the studio at four o'clock, Henry's old Saab convertible was parked on the double yellow lines, and he was chatting – definitely flirting – with a traffic warden. The woman's smile disappeared as Clara grabbed Henry's arm.

As they drove off, Clara laughed and said, 'You're incorrigible, Henry Shawcross. While you're waiting to meet one woman, you chat up another.'

'No, no, nothing like that. Just stopping her giving me a ticket.'

'Oh yeah? More likely you just fancy a woman in uniform.'

He turned and grinned at her. 'Well … there is that.'

She pretended to slap him, he acted a wince, and they roared past the Albert Hall with the top down and Chuck Berry playing 'Johnny B Goode' at full volume.

Back in Shoreditch, Henry mixed high-octane gin and tonics while Clara showered. When Gareth Fulbright sidled onto his balcony, Henry booed him back, then raised his glass at Clara. 'Cheers!'

God, he's infectious.

And nothing like me.

Before they met, almost a year ago, her world had consisted entirely of music and musicians. Meeting Henry, brash, witty Henry, had been like arriving in a foreign country after a long-haul flight: everything was exotic – brighter, louder – and shimmered with intensity. His rudeness was irresistible, his impulsive nature the antithesis of her own ordered approach to life. He seemed to adore her, to want to show her his world, and to show her off, of course, introducing her as the greatest and most beautiful harpist in the universe, who also happened to be the sexiest woman he had ever met. What's more, having never before listened to harp music, he now couldn't get enough of it, would ask her to play for him at every opportunity, and insisted on coming to all her London concerts.

Before she knew it, Henry was an integral part of her life and she dared to believe she was in love with him. One day she might even break out of her disciplined, cloistered self to actually feel that love, but for now she had gratefully settled for passion; she longed for him when they were forced apart by foreign concert tours, missed the feeling of security she had when she was with him, that she could indeed live in the real world as well as the world of music as long as he was by her side.

'How about a bite to eat at that new place in Hoxton Square,' Henry said, 'then on for jazz at The Vortex?'

'What, more experimental jazz?'

'No. I guarantee you'll like this band. They're trad not modern, and they pump out the old favourites. But if you don't like it, we'll just leave.'

He was right. She did like the wall of sound produced by the three trumpets, three trombones, four saxophones, drums and two guitars as they blared out 'Sweet Georgia Brown', 'One O'Clock Jump', 'Smoke Gets in Your Eyes', and some she didn't recognise.

She fell asleep with 'I've Got You Under My Skin' playing in her head and woke to Henry stroking her breasts and humming 'I Want You' in her ear while rain lashed the glass doors. After luxurious morning lovemaking, Henry made toast and coffee, came back to bed and told her about the Barcelona chairs he'd ordered from Italy.

'That guy Mies van der Rohe was way ahead of his time, especially his furniture. You still see his Barcelonas everywhere, but I've nabbed some special-edition ones – upholstered with cowhide, hair and all!'

'Hairy chairs? You mean like black and white cows?'

'Yes. And a couple of nice brown ones, like Holstein Friesians.' He saw her quizzical look. 'Yeah, I know, sounds tacky, but just wait till you see them.'

'I'll take your word for it.'

He tickled her armpit. 'You musicians, you just float about in the ether, don't even notice what's around you.'

'Stop! Henry, stop it.' She tried to wriggle free. 'You're right, I'm just a philistine.'

Later, as he drove Clara back to Shoreditch after lunch and a walk along the river, Henry said he needed to see a German supplier who was only in town for the weekend.

Clara practised all evening and didn't think about the dream at all.

5

Nepal

The novices' quarters were situated at the base of the eighty steps, separated from the rest of the monastery between the inner and outer walls. Outsiders were permitted in this part of the monastery, and the Mothers lived and worked here. The Mothers were women from nearby villages whose children had grown up and who chose to look after the young novices until they became juniors at the age of twelve. Each of the four Mothers spent a week at the monastery and a week at home, so at any time there were two of them to look after the sixteen boys. The boys were taught simple household chores, like laundry and cleaning, and the older ones also helped prepare lunch and dinner.

The novice's day started with meditation at sunrise in the courtyard outside their dormitory. On this particular day, the last of the sixteen novices had just taken his place as half the sun's face peered over the eastern peaks and sent shafts of light across the snow field, over the bare rock escarpment and into the trees. Minutes later, its warmth arrived in the yard and the boys relaxed their shivering bodies; their goosebumps retreated and their ears tingled.

Senior Hansen spoke. 'Greetings, one and all. Let your dreams leave you, forget the rumble in your stomachs, do not look at any other person, but let your eyes rest on the hollow stone before us. It is empty now, but fill it with your imagination and watch the water swirl round and round and round. Water is the essence of life, for without water we would not exist. In the beginning, all was water, and where there is water there is memory and potential. Remember, everything was formed in primeval water, water is the link to the life force, and what is dry is dead.'

About half an hour later, Hansen said, 'And now the water drains through the hollow stone and nourishes the earth with our greetings. Watch it go until the last drop leaves the narrowest crevice.'

Around the time the novices were at breakfast, Rinzen was studying the map that showed the routes to Barnang and Qo. Kwato's handwritten note was at the base of the map:

The routes marked ignore the roads, which would make your journey much longer. But remember, Rinzen, do not run. Many you encounter on the way will not comprehend your speed and may fear you.

Rinzen placed the map in his satchel, and looked out of the library window. His eyes traced a line from the track at the base of the valley up the steep hillside beyond. He tried to picture himself striding along the ridge, looking back to Sarmand. No, I must look forward; looking back will only lengthen the journey. What would it be like beyond the ridge? Would the villages be the same, what about the people there – would they be warm and welcoming like Chaukati, his own family village, or would they fear him as Kwato warned?

He looked around the library and remembered the first time he had been allowed to study there, as a new junior sixteen years ago. He and the others in his group had spent many hours seated around the long table; they were taught mathematics and science, geography and geology, as well as the history of the brotherhood and its place in the universe.

49

Rinzen's favourite subject had been astronomy, but what he loved most was the art of debating. As Kwato told him on his first day as a junior, building a coherent argument was the key to mastering any subject. All the intellectual tests required for a junior to progress entailed public debate. They started by debating with one other junior, under the guidance of an elder, and later pitted their wits against up to five others at a time. Rinzen soon learned that it was necessary to impress the elders with not only the clarity and economy of one's arguments but also the speed with which one responded.

To become a senior, you had to engage in two days of debates with all of the seniors and show that you could hold your own. Rinzen argued convincingly but did not win the debate on whether solipsism was false, but when he devastated his older opponents on the question 'Is there such a thing as free will?', the elders unanimously voted him a senior. Rinzen had taken a quantum approach, citing Frank Knight, who wrote about uncertainty that couldn't be quantified with probabilities. When two seniors mounted a robust challenge, he floored them with Aaronson's concept of qubits that had never been measured and had retained their original freedom. If it was possible that such qubits existed, and that some might even possess Knightian uncertainty, then predicting certain future events – possibly including some human decisions – would be impossible. His opponents offered no counter argument, and even the elders were stumped.

Just as some novices failed to become juniors, so some juniors did not graduate to seniors. And even after twenty-three years in the monastery, some seniors were not destined to become elders. Those that failed at any stage had to leave the monastery and many found work in the universities and high schools of India and Nepal. Rinzen sometimes wondered how life would be if he had to leave. Would he have to hide his physical powers, suppress his desire to run up mountains, dampen his debating skills? Such thoughts only served to reinvigorate him, to spur him on in his studies, to widen the scope of his mind and attain even greater intellectual heights.

Before he left the library, he stood for a few minutes and surveyed the dark wood bookcases crammed with books, pausing every so often when he caught sight of a favourite volume. He ran his hand along the worn surface of the long table and sighed.

~

At noon, when the meditators were due to change, Rinzen rang the bell for a meeting, and all the seniors and juniors gathered in the dining hall. Keung stood beside him as he addressed them.

'Ill fortune has visited Sarmand, and now the last of the elders is dead. Before he died, Elder Kwato told me that I must go to the other monasteries to ask for elders to come and guide us, and as a senior I must obey his instructions. He said that with his passing there will be no more wasting disease, so I will leave tomorrow.'

Some of the juniors gasped at his words, others turned to look at their neighbours. Rinzen gave them a moment to refocus.

'It will take three days to reach Qo and another three to Barnang. To return will take five days, so I will be away no more than two weeks and will hurry back to join the meditation as fast as I can. We are too few already, but now it is more important than ever that we maintain the vigil.' He walked to the end of the middle table so that everyone could see him. 'All is not right with the earth. We have noticed how the pattern of seasons has altered, how nature itself seems confused, and it is even possible that the axis of the planet has shifted. We understand that truly natural disasters are often the earth evolving, but that other devastating events, particularly connected to climate incidents, are earth's response to human's overexploiting the earth's resources. For many centuries we Samudrans have held the earth in balance, sustained its rotation, kept the sky clear, the sun shining, the rivers flowing, and the animals bright-eyed. Previous generations suffered winters so harsh that even the wells froze; landslides and earthquakes damaged Sarmand and Barnang and completely destroyed two of the monasteries. And yet the Samudrans prevailed, maintaining the continuous meditation, and will always do so. This is our sole purpose, and we will continue to prevail.'

The mouths of some of the younger brothers hung open. Some frowned, others looked at their hands.

Keung took over. 'Last night the seniors met in council. Certain changes must be made if we are to fulfil our role as one of the three. First, some seniors will act as elders until elders come from Barnang and Qo. All those who have been seniors for five summers will become elders elect. To replace them, all those juniors who have mastered the eighty steps will become seniors and remain as seniors. Some of the novices will be inducted as juniors to replace them.' He slowly turned his head and surveyed the room. 'If anyone here sees a flaw in our reasoning, please speak freely.'

Keung turned to Rinzen, so as not to appear to challenge anyone who might wish to speak. When Rinzen nodded, Keung resumed.

'Second, we talked in detail about ways we could overcome the greatest problem of all – how to maintain the meditation. Excluding novices, there are thirty-six of us, thirty-five without Rinzen. Nine are still too young to join the circle, leaving twenty-six. Many ideas were proposed, but the one most favoured was for each brother to meditate for eight hours in each daily cycle instead of the usual six. Each group will be led by one of the older seniors, and each will contain a balance of seniors and juniors. Until now, only a few juniors have joined the meditation, and then only for a few hours at a time, so this will be a departure from our usual practice. Some of our other duties might suffer, but winter approaches and with it there is less need to tend the gardens and maintain the buildings. Again, if anyone can improve on this proposal, speak freely. You are among brothers and, as ever, we must help each other.'

Amdong stood and waited for Keung to nod his acknowledgement. 'Thank you, Keung and Rinzen for your leadership. We juniors restricted our discussions to the question: how can we help the seniors to maintain the vigil? We felt it was not right for juniors to consider other matters. We agreed that we would sleep for two hours less each day and, if asked, would be pleased to meditate for more hours. We will also joyfully give up all of our leisure time and take on the seniors' share of gardening, maintenance, laundry and cleaning work.'

A shiver ran up Rinzen's neck and rippled over his shaved head. For a moment he could not move or speak, he could only stare at Amdong. A thought flashed in his head: Amdong had already achieved enlightenment. He'd heard of one or two instances of young brothers who had managed this but never imagined he would encounter one. The silence became awkward, a few murmurs started.

'You speak well, Amdong,' Keung said. 'Your words warm my heart and strengthen my resolve. But tell me – do you or any of the juniors wish to say anything on the other matters?'

Fulong, another junior, stood. 'My people live in Sunkhani, only half a day on foot from Sarmand. My brother is a carpenter, my sister can fix anything mechanical, my cousin, so they say, has green fingers. There are many more like these in all of our birth villages, and many would gladly help the monastery through these challenging times.'

'Thank you,' Keung said. 'We will talk of this at council tonight, before Rinzen departs. As you know, the monastery has always relied on the villages for support, but always outside the monastery. The cycle of our work must include physical endeavour and practical skills. But, as you say, these are challenging times.'

~

Rinzen packed a small satchel and set off before dawn. He wore his winter clothes – loose tan trousers tucked into quilted cotton boots with thick rubber soles, a matching quilted jacket over a long-sleeved cotton vest, and a rust-brown three-quarter-length hooded woollen coat. Keung accompanied him down the path to where it met the track that ran along the valley floor. The two brothers embraced without speaking and Rinzen marched north.

He did not look back.

6

London

When Clara arrived at the rehearsal room on Monday morning, Fiona handed her a Post-it note and said she was to call the number written on it immediately.

'Before you take off your coat.'

Clara lifted the handset and jabbed at the numbers. 'It's Mum, isn't it?' She couldn't hold the handset steady and pressed it onto her ear; her head seemed to float off her shoulders. The 'number unobtainable' signal bleeped in her squashed ear.

Fiona stood up, swivelled the phone. 'Here, let me.'

After two rings, a soft voice – the sort of voice you'd expect an undertaker's receptionist to have, calm and sympathetic – said something about a dental practice. Could have been Park View or Park Rise. She had to focus. A dentist? 'It's Clara Martinelli. I was told to call you urgently.' Why didn't she have a mobile phone?

'Oh yes, Miss Martinelli. I'm sure it's nothing to worry about, but your mother passed out in the waiting room, so we called the paramedics. As I say, I'm sure there's nothing to worry about, but as a precaution they've taken her to Homerton Hospital for a few tests. Your name was on Mrs Martinelli's patient information form.'

When Clara didn't say anything, couldn't say anything, even though she knew she should ask some questions, the voice continued. 'I tried your home number, but there was no answer. It was very thorough of Mrs Martinelli to list so many numbers for you.'

'She's scared of the dentist.' The act of speaking opened the tap. 'What time did she collapse? Are you sure she didn't just faint? Did they carry her out on a stretcher?' God, she's all alone. Screaming through London, sirens blaring. She felt Fiona's arm around her shoulders.

'They left half an hour ago, but no, no stretcher. The paramedics were very calm. I'm sure it isn't an emergency.'

Fiona took the wet handset, said, 'Thank you. Clara will go to the hospital right away,' and slammed it onto the cradle. 'Wait one second, Clara. I'll come with you.' She put her head round the office door and said something, then grabbed her coat and Clara's elbow, marched her out into the breezy street and hailed a taxi.

Clara stared straight ahead through the cab windscreen and willed herself not to think the worst. The dental receptionist had said it wasn't an emergency, but what did she know? They wouldn't have rushed her mum to hospital if everything was all right. She was unconscious, that had to be bad news, worse than fainting. Clara released the side grab handle, wrist throbbing from gripping so tight: her right hand. Idiot. She could strain it doing that. She shook it, massaged her forearm. It was probably just fear that had made her mum pass out – the body did that, a sort of self-preservation strategy. But what if she's got a massive brain tumour …

'Sorry, ladies, I know we're in a hurry, but there's traffic on every route just now.' The cab driver half turned.

Fiona leaned forward, thanked him and put her hand on Clara's. Clara turned and smiled, hoped her look said, 'Please don't say anything,' and, looking past her, saw they were only on the Marylebone Road. Miles to go, and her mum was all alone.

Grace was still undergoing tests when they arrived. The A&E nurse said her blood pressure was normal, the ECG was clear and her eye health was fine. They'd taken blood and sent it for testing straight away, and in the meantime – to rule out the possibility of a stroke – they'd managed to get her a slot for a CT scan of her brain, which was where she was now.

A stroke! Clara hadn't even thought of that.

Just as she and Fiona got to CT reception, Grace walked out, fully clothed and smiling. Smiling! That had to be good news, surely?

'Hello, darling, thanks for coming.'

Clara couldn't speak. She strode across the room and flung her arms around her mother just as the tears burst from her eyes. Grace patted her back. She pulled away but kept her arms around her mother. 'Oh, Mum. How are you? Do you want to sit down?'

'I'm fine. And now I'm causing everyone so much trouble. Shouldn't you be rehearsing?'

'Never mind that, what did the doctor say? Do you have to stay in hospital?'

'No, of course not, I probably didn't drink enough water this morning, got a bit light-headed, that's all.'

'Yes, but what did the doctor say?'

'That I'm to go home and she will ring me as soon as the radiologist has had a good look at the CT scan and she has the blood results.' Grace smiled at Fiona.

Smiling again? Why wasn't she worried – was there something wrong with her brain?

'Sorry, this is Fiona, from the rehearsal rooms. She insisted on coming with me.'

'That's nice. Thank you, Fiona. Clara does sometimes overreact …'

57

'Mum, did you hit your head when you collapsed at the dentist's?'

'"Collapsed" is a bit of an exaggeration. But no, I just slumped on the carpet.'

'Oh, Mum.' Clara hugged her again.

'Look, I'll get the bus home and you can go back to the rehearsals.'

Clara pulled away. 'Not going to happen. We'll take a taxi home, and I'll stay with you, make sure you don't have another—'

'Episode?' Fiona said. 'I do think Clara is right, Mrs Martinelli—'

'Grace.'

'Grace. I'm sure Roland will understand.'

Back at Grace's house, Clara checked that the landline was working and the volume was turned up high, then rechecked it every half hour for the rest of the afternoon. She twitched and pointed at her wrist all the time her mother was on the phone to Lawrence. Grace told him she had fainted and that the doctor had told her she needed to rest, so she was afraid she would have to cry off their Thames tour. And no, she didn't need anything, Clara had kindly offered to stay over.

'Fainted?' Clara said when Grace finally put down the phone.

'There's no need to worry him, is there? After all, it's probably nothing.'

After breakfast the next morning, Clara took a very quick shower. When she emerged, Grace was on the phone to the hospital. Clara mimed that she wanted to talk to them, but Grace ignored her, carried on writing on the notepad, finished her series of 'I sees' and put down the phone.

'And?' Clara said.

'The CT scan showed …' – she passed Clara the notepad with words that didn't make any sense to her: *abnormal hypodense area within the posterior sagittal sinus* – 'and they want me to come back for a... What does it say on the notepad?'

'CT venogram.' Clara dropped into the armchair opposite Grace.

'At noon today.'

Must stay calm, don't want her to be worried. 'Hypodense area' doesn't sound good.

'They're going to put iodine in my blood before I have the scan. Apparently, it shows things more clearly.'

~

Clara went through the week in a daze. Grace insisted she go to rehearsals, and somehow she played in the concert on Saturday night. Even though the whole orchestra – and Roland Peach, of course – were relying on her putting on a virtuoso performance, she was immune to the pressure: there was no room left in her to worry about her fellow musicians as all her anxiety was reserved for Grace. Or was it for herself, her selfish self paralysed with fear about what would become of her if anything serious happened to her mother?

The second CT scan had showed a blood clot in the posterior sagittal sinus and Dr Bland had put Grace on anti-coagulants. This meant Grace had to go for daily blood tests at the GP surgery in Crouch End, even though she insisted that she felt perfectly normal. She also had to have yet another scan, this time of her chest, abdomen and pelvis.

Grace came to the concert and sat next to Henry, who was under strict instructions to keep a close watch on her and not leave her side under any circumstances.

Before the results of the body scan had been analysed by the radiologist, Dr Bland telephoned, and Clara pressed her head next to Grace so she could hear what she said. 'We are not sure that it is a blood clot. It could be something called an arachnoid granulation.

'I see. And is this arachnoid gran … thing a problem?'

'We will need you to have yet more scans, I'm afraid.'

So, yet again, Clara went with Grace to Homerton Hospital. Each time there was another set of tests or scans, she was even more convinced that Grace had some ghastly terminal condition lodged in her brain, and it was only a matter of time before they found it. Each time, as they waited for the results, Grace became calmer, more sanguine, while Clara's own mind became crowded with fear and anxiety, as though she were already grieving the loss of her mother. Having never considered it before, she now found herself imagining a motherless world in which she would be unable to function. But she couldn't get beyond the thought that she needed Grace's guidance, her love, her attention, her … everything.

Meanwhile, Grace held Lawrence at arm's length, telling him there was nothing to worry about.

Against Grace's wishes, Clara had moved in with her after the incident at the dentist's and only returned to her flat to practise the harp and collect clean clothes and the mail. She told Henry she wouldn't be able to see him, much as she wanted to, until she knew what was wrong with her mother.

On Friday, two days after the MRI scans, just as Clara was about to go to the flat, the hospital called yet again. As she listened to her mother's side of the conversation, her throat tightened, the room darkened, and she couldn't move, couldn't cross the room to listen to what they were saying. She just knew it was bad news, knew it was the worst news.

Grace put down the phone and sighed. 'The good news is that I don't have a blood clot, but they want me to go to the hospital yet again. This time it's in the respiratory department. But listen, darling, you really must get back to your practice, you've spent far too much time trailing around with me – much as I love having you there.'

'How can you be so calm, Mum?' She heard her own screeching voice and immediately wanted to erase it. Her head was so hot and full, it was ready to burst, but she shouldn't have said that, she should be strong and supportive, not a weedy little girl.

'I know you're worried but I'm not you see. What will be, will be.' Grace stood and crossed the room to take Clara's hands in hers. 'And the good thing is, they haven't found anything ominous yet. The way I look at it, I'm having a very thorough MOT!'

'MOT! Mum, they don't seem to know anything. First one thing, then another. Come for this test, then this one. Let's try this scan and that scan. When will it all end?'

'Clara, Clara, please don't work yourself up. Look at me – do I look like a woman with some dreadful illness?'

Clara kept to herself the certain knowledge that dying people often looked their best just before they breathed their last.

'Well, do I?'

'No, I suppose not.'

'I'm much more worried about you. Those bags under your eyes. I know you're not sleeping – I hear you prowling around in the early hours. So' – she squeezed Clara's hands – 'why don't you go home, get back into your routine, go out with Henry and have some fun ...'

'Fun? While I'm worried sick about you?' The tears she'd forbidden herself gushed down her face. Pathetic. No self-control. What would Papa have said about that? And she was keeping her sick mother awake worrying about her. How selfish could she get.

Clara pulled away her hands and wiped her face. 'When is this appointment? I'm coming with you. Please.'

'Very well. We'd better get going then.'

Dr Muriel Falconer was reassuringly middle-aged and carefully explained, with scan on screen, that there was a lesion in Grace's right lung, which might or might not be benign. The only way to find out was to have a biopsy.

Clara nodded, wanted to bawl her eyes out. She had lung cancer. How could she? She'd never smoked.

'Shall I explain the biopsy procedure?' Dr Falconer said.

'Yes, please,' Grace said. Cool, serene Grace.

'While you're inside the scanner, we insert a long needle into your lung and take a small sample of the lesion.'

'That sounds rather painful,' Grace said.

'No, not painful, but there are risks. On rare occasions, the lung collapses. If that happens, you'll need to spend some time in intensive care while we reinflate it. And there is a very small risk that we won't be able to do that.'

'And then what happens?'

How was her mum managing this coherence?

'There is a remote chance that the patient will die.'

'But very remote, yes?' At last Clara had found her voice.

'Yes, very rare indeed.' Dr Falconer smiled. 'Would you like some time to think about it, Mrs Martinelli? Discuss it with your daughter?'

'No, thank you. I don't need to think about it. I won't be having the biopsy. But thank you very much for going to all this trouble.'

'Wait a minute, Mum.' Clara turned away from the doctor and took her mother's hand. 'Shouldn't we at least discuss it? If you don't have the biopsy, you won't know what this thing is. It might not be benign.' She just couldn't say the word malignant.

'No, I've made up my mind. If I do have lung cancer, I won't be having any treatment, so why risk dying in ICU just to find out?'

'Well, it is up to you, of course,' Dr Falconer said. 'I respect your decision, Mrs Martinelli. But you could consider coming back in three months for another scan, so we can see if there are any changes.'

'Thank you. I will consider that. Now, Clara, we've taken up too much of Dr Falconer's time already. Shall we go?'

In the taxi back to Crouch End, Clara realised her mother had thought all this through before the appointment with Dr Falconer, while all she had done was panic. Grace had been one step ahead all along, and now it was too late to catch up. But that wasn't going to stop her trying.

On Saturday, while Clara was yet again trying, in vain, to breach her mother's defences, the phone rang. Clara grabbed it first.

'It's me,' Julia said.

'Julia! You're back! Thank God.'

'Henry told me about Grace. How is she?'

'Sanguine. Look, I'll call you back.'

'It's all right,' Grace said. 'I'm just popping out for some fresh air.'

Code for 'getting away from my pest of a daughter', Clara thought.

She told Julia about the tests, the diagnosis, her mother's refusal to have the biopsy.

'God, you must have been so worried,' Julia said.

'And still am. Don't you think she's being stupid about this? I mean, she's only in her fifties. Surely it makes sense to have the biopsy, even if there is a miniscule chance of her lung collapsing.'

'It must have been a real rollercoaster for poor Grace.' Julia paused.

Clara could almost hear her thinking. And how she needed Julia's razor brain. To think that two weeks ago she'd been worried about a stupid dream, and now ...

Julia continued. 'By the sound of it, she's been told one thing then another almost every day for two weeks. My bet is she's putting on a show for you, and probably Lawrence as well. I reckon she's as worried as you are and doesn't know what the right thing to do is.'

'In other words, stop bothering her,' Clara said. Julia was right of course, as usual. In a matter of minutes, she had analysed the situation, taking into account the personalities of her and her mother, and come up with the makings of a plan of action ... even if it meant starting with inaction.

'See you on Monday?' Julia said.

'That would be great.'

'We could go through all the oldies, take your mind off things.'

Clara didn't mention anything to do with Grace's diagnosis for the rest of the weekend. They did some more photo sorting for the baritones book and Clara cooked a full roast lunch and then returned to her flat on Sunday night.

Still panicking.

7

Nepal

Five hours later, Rinzen arrived at Sunkhani, where several of the brothers had been born. A group of young children were flying kites on the hillside next to the track. They called to him, frantically winding the strings of their kites as they rushed to be the first at his side. Rinzen laughed and walked on, but one of the smaller girls tugged at his coat. Her dark eyes sparkled under an unruly mop of raven-black hair.

'Wait, wait, my mother will bring food and water.'

He turned to the girl and smiled. She was barefoot and wore only a thin red-and-blue-striped dress but didn't seem to be cold.

A woman, presumably the girl's mother, appeared in the doorway. 'Brother, please rest with us for a while before you continue your journey. There is food and water for you. And tea, of course.'

Rinzen followed her through the heavy wooden doorway into the courtyard. The single-storey house, built with the same mud bricks as the outer walls, spanned the courtyard. The totem of the Samudran brotherhood – a pole with blue and white stripes signifying water and clouds – projected from the wall next to the door.

'I see you have a son at Sarmand,' Rinzen said.

'Please sit, brother. Yes, my second son, he is in his fourth year with you. His name is Pasang – perhaps you know him?'

'Yes, of course. A fine young man. He will become a junior tomorrow.'

The woman frowned. 'That's one year early, is it not?'

Rinzen hesitated. Should he tell this mother about the wasting disease, reassure her lest she hear about it and worry for her son? 'Yes, but he is ready.'

The woman gave him tea and *momos*, watched by a row of awestruck children who leaned in through the open window. When he left, the children made to follow him, but the woman called them back.

Outside the village, he branched west off the valley track. The path zigzagged up the hillside and offered more and more distant views of Sarmand until all he could see was the outline of the hill on which it stood, overshadowed by the snow-capped mountains beyond. He paused at the crest, raised his right arm in salute, then turned to enter unfamiliar territory.

The little-used path descended into a thickly wooded valley. In places, the dense foliage impeded his progress, and it was already mid afternoon when he emerged onto a soft sandstone incline where there was no sign of a path. He consulted Kwato's map and struck out towards the gap between the two highest peaks. Faced with such a long, steep ascent, it was hard to resist sprinting to the top. After all, his body was trained for this, and he and Keung loved nothing more than the challenge of high peaks, the steeper the better. As his mind strayed onto what he would say when he arrived at Qo, he realised he was running at three or four times the speed of an average man; he scanned all around for observers and continued at a slower pace.

He reached the high pass in time to see the last crescent of the sun sink behind the mountain range ahead, and sat on a ledge to gaze at the wash of oranges, mauves, reds and yellows fanned across the immense sky. A shiver fluttered through him. Was it fear, or simply the colder air at that altitude? He told himself it was the latter and risked running and leaping down to the treeline so he could gather wood for a fire and find some shelter for the night.

The fresh pine crackled in the flames, but that did not obscure the sound of stealthy footsteps approaching. They stopped a few metres from the fire, their owner hidden from view in the dark wood. Hidden from the eyes of ordinary men, but not from a Samudran senior.

'You are welcome to share the fire,' Rinzen said.

The man did not move.

'You have nothing to fear,' Rinzen said. 'I will be on my way at dawn.'

'But I do fear you,' the man said. 'Who would not fear a being who can fly through the air and see in the dark?'

It was Rinzen's first day and he had already ignored Kwato's warning. How could he explain himself without betraying the oath he'd taken as a junior, that he would never, under any circumstances, reveal details of his physical and mental skills?

'You may join me as long as you do not ask me to explain myself. Or you can choose to walk away. In either case, I will not harm you.'

The old man, dressed in ragged clothes and barefoot, turned and walked away.

Rinzen poured water into a wooden bowl, focused his attention, and meditated for four hours: in the moments before he entered the trance, he had a vision of his fellow brothers meditating in the inner temple. He could clearly see each individual, but he told himself that this was his imagination, for even a trained senior on the cusp of becoming an elder did not have the power of transposition.

Later, as he lay on his back in the dark woods and drifted towards sleep, the same musical refrain that had floated in the air at Kwato's funeral pyre – like a waterfall during the thaw – seemed to beckon him.

~

For the next two days Rinzen walked at a normal pace, stopped whenever he imagined other men might have needed a rest, and resisted the urge to race up the most impressive mountains he had ever encountered. He silently recited Ryōkan poems as he walked, and tried to recall every detail of Kwato's teaching, from when they were first introduced twenty summers earlier, to the elder's last words. He wouldn't go wrong if he took his lead from Kwato. When he meditated on the second night, again he saw his brothers in the inner temple, among them Keung and Amdong. A smile lit Keung's face as he turned towards him. Rinzen thought: we are kindred spirits.

Although the map was very old and many of the paths had disappeared, Rinzen was able to navigate by the rock formations, and he arrived at Qo, as Kwato had predicted, on the evening of the third day. The highest of the three monasteries, Qo was just above the treeline but still below the snowline and was perched on a peak; its buildings hugged the topography as though they had grown naturally out of the rock, an illusion reinforced by the consistent use of blocks made from the soft red sandstone of the surrounding range. Indeed, the rock was so soft that the hills and mountains had rounded peaks and when the wind got up, the air was permeated with sand.

The only path up to Qo, carved into the rockface, narrowed to no more than a ledge in places, and twice, where it had been washed or eroded away, was replaced by wooden galleries bracketed to the rocks. Despite the exertion, Rinzen felt the temperature drop as the path wound ever upwards. It appeared to ascend the mountain adjacent to Qo, but as he could see no alternative approach he pressed on. He had almost circled the edifice close to its summit before he saw that a ridge connected the two peaks. The land dropped away steeply on both sides, but the path was paved and bordered by a wire at waist height – presumably to give comfort in high winds. The seniors must love this, thought Rinzen, imagining the many games that could be enjoyed among the knife-sharp ridges.

The monastery gates, supported by two monolithic stone towers, guarded the far end of the ridge. The brothers of Qo had a reputation for fine woodcarving, and the quality and inventiveness of their work was beautifully displayed in the design of the massive gates. Many of the twenty-four panels depicted scenes from the mountain world: a pair of eagles about to take flight; a waterfall cascading into a pool that miraculously reflected the mountain peaks; ripe fruit hanging from three trees that invited you to pick and eat it; a child laughing as he swam in a wide stream. Other panels were more abstract, carved with intricate, knotted patterns that drew your eyes inside them, and one, in the centre of the left-hand door, seemed to grow out of the wood to form a delicate cage containing a songbird, balanced on a slender branch, that nodded in the wind.

Rinzen knocked and the gates opened at once.

'Welcome, brother,' the senior said. 'My name is Jetsan, please come in and join us.'

'And I am Rinzen, from Sarmand.'

Rinzen laid down his satchel and they embraced like old friends. Rinzen felt the other's warmth and let out a sigh: had he held his breath since leaving Sarmand?

'We are about to eat, so you will meet everyone,' Jetsan said. 'I am reluctant to welcome a brother with bad news before good, but all is not well in Qo. A disease has carried away our elders and there are only two still alive. Elder—'

'No, that can't be!' Rinzen said.

'When we saw you approaching, we thought that one of the other monasteries had somehow heard of our plight and sent help.'

'I came to seek your help,' Rinzen said. 'There are no more elders at Sarmand.'

The two brothers walked in silence up the eighty steps, passed through another set of carved doors in the inner wall and entered the dining hall. Like Sarmand, this was a simple room with stone floors and walls, four long, narrow windows and three rows of refectory tables. But in Qo the tables had a lustrous golden patina as smooth as glass and were supported on finely fluted legs. The brothers had waited for them and rose from the benches as Rinzen and Jetsan entered.

An elder moved away from his bench and came forward, arms extended. 'Welcome, brother, I am Elder Nawang. Please join us for our meal. There is a basin in the corner for you to wash your hands.' The elder's eyes were watery, his skin like crumpled cardboard.

Rinzen bowed. 'Thank you, Elder Nawang. I am Rinzen, a senior from Sarmand.'

'I know who you are, Rinzen. Elder Kwato has spoken of you many times. Always with great affection.' The elder took a senior's arm for support. 'We will speak later, after the meal.'

As was customary, room was made for the visitor in the centre of the middle table. The junior opposite poured water and gave him a generous helping of stew. As soon as they started to eat, the junior asked, 'What was the journey like? Did you travel across the mountains to get here? Was it the first time you ventured so far from home?'

The boy reminded Rinzen of Amdong – inquisitive, hungry and impatient for knowledge. The other brothers nearby looked up and waited for his reply.

'Before this journey, I had only ever travelled to my home village a day's walk from Sarmand, so I was apprehensive about venturing across the mountains. I needn't have been worried. It is true that I saw the vastness of the world from the high peaks, drank water from the pools of waterfalls twice as high as any I'd seen before, meditated under the stars, and met kindly people in the villages I passed through.'

He drank some water, smiled at the junior. 'But I recalled the wise words of Elder Kwato, who said that there is no need to travel to experience the wonders of the world. We are privileged to have the training of mind and body that life in the brotherhood offers. Once trained, we are among the few who can fully experience what it is to be alive, and during our lives there is more to discover within the realm of our sanctuaries than we can ever hope to know. Why interrupt this process with external experiences?'

Rinzen stopped, aware that the whole room was now silent, that even the two elders were listening to every word. He felt the blood rise up his neck and into his face, and he looked down at his bowl.

'Let the brother eat, will you.' Jetsan laughed. 'He has walked for three days and he must be tired and hungry.'

After the tables had been cleared, Jetsan took Rinzen to the elders' quarters and knocked on a door. They entered and Jetsan gasped at the sight of Nawang slumped in an upright wooden chair. 'Master, may I help you into bed?'

'Thank you, Jetsan, but first I will speak with Rinzen. Please ask Elder Yonten to join us. Now, Rinzen, what of the other elders at Sarmand, how do they fare?'

Rinzen took a deep breath. 'The reason I am here is that all of our elders are dead, and we are struggling to maintain the meditation.'

'Such grave news. Kwato, our guide, no longer among us.' It was hardly possible, but more light seemed to drain from Nawang's eyes. 'We have already buried all our elders except Yonten and me, and we are both close to the end. It is strange that this wasting disease only affects older brothers, or are things even worse at Sarmand?'

'No, the same, only the elders.'

Elder Yonten entered, supported by Jetsan. Rinzen positioned a chair for him, then bowed to the elder, who took his hand and held it while he spoke. 'You must go to Barnang, see if it is the same there. And if it is …' Yonten's words trailed off, and his eyes closed for a few seconds. 'If it is, then we must combine the monasteries to make two strong centres. When we two die, Qo must be closed until there are enough elders to reopen it.'

'Leave Qo!' Jetsan said, and then, 'Sorry, of course we must do as you say.' The senior's eyes reddened and Rinzen sensed him holding back his tears.

'Barnang is deep in the forest,' said Nawang. 'We must hope that all is well there.'

~

When Rinzen joined the Qo brothers in meditation, he entered the trance as easily as at Sarmand, feeling kindred spirits all around him. Again, he sensed the brothers of Sarmand, could have named those present, and took heart that no matter what happened he would always be with them.

Afterwards, he and Jetsan went to Jetsan's cell. They shared their worries about the wasting disease, both voicing their fear that soon they would be at the end of their novitiate and would either become elders or fail the test and have to leave the brotherhood. Right now, both futures looked bleak, for if they did become elders, would they too be afflicted and die?

For a time, both seniors were silent, until Jetsan broke their gloom. 'Who will give us the test if there are no elders to judge us? And since we cannot be tested, we cannot become elders, and we cannot be banished either. We will remain seniors forever.'

It didn't feel right to laugh, but laugh they did, then Jetsan changed the subject, wanted to know all about Sarmand, and whether Rinzen could already bound up the eighty steps in one leap.

'I think I can,' he said.

'You mean you know you can, don't you? You've done it, haven't you?'

'What about you? Have you?'

'Yes,' Jetsan whispered.

'Me too,' Rinzen said. 'Early one morning while the others were asleep, my friend Keung and I both performed the Elder's Leap. I felt my heart would burst with joy. All I wanted was to do it again, but Keung – not usually the sensible one – persuaded me that would be wrong.'

'Ah, I bet Keung is a master of the debate, to persuade one such as you to change your mind.'

'What do you mean, Jetsan – "one such as you"?'

'You must know, Rinzen, that you are already well known in Qo, and I expect in Barnang as well. Your master told our elders that you are the most talented senior – no, the most talented brother – he has ever met. I know we are not meant to compare ourselves, but I don't see anything wrong in it. You will never find a true brother who is envious of another, so why not say out loud, "This brother is magnificent, he is better than I am at all our tasks"? For such realisations will only make us strive even harder.'

Rinzen stared at Jetsan, his mouth open, his face hot, and turned away slightly, so Jetsan would not see his tear-filled eyes. That Kwato had held him in such regard was— He felt Jetsan's hand on his shoulder.

'You grieve for your master, don't you?'

Rinzen nodded. 'I know his death is just part of his journey, yet I—'

'But you and he were together in this lifetime.' Jetsan spoke softly. 'You feel sorrow at your separation, it's only natural.' He paused for a moment. 'Even for a Samudran.'

'Thank you, Jetsan. And I am no better than you. You are wiser than I will ever be.'

'Ha.'

'What about that ridge you have here – that must be great to run down.'

'We don't only run down it,' Jetsan said, 'we cartwheel up it! I wish you could stay longer; I could show you the best tracks. There's one route where you have to cross a wide gulley, so not only do you have to cartwheel at high speed as you approach it, but you also have to judge the exact place to take off from, otherwise—'

'It's mashed brother for breakfast.'

8

London

As she left her harp to join the conductor in a bow at the front of the stage, Clara saw her mother lying in a hospital bed. She also saw the Wigmore Hall audience, standing, clapping and cheering, but she couldn't hear them. All she could hear – and see – was her mother's horrifying death rattle. Then silence.

Clara's eyes snapped open beneath her sweat-wet, overheated forehead. Her cold, damp chest heaved as her ribcage fought to contain her swollen heart. Blood surged to her head in sickening waves.

I have to sit up or I'll drown in my own blood.

She kicked aside the duvet, swung her legs over the edge of the bed and pushed herself into a sitting position, elbows on knees, hands tangled in soaking hair.

Breathe. One, two, three, four, long breath. She tried opening her eyes and saw her harp towering over her: the Lyon & Healy of course, the dream-harp. She propelled herself towards it and straddled the stool. As soon as she touched the strings, her heartbeat slowed and her jaw unclenched. Should have listened to my instincts last time I had the dream. If I had, Mum wouldn't have that arachnoid in her brain and that ... that thing in her right lung. Her whole body shivered just thinking about it.

Without thinking, she started to play 'Habanera' from *Carmen*. She hardly ever played it, but she'd known it so long, the fingering and pedal changes came automatically, as simply and unconsciously as brushing her teeth. Her papa had liked her to play it for him, and she played it for him now. And for her mum, to heal her, to avert her death. The harp was what bound them all together, even after her father's death; it was what had made it possible for her and her mum to carry on afterwards; it gave them a purpose, a way to never forget him. They had both lived their lives around her harp playing: the harp always came first, more important than her schooling and her mum's teaching, more important than holidays or games or money or ... anything else.

And it was still the same: her mum might have Lawrence and she might have Henry, but if they had to choose, both of them would say that the harp came first. Always.

This time she would not ignore the dream. She would follow its message and would play the harp without stopping. She could and would avert the dream's terrifying finale.

She played louder, plucked the strings harder, drowned out her thoughts by filling the bedroom with beautiful music. By the time she played the final note she was completely calm, even though she knew she should be panicking. Which obviously meant it was the right thing to do, to follow the harp as they all always had; she, her mum and her papa. Always had, always would.

She stroked the strings and played 'Habanera' again. There was no hurry; she wasn't going anywhere.

After she'd played it for the third time, she wondered how easy it would be to move the harp from the bedroom to the kitchen. She stood up and was about to tilt it onto its castors when a dreadful thought shouted in her head. Negotiating the harp along the corridor would not be easy, given it was two metres high and a metre wide, and during that time she wouldn't actually be playing it, would she? The dream had told her she had to play her harp non-stop. But how could she do that? Even if she didn't relocate the harp, she still needed to sleep, to cook, to eat. How could she possibly act on the dream's message?

The blood drained from her head and she could barely lift her arms, could hardly hold her hands on the strings, let alone play at performance level. How would she travel to rehearsals and concerts if she had to play all the time?

Tears streamed off her chin and dripped onto the soundboard. Mustn't let it get wet.

Then there were all the other things she had to do – her yoga, taking a shower, spending time with Julia and her mother, making love with Henry. All impossible!

OK, OK, she had to calm down, think clearly. She closed her eyes, went through the yoga teacher's breathing exercises, tried to empty her mind ... She stroked the strings, felt her fingers lose their stiffness ... Right ... So, she couldn't play the harp all the time, but she must not, could not, ignore the dream's message. She should start with that, work it out.

Start with the dream's key message.

She interrogated herself. What had actually happened in the dream? She was on stage, she came to the end of the piece, stood next to the harp and took her bow, right hand still on the neck. She always rested her hand on the harp when she took her first bow – it was a way of acknowledging the harp's own brilliance, of having the audience applaud the harp both in its own right and as an extension of her. Then she joined the conductor at the front of the stage for the additional bowing and applauding of the others, before walking off.

It was only when she'd joined the conductor at the front that she'd had that appalling premonition of her mother's horrible, imminent death. When she'd stepped away from the harp. When she'd... cut physical contact with the harp.

That was it! That was the key. As soon as she'd detached herself from her harp, her mother's suffering had begun. It wasn't non-stop playing that the dream was advocating. No, its message was more subtle, less unreasonable. She simply needed to demonstrate her total commitment to the harp, her *attachment* to it.

It would be impossible to play the harp twenty-four hours a day, but it would not be impossible to maintain physical contact with the harp 24/7.

It would be bloody difficult, but she could manage it. And of course, she would still play it as much as possible – more than she did at the moment. That was the point. But the main thing was she should not let it go. A part of her must remain attached to the harp at all times.

She could manage that.

She kept playing while she examined this interpretation from every angle, reviewing the dream from its start to its terrifying end, and after a long time – impossible to say how long – she was convinced that this was the only possible diagnosis.

Nevertheless, Clara's heart pounded as she tilted the harp onto its front castors and guided it through the wide double doors into the hall. She used her left hand to pull it while she tried to keep playing with her right hand and steer it at the same time. She only ever used the front castors to fine-position the harp in the bedroom, and for minor stage moves during performances. Her usual moving procedure was to wrap the instrument in its protective covers and strap it to the trolley while still in the bedroom, then push the trolley through the ceiling-height double doors and the entrance doors directly opposite, onto the landing and down in the lift. The flat had been altered for the harp to be played only in the bedroom, and she had never tried to move it along the corridor and through the single door into the living room.

The harp towered over her, its long neck nearly the full width of the hall, the column stout and gaudy in the enclosed space. She tilted and turned it, but she misjudged the arc and the capital caught the wall. She eased it away but only succeeded in bouncing the top edge along the wall. She slumped next to it, exhausted and hungry, but continued to pluck the strings, albeit discordantly. How would she manage? If she couldn't even move the harp from the bedroom to the living room …

She would, she'd have to. Of course she could move the harp; she just needed to relax, take deep breaths, do everything slowly.

Before she tried again, she repeated her examination of the dream – her argument further supported by the failed attempt to manoeuvre the instrument while playing it – and told herself to have some self-belief, stick to her resolve, and get on with it.

She let go of the strings and pulled the precious instrument into the living room/kitchen and managed to make coffee and even to toast the sliced bread. Julia would have been proud of her. The question 'How would I slice bread using one hand?' passed through her mind, but she ignored it and savoured the double espresso with eyes closed as she plucked a lazy 'Greensleeves'.

A sudden anxiety caught her: what if her mother was already dead? She frowned, gripped by a terrible thought that refused to remain hidden in her subconscious. If her mother was dead, this burden would be lifted. The thought popped up like a mocking automaton, finger-wagging, intimidating. She was cruel, heartless, foul.

The phone rang in her mother's house. After six rings, Clara felt the sweat slimy on the handset; after eight, a blush welled up from her neck into her hair, her ears, her temples. She had willed her mother to die and her mother had died. After twelve rings, her mother answered.

'Mother, where were you?'

'And hello to you too, Clara. Why so much hurry? You're not in a rush today, are you? If you must know, I was in the downstairs loo. You sound a little fraught, darling.'

'Worried about you, Mother.' Clara stood, caressed the strings but made no sound. 'I do wish you'd have the ...' But she stopped before mentioning 'biopsy', held onto Julia's wise words.

'Please try not to worry about me, Clara. I'll ... Oh, there's my bell, better go, don't forget to do your practice, and your breathing exercises. Bye.'

Not dead then, thought Clara. God, she was so exasperating, but what would I do without her? If Julia had had the dream, she would simply accept it as her fate and get on with it. She would think methodically, work out how to do all the menial chores while attached to a very large musical instrument that weighed over forty kilos, and then get on with her life.

Clara plucked the strings, moved up and down the scales, and found herself playing 'Blue Moon' at a mournful pace, softly, almost inaudibly. She heard the words in her head and let a tear slip down her cheek ... Stop it. Don't get sentimental, work out how you're going to manage everything.

She practised moving the harp around the living room. It glided smoothly over the oak floor, but when it snagged on the rug in the middle of the room, she moved the coffee table and rolled up the rug, then sat on the sofa with the harp beside her, her right arm on the sofa's armrest, her fingers on the strings. Images of a blue moon filled her half-asleep vision; she walked towards the moon and the image gave way to a distant figure playing enchanting music on the harp, not her harp, it wasn't her playing; it was Henry, frowning, intense, all his focus on the complicated piece. Clara looked away, stared at the ceiling, her left hand in her lap, her right hand flopped over the arm of the sofa, not even touching the harp, nowhere near the harp strings.

She retched, an acrid taste swelled in her mouth and fizzed inside her nostrils then burst against her sinuses. And still she did not move. All she could do was stare at the harp, prevented by an invisible force from grabbing hold of it. She wanted to play her sweetest tune, wanted to pull her mother back from the brink, but all she could do was think about moving, imagine herself moving, and yet remain unmoving, sinking deeper into the blood-red sofa. Would blood trickle from her mother's mouth when she died? Would she, Clara, be there at the end, or would she fall asleep, loosen her grip on the harp and let her mother die alone while her selfish daughter slept away the morning?

Finally, Clara woke enough to sit up, pull the harp towards her and play 'Hallelujah' at full volume. In future she would have to rest while seated on the stool, slumped over the harp. She resisted the urge to telephone her mother again: although she suspected that her short disconnection from the harp had probably gone unnoticed – cosmically speaking – her uncertainty made her nervous and clumsy, and it was with great difficulty, and a series of minor bumps to her beloved instrument, that she managed to manoeuvre it into the bathroom, only to discover that there was no way she could stand in the shower and keep in contact with it. Stripped naked, she splashed water from the basin under her armpits and between her legs, dried herself roughly and doused herself liberally with eau de cologne.

She sat down on the playing stool to think about the easiest clothes to wear. The smooth wood of the soundbox felt warm against her body, seemed a perfect fit against her breast and shoulder, and she recalled the time she'd played naked, in this same place, while Henry drank champagne, smiled appreciatively at her and waited for a pause to deliver a rare compliment. She wanted him to be there now, to walk up behind her, brush aside her long black hair and kiss her on her naked neck, whisper how he adored her olive skin, ask her to keep playing, stroke her body, rest his heavy hands on her, and kiss her lips as she stroked the strings until the whole world hummed 'Ave Clara'.

She took it as a good sign when Henry answered his phone immediately.

'Clara, darling, you're back home. How's Grace?'

'Not good news … but I'll tell you later. Can you come round later?'

'Tonight, yes of course, I'll cook.'

'I had that horrible nightmare again. About Mum dying …'

'You'll be fine after you've had a shower. Come down to the shop and have a coffee, I'll make a fuss of you.'

'I can't.'

'Busy day? Even better.'

'No, I can't leave the harp. The dream. Last time I ignored it, look what happened to Mum.'

'Oh come on, Clara. How could you being away from your harp have caused her collapse at the dentist's … and the rest?'

'I just know it did, and if I let go of it, she'll die.'

She heard a whisper – it sounded like 'What bollocks.'

'What was that?'

'Nothing. Look, I've go to go, another batch of those Barcelona chairs is just arriving. See you later. And Clara …'

'Yes?'

'Nothing. Bye.'

She could tell he'd forced himself to shut up, resisted telling her to pull herself together or something even ruder.

~

When the doorbell rang, Clara ignored it. She held her breath after the third persistent ring, and only noticed she was crying when a tear rolled onto her lower lip. She didn't want to spurn her mother, but she had no choice. She would notice her dishevelment, would want an explanation for her attachment to the harp while she made them coffee, would not leave until she'd wheedled out of her the exact nature of her affliction, its origin and its implications. The thought of which was more than Clara could bear. So Clara cried and while she cried she laughed at the paradoxical situation: always the devoted daughter, she was now completely in thrall to her mother, having sworn to attach herself to the harp for evermore for the sake of her mother's mortality; meanwhile, she couldn't see her mother to allay her fears that some terrifying illness had befallen her only daughter. After all, what would Grace do without Clara? What good was a devoted mother without an offspring to nurture?

Clara guessed her mother would take the short walk up to Henry's furniture showroom on Curtain Road. She called him. 'Henry, you miserable sod, couldn't you be a bit more understanding? Don't answer, I'm not talking to you. I just want to make it clear that you are not to tell Mother about my resolution. In fact, don't tell anyone, not even Julia. You'll only make me out to be a madwoman, and how would that reflect on you? Don't answer. Henry, is that clear, don't tell anyone, understand? Don't answer that!'

She put down the phone, satisfied that she hadn't had a conversation with Henry, had merely given him instructions. She played the first few bars of Cole Porter's 'I've Got You Under My Skin', hummed the lyrics with eyes closed and played louder but failed to chase Henry from her mind.

Dressing had been complicated but not impossible; she'd chosen a sports bra without a clasp, no tights and a simple shift dress to wriggle into one arm at a time. How would she dress for the stage, how would she even get to the concert hall when she could hardly manage to get around the flat? She needed help, Julia's help; Julia would be good on the practicalities. But what would Julia say about the dream? It was still undefined, blurred around the edges, as dreams usually were, but instead of forgetting all but the uneasiness after a disturbing dream, it kept acquiring more detail as she recollected it: the conductor beaming at her as she took her bow, his red face, sweat pouring from his forehead; the coolness of her new midnight-blue satin dress against her bare legs; snatches of the piece she'd played, *Toccata and Fugue in D Minor*. Julia, like her mother, would need to be convinced. An unconvincing explanation would lead to concerns about her sanity, talk of convalescent homes, the need for a long vacation, worries over Henry's influence.

The bedside clock showed 11.05am and the curtains were still closed. She dragged the harp behind her and opened them. The full-height glass doors overlooked the communal courtyard below, and the helmet of the 180-metre-high Gherkin sparkled against the clear blue sky above the building opposite. She slid open the door and put one foot onto the balcony, impeded from further advance by her grasp of the harp and the raised sliding-door track. A ramp of some sort was needed. She leaned into the open air, checked that Fulbright wasn't ogling her and closed her eyes, breathing deeply.

The doorbell roused her from her reverie. Moments later the front door opened. 'I've brought Grace to see you, Clara,' Henry called out from the landing. 'Can't stop, important meeting back at the store.'

'Henry!' she shouted. 'Henry, wait ...'

'I'm sure you'll see him later.' Her mother walked into the bedroom, all prim and smart and efficient next to Clara's unkempt explosion of dress and unbrushed hair.

'Mother, do come in for a minute. I'm practising, as you can see.'

'Yes, do carry on. You look tired out, darling. Shall I make you something, a nice fruit salad perhaps? I bought panettone, but perhaps we should leave that for later? What do you think? Mmm?'

She was babbling. 'Fruit salad would be lovely, Mum.'

Grace smiled. 'Then fruit salad it is.'

The moment her mother left the bedroom, Clara wheeled the harp around the room, picked up her discarded nightie and the jumble of yesterday's clothes and stuffed them into the laundry basket by the bathroom door. Making the bed was almost impossible with one hand, and she settled for straightening the duvet and pulling the cover vaguely into place.

'I'm pleased to see you've got straight back into your routine,' Grace called from the kitchen.

'You know me…' Clara kicked a stray pair of knickers under the bed, then thought how out of character that was. '… discipline is my middle name.'

Grace came into the room, wiping her hands on a tea towel. 'I wanted to thank you for your help with all those hospital visits. It was very kind of you.'

'I wouldn't have let you go through all that on your own, Mum.'

'And then you came home and you had a dream.'

'I'll kill Henry!'

'I would have found out soon enough. Besides, Henry only told me because he's worried about you. As I am. Now why don't you leave the harp for a few minutes, come next door and eat a lovely fruit salad. If it looks like I'm about to die, you can rush back to the harp and save me.'

The words pierced her. Tears rose unbidden, unwanted and thankfully unshed. 'I can't believe you said that, Mother. What have I done to deserve your scorn? I try my best: I practise every day, almost always get my eight hours' sleep, eat all the right food, do the exercises morning and night, and all you can do is side with Henry.'

'I'm not siding with Henry, Clara. But from what he's told me, you had a dream that you can't leave the harp for one moment for fear that I'll die. Well, that's, that's …'

Grace's words died as soon as she had the nerve to look her daughter in the eyes.

'Nonsense?' Clara said.

'Well, yes. But you're right, it's wrong of me to jump to conclusions without hearing about this omen from you first hand.'

'I think you'd better leave.'

'Oh, darling, don't be like that. I'm sorry I mocked you, I should know by now how sensitive you are, shouldn't I?' She patted Clara's right arm. 'Look, I really would like to hear about this unusual dream. It must have been very powerful to have this lasting effect on you.'

'And then you'll go?'

Grace nodded.

'Without trying to bribe me to stop by feeding me cake?'

'Very well, but only today.'

Clara included all the details about the piece she'd played and watched Grace's reaction. She could read her face, could see she was dying to tell her to 'grow up' or 'stop being silly'. She doesn't even realise she's opening and closing her mouth like a bloody goldfish. 'OK, Mum, I think you should go now. I need to think about my dream, and if you stay we'll only argue and then we'll both get upset, and it's already bad enough that Henry has gone all moody on me.'

'He just wants things to get back to normal.' Grace spoke quietly, as if by whispering she could creep up on Clara's defences and breach them.

'All Henry wants is an easy life – as soon as things don't go his way, he gets all huffy about it.'

'That's not fair. I know for a fact that Henry is something of a philanthropist in this area.'

'Huh!'

'Well, you just ask his staff, or that boys' football club on Pitfield Street.'

'What? How do you know so much, Mother? How do you know about boys' football clubs?'

'He sponsors their uniforms, if you must know. And yes, you're right, I think I will go now. Leave you to think things over.'

As soon as she heard the front door close, Clara pulled the harp towards the balcony doors and looked into the courtyard below. She prepared a smile and held it in position until her mother had looked up and waved, as she always did.

She positioned the harp in the middle of the bedroom and played the first few bars of Handel's *Water Music*. It would be easy to bury herself in the music, but she had practical matters to consider if she was to manage for more than a few days. The shower was the first thing. And maybe some proper wheels on the harp. And how to get to work, of course. At least she had two weeks before the next run of concerts. Then there was shopping – although she did know people who bought everything on the internet. She could try that. Even Henry wouldn't object to doing a bit of easy supermarket shopping. So, in terms of urgency, the shower was top of the list.

She called the builder, Martin McCarthy, and arranged for him to visit the following morning.

~

Julia dropped her helmet and violin case on the sofa and encircled Clara in her arms. She held her for far longer than their usual brief embraces. She half pulled away and frowned at Clara. 'You look knackered. Sleepless nights by the look of it.'

'And you're radiating health and vigour.' She looked at Julia's perfect bouncy hair. Her own unwashed, uncombed mop must look disgusting.

'I haven't been through what you have with Grace.'

'I just can't get Mum's condition out of my mind. I wish I was like you, able to look at things with a cool head.'

'Not sure that would apply if it was my mum.' Julia smiled, stepped back and swept a loose hair off her forehead. 'And I hear you also had a dreadful nightmare.'

'Bloody Henry, I told him not to tell you.' She slumped onto the harp stool, then jerked up her head. 'What did he tell you? No, let me guess – he asked you to get me to pull myself together.'

'Something like that, but you know me.'

'So you're not going to tell me to snap out of it.'

'Dunno. You haven't told me about the dream yet.'

Clara put in every detail she could remember, while Julia listened, her impassive face giving nothing away.

After a few moments, Julia said, 'I hate to sound like a stuck record, but I think what I said about Grace applies to you too. Think about it – I've never met anyone who is so close to their mother. It's an understatement to say that you depend on each other. You see each other almost every day, she still helps you with that ghastly regimen she designed for you, she cooks and plans and keeps you at it.' She knelt on the floor next to Clara and put her hand on hers. 'When she passed out, and then the rest happened, you feared the worst – still do, I'm sure. You've just gone through hell with your mother, so it's not surprising you had a nightmare about her dying.'

Clara pulled her hand away, leaned the harp towards her, and plucked the strings with both hands. She didn't look at her friend. 'Shall we play then?'

'All I'm saying is you need time to get a perspective on this.'

'I had the same dream a few weeks ago, before Mum collapsed. I didn't act on it then, and look what happened.' She turned to look at Julia, saw a crinkle around her mouth.

She finds it funny!

'Look, you're my best friend, and I'll do anything for you …'

Maybe the crinkle wasn't a suppressed laugh.

'… but you know me, what did you expect rational old Julia would say when you told me you were going to remain attached to the harp forever?'

Clara started to speak, but Julia carried on. 'But I'm not going to try to persuade you to let go of the harp, I'm just saying I'm not going to enter into this whole omen interpretation with you. I'm going to wait a while, see whether time passing leads you to see the dream from a different angle.'

Clara thought she'd wanted Julia to help her with the practicalities of life attached to the harp, but now she was face to face with her what she really wanted was for Julia to apply her mind to the problem, to find a way to convince her to let go of her harp. She wouldn't be Julia, wouldn't be her best friend, if she just agreed with her. No, Julia wouldn't abandon her to her fate without a fight, even though that would be much easier for her.

Clara didn't want to talk any more, just needed to play, to make music, to free herself from mundanity. Julia must have sensed this, and she pulled out her violin. They'd been playing together since they'd met as nine-year-olds in the juniors' classes at the Royal College of Music. They tuned up with eye contact; words were no longer necessary. When they started to play, the notes sounded clear and pure, pitch perfect.

After Julia left, Clara closed her eyes, raised her face to the low sun that had found a route through the gaps between the surrounding buildings, and drifted into a daydream doze. She pictured her papa conducting her with his beefy hands, sleeves rolled up, intense concentration in his eyes. Soon after she'd been given her first half-scale instrument aged six, Clara was playing beyond the range of her father's teaching, so he arranged for a harp tutor to come to the house twice a week. But he'd still been there; she would sense his presence in the next room, listening, resisting the temptation to stride in and give advice.

And then a year later he had a stroke and died. Clara stopped speaking. She played her harp all the time, except when asleep or eating, and Grace did not force her to go back to school.

Clara opened her eyes and saw that it was dark outside.

Of course … That was the last time she'd been almost permanently attached to the harp.

She played a lullaby her father had taught her. He would have understood why she had to keep playing; he wouldn't have judged her or called her foolish; he would have encouraged her, suggested she use it as an opportunity to work on new arrangements of music not originally written for the harp, even to return to composing her own pieces. Because he loved her, he would have trusted her, believed in her dream as much as she did.

Why couldn't her mother do the same?

She didn't want to think about that right now. Better to do as Julia suggested and take one day at a time. She wished she shared Julia's confidence that she would soon get a different perspective on the dream, but she knew by its vividness, its fluorescence, and by the way she could recall more and more of it as time passed, that every second of it counted, that every detail was imbued with meaning.

Cause and effect: she abandoned the harp, her mother died.

Clara wheeled the harp into the bathroom and took her time applying lipstick and eye shadow one-handed. She brushed her long black hair – what her father called her Italian hair – and decided a hint of blusher was called for. All this for Henry? Who had as good as hung up on her that morning and had no doubt promptly forgotten about her. She trundled the harp into the bedroom to look for something less like a sack to wear and found her plain black dress lying neatly on the bed, courtesy of Julia, no doubt.

She had just managed to manoeuvre the harp back to the living room when she heard the door open and Henry call out, 'Hello, darling, can I come in?'

'Of course.'

He sprang through the door, all smiles and wild eyes, and planted a kiss on her newly glossed lips. 'Mmm, you taste good. I've brought food, and ice-cold Chablis. I bet you're hungry. I'll cook right away, shall I? How are you, darling? You look great, did I say that? Now, where is that huge saucepan of yours? I'll just wash this lot, then I'll open the vino and pour us a glass. God, it was manic in the store today. More of those gorgeous Barcelonas arrived, including three with hairy cowhide. My God they are perfect.' He shouted over the noise of the running water, looked over his shoulder every few seconds. 'Those Italians really know what they're doing, real craftsmen. Managed to get perfectly crisp corners on that rough skin as if it were the softest, most malleable leather. One's a black and white cow – amazing how long cow's hair is, you know – and the other's a lovely pale brown, a sort of tan colour with flecks of white. You'll have to come and look at them, try them. Not everyone's taste, but they're just so wild, they're bound to sell, even at three grand each. Sorry, I'm babbling.' He looked up from the corkscrew, she opened her mouth, he carried on. 'How are you? No, before you answer, I just want to say I'm so bloody sorry I sprang Grace on you, but you know what she's like. Ah, you're laughing. Laughing is good, very good.'

Clara managed to say 'Henry' through her laughter and her wild strumming. 'Henry, stop, please stop!'

'Sorry, I'm babbling, aren't I?' He poured the wine and walked across the room towards her. 'Here, get your laughing gear around this. Cheers.'

'Cheers.' Clara raised her glass, turned away from the harp so it was almost behind her, her left arm stretched back, barely stroking the strings, her face turned up towards Henry. 'Thanks.'

'Now I'm going to cook. You could play something– how about 'Hey Jude'?'

As she played, she allowed herself to think that everything would be all right. Henry had actually apologised, he was bursting with enthusiasm, he even wanted her to play … He might be forty, but he was just a big kid really. She caught his eye and smiled. They were such an odd couple, he the working-class boy who'd served an apprenticeship in his father's reproduction furniture workshop in Bethnal Green, she the middle-class girl who'd spent her whole life playing music to the exclusion of everything else. She moved seamlessly on to 'Yesterday'.

Henry lifted his face to the ceiling and sang. His mess of tawny hair fell away from his face, the light caught the stubble on his chin, the pot steamed on the hob, and a delicious aroma of wine and herbs filled the air.

Everything had changed since yesterday.

When he came to the line about believing in yesterday, Henry glared at her. He looked away immediately, but she'd seen the resentment in his eyes. This was all an act, all this 'darling' and 'you look great'. Why? It was so unlike him to put on an act – one of the things that had attracted her was his brutal honesty, that he spoke without thinking, even if what he said was often rude. Maybe she'd seen wrong. He whistled in the silence, sliced a baguette, dropped a sliver of potato into the chip pan to test the temperature. Her stomach grumbled.

'Nearly ready,' he said. 'The chips will be done in ten minutes. More wine?'

'No, thanks.' Clara raised her glass. 'But it is delicious. You didn't cook with it, I hope.'

'No, I used up that half bottle on the side – the Sauvignon plonk.'

She laughed at their in-joke. Maybe things were all right. She wheeled the harp to the dining table, which was set at right angles to the kitchen island, and used her right hand to move the things Henry had assembled on the counter: bowls, cutlery, breadbasket, mayonnaise, salt and pepper, wine, paper napkins. He emptied the chips into the white porcelain bowl and turned his attention to the mystery dish in the large two-handled saucepan. His body obscured her view of the hob.

'And now, my piece of resistance, all the way from Brussels …' He spun round the end of the counter and placed the steaming pan on the mat in the centre of the table.

Mussels.

Clara stared down at the pan.

'Come on,' Henry said. 'Sit down and dig in.' He grabbed an empty bowl for the shells.

'How exactly?' she said.

'Surely you can leave the bloody harp while you eat!'

'You could at least take them out of the shells for me.'

'You take them out of their damn shells.'

'I think you'd better go, Henry.'

'What? You're kidding. Leave this exquisite *moules marinière?*' He spooned a dozen mussels into his bowl, picked one up in his left hand and extracted the mussel with the fork in his right hand. 'Delicious. Come on, I'm sure your mother won't notice.' He grinned at her, but his eyes accused, challenged.

'God, you're a selfish pig.' She stood, pulled the harp closer. 'You haven't even asked about my mother.'

'Yes I have. On the phone earlier.'

'Yes, then immediately swore at me about my dream.' She yanked at the fifth octave, then again. It cracked the air, wounded her ears. 'Look, you bastard, I lost my dad when I was seven, I'm not about to watch my mum go as well. And you, you just—'

'What? I just sit here and piss on your stupid obsessions? You need to grow up, woman. It was only a fucking dream, get over it.'

She stared at him, her eyes narrowing at the sight of this stranger, this evil conman. He could do what he liked, say what he liked, she'd taken her last insult from him. 'You can eat all you want. Then go.' Without looking at him, she tilted the harp onto its front castors and pushed it through the hall doorway and along to the bedroom. She didn't slam the door.

She sat on the edge of the bed with the harp between her knees. She would need another harp stool so she didn't have to lug the one she had from room to room. She heard Henry's curses and played 'All I Have to Do Is Dream' as loud as she could, played it again and again without pause, her resolve hardening, her eyes dry.

9

Nepal

Although Rinzen left Qo before breakfast, the monastery walls were lined with brothers, their right hands raised, their hopes resting on his mission. As soon as he rounded the peak, the rough track – no wider than a donkey's back – was plunged into deep shadow. He paused, let his eyes adjust to the gloom, and then set off at full speed; he flew along the track, leaping the narrower stretches, letting the cold wind blow away his worries about the brothers at Qo and the prospect of them having to leave their beautiful monastery.

When he stopped at the valley floor to consult his map, his legs started to shudder. At first he thought it was the effect of the steep descent on his calves, but the shaking intensified, the path before him vibrated, his teeth chattered and a low rumble vibrated from deep within the rocks beneath his feet.

No! Not another earthquake, not now, please not now!

There were no trees to fall on him, no cliffs to collapse above him, so he stood still and closed his eyes. The rumble subsided, the shaking suddenly stopped, but he remained where he stood, willing the earth to remain still.

It's a warning, he thought, a reminder of the urgency of his mission: the Samudrans were so few, the task so great.

He looked at the map and reckoned he could make it to the high pass at Khare by dusk, a full day's march over three peaks and then what looked like a steep zigzag path up the final ascent. The wind whipped the rust-red dust from the bare hillsides and stung his eyes; he wrapped a piece of cloth around his face, then strode along the track, head down, his heart thumping.

Three hours later he entered a wood and stopped to drink from a stream and have a wash. As he splashed the icy water onto his face, he heard a child's sobs coming from behind a tree on the opposite bank. He jumped across the stream and looked round the tree. A young boy, no more than eight years old, lay curled up in a ball between the gnarled roots.

'What's the matter? Has something happened to you?'

The boy shook his head but did not look up.

'What then?' Rinzen spoke softly, knelt down and put his hand on the boy's shoulder. 'Why are you alone in the woods?'

'Not alone,' the boy said.

'With a friend?'

The boy nodded.

'And where is he?'

The boy uncurled and turned to face Rinzen. His eyes were red, his face and hair covered in mud, and even though he'd stopped crying, his whole body was shaking. He pointed into the forest. 'Over there.'

'Show me,' Rinzen said. He held the boy's hand.

The path, in places no more than a low tunnel through the dense undergrowth, led to a small clearing with a large shaft at its centre. The boy pointed at the hole.

'He fell in there,' he said. 'It was my fault!' He wailed, calling out a name Rinzen couldn't catch through his sobs.

They looked over the edge. The shaft was about two metres wide and so deep it appeared bottomless. It steep sides were wet and muddy from recent rain. Rinzen focused on the blackness, let his eyes adjust and saw no sign of the friend at the bottom of the shaft. As he peered into the gloom, he discerned a further channel sloping away from what appeared to be the base, out of sight for even a Samudran senior.

He dropped his shoulder bag on the ground and crouched down to the boy's level. 'I'm going into the hole. I want you to look after my satchel while I'm gone.'

'No, please don't leave me.'

'You were brave to bring me here. Now you must be brave again. You want to see your friend, don't you?'

The boy nodded, and Rinzen leapt over the edge of the shaft. He jumped from one side of the well's wall to the other until he reached the false base. He peered into the treacly darkness and called out, but there was no reply, not even a groan. He braced himself for what he might find when he reached the end of the tunnel.

Round the bend, he nearly fell over the body of the lost boy, lying on what looked like an iron mesh suspended over a smaller channel, possibly some sort of ventilation shaft. Rinzen crouched, put his cheek near the boy's mouth, and felt a faint breath. With great care he felt the boy's arms and legs, checked for signs of a break, then gently felt his head with the tips of his fingers – on his forehead there was a protrusion the size of a hen's egg.

He lifted the limp body and laid it down on the ledge next to the shaft, wishing he had a candle so he could see more clearly. Working only by touch, he found the meridian and applied pressure in precisely the right points. The sound of a sudden outbreath told him he'd found it, but he kept up the pressure as he said, 'My name is Rinzen, what is your name?'

He repeated the sentence many times, until, 'What!' The boy lashed out with both hands.

Rinzen caught them in his, and said, 'Don't worry, I'm here to help you. I met your friend in the forest.'

'I fell and fell and …' The boy stopped. 'I can't see anything! I'm blind!'

'No, it is very dark here, but I can see. I'll carry you back to your friend.' As if on cue, they heard a distant cry from the surface, but it sounded like a man's voice.

'What's your name?'

'Goba,' the boy said.

'I will have to put you on my back, Goba, then we'll climb up the tunnel like a pair of cats. There's nothing I like more than being a cat, but you'll need to hold on tight.'

Rinzen, with the boy on his back, bounded up the slope, then stopped and shouted up the well, 'Throw down a rope.'

While the villagers fussed over the boy, Rinzen picked up his satchel and disappeared into the woods. Goba would tell them that a magic monk had saved him, had run like a real cat up the steep tunnel. The parents would smile at the fantastic story and know it wasn't what actually happened. Otherwise why would he have needed a rope to get up to the surface?

~

Rinzen walked at a steady pace all day and stopped only to eat some of the *gwaramari* and *momos* the Qo brothers had given him. Shortly before dusk he came across a shallow cave just off the mountain track, and although the high pass at Khare was in sight he decided to shelter out of the wind for the night. As he lay down to sleep, his thoughts travelled back to Goba: perhaps he should have stayed to make sure the first boy didn't take the blame for Goba's fall? No, he'd done what Kwato would have done and left the scene before the villagers could thank or praise him.

In the morning he drank the last of his water, ate a few berries he'd collected as he trekked through the second valley, and set off up to the high pass. By the time he got there the sun was warm on his back, his shadow shrinking with each minute, and he squinted in the glare from the remains of last year's snow. The track swirled before him, his

98

stomach churned in response, and he felt a great urge to lie down and sleep; altitude sickness, he thought, and forced himself to continue to the summit, where he leaned against a snow-covered bank and closed his eyes.

The ring of the bell that woke him belonged to an old goat; its head cocked to one side as if questioning what it was seeing. Rinzen stood up slowly and surveyed the scene in front of him. Mountains to the far horizon, with high, snow-capped peaks sparkling in the sunlight. He took some deep breaths, stretched his arms to the sky, and watched a dozen eagles ride invisible air currents. He had told the inquisitive junior at Qo that travel was nothing special, but when you came across scenes like this ... No, he was on a mission, Kwato's mission, and must resist such indulgence.

He quenched his thirst with a handful of snow and ran down to the bottom of the valley, where he turned south along the bank of a river. He came across several waterfalls that fed the river's tributaries. He knew that he should wade across them in case someone saw him, but he jumped them all the same. He encountered rabbits and goats, heard the song of the crested bunting, and paused to watch a pair of mating spiders, the male bright red, its partner a dirty brown.

At the end of the valley, where the river widened, he entered a village of wooden houses decorated with intricate patterns picked out in sunset reds and yellows, lilypad greens, rich ochre from the soil around them, shades of blue from a winter sky to a deep ocean, and all the lilacs imaginable. Again there was a welcoming group of excited children, and again he was offered food and drink. His host, an old woman with her front teeth missing and a laugh like an agitated crow, questioned him about where he'd come from and where he was going. She had heard of the Samudrans but had only ever met one brother, and that was in a distant village. When he emerged from her house, the crowd of people all wanted to take his hand in friendship;

perhaps they thought that the touch of a monk would bring them good fortune?

As he left, the old woman pressed him to take a small sack containing guavas, plums, a slab of seed cake and two freshly baked flatbreads.

That night, as he prepared his camp close to another river, he heard footsteps and called out a welcome.

A man about his age, wearing a long, brown woollen coat and a wide-brimmed felt hat, walked straight up to him 'Good evening, brother. Thank you for inviting me to share your fire.'

'Please sit. Would you like to share my food?'

'Surely it is for me to offer a monk food and drink?' the man said, and laughed. 'But as I do not have any food to offer you, I accept your generosity.'

Rinzen set out his simple fare on a piece of cloth and the man immediately helped himself to the flatbread, the seed cake and then the fruit. The man belched, and thanked him, then said, 'May I ask where you come from, brother?'

'I am a Samudran brother from Sarmand. My name is Rinzen.'

'I'm Chodak. I've heard of the Samudrans, but I've never come across Sarmand. Is it far from here?'

'It feels like a long way, but it's only five days' walk from here.'

'You say "home", so you were born in the monastery?'

'I've been in Sarmand for so long, it is my home, but I was born in the small village of Chaukati, not far from the monastery.'

'I'm very pleased I came upon you, Rinzen. I'm going to visit my uncle and hoped to arrive by nightfall, but I misjudged the distance. Which way are you going?'

'To the monastery at Barnang.'

'Oh yes, I know it. A beautiful place – at least it looks beautiful from the outside. It's a long journey, you'll be lucky to get there tomorrow.' Chodak poked the fire with a stick. 'I suppose you must have an important reason to visit.'

'Yes, I do.' Rinzen realised he hadn't given his mission much thought since the incident with the boys. He'd been focusing on the journey itself, checking his map, soaking up the new landscapes. Now he was only a day away from Barnang, a day from knowing whether they too had the wasting disease. What would befall the brotherhood if that was the case, if there were no more elders?

'You look worried, brother. You're frowning.'

'It's true that I'm worried. But it's rude of me to worry when you've done me the honour of joining me.'

'The honour is all mine,' Chodak said. 'But please tell me.'

After Rinzen had told Chodak about the disease afflicting Sarmand and Qo, the stranger was silent for a few minutes. He stared into the fire, which cast shadows on his creased brow, then he looked up and said, 'Ah, that is very unfortunate. We must hope that Barnang does not have this wasting disease. But it is very far from the other monasteries, so I'm sure it will be different there.'

'I hope so,' Rinzen said.

The two men sat in silence for a time, until Rinzen said he needed to meditate, and walked along the river bank to sit beneath the branches of a large willow.

When he emerged from the meditation Chodak was not there.

~

The next evening Rinzen arrived at the foot of the hill below Barnang and saw men on the trail – soldiers with rifles in front of a barricade. He stopped and ducked out of sight behind a tree. His instinct told him to wait until it was completely dark, and then to make his way up the steep hillside and through the woods around the barricade to

Barnang. Two lanterns hung beside the roadblock, and he counted six soldiers and a man with his back to him dressed in a long coat and a wide-brimmed hat. The man turned to point back along the trail and Rinzen saw the face of Chodak.

10

London

Backache woke her before the alarm clock. She slowly straightened, shook her arms, splayed her stiff fingers, rolled her shoulders and stood up. It was 6am and still dark outside, and although she had a desperate desire for a strong cup of tea, she pushed the harp into the bathroom, stripped and flannelled her whole body. Her face didn't look too bad, no black bags below her eyes, but then this was a forgiving mirror. She stared at her naked body with the harp beside her – like Terpsichore, the muse of choral song and dance, with her lyre – and considered entering the mythological world by foregoing clothes; until she remembered that Martin McCarthy would ring the bell at eight o'clock.

She felt calm and in control; today, nothing was urgent, there was no need to panic about what to eat, what to wear, how to move around outside. Something had clicked when Henry placed that pan of mussels on the table. In that moment she realised she was alone in this, that even the helpful Julia couldn't really enter into the strange world she now inhabited. Conditions of life had changed and she had no choice but to accommodate them, the first one being that she now belonged to a minority of one – people who were permanently attached to a classical concert harp. So, she had not wept over Henry's callousness, didn't even blame him for it. After all, it was a very difficult thing for anyone else to accept. After his noisy departure from the flat, she had returned to the kitchen and eaten the remaining chips and bread and had then loaded the dishwasher, cleared everything away, wiped the surfaces and escorted the harp back into the bedroom. If she had been a whistler, she would have whistled while she worked.

Martin McCarthy rang the bell at exactly 8am. In Martin's world there were only solutions, never problems, so she didn't feel awkward explaining the reason she needed the bathroom made into a wet room. She knew he'd done all sorts of unusual projects, including constructing a quarter-size replica of the Leaning Tower of Pisa in a garden in Surrey. He didn't look at her quizzically, didn't question her sanity, just immediately sketched out a solution to the problem of how she could shower while holding onto her harp.

'Would it be difficult to widen the doorway into the bathroom, and also the one between the hall and the kitchen?'

He tapped the walls. 'That's not a problem, it's only studwork. Shall I raise the heads as well?'

'Come to think about it, I don't actually need doors.'

'Then we could remove the wall above the doors as well.' He walked along the hall, tapping the wall. 'I see this room already has wide, high doors.'

'My harp store. Have a look if you like.' She pulled the Lyon & Healy towards Martin and looked through the open door. 'I wish it had been that little Celtic harp in my dream instead.'

'A lot easier to move about, that's for sure. My, will you look at the depth of finish on that black one!' Martin peered closer, and a distorted reflection looked back.

'That's my second favourite. It's a Salvi Diana, lovely mellow sound.'

'And the detail on the soundboard.' Martin pulled his reading glasses from the top pocket of his coat and leaned even closer. 'What wood is that?'

'Fiemme Valley red spruce.' A wonderful warmth spread from her belly up to her chest. 'The flower inlays are gold leaf.'

'It's … perfect. What exquisite craftsmanship. All of them, even that strange skinny one at the back.'

'That was a gift, an electric harp – you put that strap over your right shoulder and round your waist. I don't play it much. And I keep that other one, another Salvi, for sentimental reasons, even though I no longer play it.'

Martin sighed with satisfaction and closed the doors. He took the measurements he needed, promised that the whole team would be back the next day, and was about to leave when he stopped and stared at the harp with a puzzled frown. 'Would the harp not benefit from a set of more substantial wheels?'

'I'm going to call the man who repairs my instruments about that today, but his workshop is near Gloucester, so who knows when he'll be able to do it.' They both looked down at the base of the harp. 'I'll manage though. I'm getting used to lugging it around.'

'If you like, Richard could put some small wheels on it for you – don't worry, he'll do a neat job, no damage.'

'Have I ever told you that you are the best builder in London, if not in all of England, Martin?'

'Now don't make me blush. We'll be here mob-handed in the morning. Joel loves your harp playing, you know. So do I of course.'

'Then I'll play to them, any tunes they like.'

~

During the following week, while the builders worked on the bathroom, Clara played their requests and camped in the living room. Joel, the plumber, who was particularly keen on her harp playing, also had a fine baritone voice and sang along to many of the old favourites.

Each night after the building team left, Clara rested, cooked and ate the food delivered by Ocado, and then started on her own composition. She had intended to work on classical pieces not yet arranged for the harp, but instead found herself composing longer and longer interludes of her own devising. The sounds flowed from her fingers and hung in the air like mist; the notes never jarred, the tempo changed only imperceptibly, and she had no need to concentrate on what she played. It was as though the new compositions were already familiar, already learned and practised and perfected. She didn't dwell on why this was, or on anything else. While she played this new music, she was released from the tyranny of thought, freed from anxiety; she floated on the waves of sound, submerged in the music, which stayed in the room long after she'd played it. When she emerged from these trances she had the sensation that layers of herself had peeled away.

While in this state one night she thought kindly of her mother, thought of all the sacrifices she had made for her, and telephoned to apologise for her recent moodiness. 'The building work will be finished tomorrow,' she said. 'Would you like to come over for lunch the day after?'

'Do you mean on Saturday?'

Clara had no idea if that's what she meant. 'Yes, Saturday.'

'I thought you and Henry got together on Saturday.'

'Yes, usually, but …'

'But what, darling?'

She took a deep breath. 'Henry and I argued last week, and we decided to give each other time to get used to things. I'll probably call him next week.' Had she managed to sound light-hearted?

Silence.

'Mother?'

'I see,' Grace said.

How could a simple 'I see' be so exasperating?

'I'm sure you'll sort it out, Clara. Please tell me you're not still refusing to let go of the Lyon & Healy.'

'No. That's why I've had the builders here. As you know.'

'I'm so worried about you, about this … this obsession. Think about it – how can tethering yourself to a harp possibly affect anything, let alone another person?'

'I have thought about it, and I know that it does. Look how central the harp has been in our lives.'

'That's completely different. That's your calling, and now your profession.'

'All I know is that when I didn't follow the message of the dream the first time, you collapsed and they found something wrong in your brain and in your chest.'

'For God's sake, Clara! Listen to yourself. You really must stop this, before you go completely mad.'

'Thank you, Mother. See you on Saturday.'

Clara stared at the phone. She'd just hung up on her mother for the first time in her life. It felt wrong and right at the same time.

The new swivel wheels made it easier to manoeuvre the massive harp, but she felt no inclination to take it outside the flat; the furthest she'd been was onto the balcony, using the ramps Richard the carpenter had installed. She used them now, took several deep breaths, and gazed up at the starless sky. Fulbright's flat was in darkness, thank God.

An icy gust sent a shiver through her and she turned to go back inside. As she did, she caught a glimpse of something, a flash of light, or possibly the reflection of a light, in the blank blackness of Fulbright's sliding patio door. She froze, leaned forward and stared at the glass. Her heart pounded; spidery nerves tingled on her scalp. Suddenly a light came on and Fulbright, close to the glass, gawked at her. She fell back, crashed against the harp, grabbed it as it fell towards the stone tiles, scraped its body against the wall and wrestled it back into an upright position. Panting heavily, she pushed it back through the doors, slammed them closed and yanked the curtains across.

If Henry had been there, she would have got him to talk to the creep. She wanted Henry to understand, needed him to. She paced around the room, circled the kitchen island, eyes averted from the harp.

He had called a few times since the mussels fiasco, and what had she done? Told him she was too busy to talk. She picked up the phone and called his mobile. When it went straight to voicemail, she left an apologetic message. Then she took three long strides across the room, slid her hand between the curtains and opened one of the balcony doors, pulled the harp towards her stool, started at C major and ploughed through the cycle of fifths again and again, determined to drive Fulbright back into his hole, to wipe that leer off his ugly face.

~

After Martin McCarthy's team had completed the bathroom on Friday afternoon, Clara opened some sparkling wine and began playing ragtime songs. On the third bottle, Joel requested 'Old Man River' and sang along; the others maintained a respectful silence before erupting into loud cheers and shouts for more. Martin was pressed into singing 'Danny Boy', and the two Irish labourers looked almost tearful as they hummed in the background.

As soon as they left, she stripped naked and pushed the harp into the bathroom. Martin had built a two-metre-high wall that jutted into the room, with the shower one side and a dry place for the harp on the other. The wall had a hole a little above Clara's shoulder height, through which she could reach her arm to touch the harp. The idea was that any water that landed on her right shoulder would trickle down her body rather than along her arm. The new shower rose in the ceiling meant she didn't have to turn around to get a proper drenching, and the water ran onto the tiled floor and into a gulley. Martin had also installed three dispensers on the back wall, for shampoo, conditioner and shower gel, all of which could be operated with one hand. To protect the harp from excessive humidity, the powerful extractor fan sucked away the steam.

Clara laughed as the power-shower massaged her aching head and shoulders. Her hair was so matted with building dust that the water ran cold by the time she'd rinsed away the last of the conditioner.

~

On Saturday morning Clara pulled on her Levis and a thick Guernsey jumper and made her first trip outside the flat in two weeks. She came out of the lift, turned right and paused at the edge of the cobbled courtyard. Silver threads of sunlight transformed the ground into a sea of stone waves that glistened and glittered. She looked back with longing at the lift, but she'd spent at least half an hour working up the will to go out, had decided to make it into a mission to buy lunch for her mother's visit from the Italian deli on Charlotte Road. She pressed on.

The harp swerved like an airport baggage trolley with a faulty wheel, following the line of least resistance, bumping and bouncing on the cobbles so violently that she worried it would shake apart. She persisted, found it easier to pull rather than push; one cobble at a time, she edged towards the gateway onto the pavement. Now that it was outside, the harp looked enormous, outsized, its presence in the open air as absurd as someone taking a bath in the middle of a zebra crossing.

Once she was under the arch, the going improved; she was relieved to see there was no one in the short street as it would be impossible to pass someone on the narrow pavement. At the corner with Phipp Street she stopped and looked towards Great Eastern Street – a constant stream of traffic in the background, a press of pedestrians nearer to her. She carried on, apologised to the woman with two overfull shopping bags who had to step into the road. She smiled at Clara, which encouraged her to go on, barely pausing as she turned into Great Eastern Street and weaved through the stream of pedestrians towards the traffic lights. Without exception they stared at her; some laughed and pointed, others refused to give ground as she approached. She progressed slowly, 'Excuse me' and 'Sorry' popping automatically from her mouth.

By the time she got to the traffic lights her face was florid and her legs ached with the constant need to brace and twist. To make matters worse, she seemed to have acquired some followers, a group of boys under ten who harassed her with questions like 'Won't you give us a song?' and 'Are you mad, miss?' Glares had no effect, so she focused on the pedestrian lights. The moment they changed to green she pushed the harp, but it caught in a rut at the edge of the road and tipped forward. A man jumped past her and grabbed the column, but her own forward momentum dumped her onto the road beside him. Two pairs of hands immediately held her arms, pulled her gently to her feet.

'Are you OK? Are you hurt?' asked one of her helpers, a willowy young woman with a riot of fair hair.

Clara looked at her concerned face. 'Thanks, I'm fine. You are all so kind.'

'The lights have changed,' the man said. 'We'd better get your harp back onto the pavement.'

He and Clara moved the harp to the back of the pavement, and the two young women came along.

'Are you all together?' Clara asked.

'Yes, we're on a break from our life-drawing class,' the tall young woman said. 'Where are you going with this beautiful harp?' She stroked the curve of the harp's neck.

'To the deli on Charlotte Road.'

'That's where we're going. To Charlotte Road, it's where the Prince's Drawing School is. We could help you if you like.' She looked at the other two.

The other young woman nodded. 'Of course,' the man said.

They laughed and chatted as they all marshalled the harp. When the tall girl called out 'Mind out, harp on the move!', the reactions from passers-by changed from frowns of incredulity and impatience to jocular and helpful acceptance that the magnificent instrument had right of way on the busy pavement.

The friendly artists left her at the delicatessen and crossed the road to their college, waving and shouting their goodbyes as they went. The deli owner, who was either a naturally generous soul or had been infected by the youthful vigour of the two girls, offered to serve her from the door, and even found a bag with a long handle she could sling over her shoulder. Thus buoyed, Clara set off towards home.

She hadn't gone more than a few metres before the harp veered across the sloping pavement into the path of an old man with a stick. 'Watch what you're doing,' he snapped. 'You'll injure somebody, you will. Bloody idiot.'

Blood rushed to her face. She stopped and looked down the length of Charlotte Road – such a long way to go, and every centimetre an agony.

'It's OK,' the tall girl shouted from across the road. 'I'll help you.' She dashed over and steadied the harp with both hands. 'It will be easier if we both push it. It's so beautiful, but don't you usually have a cover and a trolley? My friend does, and even then it's still tricky to move it about.'

'Thank you,' Clara said. 'Thank you so very much.' She failed to keep the sob from her voice.

'It will be OK now, don't worry.'

The girl also blushed. Empathy, Clara supposed. Such a good person. 'What's your name?'

'Gail.'

'Mine is Clara, Clara Martinelli. But don't you need to go back to your class?'

'It's an open class, they won't mind if I miss some of it.' She looked down the street. 'Where to next?' she said brightly.

Clara laughed. 'What luck, meeting you. And yes, I usually do have a proper trolley and a thick cover, but not today. I live about five minutes away. Well, it's five minutes without a harp to push.'

When they arrived at Clara's building, she invited Gail in for coffee and was pleased when she accepted. It seemed much easier to be with a stranger than to deal with the judgement of her mother, her lover, even her best friend.

Gail poured the coffee and joined Clara on the sofa. 'Do you play in an orchestra?'

'Most of the time. Sometimes I do solo performances.'

'I don't suppose …'

Clara smiled. 'What don't you suppose?'

'Would you play something? Only if you're in the mood, of course.'

'What would you like me to play?'

'Anything. I love the sound of the harp.'

'I'll just tune it – all that shaking about will have put it badly out.' She plucked the strings and tuned the harp. 'OK, now let's see.' She considered tunes that Gail probably knew, then realised she wanted to play something special for this angel who had come to her rescue, who didn't ask awkward questions, who accepted things as she found them. 'I'll play something I guarantee you'll never have heard before.'

Clara closed her eyes and played her own composition. Again, the chords floated in the air, but also tumbled like a waterfall from the Lyon & Healy. As she played, she found variations on the theme presented themselves; she allowed them to materialise, to cascade from the strings in a whirlpool of sounds that twisted and spun to the edge of infinity before bursting as a brilliant fountain, each note expiring before it landed but leaving an imprint for the next to follow.

She opened her eyes and saw Gail face up on the floor, her face devoid of all anxiety, eyes closed, arms outstretched, as though she were about to levitate.

When Clara stopped, Gail whispered, 'Thank you', and slowly sat up. Her eyes had a faraway look about them, like someone just emerging from a deep meditation. 'I'd better go,' she said. At the door, another whisper, as if speaking too loud would break the trance. 'I've never heard such beautiful music.'

Neither have I, thought Clara.

She stayed on the sofa, gazed at the wall and fantasised about having Gail's help to get around, go shopping, go to rehearsals, even go on tour. They would laugh at the absurdity of it but would tell the world to go to hell. She wouldn't want her to give up her art studies, but Clara could accommodate that, could organise her life to suit. Everything might be all right then; it would be possible, wouldn't it, to live a normal life?

She shook her head. What a stupid idea. The girl wasn't her servant, she had her own life ahead of her, what would be in it for her?

The doorbell rang. She'd come back! She rushed across the room to the entryphone and picked up the handset. 'Gail?'

'No, darling, it's me.'

It took a couple of seconds to register that it was her mother's voice.

'Mum!' she shouted. 'Sorry, come up.' Moments later, she heard two voices as the flat door opened.

'I've brought Lawrence with me. I hope you don't mind.'

Did she mind? Perhaps with Lawrence Greene there they could avoid the elephant in the room and have a pleasant lunch? 'No, that's lovely. Hello, Lawrence, please come in.'

He marched into the living room, came straight up to her and kissed her on both cheeks. His lined, leathery face crinkled into a smile. 'Good to see you, Clara. Sorry I missed your last concert, had to be elsewhere.'

'Anywhere interesting? Silly question, you always go to interesting places.'

'Nepal this time, then Bhutan. Studying the Himalayan honey gatherers.'

Grace smiled at her, took her free hand and squeezed. 'You're looking well.'

What's this? thought Clara. A new tack, or was it just for show in front of Lawrence? 'Hi, Mum.'

Grace looked at Clara's feet. 'Have you been out?'

'Yes, I went to the deli to get the lunch ingredients. *Penne alla pesto*, Parma ham, nice Italian bread.'

'What, with the …?'

'Mmm hmm. A bit tricky, but I managed in the end.'

Grace's smile evaporated, and Clara wheeled the harp across the room to the kitchen and filled a pan with water. 'Actually, a very nice young woman helped me.' She turned the gas knob, waited for ignition, put the lid on the pan.

'Would that be Gail?'

'Yes. She left a few minutes ago. I thought she must have forgotten something.' Clara looked vaguely around the room. The others followed suit, in silence.

'Mum, why don't you go and admire the bathroom while I put on the pasta? Lawrence, would you mind laying the table?'

'Of course. Point me at the necessaries.'

Grace didn't move, seemed a bit confused, had probably expected to find her daughter a nervous wreck after two weeks attached to the harp.

During lunch, Grace prompted Lawrence to talk about his anthropological investigations in the Far East.

Clara watched him while he spoke. Were they in love? They'd known each other for at least five years, but lately he seemed to be far more present in Grace's life. There'd been a lot more sentences that started 'Lawrence and I went to …' in the months since Clara had moved out of home and into her own flat. Perhaps her mother had begun to reclaim her own life after focusing on Clara's for twenty-six years? She wouldn't blame her: Lawrence was a good-looking man, the classic English sportsman, broad-shouldered, confident, upright like an ex-soldier – even though he wasn't – and with that attractive swarthiness of a man who'd spent a long time outdoors. And he was very clever, could speak all those languages, had travelled all over the world.

No sooner had he finished an interesting story about the warring tribes of Papua New Guinea than Grace asked him to tell Clara about the honey collectors of the Himalaya.

'OK, but instead of the honey gatherers, I'll tell you about a tribe I think you may find more interesting. The elders of the Matsigenka, who live in the high Andes, wear large headdresses all the time, day and night. This elaborate headgear – about one metre square – means they have great difficulty moving about in normal buildings, so they live in specially adapted houses with enormous doorways and beds made for giants. I spent some time with them a few years ago but wasn't able to establish when and why this tradition began.'

He told them more about the Matsigenka, but Clara couldn't concentrate; all she could think was: He's on my side! He could persuade Mum to let me be.

'Seeing the alterations you've made to your flat made me think of them,' he said, as though in confirmation. 'And now I really have talked enough.'

Grace glowered at him, fidgeted in her seat. 'Well, we'd better be going anyway.' A frown gathered, as though she were about to relate some dreadful news.

'What is it, Mum?'

'It's just that I'm still very worried about you.' She looked down at the table. 'I had hoped that after a week you would have put that dream of yours into perspective and everything would be back to normal. But I can see you have got used to it, have had all this expensive building work done to make it easier, even put new wheels on your precious harp, and … and it's all my fault.' Grace looked at Lawrence, then turned to Clara. 'You're doing it all for me, even though I don't want you to.'

Clara did not look away. She was causing her mother all this anxiety but couldn't do anything to stop it. She had attached herself to the harp in order to prevent her mother's death, but by doing so she was making her mother so stressed that she might actually be hastening her demise.

'There's no harm in Clara being attached to her harp,' Lawrence said. 'Look, Grace, she's happy, and she's managing to cook and eat and wash and dress. She even went shopping. We in the West pay scant attention to our dreams, but others feel very differently – Native American Indians, for example. Like the Naskapi of the Labrador Peninsula, who live in such isolated family groups that they rely on their own inner voices and unconscious revelations to guide them – much like our Clara is doing here. In fact, the major obligation of an individual Naskapi is to follow the instructions given by his dreams. They help him to foretell the weather and give him invaluable guidance in his hunting, upon which his life depends.'

'Oh, Lawrence, you and your blasted tribes … But it's still not right, is it?' Grace turned away from Lawrence, a look of disgust on her face.

Foretell the future, Clara thought. That's what the instruction in her dream was all about.

Grace leaned across the table and held Clara's hand. 'Will you do something for me, darling?' Her frown deepened as she looked at her daughter. 'Will you indulge me and agree to see a psychotherapist?'

Clara's hand twitched under her mother's, but she resisted the urge to pull away.

'Just to see what she thinks is going on,' Grace continued. 'She might be able to help you understand why you're doing this.'

She thinks I've lost my mind, thought Clara. She can't forget those two years I stopped speaking after Papa died; even though I was only seven, she thinks that showed I'm vulnerable, that I might be heading for a breakdown. 'I'm seeing a hypnotherapist next week. Julia thinks I should.'

'I see.' Grace pursed her lips in that way Clara knew so well. 'I'll pay for the psychotherapist.'

'OK, Mum, I tell you what. If the hypnotherapist doesn't help, I'll see your psycho person. OK?'

'Thank you, darling.' Grace withdrew her hand, got up and cleared away the dirty dishes.

Clara pushed away from the table, sat on her stool and played the theme from *Chariots of Fire* while the two of them washed and dried, wiped and tidied. She had half a mind to bring up the issue of her mother having the biopsy. She could pose it as a quid pro quo – you have your test to please me, and I'll see the therapist to please you. But it would only lead to another argument.

She watched them as they walked across the courtyard. Her mother's arm hung free, not through Lawrence's, and her head was bowed. She did not turn to wave.

11

Nepal

A flash of light sprayed the trees around him, then more torchbeams lit up the path below. He moved deeper into the woods, crouched down and listened, heard soldiers' voices inside the wood further up the hill. Had the soldiers seen him, and were they now searching for him? There wasn't enough time to employ Standing Still, so he climbed a tall oak tree and lay along a branch, peered through the thinning autumn leaves and strained to hear them.

There came the crackle of steps on fallen leaves – surely too delicate a sound for a soldier's boots, however stealthy. It moved to the other side of the tree; the man would pass him by. But then it stopped, and all he could hear were the soldiers on the trail. Rinzen held his breath and didn't dare move, not even his head. Was that scraping noise behind him a squirrel? An owl?

The whisper sounded like a shout in his sensitised ears. 'Hello,' it said. 'I'm a brother, right behind you.'

Rinzen's muscles tensed; he curled his toes so they pressed down on the branch, ready to leap. He slowly turned his head: a man was crouching at the end of the branch, his back against the tree trunk. He was dressed in a brother's maroon jacket, wore boots similar to his own, and his eyes shone in the darkness. Definitely a Samudran brother.

'What are you doing here, brother?' the other asked.

'I am Rinzen, a senior from Sarmand, on my way to Barnang.'

'My home,' the brother said. 'The soldiers are close. Let's get away from here.'

Rinzen followed him down the tree. They walked in silence for ten minutes along the contour of the hill, climbed up a crevice in a rocky outcrop and onto a ledge behind the rock, hidden from view. They sat cross-legged face to face, and the brother introduced himself as the senior Lobsang.

Rinzen knew the answer, but he asked anyway. 'Why are the soldiers on the trail?'

'They've heard about a disease that's killed the elders, and they fear it will spread to the villages nearby. No one is allowed in or out of the monastery.'

Thoughts tumbled in Rinzen's head; his heart rattled in his chest. The worst had happened: Barnang had been hit too. No more Samudran elders. What would become of them, what would happen to the earth?

'The last two elders told me to go to Sarmand and Qo to seek help from the elders there,' Lobsang said. 'But seeing you here, all the way from Sarmand ...'

'You're right.' Rinzen clasped his hands together to stop them shaking. 'Sarmand and Qo have the wasting disease. The last two Qo elders are close to death, and we bade farewell to the last of our own elders a week ago.'

'Then ...' Lobsang looked down at the rock.

Rinzen told Lobsang that the elders of Qo had decided to close the monastery if Barnang had the wasting disease. 'I suppose we need to get a message to your elders,' he said. 'And take their instruction.'

They remained silent for some time. Rinzen couldn't harness the thoughts that flew about his head in snatches. His teeth ground together, pains spiked in his skull. There is no solution. Can't think. Can't sit here and do nothing. Act, come on, what would Kwato do? Control himself, for a start.

Of course I'm not ready for this, how could he think I was? He closed his eyes, took long slow breaths. This is panic. Where's your self-control? Come on, come on ...

'Have you heard about these brothers in Columbia?' Lobsang said. 'The Kogi. They enter the spirit world through concentrated thought and meditation.'

Something to latch onto, to silence the cacophony in his mind. 'My master spoke of them. He said they ... are like us.' He racked his brain, tried not to get emotional at the memory of Kwato's deathbed. 'Like us, they believe all things in nature are linked. And ... they too meditate to keep the world in balance.' Rinzen's voice wavered, but then he opened his eyes. 'Of course, you're right. Well done. Good thought. Elder Kwato told me all would not be lost if our meditations were weakened, that these Kogi would continue our work.'

Lobsang leaned forward, locked eyes with Rinzen. 'Perhaps we should go to see the Kogi, ask them to send some of those they call *mamas* to help us? What do you think?'

'But Columbia is on the other side of the world!' It would take many months to reach South America; there would be seas to cross, strange places to pass through. If it was such a struggle to leave home for these few days, how would he manage to be away from Sarmand for so long? 'Is there no other way?' he said, half to himself. 'Let's try to think of another way ... Shall we meditate – perhaps an answer will present itself?'

Rinzen took the wooden bowl from his bag and poured in a little water. The two brothers entered the trance. When they emerged some hours later, the moon, almost full, illuminated the forest.

Rinzen looked around him. Heartbeat steady, mind clear. Panic over. Must never let that happen again; his brothers depended on him.

Kwato depended on him.

'I know another way into Barnang,' Lobsang said. 'It's longer, but we'll be unlikely to meet any soldiers.'

They climbed higher, then skirted around the hill and traversed down a steep slope. Halfway down, Lobsang pointed east to the outline of Barnang on the next hill. As they neared Barnang he could see why Lobsang was confident there would be no soldiers – a sheer cliff, at least a hundred metres high, rose from the valley floor to support the monastery walls. It reminded him of the west side of Sarmand.

'Perhaps you should wait here,' Lobsang said. 'In case the soldiers come before I get back.'

Rinzen nodded and watched Lobsang scramble up the rockface. With his back to the cliff, he set his legs slightly apart and focused on Standing Still. The bright moonlight tinted the world a pale monochrome and carved deep shadows into the bark of the ancient sandalwood that loomed above him. He let the tree's fragrance wash over him, let its shadow cloak him, felt his feet drawn into the soil as though some unseen agent was tightening an invisible rope. He waited, waited, waited. Suddenly weightless, he watched the statue of his body from a great height. Even Lobsang walked straight past him when he returned from Barnang. 'Here,' Rinzen whispered in his ear, and Lobsang leapt away. 'Sorry,' Rinzen said. 'Not the right time to play tricks.'

Lobsang laughed. 'Hard to resist though, especially after I sneaked up on you.' He leaned closer to Rinzen. 'The elders want me to go and see the Kogi *mamas*. They would like you to go too, but when I told them your name, they said it was up to you, that they would not presume to instruct you as they would one of their own seniors.' He smiled at Rinzen, put his hand on his shoulder. 'It seems you are held in high regard.'

'I'm not an elder, I'm simply a senior, like you. And I don't know why the elders think so highly of me. Earlier, I

121

panicked while you were calm, and it was you who thought of the Kogi, not me. And if your elders want me to—'

He saw the flash before he heard the bang, felt the bullet graze his leg as he leapt aside. The clean air was shattered by gunfire. The two brothers sprinted along the base of the rockface, did not hesitate as they leapt over the massive boulders in their path, and realised too late that they were headed directly towards the main army contingent on the trail.

'This way,' Lobsang shouted, and took a sharp left towards what appeared to be another sheer cliff in front of them. If they scaled the rockface, Rinzen thought, the soldiers would pick them off with their guns, but still he followed Lobsang, who turned and yelled, 'Jump when I say so,' and sped on. 'Now!' he shouted, and took off over the hidden rift in the valley floor. He landed five metres sooner than Rinzen, who, not knowing how far he needed to jump, had leapt further than he thought possible. It was hard to tell if the gunfire behind them was near or far. Doubled over, the two brothers ran on.

The cliff before them was not as monolithic as it looked from afar, and Lobsang ran straight at it and round a vertical rockface into a deep gulley that zigzagged its way to the summit. Before they reached the top, Lobsang stopped and leaned against the rock. 'I saw that bullet, Rinzen. Are you hurt?'

Rinzen checked his leg. 'No. Look, just a graze.' He started to shake; his whole body vibrated as though the ground itself was oscillating.

'Sit, my brother.' Lobsang held Rinzen's arm, guided him to the ground. 'Drink some water.'

Rinzen couldn't speak; his teeth chattered as he tried to drink the offered water. He lowered his head and tried to calm himself, tried to cut through his fear with the power of concentration. Clearly, Lobsang was an accomplished brother. How did he stay so calm?

The shaking subsided enough for him to look up, and he saw that tears were pouring from Lobsang's eyes. 'Sit with me,' he said, reaching for Lobsang's hand.

Lobsang slid down, and the two brothers leaned against each other. 'You nearly died at Barnang. How could I have let that happen to our guest?'

'You saved my life,' Rinzen said. 'Your thinking was quick when mine was slow, your mind was clear when mine was in disarray, you ran so fast, you pulled me in your wake.'

'Blind panic,' Lobsang said, and they both laughed, but softly. 'Look, dawn is nearly here, and we're not out of danger yet.'

'I fear I made a terrible error of judgement yesterday,' Rinzen said. 'I met a man on the way and told him about the wasting disease at Sarmand. I told him my name and that I was going to Barnang. And then, before you climbed my tree, I saw him again – telling the soldiers about me.'

'Our training is based on trust, Rinzen. We approach everyone we meet with compassion and honesty and would rather assume the best qualities in our fellow man than treat them with suspicion.'

'But I know so little about the world beyond Sarmand.'

'Come. We must go. Let's get away from here and make a plan.'

'I have to get to Sarmand before the soldiers get there. And you, Lobsang, will you go to Qo and tell them?'

'I will. And after that we can go together to see the Kogi.'

Rinzen shook his head. His throat tightened. 'It's too dangerous. These soldiers will search for two brothers travelling together. It would be better to split up, take separate routes. We'll need money, different clothes.'

Lobsang muttered something, then said, 'Now who is thinking clearly? You are right of course. I have some money from Barnang with me, and a map of the world, but I didn't think about the clothes. I could go to my village, ask my father?'

'Good idea. I'll do the same.'

Lobsang spread out the world map and they traced the most direct routes to Columbia. It looked about the same distance whether one travelled east or west.

'So, shall I take the way west, and you the east?' Rinzen said.

Lobsang nodded.

When they reached the summit of the hill, Lobsang scratched a rough map for Rinzen in the dirt – the first day's walk towards Sarmand avoiding roads. After that, Rinzen would need to rely on Kwato's map.

As they parted, Rinzen said, 'See you in Columbia.'

Part Two

One Light Step

Water is the driving force of nature

Leonardo da Vinci, *Codex Atlanticus* (folio 154)

12

London

Clara did not get used to sleeping draped over her harp. Her nights were broken into uneven waves of sleep and wakefulness, and often she was unsure which state she was in. Dreamlike episodes turned out to be memories, and waking thoughts became scenes that spiralled out of control. There was no clear narrative to any of them, just an exhausting assemblage of nonsense. The one rather lovely scene that stayed with her was of a beautiful snow-capped mountain range – which she assumed came from one of Lawrence's descriptions – with a solitary figure bounding along the ridge.

As she looked at her puffy, misshapen face in the mirror on Monday morning, she decided that she wouldn't leave the flat unless it was absolutely necessary. After breakfast, when her aching shoulders had eased and her head had mostly cleared, she called Roland and said she didn't feel up to coming to the full orchestra rehearsal. As all the pieces were familiar to the orchestra, he agreed that she could practise at home.

Next, she called Julia's hypnotist and asked him if he would treat her at her home. He disputed the word 'treat' but agreed to come the next day.

~

Matthew Cleary looked nothing like Clara's idea of a hypnotist. He wasn't dressed in tartan trousers, a red satin waistcoat and a pink bowtie. And he didn't have rosy cheeks and a handlebar moustache. He looked more like a young estate agent with his grey, close-fitting suit, crisp white shirt and pale paisley tie. He sat on a dining chair, his back straight, his knees together; his black shoes were polished to a mirror and matched the cleanliness of his unblemished face and just-cut hair. He was unremarkable in every way, and Clara wasn't sure whether to be impressed or disappointed.

And then he opened his mouth and spoke like Richard Burton reading *Under Milk Wood*. He explained something, but Clara was too focused on the timbre of his voice, its baritone resonance, to pay any attention. As far as she was concerned, he could say anything, could talk all day if he liked.

'Before we start, do you have any questions, Miss Martinelli?'

'Clara, please.' She shifted on the harp stool, brushed the strings with her left hand. 'Sorry, could you tell me about hypnotism before you actually hypnotise me?'

'But I ... Never mind. Yes, of course.'

She found that if she stared at him and forced herself to concentrate, she could listen to the words he spoke. Did he know he had this voice? He must do, but he behaved as though he were just an ordinary man.

'... just as though you were dreaming. To put it another way, the REM state can be – and routinely is – activated outside the dream state. We all flip in and out of trance states many times a day and this is intimately connected to the REM state. A trance state is a focused state of attention, a state of utter absorption.'

'Yes, I know what you mean.' Clara thought of how she felt when she played her new composition on the harp.

'And,' he continued, 'the most absorbing trance state we ever enter is a dream. But the trance state most people are familiar with is that of hypnosis. I could say a lot more about why hypnosis can help people with addictions, phobias, and so on, but would you mind telling me why you asked me to come to see you?'

'My friend Julia thinks you might be able to help me understand this strange dream I had.'

'I see. Has this dream caused you distress, or …?'

'In fact, I had the same dream twice. The first time I wondered whether it was an omen, the second time I was sure it was.' As soon as she said this, she realised how ridiculous she must sound, but she carried on. 'When I woke from the dream the second time, I knew that if I didn't play my harp all the time my mother would die. But then I realised that I couldn't actually play the harp twenty-four hours a day – I would need to sleep, eat, wash, and so on – so I examined every detail of the dream and realised that it was when I lost physical contact with the harp that I had the premonition of my mother's horrible death. So, the key message of the dream was that I must remain permanently attached to my harp.' She grinned idiotically. 'Crazy, isn't it?'

'Dreams are our way of dealing with the events of the day,' he said. 'They are metaphors for our waking expectations. So, no, I don't think it's crazy. What we can do with hypnosis is let you access your subconscious self while you're still awake. When you're hypnotised, you become suggestible and the hypnotist can communicate directly with your subconscious mind. Perhaps through that route you can come to have a better understanding of your dream.'

'OK …' Clara wasn't sure she understood, but how could she not trust that voice?

He asked her to tell him her dream in as much detail as she could remember.

'We – the orchestra – are at the Wigmore Hall. The house is full, and all of us musicians are in complete harmony, playing sublimely. I feel at one with the music, never played so well. I guess that can happen in a dream – I mean, anything is possible, isn't it?'

'Yes, that's right, anything,' Matthew said. 'May I ask, where are you on the stage?'

Clara closed her eyes. 'I'm almost centre stage, close to the conductor, beside the violins. The conductor's baton appears to float, as though it is moving his arm rather than the other way round. His silver ring glints like a firefly under the lights, but I can't see his face clearly. His shoes are so highly polished they reflect the lights. I glimpse his red socks as he shifts his feet … He's almost dancing.' She opened her eyes and looked at Matthew.

'Do you recall more details the more you focus on the dream?'

Clara nodded, closed her eyes once more. 'We play our last piece, Bach's *Toccata and Fugue in D Minor*. I see the violin bows move precisely in time, all at the same angle as they play me into my solo. The lights dim to darkness, leaving only the conductor's lectern light and a spotlight on the harpist, on me.' She frowned, couldn't quite see the scene. 'I must be playing, but I can't see myself.'

'That's OK. What are you wearing?'

'My midnight-blue full-length dress, the new one with the plunging neckline, and … Sorry, is that too much detail?'

'No, the more the better.'

'Right. The Zambian malachite necklace, no rings, no bracelet of course. I have my hair up, pulled back from my face, the silver clip. Oh yes, black suede shoes, no heels. No tights. Too hot. That's it.'

'Any make-up?'

'Naturally. But not much, postbox-red lipstick, a touch of eye shadow, a little blusher.'

He didn't smirk or show surprise, just looked at her with his dark, almost black, eyes, but she wasn't unnerved; his look was comforting, passive rather than aggressive, and she wondered whether the hypnotism would involve looking into his eyes.

'So, you are playing the last piece of music ...'

'I start to play my solo in the spotlight, and I see, in the silent darkness beyond, another spotlight focused on a figure lying in a hospital bed. I play on, but I can't hear the notes. The figure in the bed sits up and looks at me, holds out her hand, her face creased with pain ... It's my mother's face, my mother's pain.' She closed her eyes, the better to concentrate. 'Somehow, I play on, and when I finish, the spotlight stays on me as the applause starts. The conductor turns to the audience, the stage lights go up, he invites their applause with his open palm towards me. My fellow musicians stand and applaud, the audience stand. I stand and take my first bow with my hand resting on the harp's neck as I always do. I step away from the harp, the conductor steps off the podium and takes my hand, leads me to the front of the stage, stands aside and again does that thing with his open palm. The noise in the hall gets louder and louder, shouts of "Bravo! Encore!", and I think even the stamping of feet. I blush, bow again, then offer my palm towards the conductor. More cheers for him. I turn to the orchestra and clap my hands; the conductor does the same. I'm faint, I can't hear the applause any longer. I can see the audience clapping, but there is no sound. I don't know what to do next, so I walk off stage. Just before I go backstage, I turn and see my mother lying back on the bed, and I hear a horrible rattle from her throat. Then silence. I freeze, I try to move, but I'm paralysed. Everything goes dark. I wake up.'

Clara tasted salt in the corner of her mouth, and quickly wiped away the tears.

'I'm sorry it was necessary to put you through that,' Matthew said.

'No, I'm fine. I like thinking about the dream. I discover more details every time.'

'It's certainly an interesting dream. I expect you considered several interpretations.'

'No, not really,' Clara said. 'I just knew that's what the dream meant.'

'Well, if you're ready, we can start the session. Remember, you will be conscious when you are in the trance state, and there is nothing to worry about, you cannot be made to do something you don't want to do. But you do need to sit comfortably. Perhaps if you place the harp next to a dining chair and rest your right hand lightly on it.'

She wheeled the harp over to the chair he'd moved into the middle of the room.

'Take a deep breath and relax. Breathe in … and breathe out. Let your shoulders drop, feel your legs relaxing, your feet soft on the floor. Now, I'd like you to pick a point on the wall over there and stare at it, focus your attention on it.'

As she followed his voice, her body deflated.

'There is somewhere in the mind where awareness is created, and I want you to focus your attention on that part of the mind.'

As Matthew Cleary touched her shoulder, Clara felt the last of the tension leave her, as though he had released the valve of the balloon that was her body.

'It doesn't really matter if you hear every word I say, it's your subconscious mind I'm talking to now, where all your previous learning in life has existed. I want your subconscious mind to consider the dream that convinced you that if you let go of your harp your mother would die. Look at the fine details of your dream, at the events in the dream in microscopic detail.

'You have played the last notes of your solo, the audience bursts into spontaneous applause. Is it hot under the lights? Feel the sensations, on your skin, your face, the sounds around you. After twenty, thirty seconds, you bow, the applause carries on, forty seconds, you bow again. Picture your mother while you bow – because it is a dream you can see where she is while you bow before the adoring audience. She lies in a hospital bed, seriously ill. Do you want to be by her side, or do you want to be here in the Wigmore Hall, taking your bows, shaking the conductor's hand, feeling the slight dampness of his palms? The clock ticks … fifty, sixty, sixty-one.

'In this state of complete relaxation you can experience your dream once more, or you can change elements of the dream. You might want to try holding onto the harp instead of walking off the stage, and see whether in this scenario your mother still dies. Or you could try to change the outcome of your original dream, see if you can picture yourself walking away from the harp and your mother getting out of bed, fully recovered from whatever afflicts her. It is your dream; you can make anything happen.

'In a moment you will wake. I'm going to count to five and you'll wake feeling as though you've had the best sleep ever, you will feel invigorated, better than you've ever felt before.'

Clara felt rather than heard the click of his fingers, snapped her head up, eyes wide, the world brightening with every second.

'Well?' Matthew said. 'How do you feel?'

'Mmm … I didn't expect anything like that.'

'How do you feel physically?'

'Great.' She shook her legs, then her arms – the muscles were toned, her arms strong enough to lift the harp over her head and run down the centre of Old Street. 'I feel strong, full of energy, and no shoulder ache.'

'How about mentally?'

'Clear, crystal clear. I saw the dream again; it was so strange. I was a spectator as well as a participant in my own dream, although I still couldn't see myself in the spotlight.'

'And do you feel like letting go of the harp now?'

'What? No, definitely not. I could never do that, not after ...'

'After what?'

'After what you showed me.'

'I didn't show you anything, I just took you somewhere you could see for yourself.'

'But you must have done something, how else would I feel like this? I can't remember feeling so ... so awake. Does that make sense?'

'Yes. Hypnosis allows you to enter a state of such utter relaxation that not only your muscles but also your mind feels rejuvenated afterwards.'

Clara's grin stuck to her face like a mask.

~

To prolong the mood, she played her own composition as soon as Matthew left. The music, this particular music that she had not written down but could remember perfectly, induced a similar trance state to the hypnotic one. The music emanated from somewhere deep inside her, the sounds bypassed her ears to connect directly to her heart. Playing involved no effort of will, no necessity to recall the chords, the pedal changes, the trills and glissandos. Her trance deepened as she played, until even the awareness that it was she who was playing evaporated. Waves washed over her, each wave higher, wider, longer, more perfectly formed than the last, until she was simply a particle of the surf that ebbed and flowed without resistance, dissolved in an ocean of pure, unexamined experience.

A false note – a string out of tune – switched her back like the click of Matthew's fingers. A glance at the kitchen clock told her she'd played for over two hours without a break, but her shoulders didn't ache, her arms and hands showed no signs of the usual fatigue, and when she stood up to stretch her legs there was not a hint of stiffness. If anything, she was even more invigorated than when she started. She smiled at the thought of the next hypnosis appointment, ate some bread and cheese and drank at least a litre of water, then sat down to start Britten's *Suite for Harp, Op. 83*, the first of the solo pieces on Roland's list.

Five minutes in, and her face flinched with each note, her fingers stiffened, and a dull ache intensified in her temples. She stopped, stared at the strings, her heart pounding. Perhaps she just wasn't in the mood for this piece? She tried the softer tones of Beethoven's 'Variations on a Swiss Song', but after the first few bars she was grimacing again. She was tired, that was it, even though minutes earlier she'd felt as though she could play all day.

Clara stood and wheeled the harp a few times around the room, pushed it to the bathroom to have a pee, sat on the harp stool in the bedroom and closed her eyes: this was ridiculous, of course she could play these pieces that she knew so well. The opening of *Rhapsody on a Theme of Paganini* felt right – what a relief. Her fingers flowed through the notes, but after a minute or so she found she slipped into a variation of her own composition and began to disappear. She stopped, wheeled the harp next to the bed and lay down.

During the afternoon she tried more of the concert pieces, but either the notes jarred like pinched nerves or her fingers refused her direction and instead plucked the notes of her own expanding composition. By the time the gloom of evening had descended like a fog on the bedroom, any residual effect of the hypnosis session had worn off. She lay exhausted on her bed, gazing at the ceiling, and tried not to think about the consequences.

Clara fell asleep and woke sometime later curled up in the foetal position. She had a vague idea that there was something wrong, and with eyes still closed tried to figure out what it could be. She opened one eye, saw the harp by the bed, saw both her hands flopped on the duvet, and closed her eye. Seconds later the realisation hit her like a tornado and propelled her off the bed, towards the instrument and into a crumpled pile on the floor. She scrambled up, still mostly asleep, clutched the harp's body with both hands and trundled it towards the living room. Her mind snatched at thoughts. Was her mother dying right now because she'd let go of the harp? Did she want to play the harp anymore? You played for someone to listen, didn't you? Her father, her mother, not herself. And if there was no one to listen, why should she bother to play? It was so hard to keep it going. She could choose herself instead of her mother, she could let her mother die by stopping. Was she already dead?

As soon as her mother answered the phone, she cut the call and dropped onto the chair that Matthew had placed in the middle of the room, her left hand draped like an asp over the harp.

~

It was two weeks since she'd seen Henry, and they paced around each other like wary cats, waiting for the other to make one false move. While they ate the vegetarian thali he'd bought at Diwana Bhel Poori, she told him about the hypnotism and said she'd decided to see Matthew twice a week, in the hope that she could overcome this imperative to hold onto the bloody harp. He laughed at the 'bloody', said it was the first time she had ever cursed her instrument. She could tell he wanted to say something else and winkled it out of him that he was relieved she had a therapist.

'But I have to tell you that while I was under, I re-examined the dream from every angle and came out of the trance even more convinced that I had to keep hold of the harp.'

Henry took a large gulp of lager, crossed his left leg over his right, and turned away.

Bugger him, she thought. She hadn't intended to tell him, but damn him if he wouldn't even look at her. 'Something else happened today,' she said. 'I couldn't practise the pieces for the next set of concerts. My hands wouldn't play properly, the sound jagged in my head.'

Finally, he looked round and scowled.

'I resigned from the orchestra.'

'You what? Resigned? God, Clara, you're a fucking mess.'

She looked up at him. The veins in his neck swelled, his face reddened, his temples pulsed. He'll burst any second, she thought. Funny how his mouth opens and closes like a ventriloquist's dummy.

Henry grabbed his leather jacket from the back of the chair and stepped away from the table. Clara scooped a spoonful of sweet yellow dessert from the small metal bowl and slowly, deliberately, put it in her mouth.

'Call me when you've come to your senses,' he said.

13

Nepal

Rinzen ran so fast that his satchel flew behind him. He ran along winding paths and alongside streams, up steep slopes and through thick woods, leaping over every obstruction. Whenever he spotted a village, he veered off the path and took a wide detour. Even so, it was possible, even likely, that some people had caught sight of him, that they went home and told their friends and family they'd seen a demon dressed as a monk flying across the countryside. They might even have been so afraid they locked their children inside their houses, and if they had, he was sorry to have caused such anxiety. But he had no choice. Soldiers would be sent to Sarmand. They would knock on the gates and demand entry. He had to get there first, warn his brothers, help them prepare for the assault.

He was going so fast that it was only noon when he reached the point Lobsang had thought he'd achieve at sunset, but he ran on and only rested long enough to drink some water or check Kwato's map. He gave his full attention to the journey, blocked out all the fearful thoughts that shouted for his attention, and continued in this manner until late in the night. Tonight he was grateful for the light of the full moon. When the moon set, he decided it was better to rest than to meditate.

At first light he ate the last of his bread and raced on. After a few hours, his stomach grumbled from lack of food, his legs refused to run any further, and a sickening dizziness worsened as he walked. He staggered into a village and collapsed by the well.

When he came round, he was on a bed in a room decorated with silk wall hangings that depicted the four seasons in the Himalaya. A Buddhist monk was sitting on a stool next to the bed; he moved beads through his fingers and smiled at him.

'I will ask for some food for you,' the monk said.

Rinzen nodded and closed his eyes. Glimpses of a dream refused to take definite shape in his mind. Keung had been there, they'd been running along a mountain ridge, accompanied by the exquisite string music, like water tinkling into a mountain pool, that became more distinct each time he heard it. They'd come to the edge of a cliff so high it could have been the edge of the world, and they'd run straight over that edge … Then he'd woken up and seen the monk and the beautiful room. Surely not the monk's room?

'Ah, he's asleep again,' the monk said.

'No, I'm awake. If there is a little food, I'm very hungry.'

A woman who smelled of fresh roses and was dressed in silks even finer than the wall hangings knelt next to the bed. 'Help him to sit up, please,' she said.

The monk pulled him up the bed. The woman placed a towel and a bowl of warm water on his lap and lifted his left hand into the water. Her hands were cool and soft. He looked at her face – such smooth skin, an unblemished chestnut, and dark, almost black eyes. She glanced up from drying his hand and caught him looking at her. She smiled and took his right hand. Rinzen's heartbeat quickened, and he wondered if she'd noticed.

'Please close your eyes while I wash your face.'

When she'd dried his face, his eyes followed her across the room, watched her place the bowl and towel on the table and return with a tray of food.

'Thank you,' he whispered.

'I will leave you to eat. Please ask if you would like some more.' That smile again.

After she left, Rinzen said, 'Will you share this delicious food, brother?'

'I have eaten. This is for you. And then you can tell me who you're running from.'

Rinzen looked at the monk, gripped the sides of the tray and made to get up. The monk put his hand on Rinzen's shoulder. 'You are weak, you need to eat, and rest.'

'But I have to go. I have to get to Sarmand. I have to …' He fell back, let his hands flop onto the bed.

'Eat now,' the monk said. 'Perhaps I can help you?'

'Thank you. You are very kind, but I can manage.'

He ate all the food on the tray: the rich vegetable soup, the freshly baked bread, the bowl of savoury rice, the slices of fruit.

'You are a Samudran, aren't you?' The monk took the tray to the table.

'Yes,' Rinzen said. 'And you, brother, is your monastery in this village?'

'It is. The family sent for me after they'd carried you into their house. This is the house of a wealthy family, as you can see.'

'How did you know I was running?'

'A boy from the village saw you in the hills. I know you Samudrans only run like that when there is an urgent problem. And a problem for the Samudrans is a problem for all of us. There are many similarities between our orders, but some crucial differences too … your particular talents, the continuous meditation … but we are kindred spirits.'

After the traveller Chodak's betrayal, Rinzen was reluctant to say anything about his mission, even to a

Buddhist monk. 'I have to get to Sarmand as soon as possible. You are right, the matter is very urgent.'

The monk leaned closer. 'Do not say anything about Sarmand to our hosts. The army were here today, on their way there.'

Rinzen threw back the bed sheets, jumped up, pulled on his boots and cast about for his satchel.

'Here, by the wardrobe,' the monk said. 'Your coat is inside. I would offer to come with you, but I would only hold you back. But if you ever need my help, you know where to find me.'

'Thank you, thank you.' He stopped, faced the monk. 'I don't know your name.'

'My name is Kunchen. Come, I will tell our host you have to leave. But you must be careful. Do not travel by the roads.'

The beautiful woman was waiting in the hallway, holding a cloth bundle. 'You should rest, brother,' she said, 'but I can see you're in a hurry to continue your journey. We have prepared some food for you.' The smile gave way to a look of concern. 'Your lips are pale. Can't you stay a little longer?'

Rinzen bowed and took the offered food. 'You are very kind. I will not forget your generosity, but I am needed elsewhere.'

'There is a boy outside the back door,' she said. 'You can trust him. He will show you the way to the path you should take.' She touched his hand and looked at him with her dark eyes. 'None here will betray you to the army.'

So, she knew.

He nodded, confused by the heat in his chest, and followed her to the back of the house.

The boy, about ten years old, he guessed, jumped up and set off along the rear alley. They turned uphill through the narrow lanes, past smaller, less opulent houses. The aroma of freshly baked bread came from one house, the sound of a hammer from another. Three women, young mothers with babies strapped to their backs, stopped talking as they approached and bowed their heads. He did likewise and pressed on, his limbs loosening in the cool of the late afternoon. At the edge of the village, a path ran along the side of three small fields terraced into the near vertical valley.

The boy stopped and pointed at a higher, even steeper hill beyond. Rinzen watched the boy until he was safely back in the village.

That evening he walked until it was dark, decided not to risk a fire, and meditated for some hours. He sensed Keung in the inner temple of Sarmand, and wished again that he had telepathic abilities.

He woke long before dawn, rested and feeling robust, and walked until the sky began to lighten. Then he ran for an hour, rested for a few minutes, and walked for an hour. He repeated this pattern all day, making sure that he ate and drank every few hours.

~

As he feared, the army had camped on the trail up to Sarmand, about a hundred metres from the outer wall. The darkness was to his advantage. If he went in a wide arc around the monastery, he could descend a favourite gulley to the base of the escarpment. He set off away from Sarmand but hadn't gone more than ten paces when a terrible thought stopped him. He ducked behind a tree and leaned against its warm trunk. What was happening to him? He was behaving like a soldier himself, all this sly thinking. If he wasn't careful, he would lose his centre, disperse his training. And what about his judgement? His first reaction when the monk Kunchen had offered to help had been to deceive him, to mistrust him, a monk.

Was that a snapping twig? Soldier or animal? He slowed his breaths, calmed his heartbeat, prepared himself for combat.

'I'm on the other side of this tree,' Keung whispered. 'What took you so long?'

'Shh.' Rinzen moved silently around the tree until he was in front of his friend. He pointed to where he'd heard the noise, and Keung nodded, pointed up, and swung himself onto the branch above. Rinzen followed.

A few seconds later they were looking down on a man with a rifle and dressed all in black. Another similarly dressed man appeared beside him. The second one pointed towards Sarmand and they moved away, almost as silently as brothers. Keung put his mouth close to Rinzen's ear. 'There may be more like that. We'll have to watch out.'

When Rinzen turned to look at him, he could see that mischievous look in his eyes. They dropped to the ground and crept over the familiar territory to the gulley, along the valley floor and up the escarpment to the base of the monastery wall. Keung mimicked the hoot of an owl and a rope was lowered from the window of one of the senior's cells. Minutes later they were safely inside.

Keung hugged him. 'You look like a wild man.'

'It's been a long journey from Barnang,' Rinzen said, 'and not without incident. Hello, Dachen, thanks for the rope.'

'Good to have you back.' Dachen forced a smile. 'You must be exhausted, and hungry. I'll prepare some food.'

'Thank you, we'll follow in a minute.' And then to Keung, 'Tell me, did the soldiers come inside the monastery?'

'No, I think they're too scared of the wasting disease to enter. They've forbidden us from leaving Sarmand because of it. We told them that the last of the elders was dead and that no one else had any symptoms, but they said it made no difference. Then they ordered us to line up on the outer wall and a man who was with them looked at us.'

'Was he wearing a long brown coat and a wide-brimmed hat?'

'That's him. He knew who you were, asked for you by name. They said that as you'd travelled far from Sarmand they needed to have you tested to see if you had the disease, that we must tell them if you returned.'

'Keung, nearly all the elders at Barnang and Qo are also dead, and the four or five who are still alive are dying.'

'I thought so.' A shadow swept across his animated face. 'The Samudrans have overcome trials in the past, and we'll do the same this time.'

'We have to.' Rinzen said, and told Keung all about his journey.

They walked together to the dining hall, where all the seniors and juniors were waiting to embrace him. They agreed to have a full meeting after breakfast, and Rinzen and Keung were left alone.

'How did you manage to come back two days early?' Keung raised an eyebrow. 'I bet you ran.'

'I had no choice, did I? Don't tell me you wouldn't have done the same. Come to that, how did you know to come and get me tonight?'

Keung tapped his head with his finger and grinned.

'Well, thanks. I needed you.' Rinzen stood and paced up and down the room. 'I'm worried about the way I'm thinking. All this sneaking about to avoid being shot has made me distrust strangers, even a Buddhist monk I met. I don't want to lose myself in fear and cunning.'

Keung got up and put his hands on Rinzen's shoulders. 'Even though you were several days' away, I felt your presence in the inner temple: I always knew when you'd entered the trance and were with us. And I know you will leave us again.' Rinzen opened his mouth to speak, but Keung continued. 'Wait. I know this, and when you're ready, you will tell me why. But *you* must know this – as long as you enter the trance every day, it won't matter what you need to do to survive in the lands beyond Sarmand. Each night when you meditate, I will be there supporting you, because from now on I will always go to the inner temple and start my meditation at dusk.'

Rinzen wrapped his arms over his friend's and nodded.

'If only we were telepathic,' Keung said, and Rinzen laughed.

'The Barnang elders have sent one of their seniors to seek help from the Kogi in Columbia.'

'Ah yes, Kwato told you about them. And ...?'

'That's where they asked me to go. Do you think I should?'

When Keung twisted his mouth, Rinzen knew what he thought.

'An elder's instruction, and you doubt it?'

'No, but they said it was up to me.'

'They sound more polite than our elders! Probably thought you were out of their jurisdiction, being from Sarmand. And they did ask you, which is the same as an instruction.'

~

At the meeting the next morning, Rinzen told the others what he'd found at Qo and Barnang. 'As I speak, the senior Lobsang, a brother with superior talents and a strong spirit, is already on his way east to find the Kogi. And I will go west with the same intention.'

His words seemed to jolt the assembly. There had been absolute silence a few minutes before, but now some of the juniors whispered to their neighbours, and even his fellow seniors looked shaken.

'I see you would like to speak, Amdong.'

145

Amdong looked directly at Rinzen. 'Brother Rinzen, I am in awe of your composure and hope that one day I achieve a similar inner strength. In the world outside, you have faced violence and betrayal but have also had your compassion repaid with the kindness of strangers. But as you travel further from Sarmand and leave the land of Samudrans and Buddhists, I fear even your great strength will be tested. Would you consider choosing one of us to accompany you?'

'Thank you, Amdong. Even on my relatively short journey between the three monasteries I have felt fear and loneliness and experienced doubts about my judgement. But then I returned to Sarmand, and a wise brother' – he put his arm around Keung's shoulders – 'counselled me. He told me that you would all be with me, that a Samudran brother is never alone, even on the other side of the world. And each night I will enter the trance with you.' He paused, smiled at Amdong. 'You were in the circle last night, Amdong. Did you see me there?'

Amdong laughed. 'I thought that was just wishful thinking.'

Welcome laughter – subdued, but laughter nevertheless – dissipated the gloom.

'Sarmand cannot afford to have two of us away. No, I will go alone. Yes, Amal?'

'What about those soldiers? They will hunt you. And those ones Keung told me about, all dressed in black and as stealthy as brothers?'

'Not quite as stealthy, but, yes, a worry. I believe they think I am still on my way from Barnang – it took me two days less than it should have – so if I leave in the middle of the night, after the moon has set, I should be able to avoid them.'

~

Rinzen and Keung laid out the world atlas on the long table in the library. They opened the first page, a map of the world, and looked for Columbia.

'It's on the other side of the world,' Keung said.

'How far, do you think?'

'Must be over 15,000 kilometres.' They both stared at the map until Keung said, 'You'll need strong boots.'

'Very funny,' Rinzen said. 'It might take months to get there.'

'You'll need money. You must take all our money.'

There was a knock at the door, and Amdong entered. 'Please excuse the interruption, but I thought I might be able to help with your journey.'

'Come in, Amdong. But as I said, I think it's better if I travel alone.'

'I meant with your route across the world – or at least through India. My uncle works on the Indian railways. He was at my home when I visited last year and delighted in telling us stories about his travels. He works on the Darbhanga to Mumbai line.'

'Show us on the map,' Keung said.

Amdong pointed at the map of India. 'My uncle's train starts from here – Laheriasarai station in Darbhanga.' He traced the track across India to Mumbai. 'And ends here, at Lokmanya Tilak Terminus in Mumbai. It takes almost two days, but you don't have to change trains. Many ships go from Mumbai to places all over the world.'

All three brothers studied the map. 'It's five days walk to Janakpur from my parents' village,' Rinzen said. 'And it looks like another two or three days to Darbhanga.'

'I could write a letter for you to take to my uncle,' Amdong said. 'Of course, he may not be there at the same time as you ...'

'Thank you, Amdong. I don't speak Hindi or Urdu, so I'll need all the help I can get.'

147

'My uncle says that many speak Maithili and Nepali in Darbhanga. And your English might be useful too.'

'You'll want to speak to people in Maithili, not Nepali,' Keung said. 'Many Indians speak Maithili, so once you are inside India you can pretend to be from Darbhanga. Say you're a schoolteacher.'

'Do you think the Indian army will be after me as well?'

'Who knows?' Keung turned back to the atlas. 'Now, let's look for the name of the main port in Columbia.'

While Amdong wrote the letter to his uncle, Rinzen and Keung looked through the maps in the trunk below the window and found a folded map of the world and some detailed maps of the region down to the Indian border. At the bottom of the trunk they found a brass compass and a stout folding knife in a leather pouch.

When Rinzen returned to his cell to pack he found that his fellow seniors had left various items of laymen's clothing neatly folded on his bed. He tried them on, imagining what a rural schoolteacher might wear, and decided on a collarless shirt, a short woollen jacket with toggle fasteners, and the least baggy of the three pairs of thick cotton trousers on offer. His own overcoat was a common design worn by brothers and laymen alike, and he would have to hope that his parents could furnish him with a suitable pair of boots.

In any case, his father – a schoolteacher himself – would help him with his disguise. He stopped packing, stared at the cell wall, felt a shiver run down his back – his father, his mother, he would see them in a matter of hours. He was actually going to leave Sarmand again … but this time to travel across the world. He slumped onto the bed and let his head drop forward. How had it come to this? What would happen to the brotherhood? He didn't have a passport, had no idea how much things like trains and ships cost; he didn't even know the price of *momos*.

He stood up and leaned his head against the wall, his mind a jumble of thoughts and emotions: he was afraid to

148

go; it was his duty to go; he wanted so much to stay; the future of the brotherhood, and their work to keep the planet turning, was in his hands; it would take too long; he lacked courage, was uncertain of how to deal with people, his fear would be clear to everyone he met; Keung should go, easygoing, quick-witted, compassionate and friendly Keung would do a much better job than he would; Kwato had chosen him, the Barnang elders said that Lobsang and he should go. And who was he, a senior, to doubt the wisdom of the elders?

He groaned out loud and heard an answering groan from the other side of the door.

'Come in, spy.'

'You think too much,' Keung said. 'Your one aim is to get to your village, ask your parents to help you, let your mother make a fuss over you, let your proud father shake the hand of his fine son.'

'But what about after that? I have to cross the border undetected, find this one train I need to take among all the many—'

'No, no, my friend. That is not your aim today. That is your aim tomorrow. Do not think about tomorrow's aim until tomorrow. OK?'

'I know you're right, but I doubt myself.'

'As well you might. I doubt you too. That's why my spirit will be with you, to whisper in your ear every time you're about to make a wrong decision, or say something stupid or mistrust a person who trusts you. Shall I go on?' He cocked his head to one side and grinned.

'I don't know why I put up with you, I really don't.'

'I do. You need someone superior to aspire to.' He ducked Rinzen's high kick, leapt onto the bed and disrupted the neat piles of clothes. 'You look great as a schoolteacher, by the way. Good practice for when you fail the elder tests.'

'Good idea. If I become a teacher, I won't have to listen to your inane banter.'

This time Keung jumped up to avoid the low kick and landed like a cat in the gap between the bed and the wall.

'Let's get out of this cell,' Rinzen said. 'You can give me more of your sage advice as we stroll around the cloisters.'

'One more thing before we do that.' Keung's grin turned into a frown. 'Kwato did not doubt you, and neither did the elders of Barnang. When you're faced with peril or indecision, imagine what Kwato would do.'

14

London

Clara hadn't actually resigned from the orchestra. She'd tried to, but Roland Peach had refused to accept it, said he understood all about burnout and suggested she sit out the next concert tour. They would talk again after that. She agreed and requested that Roland ask the other musicians not to contact her for a while – she needed peace and quiet, to be left alone.

It was anger that had made her tell Henry she'd resigned. He was too damned selfish, could have shown more grace, more understanding, could have waited until she'd had more therapy sessions before he passed judgement. Stuff Henry.

She caressed the harp strings, barely making a sound, and thought about her new composition. Before this piece, she'd never experienced a trance state while playing; even when rehearsing pieces from memory, she needed to remain alert, to watch her fingers on the strings and focus on the pedal changes. Impossible to drift off and disappear into the music –

The telephone interrupted her thoughts.

'Hello, darling,' her mother said. 'How are you?'

'Fine, thanks,' Clara said. 'Mum, did you know that some artists – Kandinsky among them – actually see some pieces of music as colours rather than hearing it as notes. Isn't that interesting?'

'Yes, very interesting.'

'It's called synaesthesia.'

'I know that. You know I know that. Why are you suddenly so interested? You never have been before.'

Clara could hear the frustration in her mother's voice. 'Why shouldn't I be? I was just thinking about how I feel when I play—'

'Is there anything else you want to tell me?'

'I'm still holding onto the harp.'

'I see.' Silence on the line, then, 'Even after your hypnotherapy? So it didn't work.'

She could hear the unsounded tut.

'You want to know how I got on with the hypnotist?'

'Only if you want to tell me, Clara.'

This expression was almost as irritating as 'I see'.

'He, Matthew, is also a psychotherapist, and he often uses hypnotherapy to help his patients. I'm going to see him twice a week rather than seeing someone else as well.'

'Is that what you are: a patient?'

Clara gripped the phone tighter. 'Yes, of course. I have something called "harpitis". Quite rare, only known to affect one in nine billion people, namely me, but quite treatable all the same.'

'Come on, darling, less of the sarcasm. We don't need sarcasm. What's his full name?'

'You want to check on him, don't you?'

'Never mind, I'll ask Julia.'

'His name is Matthew Cleary. Feel free to check his credentials with your psychotherapist.'

'She's not my psychotherapist, but she may as …'

'As what?'

'Never mind. I'll check on him and call you back.'

Did her mother, she wondered, ever experience the tranquillity of utter absorption? Probably not, at least not since she'd become a mother.

Clara stroked the harp strings but resisted the urge to lose herself in the rhythms and cadences of her mysterious new composition. She'd thought about writing it down, but feared this would break the spell, that if she recorded the notes and chords she would destroy its spontaneity. In any case, the music emerged so naturally, she could no more forget it than forget how to breathe.

She ploughed through her scales, starting with C major, moving up to C sharp major, then back down a fifth each time. With each round she played louder and faster, until during her fifth or sixth round the G string in the second octave broke. This would usually have irritated her, but today she almost welcomed the chance to do something practical.

She wheeled the harp across the room to the vintage teak sideboard – a gift from Henry – and looked at the framed black and white photograph on the wall above it: herself as a toddler seated on her father's knee. He wore a black suit, white shirt and white bow tie, and his baritone's chest swelled inside the suit's lapels. His thick black hair, usually an unkempt mass, was slicked back with hair oil and his fleshy lips parted in a wide – she thought proud – smile. She examined his face closely, to confirm that his eyes were also smiling. His right arm encircled her tiny form and rested on the outside of her thigh; an inch of starched shirt cuff protruded from his jacket and revealed a silver cufflink in the shape of a concert harp. Her three-year-old self was balanced on his lap, her face turned up to stare adoringly at her papa.

Looking at this photograph sometimes brought tears to her eyes, tears of longing, tears of loss; other times, like now, she experienced the heat of pure love, as if she could literally feel the hot blood being pumped through every artery, every tiny vein. Her fingers tingled, and her bare feet felt suddenly hot on the cool oak floor. She felt like dancing, waving her arms in the air and losing herself in loud soul music – Marvin Gaye's 'I Heard It Through the Grapevine', played at full volume in that club Henry had taken her to somewhere near Brixton. Damn Henry.

She opened the top drawer of the sideboard and sifted through her spare set of strings. Then she bent over the harp, extracted the broken string from the back of the soundboard, stood up, unravelled the top of the broken string from the tuning peg and threw it on the armchair. She ripped open the new packet, placed the string anchor on the sideboard and unwound the string. She worked fast, threaded the end of the string through the top of the soundboard, retrieved the end from behind and, hardly looking at it, created the double loop, inserted the anchor, pulled the string through the soundboard and looped it over the tuning peg. She estimated the excess string and snipped it to length with the cutters.

She stopped. How could just that one thought about Henry have brought her down so quickly? So what if she missed one concert tour? The sooner she forgot about him the better. It would be hard, yes, especially when she was surrounded by things that reminded her of him, but if he wouldn't accept her for who she was, the selfish sod could go to hell.

Clara resumed her work on the string, overtightened it just the right amount, stretched it, listened to the note and tightened it again until it was perfect. She checked the tuning of the whole harp, made minor adjustments with the tuning key and sat down to play another variation of her composition.

~

The following day her mother called to tell her that the other psychotherapist approved of Matthew Cleary. Apparently, he had a sound reputation, even though his methods could be considered unorthodox.

She put down the phone and stared at it. Something was wrong.

'I don't care,' she said to the empty room. 'I don't give a damn whether you approve or not, Mother!'

What? Really? After needing your approval for everything, forever, are you finally getting out of my head?

Her head lightened, brightened, and she danced the harp around the living room; her feet would leave the ground at any second, she'd float off with her harp like an angelic cherub, or like Hermes with his lyre at the moment he created it. He would have smiled with joy at the sweet music it made and played it to the heavens as she did now.

She glided through the balcony doors, filled her lungs with the cool fresh air and looked for Hermes in the ancient sky. Her hands played the harp on their own, the notes cascaded around her in sparkling colours. Hermes was gazing down at her; she could feel his eyes seeking her out and she cast about for them – only to meet Fulbright's through the glass doors of his kitchen. The music stopped, her mouth formed a scream, but the sound stuck in her throat.

There, next to Fulbright and seated in an armchair facing out, was her mother.

Clara stared at her, tried to make sense of the sight of her in Fulbright's flat.

Fulbright was standing behind Grace, his face crumpled into what she took to be a grin rather than a scowl. He nodded. Nodded! Her mother had conspired with that disgusting man – how could she?

God, she's spying on me!

She heard Matthew's footsteps cross the courtyard, then the entryphone buzzer. She shoved the harp up the ramp and into the living room, lifted the handset, pressed the enter button, then left the harp to walk back and slam shut the patio door and close the curtains.

Matthew suggested they talk some more about Clara's past before the hypnosis session. 'I'm not saying that some particular event has caused you to interpret your dream the way you have, but it might help you get a clearer perspective if you were to talk about your relationship with your mother.'

'She's spying on me from my creep of a neighbour's flat. Is that a good start?'

'What? Have you seen her?'

'Yes, take a look for yourself – to the right from the balcony. She's not even trying to hide.'

'I'll take your word for it. Could she just be visiting your neighbour, as his guest, I mean?'

'Impossible. She thinks he's a lecher, and she warned me to keep away from him.'

'Why do you think she's watching you?'

'Good question.' Clara ran the back of her fingers across the harp strings. 'I've no idea …' She pushed the harp to the kitchen sink, poured a glass of water and gulped it down. 'And now that she's spending more time with her man, and openly going about with him …'

'Yes?'

'Really, I have no idea what she's up to. Probably doesn't know herself.' How stupid to think she could get her mother out of her head. She dropped into the dining chair and looked up at Matthew. 'Maybe she's worried about me. We're very close, you see.' She told him about her upbringing, the focus on harp playing to the exclusion of everything else, how she and her mother had lived in a sort of bubble after her father died.

'Do you think she's worried you might harm yourself?'

'No, not that. But she did say that my "obsession", as she calls it, would lead to total madness – or words to that effect.'

'Why? Has something similar happened before?'

'My guess is that she thinks I'm ... emotionally fragile. Because I stopped speaking for two years after Papa – my father – died.' Should she ask him about that? Better not, not yet, it would just confuse things.

'And there's been nothing since then?'

'Not that I can think of. Look, I'll call her later, ask her what she's up to. Maybe she's got some sort of explanation.'

He started to ask something, but she interrupted. 'Could we start the hypnosis now? I want to see if I can find a new way of looking at the dream.'

Moments later she entered a deep trance, and there was only Matthew's mellow voice, soft as a silk caress. She experienced his words as musical notes, perfect chords in tune with her taut muscles. The last of the tension shivered away. She sensed rather than heard what he said. He'd said that didn't matter, and she believed him. She would believe anything he told her, do anything he told her. The dream appeared on a screen that floated in the curved air. 'Five, six, seven,' Matthew said, and after that he either stopped speaking or she was out of hearing range. She watched herself standing next to her mother's hospital bed, both arms loose, hands resting lazily on the bedsheet next to the prone figure. This dream-Clara watched the Wigmore Hall concert, heard but still could not see the other dream-Clara playing the harp.

'I'm in the hospital,' she said. 'I can smell it, that hospital smell, that mixture of antiseptic and overcooked cabbage. Julia calls it "cauliflower au Dettol". But I can hear myself play that final solo. Mother is breathing evenly, peacefully asleep, her face smooth, worry-free. I feel ... apathetic, limp, like a rag doll, and I don't have any interest in that Clara playing the harp. All that bowing and feigning modesty, when really she loves the adulation. What a hypocrite! She pretends that all she's interested in is the music, but what she really likes is everyone telling her how brilliant she is.

She loves them to fawn over her, loves the standing ovations and bouquets of flowers. I gaze at Mother. Her complexion darkens, wrinkles gather in twists of agony around her eyes and mouth; her mouth opens as she gasps for air. I want to help her, but I can't move, all I can do is watch her try to sit up, gulping. Horrible rasping sounds are roaring from her throat. I must help her, but my arms won't move. Why can't I move?'

'One, two, three, four, five, and wake up.'

The click of his fingers snapped her back to her flat, to the chair, and to Matthew himself, who was frowning and holding her harp at arm's length as though it were a dangerous beast.

He held her gaze for what seemed like minutes but might only have been a heartbeat. 'How do you feel, Clara?'

'Confused.'

'Yes.' He stood up. 'Water, I think. I'll get you a glass of water. Would you mind?' He pushed the harp towards Clara.

'How come you were holding my harp?'

'I'll just get the water.'

She sipped the water; found she was thirsty and emptied the glass. 'Thanks. Tell me, was I speaking aloud?'

'Yes. Do you remember what you said?'

'Clearly.'

'You don't seem surprised by it, by there being one version of yourself openly despising the other version.'

'Never mind that – why couldn't I help my mother?' She rested both hands on the harp strings. 'The good me, the me that lives for the music like my parents wanted, should have been able to help my mother.'

'So the good you is the one who does what your parents want? And is there a bad you?' His face had relaxed back into its normal state, but like a calm sea after a storm, there were still eddies if you looked closely.

'Perhaps I shouldn't have said "good".' She looked at the floor between them. 'My father detested celebrity; he used to tell me that a true artist has no time for fame, a true artist only wants to practise their art, to perfect their art, to examine themselves through practice. He said that fame corrupts art, a phrase my mother was fond of using whenever I got excited about winning prizes or receiving praise from eminent musicians.' Clara's head snapped up. 'Did you take the harp from me?'

'You pushed it away. I decided to hold it, ready to give it back to you the moment you came out of the trance.'

'I can't remember doing that. Unless it was the me at the Wigmore leaving the harp behind? It was very strange, there being two of me at the same time.'

'And one of you, the one who you were conscious of, was unable to help your mother.'

'Yes. Why do you think that was? I did want to help her, but I couldn't move.'

Matthew held her stare, seemed to be considering how to answer. He took his time. 'I'm sorry, I don't have a direct answer for you. Not yet. I hope the answer will emerge as we talk more, but we may not get to the answer today.'

Clara nodded.

'While you were under, you seemed very familiar with the Clara who likes all the attention – the flowers, the standing ovations. Do you, like your parents, see those things negatively?' His hands were resting palms down on his knees like a pair of kidskin gloves, perfectly relaxed.

'That's what has been drummed into me all my life, so I can't help seeing it that way, even if part of me loves it. Enjoying the attention is like a guilty secret, if you know what I mean?'

'Yes, I can see that.' His right index finger twitched. Just once, but it was definitely a twitch. He looked at her face while he spoke, but avoided her eyes.

'When you were young, your parents saw it as their role to guide you, to give you a moral framework. That's perfectly natural. What strikes me as unusual about your childhood – and I'm sure you're aware of this – is that this framework was intimately connected with playing the harp. Unlike most children, who will move from one activity to another very quickly and grow out of their toys or games as they mature, you have always played the harp, almost to the exclusion of everything else. Through all your stages of maturity, the harp has been at the centre; it is associated with all your beliefs, and your moral framework is almost literally attached to you as a harpist. Early lessons – such as that fame is bad and artistic perfection is good – are deeply embedded, making it hard for you to believe in your own opinions.'

Matthew paused, perhaps to let what he'd said sink in. He allowed his eyes to lock onto Clara's. Her tongue felt like leather, but she didn't reach for the glass of water; she focused on his eyes, waited for what that voice would say next.

'Before our next session, I think it would clarify things for you, perhaps give you a different perspective on the meaning of the dream, if you were to think about some of the ideas and beliefs that you received from your parents but that you – the mature you – are no longer sure you agree with.'

'So, no simple answers then?' She wondered whether her raised eyebrows and grinning mouth made her look quizzical or just a little crazy.

'Maybe next time.'

~

Clara rang her mother and asked why she'd spent three days watching her from the lecher's lair.

'He's not so bad, darling. And he makes very good coffee.'

'But why are you watching me, Mother?' Not 'Mum', not under the circumstances.

'I'm worried about you, darling. Are you eating properly? Shall I cook you something nice?'

'No, thank you.'

'And how is the hypnotism going? Any insights?'

Clara heard a sucking sound from her mother, and gripped the receiver harder.

'But why are you watching me?'

'I'm so worried ...'

She heard her mother's voice crack, held her breath, waited.

'I ... I can't bear to see this happening to you, but I can't be with you, can't pretend everything's all right while you insist on remaining attached to your harp. Oh, darling, won't you please stop.'

Now she could hear the sobs; they pierced her, sent a shiver through her head, down her neck. And she'd been so sarcastic to Matthew about her; she'd betrayed her to him, made her out to be a harridan, no better than a prison guard, forcing her to practise, practise, practise for her own evil ends.

'Oh, Mum, forgive me. I would stop if I could. I am trying this therapy, and he's very clever. Maybe ...'

'Maybe?'

'Nothing. Watch me from Fulbright's if you want, I won't moan about it again.'

15

Nepal

Shortly before Rinzen entered the inner temple to join in the evening meditation, Keung handed him a card. On one side there was an ink drawing of the Well of Life in the cloisters, on the other a quote from the Buddha:

Do not dwell in the past, do not dream of the future, concentrate the mind on the present moment.

In tiny letters at the base of the card, Keung had written:

The wise Keung says: Start your journey by taking one light step ... and then take another.

The words rang true, but they were only words – he needed to internalise their wisdom, remind himself of his training, allow his self-confidence to overcome his doubts.

Before he entered the trance, as he focused on the simple bowl of water in the centre of the circle, the positive energy of the brothers coursed through him. His veins were hot, his heartbeat slowed, every meridian trembled. He felt weightless, then unaware of his physical body, a pure spirit moving in rhythm with the pulse of the earth. There was no longer a solitary man named Rinzen; he – whoever this 'he' was – was one of a unity of Samudran spirits, practising what they did best and doing it in harmony.

When one of the juniors relieved him in the middle of the night, he continued to feel that harmony, that belonging. He stood for a while in the cool, dimly lit temple and etched the sensation on his mind and body.

~

At one in the morning Rinzen climbed down the rope to the base of the west wall, gave a silent wave to Keung at the window above, and ran down the escarpment to the valley below. As he flew down the slope, he recalled the first time he'd attempted the feat as a junior. The slope was not far off vertical, and he'd been certain he would leave his legs behind and topple headfirst down the escarpment. It took tremendous concentration and all his strength to remain upright. His teacher had told him to imagine that his head was a balloon from which his body hung, but the first few times he did it, his head had felt more like a heavy cannonball, and his feet – bent at such an extreme angle – had ached for days afterwards. This time, in the moonless night, he had to rely on his memory to navigate a safe route down, and his bag, considerably heavier than the last time, added a further handicap.

As he neared the base, he sensed movement off to his left; he veered sharp right and ran along the hillside, about twenty metres above the valley floor. He glanced down and couldn't believe that two men were keeping pace with him. Was it those men in black again? He couldn't be sure in the gloom, but who else could keep pace with a Samudran brother in full flight? They must have watched him descend from Sarmand. Soon he would run out of hillside and their paths would cross. Could he outrun them on level ground? There was now only fifteen metres between them. Should he turn, run back up the slope? Were they armed? He glanced down to check, glimpsed a third figure gaining on the others, saw his two raised arms, watched him take off into a long low jump, land with a foot on the back of each of the others, and then leap again as the two crashed to the ground and tumbled into each other.

Rinzen stopped. The single word 'Go!' came from Keung's mouth, but Rinzen saw his pursuers were on their feet again and running towards Keung. He dropped his bag, called out to Keung and leapt towards the sprinting spectres, but he'd misjudged and landed short. He stooped, grabbed two handfuls of sand from the old riverbed, and ran on.

Keung was outrunning them, but he couldn't outrun a bullet. One of the men stopped, shouldered his rifle, took aim and fired just as Rinzen crashed into him and sent him through the air to land splayed out, face down. As he turned over, Rinzen crushed the sand into his eyes and punched him on his right temple. The man went limp and Rinzen ran on, his mind in turmoil, his gut churning – had he been too late to stop the man killing Keung?

Faster, he had to run faster than ever. The shot would have been heard; more soldiers would come. He was gaining on the second one, only thirty or forty metres away, but the man stopped abruptly and pointed his rifle down. Twenty metres. The man was standing over Keung, who was lying face up on the ground. Rinzen's scream split the cold night. Ten metres. Keung's leg jabbed out at lightning speed and connected with the man's throat and jaw with a sickening crunch. He flew backwards and landed at Rinzen's feet, unaware of him until it was too late to do anything about the sand rubbed in his eyes and the knockout blow to his temple.

'Go,' Keung repeated. He leapt up and raced back towards Sarmand, one arm waving.

Rinzen retrieved his bag and ran at full speed for an hour, along the valley, over one hill and up to near the top of the next, where he stopped, crouched down, and listened.

He stilled his breath, waited for his heartbeat to steady, and focused all his attention on listening for the slightest sound of his pursuers. When he was satisfied that they hadn't followed, he turned south and joined the familiar path towards his parents' village, where he knew the army would be waiting for him.

Ordinary soldiers couldn't run like those two, and there might be more like them in Chaukati. But there was no question of turning back now – the army would realise he was one of the two brothers who'd attacked the two men in black and would be even more determined to capture him.

It was still dark when he arrived on the hill above the village, but he could make out the general shape of the houses and, on the edge, the school where both his parents taught. He crept down the slope, climbed the outer wall of the playground and crawled under the veranda in front of the school building. He wrapped his coat around him, laid his head on his bag and watched the gate.

He tried not to think about what he'd done to his pursuers, told himself that he'd had no choice. But he'd never hurt anyone before. Of course, all seniors knew the weak points on the human body, it was part of their training, but how had he known to attack like that? And Keung had done the same. Was it the instinct for self-preservation or the result of twenty years' conditioning?

He dozed off, only to be awoken by the sound of the gate creaking. His eyes snapped open, his heart raced, his body shivered in the icy air. This was a stupid place to hide – there was only one way out! If they conducted a proper search … But it was, as he'd hoped, his father arriving his customary hour before school started to prepare for the lessons. The tall figure walked across the yard, his back as upright as a marching soldier, but his face looked drawn, pale, his eyes heavy below an anxious frown.

'Father,' he whispered, as his father mounted the steps.

His father did not pause, just said, 'There's a soldier outside the gate. Crawl to your right, there's a hatch to the space below the classroom,' and proceeded to unlock the school building.

Minutes later, Rinzen embraced his father in the back corner of the classroom.

'Come, we'll be safe in my office.'

They sat on opposite sides of the simple plywood desk, and Rinzen's father produced a flask of tea, a pile of rotis and a pot of his brother's honey. 'Eat, Son. Here, have some tea. They came to look for you last night, said you have a fatal disease and that we must detain you if you came home.'

Rinzen sipped the sweet tea, cupped his hands around the glass. 'We face disaster, Father,' he said. His eyes filled with tears.

His father was at his side in a moment, crouched down, his hand on his son's shoulder. 'Are you ill, Rinzen?'

'No, no. I am well. There is no more disease.' His leaden head dropped to his chest.

'All right. Now eat quietly, drink some more tea, then tell me what has befallen Sarmand.' His father sat in his chair and watched his son eat.

Rinzen was happy to obey his father, to have time to collect his thoughts. He supposed the sudden emotion arose from a childhood yearning to be comforted by his parents.

After eating, he told his father about the wasting disease, about his journey to Qo and Barnang, and about the order to seek help from an ancient tribe in South America.

'So the future of the Samudrans rests on your shoulders,' his father said. 'Your father would say he was enormously proud – if pride were not a sign of weakness in Samudran brothers.' His smile obliterated his anxious frown and set his eyes alight. 'You will need money for your journey, and maps, and less conspicuous boots, I think.'

His father stood, paced around the small office, and looked out of the window towards the gate. 'Your mother will be here in a few minutes, and then the children will come in half an hour. Before they arrive, we must think of all the things we need to do today, then you can sleep in the book store ... Ah, here she comes now.'

She came directly to the office and put her arms around Rinzen's waist, buried her face in his chest. It was four years since he'd seen her, and now, instead of his visit being a cause for celebration, he'd brought trouble. He waited for her to release him, held her away from him, looked at her raw, red eyes. 'I'm sorry, Mother.'

'No, Rinzen, there's no need. Let me look at you.' She leaned away but kept hold of his arms. 'You look well enough, a little tired perhaps, but your eyes are bright, your skin healthy. Are you sure you have this disease?'

'He doesn't have it – only the elders were affected,' his father said. 'Now listen, we have a lot to do and not much—'

'You don't have it? Sure?'

Rinzen smiled. 'Yes, Mother, I'm sure I don't have it.'

'Why are you crying?' his father said. 'I thought you'd be happy.'

'I am, I am.' She broke away from Rinzen and pulled a cloth from her coat pocket. 'Of course I'm happy.' She blew her nose. 'Why do you think I'm weeping?'

'Ah, yes,' his father said. 'Tears of happiness, I suppose. I will never understand. Now we really have to—'

'Wait, have you given him some food?'

'Yes, of course I have. Now, look, the children will be here soon.'

Ignoring Rinzen, his parents batted back and forth a list of who would do what and when, and how they would avoid detection by the soldiers. Then suddenly there was silence.

They know each other so well, thought Rinzen, that they only need these few words to come up with a comprehensive plan. He laughed.

His mother frowned at him. 'What is so funny, may I ask?'

'Nothing, Mother. I'm just so happy to see that my parents love each other so deeply.'

'Yes, well.' His father turned over some of the papers on his desk.

His mother blushed, took Rinzen's hand and led him to the book store, where she made up a rudimentary bed from the pile of blankets used by the pupils on particularly cold days. She brought him a jug of water and some fruit. 'We'll come and see you after school, at about two o'clock.' She stroked his cheek and gazed into his eyes. 'Try to sleep, Son. You look so tired.'

He hugged her to him and inhaled her scent, a scent that took him back to his early childhood and falling asleep in her arms. Beneath the surface fragrances of myrtle and yak's milk, flour and honey, there was her unique scent, and he wished he could bottle it and carry it with him.

Rinzen lay on his back and stared at the cedarwood ceiling. He'd never been in this room; the elders had come for him when he was still very young, too young even to have started at the school, and he'd only visited it a few times since. It must have been hard for his parents to agree to let their only child join the Samudrans, and his subsequent visits had been so infrequent that they were almost strangers to him. And yet they behaved as though he'd been around them all his life; they were affectionate and loving and keen to do anything for him.

He closed his eyes and let the warmth of his mother's smile wash over him, and when he awoke, there she was, kneeling next to him, smiling.

'You needed that,' she said. 'No, don't get up. I've brought some *dal bhat* for you. Your father and I will get what you need this afternoon, but you must stay out of sight. These soldiers are watching us, so I'm not sure what time we'll come back.'

'It will have to be before dark.' His father spoke from the doorway. 'They might suspect something if they see us coming to the school at night.'

'Father, have you seen any soldiers dressed all in black?' He pushed back the blanket and stood up.

'No, who are they?'

'Some sort of special unit, I think. Very well trained.'

'I haven't been around the village since the army came yesterday, but I'll have a good look this afternoon. Now rest, and if you like, you can read this book.' He handed Rinzen a slim volume, *A Short History of India.*

His parents stood together and looked at him as though they were trying to imprint an image of him on their minds.

'Listen, if they come and search for me, even if I get away, they'll know that you hid me. We cannot let that happen. When I see it's safe to do so, I'll climb to the top of that tall, solitary, pine tree. You know, on the hillside, the one without any low branches. Perhaps you could send someone there after dark?'

His mother's eyes filled with tears. She held his hands and said, 'Be careful, Rinzen, not everyone in the world is kind like you.' She stood on her tiptoes and kissed him.

He felt a tear on his cheek, her tear, and his heart pounded against his ribs. He had to avoid crying, had to be strong in front of his father, whose face betrayed his grief at their parting.

'Goodbye, Father.'

He offered his right hand, but his father embraced him, held him tight, then broke away suddenly.

'I know just the boy to send. And let's not say goodbye but do as the French and say *au revoir.*'

'*Au revoir, mon père.*'

'Come, Dhanya, there is much to do before nightfall.'

~

169

It wasn't a boy that came to meet Rinzen at the pine tree but his own father. Rinzen had concealed himself in the evergreen foliage high above the ground. He scanned the surroundings for signs of soldiers and jumped the fifteen metres to land in front of his father, who, if he was impressed, didn't show it.

'Firstly, no one has seen any soldiers dressed in black. Here's a parcel of food from your mother, and this is the map to take you across the border and on to Darbhanga. There's only one short stretch of road, otherwise it's all remote paths. Everyone I asked gave me money and wished you well. I don't know how much things will cost once you leave India, but this should take you a long way towards your destination. And here are some boots, a little worn but strong and in keeping with the rest of your disguise.'

'I'm meant to be a schoolteacher,' Rinzen said. 'My friend Keung's idea.'

'Mmm, I suppose you could pass as one of the new generation of teachers, but I certainly wouldn't wear such an outfit.'

'Ah.'

'You'll be fine. Here, take my passport. In case you have to flash it at someone.'

'No, Father, I can't take it. It took you so much effort to get it. Really, I don't—'

'I insist. Please. You're risking your life for the brothers, for humanity. What's a bit of cardboard and paper compared to that?'

Rinzen tucked the passport into his pocket, sat down and tried on the boots. 'Perfect. Whose are they?'

'Rajeesh's son. He's a good man. He came with me to the edge of the village to check I hadn't been followed and will meet me on my return.' He glanced towards the village. 'We are very exposed here.'

Exposed. Precisely how Rinzen felt.

16

London

On Saturday lunchtime Gail the art student came round to ask if Clara would like her to help with her shopping. Clara thanked her for her kindness and explained that she didn't want to go outside for a while.

'But you're very welcome to visit me when you come down for your art class.'

After Gail left, Clara's stomach turned as she realised that this must have come across as condescending, as though it were a great privilege to be invited into her presence.

I push everyone away, she thought – first Henry, then Julia, and now that sweet girl.

She played non-stop for three hours but failed to dissipate the gloom.

~

When Matthew arrived for the next session on Monday morning, he had hardly sat down before Clara said, 'You seem to think that my parents were tyrants who forced me to practise the harp all the time. Perhaps I gave you that impression, but it wasn't like that. My father was a kind, gentle man, very affectionate. He never shouted at me or made me do anything I didn't want to do.'

She interlocked her fingers and stretched forward until they clicked. 'It's true that he believed that when someone was blessed with a particular talent, they had a duty to make the most of it, but I know that if I'd shown any signs of distress, he wouldn't have insisted I continue.'

Although Matthew's placid expression didn't change, there was something about the light in his eyes that told her he was carefully considering how to respond. She ran her tongue through her lips and waited.

'I assure you I'm not judging your parents at all. In a way, I was stating the obvious – that the harp has been present throughout your life, that it's associated with all the natural processes you've gone through as you matured, and that this is rather unusual. And now you are physically attached to the harp to prevent your mother's death.' He paused, drank some water. 'Was your mother always as committed to your harp playing as your father?'

Clara looked down and finger-drummed the table with her left hand. 'My mother is exasperating, but I know she loves me, wants the best for me, has sacrificed many years of her life to help me and look after me, years when she could have found love or developed her own career.'

She ran her hand through her hair and realised she hadn't brushed it that morning. She must look a mess. And he was always so ironed and fresh.

'She's always tried to keep in the background, never boasted about me like the other Royal College mothers. After my dad died, I think she saw it as her duty to carry on his work, but no, I don't think she was in complete agreement with him when I was very young. She thought I should play with other children, go to ballet and all that, but I didn't want to do anything apart from play the harp. Maybe I did it to please my father, but I don't think I could have kept it up if it was just for him.'

Matthew nodded. 'You know,' he said, 'I wonder … No, maybe not. Um…'

'What were you going to say?'

'It's not strictly professional, but everything is about the harp, and I've never heard you play. Of course, I bought two of your CDs and listened to those – very beautiful – but ...'

'I'll play something if you like.'

'Thank you.'

Did he blush or was it just the light on his face as he looked down?

She checked the tuning, made some minor adjustments and settled herself on the harp stool. She started slowly, softly, played in the first and second octaves, let the notes linger and overlap; she moved into the third and fourth octaves, increased the volume but held the slow pace so her audience of one could appreciate each note. It felt like a suitable introduction to the first bars of her own composition, or rather a variation on her composition, as she never seemed to play it the same way. She settled into a rhythm that suited this mood, closed her eyes and allowed the music to flow through her; notes and chords layered the air. Her arms moved, her fingers plucked the strings, her feet shifted between the pedals, all of their own volition, without effort or conscious direction.

Sometime later, she opened her eyes and said, 'Sorry, did I go on too long?'

Matthew's eyes were closed and he didn't answer.

'Matthew?'

'Yes. I mean no, not too long.' He opened his eyes, their lids heavy. 'That music isn't on your CD. There's nothing like that on your CD. I didn't know music like that even existed.' He shook his head, widened his eyes, smiled at her. He was definitely blushing now.

'It's my own composition. That was the world premiere!' She laughed and it felt strange. When was the last time she had really laughed?

Matthew laughed along with her, probably to cover his embarrassment.

'I'm honoured then,' he said. 'And I feel like I've had a spiritual experience. It probably sounds clichéd, but your music lifted me out of this physical world. I was flying like a Chagall figure through a different dimension … And the colours were sublime, swirling and twisting with that impossibly beautiful music.'

'Now you're making me blush. It's a work in progress, never the same.'

'And don't you want to share it with the world? Sorry, not a fair question.' He straightened his already straight tie, smoothed his already smooth trousers, and pretended to clear his throat. 'Thank you, Clara. Very much. Now, this is your time, not mine, so shall we continue?'

Clara smiled. Like a Chagall figure, eh? And he saw the colours. This man is a kindred spirit.

'I did think about my beliefs and opinions, like you asked. And it's true, I've had very little experience of forming my own judgements. For example, even when I really liked a particular tutor and felt I learned a lot with them, my mother would overrule me and dismiss them if their musicianship turned out to be anything less than world class.'

She paused, shifted on the stool.

'Would you like to move to a more comfortable chair?'

She detected a tone of reverence and hoped it was temporary.

'No, I'm fine here. But please pass me the water. Thanks.' She took a large gulp.

'I've come to realise that too much discipline dulls the senses, so I suppose that's a sort of judgement. Since I moved in here, over a year ago now, I've listened to a much wider range of music, and my man, or maybe my ex-man, Henry, has taken me to live bands all over London, from jazz to house, country to electric reggae, even rap and folk. Far from it somehow corrupting me musically, it's inspired me. Live poetry and modern dance too.'

'Interesting.' His eyes had been flicking from her face to the harp since she'd stopped playing, but now he stared straight at the soundboard.

Unless it was her breasts he was looking at? She hiccupped at the thought. No, he wouldn't do that. Or would he? Her low-cut T-shirt left nothing to the imagination. And he was a man as well as a hypnotherapist. A wave of heat travelled up her body, but she resisted the urge to check her chest hadn't reddened, and tried not to think about her nipples hardening. In any case, she wasn't attracted to him. Except his voice, of course, and he was definitely a kindred spirit. She had to say something, distract herself. 'I suppose what you mean is I should be more conscious of things, rather than lazily follow what I've learned from my parents?'

'Have you seen the Chagall stained glass at Reims Cathedral?' Thankfully, he stopped staring at the soundboard/breasts and looked at her face.

'What?'

'Sorry. I must apologise. Do you mind if we call it a day? I won't charge for today.'

'Why not? You've been here over an hour.'

Matthew stood, carefully repositioned his chair under the dining table, and stood in front of her. He rubbed his hands. 'I confess your playing has discombobulated me.'

Clara laughed at the word, saw it embarrassed him, and tried to stop. Giggles bubbled up around the hand clasped to her mouth. 'Sorry,' she managed to splutter.

'I'll just go, shall I?'

She nodded.

'Right, see you on Thursday.'

She nodded again, desperate to let the laughter explode from her stomach, willed him to be gone.

~

175

At their next session, instead of taking her back into her dream, Matthew asked her to return to her earliest memory of playing the harp. She agreed willingly – it would mean spending time with her papa – and entered the trance with ease.

'I am playing the piano in the front room, while Mum reads a book in the old leather armchair. The heavy red velvet curtains are closed, so it must be winter, otherwise I would be in bed. I can't reach the piano pedals, so I have long blocks attached to each foot, but they don't feel heavy, just a bit clumsy. I can't hear the music, but I am definitely playing. There's a faraway voice, but it doesn't make sense. Papa bursts in, holding a large case in one hand. He places it carefully on the floor and scoops me up and blows raspberries on my neck. I wriggle and squirm and giggle.

'"Stop, Papa, stop!" I can hear that.

'He pulls off the blocks and sets me down on the floor, kneeling beside me. "Look what I have here." He opens the case and pulls out a Celtic harp. I've never seen one before so don't know its name. "It's like a piano, but you pluck the strings instead of pressing the keys." He demonstrates, and bright music fills the room.

'Papa sits, lifts me onto his big knees, facing the same way as him. Mum passes over the harp, which he holds at its base, balanced between both our knees. I copy what he did a minute before. I copy it exactly, note for note.

'"How did you do that, Clara!" Mum's voice is all high and screechy.

'"She's a natural," Papa whispers. I can feel his heart beating against my back. It seems to be going faster with every second. "Again, Clara, play it again!"

'Now I can't feel the heartbeat, maybe it's because I'm playing so loudly, the vibrations drown it out. I stop. Mum is crying. I turn to look at Papa, see his open mouth, something liquidy pouring out the edge. I see it drip on his stiff white collar. I'm not on his knee after all. I'm standing in the doorway, I'm bigger, and there's a half-size harp next to him—'

There was a click.

'And wake up.'

Clara was screaming now, and someone was banging on the door. She stared at the man in a suit crouching next to her, holding her hand. She knew him, but she couldn't stop screaming.

'Look at me, Clara. Look at me and everything will be all right.' His voice was so mellow, like a woodwind instrument played from a high tower at sunset.

She was incredibly thirsty, but the man had thought of that and handed her a glass of water. She closed her eyes, slumped over the harp.

There was someone shouting, 'Let me in! Let me in!' Then Matthew – that was the man's name – went away and came back again. The shouting stopped.

'That was your mother. I said I'd go and get her from next door if you want me to.'

Clara shook her head, didn't want to speak. She pushed the harp to the bedroom, lay on the bed with her hand on the soundbox, and fell asleep.

When she woke, Matthew was sitting on a chair.

'You're still here.'

'I wanted to make sure you were OK when you woke up.'

'Thanks. That was horrible. I was there, three or four years old, playing the Celtic harp for the first time, and it felt like I already knew how to play it, even though I'd never even seen one before. Then suddenly I was in the doorway, looking at my dead father.'

She looked away from Matthew. 'I didn't realise I'd actually seen him dead.'

'I've never known that happen before. If I thought for one minute—'

'It's OK, Matthew.'

He raised an eyebrow. She'd never seen him do that before.

'Really. It was awful, but … it's like I've found a missing piece of me. Something that fits in a hole.'

'You've filled a memory gap, which makes you feel more complete.'

'That's it. Complete.'

'The shock of seeing him just after he died might explain why you stopped speaking. Suddenly, after being so much part of your daily life, he was gone.'

'Always there, then never there.'

'Yes. A huge, unfillable hole in your life.'

~

Over the following ten weeks, apart from the supermarket delivery man and occasional chats with Gail, Matthew was her only visitor, every Monday and Thursday morning for two hours. Julia telephoned every few days. Other acquaintances and colleagues also wanted to know what was going on, but Clara didn't want to see them while she was undergoing such intensive therapy.

The sessions with Matthew usually consisted of hypnosis and then more talk about her past, particularly her relationship with her mother. He trod lightly around the subject of her father's death, as though he didn't want to dilute the beneficial effects of the revelation that she'd been there. Rarely did a session end without some new insight.

Grace watched her six days a week from Fulbright's flat. On Sundays, Clara telephoned her mother to tell her that the therapy sessions were going well but that she was still holding onto the harp. With each Sunday, Grace's sighs became more extended, more despairing.

And then, on Wednesday 26 June, Grace stopped coming to Fulbright's flat.

17

India

The further south he travelled, the more people he met,
even on the remote paths his father had marked on the map.
Most of them were locals – farmers on their way to their
fields, people loaded down with stacks of wood twice their
own height, lines of children taking shortcuts to and from
school, market traders with overladen mules – but some
were barefoot pilgrims on their way to holy shrines, or
inspectors of one sort or another, and even a pair of
European hikers who carried everything they needed on
their backs. Rinzen greeted everyone with a smile and
'Namaste', was rewarded with friendly responses, and was
soon more comfortable travelling with a family, or a group
of farmers en route to market, than on his own. The more
people there were, the more anonymous he became. He
observed his companions and learned how to use money
and how much simple food cost at the stalls along the way.

After four days he emerged from the hills onto the
tapestry of fields on the vast plain, and the going became
much easier. On the sixth day he arrived at a village that was
officially in India but had spread across the border. The
boundary line was marked only by small concrete pyramids,
and these had either been incorporated into buildings or co-
opted as stands to dry clothes or for displaying fruit and
vegetables for sale. He walked on and was now hardly ever

on his own. His fellow travellers became even more diverse, even more colourful, and he had to remind himself not to stare at the groups of near-naked sadhus with full-body paint.

As the days passed so his confidence grew, and with each step away from the border he felt more certain that his pursuers would not find him. It was in a state of mild euphoria that he strode through the crowded streets of Darbhanga towards the railway station. Shortly before five o'clock, he joined the queue at the ticket office, and when his turn came he leaned towards the hatch and asked the ticket seller if he knew where he could find Amdong's uncle.

'This is not an information desk.' The man looked about the same age as his father, but that was where the similarity ended. Although he wore a suit like his father, this man's was shiny with age, and his dun-coloured tie was knotted around a threadbare collar. His greasy hair flopped over his forehead, almost in front of his eyes, eyes that did not even glance up at Rinzen.

'Where is the information desk, please?'

'There.' The man pointed, still not looking up. 'Closed until tomorrow morning.'

'Thank you. But Mr Shrestha works on the train to Mumbai, and I hoped I might see him today.'

'Who?' The man frowned and scowled at Rinzen.

Rinzen looked at the envelope and repeated the uncle's name.

'Don't understand you. Others are waiting.'

Rinzen turned. The woman behind him smiled at him. 'Sorry,' he said.

'No need to apologise to her. It is I who am in charge. Show me the envelope.' He jabbed his hand out, flicked his thumb against his fingers.

Rinzen held up the envelope, but the ticket seller snatched it and looked at the name. He rang the handbell next to him, and a barefoot boy ran in from the room behind, grabbed the letter and made off with it.

'No! Bring back my letter,' Rinzen shouted, and then to the ticket man, 'Where's he gone?'

'To find Mr Shrestha. Next.'

Rinzen had no choice but to step aside and wait. Some of the people in the queue stared at this man who had delayed them, who'd even had the temerity to shout at the ticket attendant, the official with the power to refuse a ticket. Why hadn't he just enquired about a ticket to Mumbai? It seemed it wasn't necessary to have any travel documents after all. He walked across the ticket hall to the station entrance, out of sight of the accusing eyes. A terrifying thought struck him: what if someone opened the letter? They would know he was a Samudran brother, wonder why he was dressed in civilian clothes, might have heard that the Nepalese Army were searching for him. He felt a trickle of sweat between his shoulder blades and closed his eyes for a few seconds, centred himself, quelled the rising panic.

When he opened his eyes, he saw the boy beside the ticket seller, pointing in Rinzen's direction. He readied himself to run. The ticket man nodded and the boy hurried off again. Rinzen took a few steps forward and stared at the ticket seller, who stubbornly refused to look at him.

'You are Rinzen?' The voice came from behind him.

Rinzen jumped three metres and spun round into a crouch, ready. Someone in the queue gasped, others murmured to each other. The voice belonged to a portly man with a smiling face and unruly thick black hair.

'Sorry to startle you. I am Adil Shrestha.' He waved the envelope.

Rinzen advanced, hand outstretched, laughing with relief. 'It is I who is sorry, sir. Thank you.'

'Come, let's go. The ticket seller will prepare your ticket to Mumbai and give it to me later.'

They walked onto the platform and along to the bridge across the tracks. Adil chuckled. 'You gave those poor people a bit of a shock with your spontaneous leap.'

'Yes, I confess I found it difficult to remain composed. I completely misread what was going on …'

'Perfectly understandable after all you've been through. I am at your service, and I will personally deliver you to Mumbai aboard the Pawan Express.' Adil put his avuncular arm around Rinzen's shoulders. The latter nodded, whispered his thanks.

They crossed the tracks, exited the station and walked the few minutes to Adil's small white house one street back from the railway lines. The front door opened onto a white-walled room with mats on the floor. Adil's wife, a small, wiry woman with a high forehead and a smile that split her face from ear to ear, welcomed Rinzen without hesitation. When Adil explained that Rinzen was a Samudran senior on an important secret mission, Chameli pressed her palms together, bowed, and called for her teenage daughter to bring a bowl of water and a towel so that he could wash his hands.

'Would you like to rest, Rinzen?' Adil asked. 'I must go to make ready the train. And then we will eat in one hour. You have come on exactly the right day at exactly the right time because the train will depart at 8.20pm sharp.'

'It will be my first time on board a train.' Out of respect, he stood up.

'We will do anything, anything at all, for the Samudran brothers. I mean to say, where would we be without your devotions?'

~

Adil showed Rinzen to his curtained berth in the second-class sleeper carriage.

'I hope you will be comfortable here.' Adil handed him a bottle of water. 'I will come and see you in the morning. We will eat breakfast together.'

'You may have to wake me.' Rinzen imagined delicious sleep in the cosy berth. 'Thanks again, Adil. Will you get any sleep tonight?'

'Perhaps a couple of hours in the dead of night. I wish you a peaceful night and a deep sleep.'

Minutes later, as he drifted into sleep, Rinzen heard the string instrument. The music wafted about, now clear, now faint, as though it were being carried by a breeze. Soft, delicate chords, like meltwater splashing over mossy rocks, lulled him into a dreamless sleep.

When he awoke, they were passing through the outskirts of a large city. Through the slatted steel window, he saw that the sun had half risen and seemed to be deciding whether to bother performing its daily arc today. His body rocked with the gentle rhythm of the train, and he felt no inclination to move. In this half-awake/half-asleep state he allowed his mind to wander. He would meditate later; right now, he would permit himself the indulgence of daydreaming. The face of the woman who had washed and fed him when he collapsed on the way to Sarmand gave way to the laughing, jumping Keung as he bounded up the mountain, disturbed mid leap by the train whistle as it slowed to a halt at Varanasi station.

He peered out as hundreds of sleepy passengers disembarked and a smaller crowd of more lively people boarded the train. A skinny boy, barefoot and mud-stained, held aloft a battered urn and shouted his offer of tea at a price Rinzen couldn't quite catch. Other vendors lined the platform, many with overfilled baskets balanced on their heads. They carried cane stands for the baskets under their arms and set these up to serve passengers through the train windows. Grapes and peeled cucumbers were on offer, as well as plastic sandals, jewellery and men's belts. They called out their wares, tried to out-shout each other as their eyes darted about for customers. There was no time for levity, so intent were they to do as much business as possible during the short time the train was in the station.

Adil took up a position halfway down the platform and surveyed the train proprietorially. He accepted and returned the greetings of station staff as they went about their tasks with great haste. Clearly, it was imperative that the train depart on time.

Adil consulted his watch, lifted his right arm and climbed aboard. Moments later, the whistle blew and the train pulled away, through the railway yards, past rows of warehouses and out into the country, where the last of the morning mist rose in feathers into the warming air.

'Breakfast time, I think.' Adil spoke from the other side of the curtain.

They picked their way through the crowded carriages: families at their breakfasts; a group of monks on a corridor bed; a noisy clutter of young men in matching T-shirts; an old man bent double, coughing and wheezing. Some passengers were still asleep behind their curtains, but even so the going was slow as they traversed carriage after carriage to reach the pantry car, where the tables were laid with starched white cloths in readiness for breakfast.

Adil introduced Rinzen to his friend Rohit, an elderly Punjabi with an impressive handlebar moustache and a wide smile that revealed a set of perfect, gleaming teeth.

'And this,' Adil said, pointing at Rinzen, 'is Akash, a family friend on his way to take up his first teaching post in Mumbai, of all places.'

'Welcome to my first-class second-class restaurant car!' Rohit said. 'Adil told me you were on board, so I have made up a special breakfast tray for you, precisely matching the one I have made for Mr Shrestha.' He beamed beneath his bleached white cap as he passed Rinzen a tray.

'This looks and smells delicious,' Rinzen said. 'Thank you very much, sir.'

'Yes, indeed,' Adil said. '*Idli podi* and *ragi* porridge washed down with *masala chai* will do very nicely.'

They carried their trays to the next carriage, to a small compartment in which the train staff were permitted to rest and sleep.

'Welcome to my first-class dining car.' Adil grinned at him. 'Please take a seat by the window and I will show you the sights as we eat our breakfast.' A few minutes later, he said, 'See there, in the distance, those black mounds? That is one of the largest coal mines in all of India. It supplies many of the power stations in Uttar Pradesh and Madhya Pradesh.'

'I have heard of such mines,' Rinzen said. He'd heard of them from an elder who had travelled through India, but he had no idea that open-cast coal mines were so enormous. The black mounds – slag heaps, he remembered they were called – stretched across the horizon like a mountain range.

'Impressive, don't you think?' Adil said.

'I have never seen such a place,' Rinzen said, afraid that if he spoke his mind Adil would be offended. He turned back to look at his tray, overwhelmed by the enormity of the Samudrans' task. It was no easy matter to look after the planet when humankind was intent on destroying it. There were mines like that all over the world that fed power plants to work the factories that made things to satisfy man's desire for more of everything, many times more than they actually needed. Perhaps Elder Kwato's sense that the planet had shifted on its axis was caused in part by all this digging and burning?

'Look, now we're passing close to the great river, the river of life, the mighty Ganges. Perhaps one day you will make a pilgrimage to Varanasi to bathe in its waters?'

The river was so wide, Rinzen could barely see the opposite bank. The morning sun blazed across its surface and made silhouettes of the sailing boats bound for Varanasi. Without the slag heaps and the plumes of smoke from the giant chimneys of the distant power plant, the scene would have been idyllic – simple, elegant craft powered by the wind floating down one of the great rivers of the world.

'Perhaps,' Rinzen said. 'But my journey has only just started.' He looked up from his tray and met sympathetic eyes.

'Yes, you have a long way to go, but – please excuse my saying so – you are the only one who has the strength to make such a pilgrimage. Years ago, when we last saw my nephew Amdong, he spoke of your special abilities, how history would tell of Elder Rinzen and his contribution to the Samudran brotherhood.' Adil paused, as if considering whether he had already said too much. He laid his hands palms down on the metal table that separated them and looked into Rinzen's eyes. 'I have refrained from saying this until now, as I know you brothers shun praise and detest comparisons, but I wanted you to know the confidence you inspire as you pass through the world.'

Rinzen nodded, determined to present an expressionless face. It would not be fitting to share his inner turmoil; it would likely be interpreted as false modesty. He knew who and what he was, a simple Samudran brother with one task: to keep this battered and bruised planet turning at whatever cost. He was no different from any other senior on the cusp of becoming an elder, and it was not a given that he would ever achieve the inner peace required to take the name of Elder Rinzen.

'Well...' Adil arranged the empty bowls on one tray, slipped Rinzen's tray under his, and rose from the table. 'I need to attend to matters before the next station stop, so please excuse me. You are welcome to sit here for as long as you like, or return to your own compartment.'

186

'Thank you, Adil.' Rinzen clasped Adil's right hand between his palms. 'For everything.'

Tears formed in the eyes of the important railway official, and it was his turn to simply nod.

After Adil left, Rinzen looked through the window, but he did not see what was before his eyes, did not feel the sway of the train or hear its rattling progress along the uneven tracks, was unaware of the cauldron of aromas that leaked from the pantry car's breakfast service. In an instant his full consciousness was focused on the inner temple at Sarmand, his fellow brothers in silent meditation while he looked on from the shadows, breathed in the delicious myrtle incense, felt the cool mountain air on his cheeks.

Winter had arrived. The cold would anaesthetise the monastery, banish the dreadful, invisible wasting disease, harden the earth that capped the funeral pyres of those many elders: in life, they protected the earth; in death, the earth would protect the remnants of their ashes. But the mountain streams would not freeze. Even below the icy surface of the many pools that marked their course, the water – the earth's life force – would flow and nourish and defy armies and all their ordinance. No matter how many stealthy men dressed in black were sent, the water would still flow, Sarmand would still stand, the meditation would not be interrupted. Even if all Samudrans were shackled, blindfolded and gagged, even if they were all locked in separate cells, still the meditation would continue. Rinzen did not think this: he felt it as a force that coursed through his muscles; it prompted in him the sudden urge to leap from the train and run alongside it. He could easily run all day and all night.

'May I enter?'

Rinzen turned to see one of the Buddhist monks they'd passed on the way to the pantry car. He half stood in the space between the table and bench, pressed his hands together and bowed. 'Please do.'

The monk's face was unlined, but his eyes betrayed the wisdom of years in devotion. 'I felt you pass us in the corridor and was compelled to follow.'

'Please sit. This is not my compartment, but I have permission to use it.'

The monk put his head out of the doorway and looked both ways before sliding the door closed and sitting down opposite Rinzen. 'I sensed your anxiety, but now I see that it has passed.'

'You are very observant.'

'It is not surprising. I hear all is not well in the north.'

'You know who I am?'

'I do, but I will not speak of it. The walls are as thin as skin. However, I will say that it is difficult to make bread rise without the baking powder.'

'Indeed, but there are other raising agents, and I can tell you that these have been successfully introduced without the loss of a single day's manna.'

The monk's face, which hitherto had been cast in shadow and had displayed no emotion, rippled with laughter lines. He laughed and slapped the table with the palm of his right hand. 'Such good news! I pray that the Well of Life remains undisturbed for many years.'

He's a Samudran, Rinzen thought. But why is he dressed in monk's clothing?

'My cousin ...' the monk said.

'Yes?'

'My cousin is a fine baker of bread.'

He was desperate to ask the name of the monk's cousin, but he controlled the urge and simply grinned at his companion.

The monk continued. 'I have something to tell you, although now I look at you, I'm not sure you need to hear it.' Rinzen made to speak, but the monk raised his eyebrow. 'Let's suppose a person is on a long journey. His reason for the journey is to find a solution to a very difficult problem. It would be natural for the person to be overwhelmed by the enormity of the task and to worry that he will never make it through the many obstacles to the end of his journey.'

Was this monk reading his mind? How could he know, so soon after his flight from Sarmand, that Rinzen was on such a quest? He leaned forward, willed the monk on. A dim light in the centre of his mind seemed to be growing brighter. If it continued like this, he would be able to see into every hidden nook.

'But if the person looks at each stage of his journey in turn, looks at each problem or obstacle on its own, then he can apply the straightforward advice of the Dalai Lama in order to reduce anxiety and act with clarity. Perhaps you are familiar with this teaching?'

Rinzen shook his head. He was all ears.

'His Holiness advises that "if the problem is such that it can be remedied, there is no need to worry about it". In other words, it's more sensible to spend your energy focusing on the solution than worrying about the problem. He also suggests that "if there's no possibility of finding a resolution, there's no point being worried about it", so the sooner you accept the fact, the easier it will be on you. This formula, of course, requires confronting the problem directly. Otherwise you won't be able to find out whether or not a resolution is possible.'

The monk brought the index fingers of both hands up to his lips, as though considering what more to say.

Rinzen waited, wanting to hear every word of his advice and keep the light in his mind brightening. It was just like being with Elder Kwato; he used to take every opportunity to remind Rinzen of his training and had always been willing to reiterate seemingly elementary lessons when the situation called for it.

The monk continued. 'Muddled thinking often creates problems when none exist. Accepting that some problems have no resolution will often enable you to bypass them or see them as unimportant.'

Rinzen was about to reply when the monk said, 'But of course some brotherhoods train their members in just such strategies.'

'True,' Rinzen said, 'but I'm sure that even those brothers would find great benefit in looking at things from a different angle and being reminded of their training.'

The monk half stood and shuffled along the table, and Rinzen did the same. 'I will now return to my fellow monks. Later, we will chant for our brothers in the north.'

At the door, the monk bowed, and Rinzen's heart was massaged by the warmth of his smile.

A few minutes later, when he passed the three monks on his way back to his compartment, Rinzen nodded but did not speak. As he weaved his way along the crowded corridors, he was loose-limbed, unimpeded; he sidestepped children and stepped over suitcases, dodged plates of food balanced on knees, chai boys shouting their prices and women queuing for the toilet, bypassed an old sadhu offering prayers on his bunk, his bare feet like plates of leather obstructing the narrow passageway. The conversation with the monk, and his own vision of the inner temple at Sarmand, had cleared his mind; instead of avoiding eye contact, he nodded and smiled at his fellow passengers as he floated along.

When he reached his bunk, the three men in the main compartment were engaged in animated conversation. They were all speaking in English, presumably in deference to the European sitting by the window. He wore tattered sandals, loose trousers that had once been white and a collarless cotton shirt of indeterminate colour. His hair was uncombed and his chin studded with a week's worth of stubble, but his eyes were bright with argument, and his long forehead lent him the look of an intellectual.

Instead of hiding himself away behind the curtain, Rinzen waited for a pause and offered his greetings to them before he sat on his bunk and faced the group. The young boy leaning against the shoulder of one of the men turned his head shyly into the man's jacket. The three men returned his greeting and continued their conversation.

The European man said, 'But you cannot get the same quality of protein from pulses and nuts – meat is essential for a balanced diet.'

'Not true,' the man with the boy, presumably his father, said. 'That is simply a myth propagated by people who cannot bear the thought of a vegetarian diet.'

'Exactly,' the third man, some years younger than the others, said. 'I completely agree with our lawyer friend. There are millions of fit and healthy vegetarians in India alone.'

'Our young student friend is right,' the lawyer said, 'and vegetarians are less likely to develop cancer.'

'Nonsense.' The European turned to Rinzen. 'What do you think, sir?'

Rinzen would have liked to speak about the Samudrans' feats of strength and endurance on a vegetarian diet, but he said, 'People grow crops to feed to animals so that people can eat the animals. Why not just eat the crops?'

'Well said.' The lawyer grinned at Rinzen.

'Ah well,' the European said, 'it seems I am outnumbered. Now, what else should we talk about to pass the time?'

Rinzen, reminded of debating competitions at Sarmand, felt a sudden pang of longing for his home. Oh, to walk around the cloisters with Keung or watch Amdong practise on the eighty steps; above all, to be in deep meditation in harmony with his brothers. 'You are a long way from your home, sir. May I ask why you have come to India?'

Everyone, even the boy, looked at the European.

'Well, let's see ... I guess I wanted to see how other people live, visit your sacred places, expand my mind, gain knowledge.'

'I see,' Rinzen said. 'Then you are wasting your time. Knowledge is to be gained not by travelling out but by travelling in.' He saw the shock register on the man's face and immediately regretted his words, words he had spoken in the spirit of debate, words which could not be retracted and which might expose the Samudran beneath the schoolteacher disguise.

'Am I not welcome then?' The brightness in the man's eyes dimmed, his brow curled over like a frozen wave.

'No, no, of course you are welcome. I ... I meant no offence, excuse me.' So easy to put a foot wrong out in this world where people did not speak their mind.

'I think our friend was just being controversial for the sake of argument.' The student removed his spectacles, took a cloth from their case, and polished the lenses. 'Am I right?' He raised one eyebrow at Rinzen.

Rinzen nodded, feared that if he spoke again, he would cause further offence.

'OK then.' The European sat back and turned to look out of the window.

The others were silent. Rinzen wanted to close his curtain and then his eyes.

'Travelling in, eh?' The European spoke without turning. 'Interesting. You mean self-knowledge, I presume. But I would say that without experience, external experience, we have no way of accessing that inner knowledge. It is only by engaging with other people – and preferably people unlike oneself, like you guys, for example – that we gain an insight into our own being. Take this clever boy here' – the boy sat bolt upright – 'if you placed him on his own in a nice house, fed him with delicious meals, kept him warm and comfortable, and let him grow up entirely on his own, his mind would become dull and he would have no means of discovering this inner self of which you speak.'

Four faces turned towards Rinzen. He would have to answer. Should he – for the sake of his mission – protect himself from further exposure, go against all his training and accept defeat in a debating contest?

'My argument does not assume the isolation you posit. If you had stayed in your own society, you would not live in the way you describe, so it is not only hypothetical but also a false analogy.'

The European's expression hardened into a sneer. He should stop, he'd turned a friendly conversation into an intellectual competition. But his mind raced on.

'Tuition from one's elders, engagement with one's peers, focused study and the training of mind and body, these are the elements that bring about clarity of mind. Clarity of mind is essential for true self-knowledge, without which we are condemned to a life of inner turmoil, unhappiness and dissatisfaction. It is not necessary to travel to learn the compassion for others, generosity of spirit and sincere empathy required to become a fulfilled human being. I argue that travel is a distraction from the search for inner knowledge: one goes from one sensory experience to the next without understanding, and the mind becomes cluttered not clarified.'

'Are you a philosophy professor?' the student said.

'Schoolteacher,' Rinzen muttered. Why was he doing this?

'Ah, here you are.' The monk had arrived unnoticed. 'I'm sorry our conversation earlier was interrupted, and I wondered whether we might continue it.' He turned to the others and soaked them with one of his smiles.

'Yes, yes, of course,' Rinzen said. 'Please excuse me, gentlemen, I hope you won't think it rude of me to break away.'

A chorus of nos freed him from the chasm he had created.

18

London

On Thursday, Clara celebrated her mother's absence from Fulbright's flat by playing her composition twice. Sometime in the middle of the night she dozed, on the edge of sleep, draped around her harp as usual, vaguely aware of a rhythmic hammering – louder, softer, louder, softer. Suddenly the volume increased, the rhythm became erratic, and her eyes snapped open. Where was it coming from? She lifted her head off the soundbox. The front door? Who? She stumbled away from the harp, still mostly asleep, and staggered to the door.

'Who's there?'

'It's Gareth Fulbright, from next door.'

'What do you want?' This came out as a shout, far too loud.

'I have a message from Lawrence Greene in Basel.'

Basel? Why had Lawrence called Fulbright from Basel? She unlocked and opened the door to a dishevelled, dressing-gowned, unshaven Fulbright. 'Sorry to shout at you. What message?'

'You are to call this number immediately.' He handed her a scrap of paper with numbers on it. 'Mr Greene tried to call your number many times. Apparently' – he twisted his mouth as he said the word – 'it's urgent.'

'God. What?' Wide awake now, her heart thumping, her mouth so dry that her tongue stuck to her teeth. 'Thank you.'

She slammed the door and rushed into the kitchen, grabbed the phone, saw at once that she'd forgotten to turn up the volume after Matthew had left that morning, and dialled the number. It was answered by the receptionist at the Hotel Euler, who put her through to Lawrence's room.

He answered the moment it rang.

'Hello, Lawrence?'

'Clara, are you at home? I've tried to call you many times. I couldn't get through to Henry either. Is he with you, by any chance?'

'No. I'm on my own. At home. I forgot to turn on the phone. What is it, Lawrence?'

'Please sit down, Clara. I'm so sorry, but I'm afraid I have some terrible news.'

The walls closed in on her as she dropped into a dining chair.

'It's Grace, Clara. Your mother had a heart attack this morning. She died almost instantly, so I'm sure she didn't suffer. I'm so dreadfully sorry.'

Clara heard his words, tried to make sense of them.

'Clara? Are you there, Clara? Oh God.'

She couldn't speak.

'Clara, please say something.' He gave her a chance to answer, then, 'I'm so very sorry. It was ... uh ... after breakfast, after we'd come back to our room to get ready to go out.'

She heard breathing, was he panting?

'Clara? I can hear you breathing, Clara. Your not speaking worries me.'

'Why?' she said. She hadn't intended to speak out loud; the 'why?' was addressed to herself.

'I'm sorry, I don't know why. She's been ... fine, as you know. Since all those hospital appointments. Worried about you, but … The … the paramedics arrived very quickly, but there was nothing they could do.'

Clara knew she should say something, but all she could come up with was 'I see.'

'I'll bring her body back to England in a few days, after the autopsy. But let's speak again in the morning. I'll have a clearer idea of when we … I … we will be free to leave.' She heard him switch ears. 'It's all quite complicated. You know the Swiss and their paperwork.'

'I see,' Clara said again, and pushed the harp away from her. It loomed over her like a gilded dragon in the unlit gloom.

'Shall I call you in the morning?'

She didn't answer, couldn't find the words.

'Clara? Please listen to me. Why don't you call Henry? Grace was sure he still loves you. Or Julia – you need your best friend at a time like this. And I will call you at ten o'clock your time tomorrow morning. OK?' He didn't hang up. 'Or please call me any time, any time at all.'

'I see.' The phone slipped from her hand as she fell to the floor and landed on the side of her knee. She toppled over, hands splayed out on the floor, legs crumpled under her.

All my fault. I killed her. In Switzerland. Heart attack. All because I couldn't do something so simple as hold onto the harp.

Her thoughts stopped. Nothing but a stare along the surface of the floor. Time passed, unnoticed. She closed her eyes and immediately saw the dream image of her mother's distorted face, her twisted, taut neck and the cavernous mouth stretched over yellow-stained teeth. A groan started deep in Clara's gut, vibrated through her chest and emerged as a scream. She scrambled to her feet, fell against the dining table, gripped its edge with both hands.

No mum to guide her, no one to tell her to sit up straight, drink more water, get some fresh air … No mum to erase her doubts, to brush her hair before concerts. When she was little, she used to love sitting in front of her mum's dressing table mirror watching her gentle hands carefully pull the brush through her unruly hair. She always smelled so nice, her unique smell, like flowers and cherries or … She raised her head and looked through the tears at the photograph of her and her papa on the far wall.

'Oh, Papa, what will we do now?'

The floor shook and her whole body juddered; even her teeth chattered. She gripped tighter, but the shaking just intensified.

She staggered to the bedroom, stripping as she went. Somehow, she managed to pull on a pair of jeans, a bra, a jersey. She grabbed the rucksack from the wardrobe and threw in an unselected handful of clothes, walked like an automaton back to the living room – thank God the shaking had stopped – and pulled her passport and purse from the sideboard drawer.

She was about to walk out of the flat when she saw the Lyon & Healy, shoved up against the living room wall, all alone. She dropped the rucksack and ran over to it, wrapped her arms around its neck. 'It's not your fault, it was me, I didn't hold you enough.' She carefully wheeled it into the centre of the room and stood back. It still looked isolated, seemed to be asking her to do something, but what? Maybe she should cover it up? It would be the first time in many months. No, that would be worse, like a funeral shroud, a body bag.

She paced around the room, cursing herself for hesitating when she was about to leave. She stopped, stared at her precious instrument, hissed at it. 'You want me to take you with me, don't you? Well you can fuck off. You, or your ancestors, got my family into this mess, and now look where I am. All alone. Like you.'

She turned her back on it, plunged it into darkness and strode out of the building.

She marched head down along Great Eastern Street, passed a closed Old Street Underground station and continued to King's Cross. She kept her eyes down, only glanced up once in a while to cross a road or check for other pedestrians. She knew what she was up to but refused to let her conscious self admit it. But flashes of realisation – that her mother, her darling mother who she could not live without, was dead – stabbed at her brain and demanded attention. She walked on, intent on keeping her body moving, focused on stupid things like what that homeless man's dog ate, what it would be like to sleep on the streets under a couple of threadbare blankets, how she salved her conscience by always giving money to every homeless person she passed. Except today.

Mum's dead.

She almost ran down the escalator at King's Cross. She hadn't run for months, couldn't when attached to a harp; she could hardly remember what it was like to move so freely ... Dead. No, not now. Later. Don't believe it until you see it. Don't believe it until you see it. In the half-empty carriage she stared at her own reflection in the window opposite and repeated this mantra. At the back of her head a new variation of her composition played. She should write it down, shouldn't she? Deaf composers heard music, but they didn't hear the sound of a barking dog or a reversing rubbish truck. Their hearts heard the notes and subtle chord changes, the instrumental arrangements and dramatic interjections. And some deaf musicians could play beautiful compositions note perfect. It was more than the vibration of musical notes in the air that allowed them to do that: they felt the music itself. Keep thinking, time will pass.

If she hadn't drunk those two cups of coffee at the airport, it might have been possible to sleep on the plane. The mantra could no longer compete with her thoughts about all the times she'd let go of the harp. Had one of these times been the fatal one, or was it simply an accumulation of small lapses in concentration, tiny errors of omission? A few times she had woken up on the bed unattached to the harp with no idea how long she'd been asleep. Then there was that time when she came out of the hypnotic trance and found Matthew holding it. After that, he'd agreed to bring her back into the present the moment she let go of it. But had the damage already been done, had she already sentenced her mother to death?

The first tear since Lawrence's phone call rolled down her cheek and tasted salty in the corner of her mouth. She turned towards the porthole window and let the tears flow for the longest time. A flight attendant leaned across and asked if she was all right. When she didn't answer, the woman pressed a handful of tissues on her.

Poor Lawrence. He'd tried to keep his upper lip stiff on the phone, but she could tell he was in shock. He'd wanted a more significant relationship with her mum for years, and now, when at last it seemed possible, when her mum had started to put her own life before Clara's career, she'd been snatched away. What an ungrateful daughter she was.

The taxi dropped her outside the Hotel Euler at 12.15. The sky-blue facade dazzled under a clear sky and scorched her sore eyes. Inside, a group of chattering Japanese tourists swamped the reception desk and Clara held back, too anxious to enter the fray. Her skin was clammy, reptilian, her heart pounded. Not enough air in there. She flopped onto one of the black leather armchairs, but still she gasped for air. She lurched onto the outside terrace, leaned against a stanchion and closed her eyes. Concentrate, slow down the heart, slow, deep breaths ... One, two, three ...

After a time, she opened her eyes and looked around to check that the world had stopped swirling. Most of the tables were full, and two waiters, one tall and blonde, the other short with a Mediterranean tan, were busy taking orders and clearing away glasses. She idly watched the tall blonde one glide from table to table, nodding here, listening there. He stopped at the furthest table from the door and leaned towards a woman wearing a sleeveless white dress.

At first glance the woman resembled her mother. Clara sobbed. The same thing had happened after her father had died: she'd caught glimpses of him everywhere – in the street, at a concert, on the bus – and always she'd been so convinced it was him, she'd raced over to have a better look. Instinctively, she did the same now, moved closer and arrived, dazed, at the end of the table, next to the waiter.

The woman didn't resemble her mother – it *was* her mother! A mother who was very much alive, smiling up at the handsome waiter and ordering a cappuccino. With Lawrence laughing alongside her.

What the hell …?

Clara jabbed her nails into her wrist and counted to ten, eyes watering with the pain.

Yes, definitely her mother. And Lawrence.

She folded, grabbed the table edge and rasped at Lawrence. 'How could you?'

Rage boiled in her brain and she banged the table with her fist. 'How could you lie to me about something like that?' she shouted in his face. 'What sort of evil, selfish, heartless …' She aimed the punch at his face, but he grabbed her hand. 'Let go! Let me go!' she screamed at full volume, twisting her hand free and catching the waiter in the gut.

The waiter stepped back; Lawrence's face darkened.

Clara turned to her mother. 'Why would you do this, Mother? Do I mean so little to you?' Tears soaked her face.

'You see, darling, I'm not dead,' Grace squeaked, as though she had laryngitis. 'You're not holding your harp and I am still alive.' The smile belied the fear in her eyes and her voice was trembling now. 'I love you, Clara. I couldn't bear watching your life evaporate any longer – no friends, no Henry, no concerts, just you, wasting away inside your flat. Like a prisoner in solitary confinement.'

'We knew you'd come, Clara,' Lawrence said. 'Not so soon, but … Forgive us for the laughter, an idle moment of levity in a sea of remorse.'

Grace stood and came towards her. 'I've done something terrible, I know, deceiving you like this, but … I'd run out of options. I … I couldn't just do nothing. And then, Lawrence and I saw this documentary, about the power of drama therapy, and it got me thinking, and …' There were tears flooding down her cheeks now, soaking the monogrammed hankie she was dabbing at her eyes. 'I see now that it was too brutal, our plan. We should have thought it through. But I love you so much, darling. I had to do something to show you you could let go of the harp and nothing would happen.'

Clara's head floated off her body. She closed her eyes to stop the spinning, gripped the table edge as the sobs wracked her chest.

'Sit down, darling. You've had a terrible shock. Sit down and we can talk about it, try to explain …'

Someone touched her hand; she snatched it away and ran. Ran through the lobby, out onto the street, and into the first available taxi.

19

India

Rinzen sat silently with the three monks. After some time, they seemed to sense he had finished berating himself, and when they started chanting, eyes closed and legs crossed, he joined in. Later, when he returned to his compartment, the European was asleep, the student was reading, and the lawyer and his son weren't there. He and the student nodded to each other, and Rinzen climbed onto his bunk and closed the curtains. He would not enter into any more debates. He would say as little as possible. Keep a low profile, the monk had said, and he was sure Kwato would have concurred. He resolved to use this as his mantra for the rest of the journey.

Secluded behind the flimsy curtain, Rinzen sat cross-legged and prepared to enter the trance. He looked at Keung's card and reread it:

Do not dwell in the past, do not dream of the future, concentrate the mind on the present moment.

First the ricket-racket of the train subsided, then the disjointed chorus of voices quietened to a whisper, drowned out by his booming heartbeat, until even that faded away, leaving just the whisper of his breath as he joined his brothers deep in the soul of the earth.

~

Adil's voice, shouting 'Stop!' pulled Rinzen from the trance. At that instant the curtain flew back and two uniformed men with full-face masks grabbed his arms. As he yanked his right arm free, a huge, hard fist smashed the side of his face. His eyesight blurred, and in the following seconds two others held his legs, while a fifth shackled his ankles. The two arm-holders pulled him to his feet, twisted his arms behind him and snapped handcuffs on him. Still reeling from the punch, he heard Adil's pleas of 'Leave him, leave him,' but he sounded far away. He turned towards his friend, but Adil was being pushed along the carriage by more masked soldiers. 'Where is your authority?' Adil demanded, but no one answered. Adil's shouts woke other passengers and Rinzen saw heads peering through the curtains as the silent soldiers carried him to the nearest door and straight into the back of a closed truck parked on the platform. He glimpsed the station sign – Igatpuri – and then, just before the doors slammed, he saw his friend the monk looking at him with an uncharacteristic frown from a few metres away.

The soldiers chained Rinzen to a horizontal bar welded to the inside of the truck. The only sound was that of air being sucked through the respirator masks worn by all the soldiers. Six pairs of eyes stared at him. Rinzen closed his and slowed his racing heart, guided his blood to his throbbing face, and focused on means of escape.

After half an hour of racing along rough roads, the truck stopped and the soldiers unchained him and marched him towards a grey, single-storey building. He looked about intently, memorising everything: the height of the perimeter fence, the lights on tall posts, the silhouette of hills beyond.

They entered a lobby and the man at the hatch took his bag. Rinzen's escort pushed him through the door opposite and held him with his back against the white wall to be photographed. Still not a word had been spoken. Perhaps they couldn't speak with the masks on? Then he was manhandled along a corridor and into a cell.

The soldiers unlocked the handcuffs and leg shackles, pushed him onto a low, hard bed, and left the room. He heard three locks tumble. Rinzen stood immediately and surveyed the white-walled cell. The bed, which ran almost the whole length of the cell, was a thin, hard mattress on a concrete plinth. A metal table was bolted to the opposite wall, an empty bucket reeked of cheap, powerful disinfectant. The door had an eye level hatch, with the flap on the outside.

Rinzen placed one of the folded blankets on the floor and flipped into a headstand, arms crossed on his chest, eyes closed, and focused on the blood as it gathered in his skull, warmed his ears, his temples, his eyes. One by one he recalled all the details of the way out of the building.

He heard footsteps in the corridor and righted himself, placed the blanket on the bed, and stood with his back to the wall that faced the door. Four soldiers, all wearing face masks, entered, ran at him and handcuffed and shackled him. As they moved away, a man dressed in a white coat who wore a mask that only covered his nose and mouth, ambled towards him. He held Rinzen's father's passport in his right hand.

'Are you Rinzen, the Samudran monk from Sarmand monastery?'

Rinzen stared at the passport. 'Yes.'

'That was easy.' The doctor looked at his eyes, seemed to smile beneath his mask. 'I need to take blood and urine samples, to check whether you have the disease that killed your colleagues.'

One of the soldiers unbuckled Rinzen's belt, pulled down his trousers and held a plastic bottle in front of him. Without looking down, Rinzen urinated into the bottle, gauging when to stop to prevent overfilling it.

'Thank you,' the doctor said. When the soldiers did not immediately pull up Rinzen's trousers, the doctor raised his voice. 'Dress the man, will you.' He passed the bottle to his assistant, took a tourniquet from him and tied it around Rinzen's upper arm.

Rinzen closed his eyes as the needle pricked his skin. His blood was sacred to him – this was an abomination. The muscles in his neck tensed, his biceps swelled, his buttocks clenched. What would Keung do? Break the bonds and flatten these rude men? They were tapping his life force, but he had to accept it. For Sarmand, he had to accept it. Kwato would. If one of these soldiers were to put a bullet in his head, how would that help his brothers?

The doctor placed a piece of gauze over the tiny wound and pressed tape over it. 'You see, if you are infected with this wasting disease, we will have to quarantine the entire train, but if you are not ...'

When you find I am not, thought Rinzen, you will send me over the border so that the men in black can have their revenge.

As he turned to leave, the doctor spoke to the soldiers. 'You can unchain him now. And do not harm him.'

When all was quiet in the corridor, Rinzen ripped the tape from his arm. A tiny bubble of blood swelled and stopped. How had he let them snatch him from the train? And then take his blood. It felt like someone was holding a burning torch against the top of his head. He lay on the bed and stared at the ceiling, but a few seconds later he leapt to his feet, the words of his monk friend clear in his head: 'It's more sensible to spend your energy focusing on the solution than worrying about the problem.'

He stood next to the slop bucket, focusing on Man Standing Still, and started to take in the faint aroma of fresh paint and the pungent disinfectant, but ... they had taken his blood, and he, a Samudran senior, had simply stood there and let them. He looked at the tiny red dot of blood on

206

his forearm and shuddered, clenched his teeth. He had to put it behind him, couldn't undo the past. Close your eyes. Clear your mind. They would soon be bringing him food; it might be his only chance. Don't think ... focus. He felt the bright light and the whiteness of the bare walls soaking into him, pictured his mind rising above his body.

A clatter in the corridor snapped him back. The food trolley? He turned, pressed his nose against the wall and inhaled, opened his eyes wide, dilated his pupils so the bright light blinded him, and disappeared as the door hatch slid open.

'Breakfast.'

'Take it.' The tray rattled.

'He's not taking the tray.'

'Let him go hungry then.'

'Let me look.'

'Is he sleeping?'

'I ... I can't see him. He's not there!'

'Rubbish, let me look ... What's happened? Has someone moved him?'

'Open the door. He has to be inside.'

'I'm not going in there.'

'Damn you, yes you are.'

The locks tumbled and four soldiers burst in, truncheons at the ready, all shouting. Then silence as they backed out of the door. A moment later they ran off down the corridor, shouting unintelligibly.

Rinzen waited until their voices became faint. When they returned, they would be sure to walk around the empty cell and bump into him. He dashed out of his cell and into one with its door ajar and lights off, concealed himself behind the open door and focused once more. He imagined the will of his brothers helping him achieve invisibility in one, two, three seconds. A record.

Minutes later, he heard the doctor's voice over the racket of steel boots on concrete. He strained to hear his words –

thought he said, 'At least he doesn't have it ...', but wasn't sure.

Two soldiers stopped in the corridor nearby.

'I've heard they can do that,' the first said.

'Do what?'

'Disappear in one place and appear in another.'

'Rubbish. That's a fairy tale, you idiot.'

That would be a good skill, Rinzen thought.

'Hey, why is this door open?' the second soldier said. 'We better take a look.'

Rinzen clenched his fists and widened his eyes in the dim light filtering in from the corridor.

'You look. I'm not getting mixed up with a magic monk.'

The light came on, a rifle barrel inched into view, then an arm stretched in. 'Show yourself!'

The soldier leaned into the room and glanced round the cell. Rinzen, now visible again, would have to disarm him and attack the other man all in one sequence. But the soldier didn't peer round the door. He joined his comrade in the safety of the corridor and switched off the light.

Ten minutes later all was silent, but Rinzen waited another hour, by which time his captors would all be convinced that he had somehow escaped and fled the barracks. He kept close to the wall as he crept along the corridor until he was outside the last door before the exit – the room where they had put his satchel. He listened at the door, then glimpsed two soldiers a long way down the corridor, walking towards him.

He pressed the handle down, eased open the door, and sprang at the soldier behind the desk. He landed behind him and had his right hand on his mouth and left hand feeling for the pressure point in his neck before the man even noticed he was there. The soldier kicked out, then went limp, and Rinzen let him slump against the chair back. He heard the voices of the soldiers in the corridor and scanned the room for his satchel.

It wasn't where the man had first put it.

Why would it be? That doctor had his father's passport, the satchel could be anywhere. He shouldn't have knocked out the desk soldier, could have made him say where it was. Now the two soldiers were at the glass doors. He couldn't leave without his satchel. The glass doors opened. Maybe he could hide in that cupboard? He pulled open the door, saw and grabbed his satchel from the shelf in the same instant, and dived through the open hatch into the lobby, landing at the feet of the two soldiers. They were unarmed, and simply stood and watched him dash out through the front doors and run at lightning speed straight towards the five-metre-high fence and jump over it.

20

London

By the time she got back to her flat, Clara's fury had subsided a little, leaving her clear-headed and decisive.

Her mother was not dead. She was far from dead, in fact. Grace had been a picture of vitality on the hotel's terrace, despite Clara having been out of contact with the harp for at least twelve hours. But that by no means disproved the message of her dream. A plant might not need rain every day in order to survive, but without any rain at all, the plant would eventually die. Like it or not, her mother depended on Clara to keep her alive, exactly like the plant and the rain. Grace just didn't realise it, wouldn't accept it. Which was why she'd got into such a state about Clara shutting herself away in her flat, why she'd dreamed up that cruel, ludicrous stunt. How could she, knowing her daughter so well, better than anyone? And she'd roped in poor Lawrence as well, the one person who'd shown a smattering of understanding towards Clara.

As Clara retuned the Lyon & Healy, a shiver vibrated down her spine. Yes, she still loved her mother. Yes, she still needed her alive. But she didn't want her mother in her life right now. She needed time, a lot of time, before she could even think about forgiving her. And space. And her harp. Nothing more.

Clara fingered the harp strings but postponed the moment she would relax into playing. Once she started, she'd become so absorbed in the rhythm of her composition, it would be impossible to think. Stroking the smooth spruce soundboard sent a tingle from the tips of her fingers to her chest.

Life was simpler now, and she liked it, preferred it to her life before.

She plucked the second octave strings, closed her eyes and heard the high notes as rainfall on a corrugated-iron roof, first a delicate drizzle no more than the weight of tears, then interspersed with bigger drops that eventually drowned out the drizzle. Her hands flew down the octaves as she chased the storm's progress, its rumbling thunder and crackle of lightning; and all the time the cacophony increasing until huge monsoon raindrops bounced off the roof to become a continuous roar.

Time passed, but she was oblivious to its passing.

Disharmonious thumps pulled her from the trance and continued after she stopped playing. It took her a few seconds to realise someone was banging on her door, just like last night. Her mother? Lawrence? She wheeled the harp into the hall and spoke through the door. 'Who is it?'

'It's Gareth Fulbright, your long-suffering neighbour, Miss Martinelli, and I can't take it anymore. I've tried every brand of earplug on the market, but your music seems to bypass them. My head aches and I can't sleep, and I beg you to be more considerate. I accept that you need to play your instrument, but playing it at such a volume at 2am is, by anyone's standards, unreasonable.'

'Oh, is it that late? I'm terribly sorry. Once I start playing …' No, she wouldn't explain herself to Fulbright, who had openly allowed her mother to spy on her from his apartment. 'Sorry, it won't happen again.'

She waited by the door but sensed he was still there. She held her breath and listened. Definitely still there. Was he thinking of saying something else? Doing something? She carefully slipped the safety chain over its keep and slid closed the top and bottom bolts on the door.

As she inched the harp towards the bedroom, its wheel caught on a postcard that must have been slipped under the door. The photograph was of one of Giacometti's Walking Men.

Dearest Clara,

I called round this morning to say goodbye. I've been asked to go on a world tour with the Aurora Chamber Orchestra. Their principal violinist has been taken ill, so it's all very short notice and I leave tomorrow.

Where could you be? I'll call you from ... somewhere!

Love,
Julia x

So that was everyone gone: first Henry, then her mother, now Julia.

~

Clara woke from a dream that had the merit of following a narrative. Accompanied by a young girl, perhaps seven or eight years old, she entered the bright white lobby of a modernist museum. They were there to look at the Giacometti sculpture gallery, but the museum seemed to be deserted. They walked across the lobby towards a narrow, unmarked white door and pushed it open. She recognised Alberto Giacometti immediately. He was instructing a woman on the precise positioning of a one-metre-high *Walking Man*. Clara greeted them and asked whether she could put some questions to Giacometti about his work.

212

'Can't you see that Monsieur Giacometti is busy?' the woman said.

'Yes, of course,' Clara said. 'Perhaps I could come back later?'

Giacometti sighed.

'I suppose everyone wants to talk to you,' Clara said.

'Yes, they do. Students, journalists, young sculptors. Too many.' He sighed again, but he did look at Clara.

'I won't take up much of your time. It's just that I really must ask you something, something vitally important.'

'Please go away,' the woman said.

'No, it's all right, Gwen, I will see her in one hour. In the roof garden.'

The next moment, Clara and the girl were in the roof garden. The girl ran around the perimeter and trailed her hand on the stainless-steel handrail while Clara stood on what seemed to be the belly of a giant sleeping Buddha in the middle of the garden. She was keeping an eye out for Giacometti when, without warning, the giant Buddha lifted off the roof, upending Clara, who had to cling to a huge metal ring to stop from falling off. She looked up and saw that the ring was attached by a cable to the gantry of a vast yellow mobile crane. Clara shouted at the driver, who responded by saying it was much too late for shouting, and drove off. She just had time to tell the girl to stay at the museum, that she would be back to get her as soon as she could.

Clara's stomach churned as the truck bounced across the land for many miles. It finally lowered the Buddha so that Clara – bruised and seasick – could slide off its bronzed belly onto the ground. 'Why didn't you let me off near the museum?' she asked.

'Orders,' he said.

'Whose orders? Monsieur Giacometti's?'

'Who? Don't know him. Gwen gives me my orders.'

Clara woke up then, worried about the young girl, still not knowing who she was or why she was with her.

Pity Matthew was on holiday, he'd know what the dream meant.

Clara recorded a message on her answer machine to say that she wasn't seeing or speaking to anyone for a while, then turned down the phone's volume, and didn't answer the doorbell or check the mailbox for the next week.

When she wasn't playing her composition, she examined her feelings, oscillating between disgust at her mother's deception and remorse for the worry she was causing her. Random thoughts about the Wigmore dream and the Giacometti one just confused matters, and a week later she was still a mess of tangled emotions and pointless circular thoughts.

One night, when even playing her composition failed to calm her down, something made her look at the photograph of her father on the wall above Henry's sideboard. She pushed the harp closer, focused on her papa's face, and talked to him.

'What do you think, Papa? Should I see her, forgive her?'

She waited for an answer, but of course no actual words came from the broad, smiling, proud face. She smiled back.

'But she'll still want me to let go of the harp, still doesn't get it. No, even though not having her with me is almost as bad as her being dead, I can't see her or even speak to her, it's too painful for her. Of course, it's not as bad as her being dead! She's still here, so just for now, I'll keep my distance.'

She stopped, leaned closer, so she could only see his eyes, and the dark, thick eyebrows, and tried to see his thoughts, glean his advice. Just her and her papa, no floor, no wall, no picture frame, just the eyes.

She did what she did out of love for you.

That night, Clara slept dreamlessly, and woke with a clear head and steady heartbeat, and without any of the stomach flutters that had plagued her since Basel.

She told Matthew about the Giacometti dream as soon as he arrived on the following Tuesday.

He placed the pile of mail he'd collected from her pigeonhole on the table. The one on top, in her mother's handwriting, and others with similar envelopes, had been hand-delivered.

'What do you think it means, Clara?'

'No, please, Matthew, don't start on the psychotherapy thing of asking back questions I've just asked you. Please just tell me straight out what you think it means.'

'My first observation is that it is possibly the first dream with a clear narrative that you've had since the original harp dream. Or at least the first one you have shared with me.'

'Full marks. Next?'

'I think the little girl is the inner you, and you are trying to protect the inner you from external dangers, but at some point, you have to let go – that's when the crane carries you off.' He paused, checked Clara's reaction.

She nodded, but her nodding was tentative, questioning, as if to say, 'Go on …'

'To you, Giacometti epitomises artistic perfection. You want to find out the secret of this perfection. But he is evasive and puts you off. His means of self-preservation, his outer shell if you like, is Gwen, who orders the crane driver to take you far away into the wilderness. Either Giacometti does not want to share the secret of artistic perfection, or he does not understand or acknowledge it himself.'

'I would never have thought of any of that,' Clara said. 'So I woke up stuck in the wilderness?'

'I suppose you did. Do you feel as though you're in the wilderness?'

'I certainly feel alone: no lover, no best friend and no mother.'

'No mother?'

Clara told him what Grace had done.

Matthew didn't respond, but she felt his eyes studying her, willing her to look at him.

'But she needs me now, just as I have needed her all my life.'

Matthew waited in his placid, detached way. She knew what he wanted to know, but this time he'd have to ask. She could also do placid. God, how childish, but …

'And now that you've been back from Switzerland for nearly two weeks, how do you feel about your mother?'

Hah! She grinned at him, but he didn't react. 'What she did was done out of love for me, and my love for her hasn't changed. If anything, I feel closer to her.'

'Closer?'

'Yes, we're both mad – me holding this huge harp to protect her, she faking her own death to protect me.'

'Interesting.'

'You know, I actually like this life attached to the harp. Life has become simple, and playing the harp is no longer an exercise in musicianship, it's my way into a trance. No one listens, no one judges the quality of my playing. I become one with the music.'

Matthew didn't say anything. He wants me to ramble on, she thought.

'Do you remember, in one of our early sessions, I dodged your questions about whether I believed, as my father did, that fame is the enemy of the artist? Well, it's true that part of me actually needs the approval, the praise, in order to keep up the discipline required to play at concert level. It spurs me on. But …'

'Yes?'

'But I also despise myself for the self-indulgence of it. It's like I lose my purity.'

'So now you are not playing concerts, you can focus entirely on perfecting your art, your composition?'

'I suppose so.' She laughed. 'And with my father's approval.'

'Perhaps you didn't need Giacometti's advice after all?'

'"What I am looking for is not happiness. I work solely because it is impossible for me to do anything else." Those are Giacometti's words – they were on a postcard that Julia gave me.'

He raised his eyebrows and his eyes lit up. 'You know, I believe you have overcome the barriers to deep meditation.'

'I wouldn't know about that. I don't feel like I've overcome anything. It feels more like I've become one with my harp.' She stroked the soundboard as if it was the silky coat of a favourite cat. Yes, she could make the harp purr whenever she wanted.

'Perhaps you've overcome the barriers without being conscious of them.'

'I still don't get what you mean. What barriers?'

'To fully enter a trance state – which is essentially what deep meditation is – a person needs to be able to disregard many of our "normal" day-to-day human emotions. They're a distraction, they anchor a person too closely to the noisy chatter of the material world. Learning to rise above sensory desire, feelings of hostility and then inertia – these are all crucial stages. You also need to be able to calm the mind and, finally, to believe that you have the ability to sustain the trance.'

She hoped he would say more so she could revel in the sound of his voice. One of these days she would ask him about that voice, where it came from, was he aware of it, had others mentioned it?

'I believe you've achieved all that with your harp, with your intense focus on your new composition.' He smiled at her, looked almost tearful. 'I haven't been able to help you to let go of your harp, and some would see that as a failure. But I don't. Through guided hypnotherapy and the examination not only of your Wigmore dream but also of your past, the events and circumstances that have made you who you are, you have come to fully accept your situation. You are no longer worried, you are fearless.'

Matthew stood and walked to the glass doors.

'You were terribly upset, angry, about your mother faking her death, but now you've understood that she did it out of love for you.'

He placed both hands flat on the glass and spoke with his back to her. 'And it seems to me you now play your music at a level hitherto unachievable; I would even say unimaginable.'

He stayed where he was, hands pressed against the glass, and Clara realised it was only the second time in all their twenty or more sessions that he had lost his habitual self-control. What he'd said made perfect sense, but she couldn't think of a reply that didn't sound trite.

The only thing to do was to play the harp.

When her composition reached a natural conclusion, she stopped playing and looked up, expecting him to still be there. Instead there was a note taped to the glass:

I think you will agree that this was our final session, but please call me if you want to see me again.
Yours, Matthew

She already missed his voice.

~

As the weeks passed, Clara became more transparent. Without conscious intention, she strived for simplicity in everything. Her weekly order with Ocado came to consist of nothing more than rice, lentils, vegetables and fruit; she wore one of three identical white shift dresses each day, so that on any given day she wore one dress and washed another, while the third dried in the bathroom; and she dispensed with underwear and – for the first time in her life

– slept naked. Her sleep was deep and refreshing, and she thought nothing of playing the harp for four or five hours at a time. Between these sessions she would leave the harp to perform a punishing set of exercises in the nude. Her biceps, already toned from years of harp practice, lost the last of their excess fat and became shapely and muscular enough to support her raised arms for extended periods. She developed the abdominals of a distance runner, with calves and thighs to match. Her fingers resembled a series of smooth pebbles with extra layers of skin to protect her fingertips: if she had bothered to try, she could have lifted her own body weight with any one of them. She drank only filtered water, always with her eyes closed so she could savour its subtle taste and focus on its rejuvenating journey through her body.

Clara's mind, as clear as her body, enabled the music she played to flow from her unimpeded by distracting thoughts or feelings. She lost her habitual self-criticism and easily reached a state of rapture, an ecstasy of pure creativity. With repeated playing, her composition took on greater internal complexity but formed its own arc that lasted exactly three hours. Often, in the moments after she stopped playing, she saw the snow-capped mountains and the solitary figure. He was more distinct each time – sometimes running, sometimes taking giant leaps along the ridge.

She thought of her composition as a piece of sculpture, like one of Bernini's works in the Villa Borghese in Rome. Her father had taken her there a few months before he died, and she'd returned several times since with her mother. Their perfection was in the details. Bernini did seemingly impossible things with marble: the statue of David, caught the moment before he unleashed his sling, varied with the viewpoint – from the right side there was the swinging movement before the release, from the front the arrest, a split second before the release, and from the oblique viewpoint there was a rhythmic balance to the whole body. Clara saw her composition as similarly multi-layered and multifaceted. It belied simple interpretation. She would never have consciously combined notes and chords in that way, wouldn't even have known how to create the layers of sounds that appeared to emanate, like the changing perspective of the sculptures, from multiple harps. For someone else to fully appreciate her composition would require them to devote to it the same absolute concentration she'd employed in its creation. An impossibility, of course.

~

When she had almost no money left, Clara called an auction house and told them she had a few pieces of early- to mid-twentieth-century furniture to sell. She chose a Cambridge company, not wanting Henry to hear she had sold his gifts, and realised enough money to pay the three months' mortgage arrears plus three months in advance. The auctioneer agreed to sell the television and most of her books and the bookcase, so that after his men had collected everything, all that remained in the living room was the Ercol two-seater sofa, the Eames lounger and footstool, the African side table that Julia had given her as a moving-in present, and the dining table and chairs. The bedroom was even more sparse – after all, what use did she have for a full-length art deco mirror, bedside tables or lamps, and the rug only impeded the free movement of her harp. She kept a few books she could not bring herself to sell, among them the one on meditation Matthew had given her and *The Art of Happiness* by the Dalai Lama and Howard Cutler.

At first, she rejected the weekly food parcels her mother left outside her door, but when, in late November, the money finally ran out, she started to accept them. It didn't occur to Clara that her mother was also paying the electricity and gas bills.

A few days before Christmas her mother left a card, attached to an enormous hamper, begging Clara's forgiveness yet again and imploring her to join her for Christmas lunch. She added a PS that Lawrence had gone off on an anthropological assignment to India after the 'unfortunate incident' in Switzerland six months ago and she hadn't heard from him since.

She'd got into the habit of leaving occasional notes for her mother outside her door – mostly Dalai Lama quotes or snippets of meditational mantras – which allowed her to maintain their relationship without engaging with it. She found a suitable quote to convey the fact that she wouldn't be coming for Christmas lunch, then called Gail and asked her to take most of the hamper's contents to Shelter's kitchen for homeless people in Hackney.

Then, on Christmas Eve, Fulbright moved out of his apartment and no one came to take his place. The professor who owned the flat on the other leg of the U was still on his sabbatical, so Clara was now the sole occupant of the courtyard buildings. Six months ago she would have found the isolation intolerable, would have feared intruders and started at the slightest sound, but now the solitude complemented the simplicity of her existence. Fulbright's departure affected her physically, as though a rotten tooth had been removed.

21

India

Rinzen landed on the far side of the road and saw that the barracks were in a valley surrounded by forested hills. As he entered the wood, he turned and saw three army trucks accelerating towards the woods, and sprinted uphill, topped the summit and ran down the other side.

Four words materialised from some corner of his subconscious: Hide in plain sight.

Hide in plain sight? What – hide, not run from his pursuers? He couldn't examine this paradox and run at high speed. He stopped near the shore of a lake, jumped onto the branch of a tree and scrambled to the top, casting about for the statement's meaning; but his conscious mind refused to focus on anything other than the need to get as far as possible from the army trucks.

He closed his eyes, took ten slow, deep breaths. Steady the heartbeat. Relax the muscles.

They had a photograph of him; they were in familiar territory, he was not; there were many of them, one of him; they had trucks, radios, probably helicopters, he only had his wits and speed.

Hide in plain sight. Invisibility was no use: as soon as he moved, they would see him. He needed to reduce the odds, needed allies to get to Mumbai undetected; but his only allies – Adil and the Buddhist monks – were on the train.

The train might still be in the station, awaiting the doctor's verdict, but surely it was madness to return to Igatpuri. Or was it?

Could he hide in plain sight by returning to the train in disguise? If he had heard the doctor correctly, that he'd established that Rinzen didn't have the wasting disease, the next thing he'd do would be to give the all-clear for the train to depart.

His reasoning, formed from years of Kwato's training, cautioned not to go back, but his instinct propelled him from the tree and into a maximum-speed sprint back over the hill and down the other side.

As he started the descent, he saw the three trucks parked in a clearing. He paused, watched two men dressed in black run up the hill adjacent to him. He allowed himself half a smile, crouched down low until he was in the dense wood, then ran towards Igatpuri.

When he was in sight of the town he stopped at a disused barn, stripped to his underwear, tied his spare shirt around his waist with the sleeves concealed, and made a mark on his forehead by spitting on his finger and rubbing it in the red earth. He went barefoot and stayed away from the roads until he was at the edge of the town. He stared vacantly ahead of him, hoped to be taken for just another Hindu pilgrim, and ignored the many pedestrians he passed. After a few blocks he came to the road beside the railway tracks.

The train was still at the station. There were soldiers – one for each carriage – on the tracks to prevent people disembarking. The entrance to the platforms was barred, and the ticket hall and courtyard were filled with people. Two Hindu sadhus with white body paint and ragged dye-splattered beards sat cross-legged at the edge of the crowd, dressed only in loincloths. Rinzen sat next to them, lowered his head, and waited.

His heart beat erratically, his muscles twitched, and a knot tightened in his gut. The army had his photograph, they could pounce any minute. What had possessed him to be so rash, to ignore his rational mind, the decades of training? To go against Elder Kwato.

It was only a few hours after dawn, but it was already hot, and the hotter it got, the more restless the crowd of waiting passengers became. Every few minutes, one section or other of the crowd would shout and throw curses at the station.

And then, without any punctuating event, the soldiers walked away, the platform gates were opened, and the crowd pressed forward.

Rinzen hurried along the length of the train and climbed unnoticed through a wide door into a windowless wagon piled high with crates and boxes. The pile on one side did not quite reach the roof, so he tossed the satchel into the gap and scrambled up after it. He lay flat on his back, his nose a few centimetres from the roof, his body covered in sweat, and waited.

As he drifted into a half sleep, he heard the wagon door slam, the whistle blow, and the train jolt into motion. He waited ten minutes then jumped down and made his way towards the pantry car. Even though he was half naked and barefoot, no one gave him a second look. He slipped into the guards' compartment and sat with his knees up on the bench beside the door. Adil didn't see him as he walked in with his breakfast tray.

Rinzen slid the door closed. 'Is there enough for two?'

Adil's head jerked round. 'Who …? Rinzen!'

'Sshh…' Rinzen grinned. 'I managed to slip away. Thought you might be worried about me. Besides, I hadn't thanked you for all your help.'

'Help? Is that what you call it? I allowed you to be snatched from my train.' He clasped Rinzen to his chest. 'Are you hurt?' He broke away and locked the door.

'No, the soldiers were not violent. I think they were worried they might catch the wasting disease.'

'Come, eat, drink. I'm so happy to see you.'

Rinzen drained the water glass. 'You probably think I'm mad to come back. In fact, I think I'm mad. But something, some impulse, told me to hide in plain sight, and then I couldn't get it out of my head.'

'Have the tea as well.' The light in Adil's eyes brightened. 'Hide in plain sight? No, not madness at all. I'd say it was inspired.' He pushed the tray towards Rinzen.

'Thanks for saying that, Adil.'

'I don't know why he did it, but it had to be Assif – the one in the ticket office, the only one who knew which berth you were in – who betrayed you. And in so doing he betrayed us all.'

'One positive thing came out of it. They now know I do not have the wasting disease. So perhaps they will leave my brothers alone.'

'Perhaps.' He sounded sceptical. 'Now, if you do not eat this breakfast you will insult my hospitality.'

'Adil, you saw me with the Buddhist monk yesterday. Please ask him to come and see me.'

'I see what you are thinking.' Adil tapped his nose. 'You will become a monk for a short time, yes?'

Rinzen nodded, distracted by the coconut and chilli bursting on his palate.

The monk, who did not seem surprised to see Rinzen, welcomed him with his radiant smile and produced a clean saffron *sanghati* from his shoulder bag. 'Please follow me, Brother Kalsang. My name is Angyo.'

Three hours later, as the train clanked and screeched its way into Lokmanya Tilak Terminus, Adil came and stood in front of the monks in the corridor, positioning his large frame so that nearby passengers could not hear what he said. 'We have arrived. Here is some food and a map of Mumbai. I wish I could help you more, but I don't know anyone who works at the docks.'

Adil started to unfold the map, but Angyo placed his hand on Adil's. 'We will go together: we know the way to the docks.'

'Thank you, brother,' Adil said, and turned to Rinzen. 'When you get there, ask for Indira Dock – one of the guards used to work at the docks and said that is a good place to start to look for a ship that does not carry containers. A container ship is unlikely to take you, and even getting to speak to someone would be very difficult.' Adil's eyes dropped, his heavy shoulders slumped, and his brow creased like a papadum. 'Here is some money for the train and a few US dollars to help you on your way.'

Rinzen stood and bowed to Adil. 'Your heart is full of love and generosity. It is no wonder Amdong holds you in such high regard. Thank you, Adil.'

The words had come out wrong, so formal, when his heart swelled with warmth for Adil Shrestha, but before he could correct himself, the big man enclosed Rinzen in his enormous arms and kissed him on his cheek. 'Must go now, must go. Good luck, brother, your light shines on the—' He broke away, turned and danced through the chaos of hundreds of passengers getting ready to leave the train. At the end of the carriage, he raised his arm without looking back.

At Dockyard Road station the monks pointed the way to the entrance to Indira Dock via the New Yellow Gate just off PD'Mello Road. They parted with a simple bow, and Rinzen sensed that any further display of gratitude or emotion would insult them.

The road was full of cars, trucks, bicycles and scooters laden with baskets and buckets; one scooter somehow carried a man, woman and two children. There was no footpath, and Rinzen, along with other pedestrians, was forced to share the busy road with the chaotic traffic. Several times he flattened himself against the wall as a truck rumbled past, hooting and belching foul-smelling fumes. How could people live like this?

He saw the sign to New Yellow Gate and turned off PD'Mello. Uniformed men stood by the entrance and checked the documents of anyone who wished to enter. He walked on and took a side road that skirted the docks' perimeter fence before it re-joined the main road. Signs to the Gateway of India pulled him on, and half an hour later he stood among sightseers looking out to sea from beneath its massive central arch.

Rinzen walked under the arch and sat on the steps that led down to the water. He let his eyes move to the horizon and stay there, but after a few minutes the noise and proximity of so many people oppressed him. The pavement along the shoreline was populated with many beggars, maimed men, women and children, some blind, others limbless, who wailed and held out their hands or a small cup to receive alms. They took him for a penniless monk and ignored him, a pointless mark among the rich pickings of Indian and foreign tourists.

After walking along the promenade for twenty minutes, he came to a disused helicopter pier with a graffiti-covered concrete bunker near the end. He sat cross-legged on the seaward side and focused on the waves near the shore, tried to watch each one break before it lapped against the pier. Gradually, he widened his vision until the ends of the waves were tiny flicks of white on the horizon. The extraneous sounds of the city faded until all he could hear was the crash and whoosh of the sea as it met the shore. His mind filled with water, so much water, fed by and feeding countless rivers. And here was that music again, the melody clearer, the notes more insistent, the waterfall growing from a trickle to a cascade, as though affirming that he was on the right path, the right watery path to the other side of the world. As his eyes alighted on the horizon, his muscles relaxed, his anxiety faded, and he was soon meditating in the company of his brothers.

When it was dark, he returned to the road alongside the docks, jumped over the fence and climbed the sheer wall of a warehouse, entering it through an open ventilation hole. He changed back into his schoolteacher disguise, slept on a wooden pallet until an hour before dawn. He put all his money in his pockets, hid his satchel in a dark corner, and used the pedestrian entrance in the large double doors to leave the building.

Indira Dock was well signed. He walked across a yard towards the warehouses that lined the quayside, passed piles of timber, stacks of bulging sacks and wooden crates, and looked for somewhere to conceal himself. To have any chance of overhearing where they were bound, he needed to be near the three ships that loomed above and beyond the warehouses, waiting to be loaded or unloaded by two giant cranes, their heads bowed as though asleep. At the end of the row of warehouses, neatly stacked but with weeds growing around them, a load of steel beams rested on baulks of timber. If he lay down, there would be just enough room to conceal himself in their midst.

In the distance, the city lights faded as the grey pre-dawn brightened. A few men appeared on the deck of the ship nearest him and an hour later the dockers started their shift. The air was soon filled with the shouts of men, the hoots of vans and the rumble of heavy trucks.

Throughout the morning, Rinzen watched the trucks roll by laden with bulky sacks that were then hoisted by the giant yellow cranes into the holds of the three ships. He listened to the dockers, hoped to hear about their destination, but most of the talk seemed to be about taking breaks and cricket matches. The sun blazed down from the cloudless sky, scorched the blue morning air to cinder-white, and baked his steel nest. The massive I-beams groaned and creaked around him and the radiated heat intensified as the day edged towards noon. His parched lips longed for moisture and he berated himself for failing to bring a bottle of water with him – again.

Soon the heat would be unbearable, and he would have to escape his oven. He checked the coast was clear on the dockside and was surprised to see a tall European among the dockers, taking photographs and talking to the men. The man ambled in Rinzen's direction, writing in a notebook. He paused next to the steel stack and tapped the pencil on his teeth, as though considering what else to write. Just then a truck careered onto the dockside at high speed and almost lost control. It swerved to avoid a group of dockers and leaned dangerously far over in Rinzen's direction. Three huge crates slipped off the tilting truck and Rinzen watched, as if in slow motion, as they plummeted towards the ground and the precise spot occupied by the European man.

Rinzen sprang at the European, grabbed him round the waist and jumped to the side. A second later, the crates smashed to the ground. The man, about the same age as his father, stood beside him, open-mouthed in surprise, and started to laugh. Rinzen joined him – laughter pulsed from deep in his stomach as the adrenalin pumped through his muscles and made his arms and legs tremble.

They laughed and stared at each other, the European's right arm entwined with Rinzen's left, each gripping the other's shoulder. The European still held the notebook and pencil. An old leather briefcase hung from his shoulder.

Finally, the man spoke – in Maithili – as he tried to catch his breath. 'Thank you. My God, you saved my life. But where did you come from? How did you ...?' He trailed off, squinted at his rescuer.

Rinzen could see he was considering the impossibility of what had just happened.

'I need to leave here now,' Rinzen said.

'Why? What's the hurry?'

Rinzen looked up and down the dock. The group of dockers who had so narrowly escaped being run over were shouting at the driver of the now stationary truck; more men were running over; a man in uniform blew his whistle.

'I just need to go. I'm sorry.'

'So, you don't have papers?'

Rinzen didn't answer. He turned to go, intending to use the chaos as cover.

'Look, you just saved my life, so why not let me help you? You can trust me. My name is Lawrence Greene, and I know my way around these docks.'

PART THREE

THE HARP AWAKENING

If you think you are too small to make a difference, try sleeping with a mosquito.

The Dalai Lama

2014

22

India

'This way.' Lawrence Greene pointed down the dock, away from the crowd that had gathered around the spilt cargo.

They made straight for the ship, the *Oracle*, docked furthest along the quay, and mounted the gangplank that led up to the deck. Greene greeted members of the crew at various points on the way to his cabin, which was up four flights of iron stairs and faced away from the dock and all the dangers that lay that way.

Greene closed the door. 'Please, take a chair. I'll get us some water.'

He poured two tall beakers from a large bottle on the small table and handed one to Rinzen, who downed it in one long gulp.

'Thank you.'

'You needed that. How long had you been there?'

'Since dawn,' Rinzen said.

'Good, you speak English. You must have found a good hiding place.' Greene sat on the other chair and studied Rinzen's face. 'Sorry, I forgot to ask you your name.'

'Rinzen.' There seemed no point in deceiving the man.

'Are you Nepalese, Rinzen?'

'How did you know?'

'I'm an anthropologist. I was in your country earlier this year. But your English is better than my Nepalese. My guess is you hid by the dock so you could board a ship. May I ask where you want to go?'

Rinzen stared at Greene's eyes, hoped to see something that would confirm his instinct to trust him.

'I might be able to help you.' Greene held Rinzen's stare. 'I could find out if any ships are about to go there.'

'I am sorry.' Rinzen stood up and stepped away from the chair. 'Thank you, sir, for you offer of help. I want to go to Barranquilla in Columbia.'

Greene whistled. 'On the other side of the world. Please, no need to stand, and do call me Lawrence.' He waited until Rinzen had sat down again. 'I'm not even sure ships go from Mumbai to Barranquilla, but I'll check with my friend the harbour-master.' He looked at the scratched face of his old wristwatch. 'In fact, if I go right now, I might catch him before lunch. It would probably be wise to lock the door behind me.'

Lawrence stopped at the door. 'I'll get us something to eat while I'm at it. Feel free to lie down, you look all in.'

'All in?'

'It means tired out, ready to fall asleep on your feet.'

'Yes.' Rinzen half laughed. 'I am all in.'

He went across to one of the two portholes and looked out to sea. With luck, he would soon be out in the middle of its vastness. Tired as he was, he was also excited: if Keung had been there with him, the two of them would have been leaping and pointing at all the extraordinary new sights. How he missed his dear friend. He relaxed his eyes, let his vision lengthen past the ships in the harbour, past the blinking lights on floating towers in the bay, and out to the far horizon. His brothers were prisoners, with armed soldiers at Sarmand's gates. They wouldn't lift their quarantine until the last elders at Qo and Barnang were dead, and even then, they'd probably wait to see if anyone else died. Keung and the other seniors wouldn't be permitted to run in the mountains; the village mothers would be barred from

Sarmand; and the tranquil atmosphere in the monastery, so essential for prolonged and effective meditation, would be disturbed.

A knock at the door rescued him from his dark thoughts.

'You were right that ships do go to Barranquilla.' Lawrence marched into the room, carrying a three-tiered tiffin box. 'But the next one is in three weeks' time and it's one of those giant container ships that don't take passengers.'

'I might be able to get on board and hide somewhere?' Rinzen pictured leaping from dock to deck in the middle of the night.

'Even if there were a way to get aboard, it's unlikely you'd remain undetected for six or seven weeks. And I'm afraid I don't have any connections with those corporate shipping companies. Let's think about it while we eat.'

They ate in silence, and when they'd finished, Rinzen said, 'You haven't asked me why I need to go to Barranquilla.'

'That is your business.' Lawrence walked past Rinzen and looked out of the porthole. 'And I'm done with meddling in other people's business.'

Rinzen stood to face Lawrence. 'When I started out from Sarmand, I trusted everyone, and then I was betrayed, so I mistrusted everyone. But many people have shown me great kindness, have taken risks to help me, and I hope I have learned who to trust.'

Lawrence spun round and looked at Rinzen with wide eyes, suddenly bright with elation or surprise. 'You are a Samudran brother?'

Rinzen nodded, smiled at the comic look on Lawrence's face.

'That explains how ... Never mind that. I hear all is not well in Sarmand, and I am truly sorry to hear it.'

'It surprises me that you have even heard of the Samudran brothers.' Rinzen's legs shuddered. He dropped into the chair and poured a glass of water.

'Are you unwell, brother?' Lawrence sat down next to him.

'Tired. It's been a long journey.'

'Rest, take the bed. We can talk later.'

'Thank you, but first I must tell you why I need to go to Barranquilla.'

Lawrence sat quite still, did not cross his legs, shift position or interrupt in any way while he listened to Rinzen's story. The only movement he made was to nod his head when Rinzen mentioned the Kogi of Columbia.

Rinzen's monologue finally came to a halt.

'That is some story,' Lawrence said. 'I'm very sorry, and I must say extremely alarmed, to hear things are so bad for the Samudrans, and therefore for all of us.' He stood up and paced back and forth between the table and porthole, hands linked behind his back. 'I see why it is necessary for you get to the Kogi as fast as possible.'

He stopped, faced Rinzen. 'Look, I have a suggestion. The *Oracle*'s captain is a good friend – I have travelled many times on his ship – and he may be willing to take you with us to Southampton in England. From there we'd be more likely to find a ship to take you to Columbia.'

'England? Isn't that much further north?'

Lawrence sifted through a pile of maps on the shelf above the desk and carefully unfolded one on the table. It was so well used that almost all the fold lines had been reinforced with tape, now yellowed with age. 'Here's Mumbai. The Barranquilla ship would go this way, around the Arabian Peninsula, up the Red Sea, into the Mediterranean, then out into the Atlantic. To get to Southampton, we follow the same route but turn north – here – when we reach the Atlantic.'

'So, not far off the route to Barranquilla?'

'Especially given that this ship leaves in two days and the Barranquilla ship departs in three weeks.'

'How much will it cost on this ship? If what I have is not enough, I'm willing to work.' Rinzen tapped Barranquilla on the map. 'But do you need to tell the captain that I'm a Samudran brother? Someone may have heard about a running brother.'

'The word you want is "fugitive".' Lawrence frowned.

'Fugitive, yes. Could you say that I'm a schoolteacher going to England to improve my English?'

'To everyone else on board, yes. But not to the captain. I cannot deceive him.'

'Of course. So sorry, I should not have asked this. You are an honest man, he a trusted friend. Please accept—'

'No need, really.' Lawrence folded the map. 'Thank you for telling me how you came to be here. We will talk more about it later, especially about the Kogi. But now I suggest you sleep while I go and see Captain Patera.'

~

Lawrence's cabin was dark when Rinzen awoke, needing to urinate. He stepped outside and found Lawrence seated in a folding chair, reading.

'Second door along,' Lawrence said. 'By the way, the captain agreed.'

He closed his eyes and pissed for the longest time. His smile burst into a laugh. He was going to sea, he would leave the land for the first time in his life, truly on his way to meet the Kogi, and in the company of a good, honest, interesting Englishman called Lawrence Greene. He splashed water on his face and dried it with the towel that rolled out of a machine on the wall.

He jumped from the toilet door to Lawrence's side, and clasped his hand. 'Thank you, Lawrence.'

'Unfortunately, there aren't any spare cabins for paying passengers, but they've cleared a small crew one for you.' They walked to the end of the corridor, turned right along a shorter one with a door at the end. 'They had to leave a stack of boxes in here – the captain uses it as a storeroom – but I didn't think you'd mind.'

The cabin was not much more than an extension of the corridor. The narrow bed ran more than half its length, leaving just enough room for a small desk and chair beneath a porthole the size of Elder Kwato's summer hat. Opposite the bed, two head-height stacks of overfilled cardboard boxes bulged alarmingly.

'If we get rough seas, which is very likely, these might crash down. Shall we make four lower stacks, do you think?'

'Yes, let me.' Rinzen lifted the top two layers as though they were empty, and placed them beside the others.

Lawrence clapped him on the back. 'I'll think of you when I need some heavy lifting done.' Lawrence opened one of two narrow mahogany doors next to the boxes. 'Wait. Do you have a suitcase or …?'

'I hid my satchel in a warehouse near the fence.'

'Probably best to get it after dark.'

'Thank you again, Lawrence.'

'Look, I hope you won't be offended, but I think you should borrow one of my shirts when we go for dinner with the captain.'

Rinzen washed and changed into Lawrence's white linen shirt, and the two men made their way up to the officers' mess on B deck. Before going in, they stepped outside to breathe the cool night air, salty and laced with the scent of fish and seaweed. Gulls called overhead, but beyond their vague outlines the stars were almost invisible in the reflected light of the enormous city.

Four places were laid at one end of a long table, but there was no one in the officers' mess when they entered. There were also some sofas and armchairs arranged in a rough circle under the forward-facing portholes, and a small bar in the corner. 'The other passengers will arrive tomorrow. Tonight, it's just you, me, the captain and the first mate.'

'What is the "first mate"?'

'I am he.' A voice with a strong accent boomed behind them.

'Ah, Christos, good to see you again.' Lawrence turned and offered his hand to a man with thick black hair and heavy eyebrows that almost met in the middle.

'And you, Lawrence. And you.' He clasped Lawrence's shoulder while he shook his hand. 'And who is this youngster?'

'May I present Arnesh Shrestha, eldest son of my good friend Adil.'

Christos released Lawrence's hand and squeezed Rinzen's with thick, muscular fingers. Rinzen squeezed back. Christos let out a roar of laughter. 'A good strong handshake. Sign of confidence. Excellent. Very happy to meet you, Arnesh.'

Rinzen bowed. 'It is my honour, sir.'

'And polite with it. I think you and I will get along just fine. Another Arnesh I met told me your name means 'lord of the ocean'. Must mean you like water!'

'It is the essence of life.'

'Indeed it is. Now—'

'I see you have introduced yourselves.' For the second time in minutes, someone had spoken before Rinzen noticed they were there. Later, when he meditated, he would centre himself once more.

While Christos was stout, with the neck of a bull, Captain Patera was tall and lean, with a square jaw and a long straight nose. Rinzen was drawn to his bright emerald eyes.

'Milos, this is the young man I told you about.'

'Arnesh, is that right?'

Rinzen bowed. 'At your service, Captain.'

'No need for formalities, but thank you. And you are a teacher?'

'A teacher with a lot to learn, Captain,' Rinzen said.

'Very good, Arnesh.' Christos slapped him on the back and almost knocked him over.

'Shall we sit?' the captain said. 'Edmundo – our Portuguese cook – is bringing the soup. Lawrence tells me you are vegetarian, Arnesh.'

'Yes, but please do not make any special arrangements for me.'

'The soup is Edmundo's special cabbage soup,' Christos said. 'And here he is now.'

Edmundo leaned between the captain and first mate and placed a large covered bowl on the table. '*Caldo verde*, good for everyone.' He glared at Rinzen. 'Next course, *peripeni* chicken and rice for three. For one, *migas de couve e feijão*.' He mumbled the words, as though they tasted foul in his mouth.

'A sort of bean and vegetable stew,' the captain translated.

Rinzen sprang to his feet and bowed to the chef. 'I am sorry to give you this extra work. If you ever need my help, I am at your service.'

Edmundo's face relaxed and his mouth widened into a smile and exposed one gold tooth. 'Well, that would be first time.'

During dinner, the others talked about many things that Rinzen didn't quite understand, either because he didn't know the words or because they spoke too quickly. The conversation was at its liveliest when they all talked at once about something called the Greek crisis and whether a Euro would collapse. He learned that both the captain and the first mate were Greek, and that the crew were from many different countries. The three men drank a bottle of red wine while they ate and sipped Scotch whisky when they'd finished.

After dinner, Lawrence kept watch while Rinzen jumped onto the dock and ran to the warehouse to retrieve his satchel. When he returned, they walked along the edge of the deck, in the narrow passage next to the holds that were half full with a cargo of cereals. They kept to the seaward side and strolled up and down a few times before perching on a metal box near the bow. The chain of white lights along the shore appeared to corral the chaos of Mumbai city, preventing it from tumbling into the sea.

They sat in silence for some time, gazing out to sea.

'Would you mind me asking why you came to India, Lawrence?'

Lawrence seemed to be considering what to say. He nodded, then said, 'I've been in Goa, doing research for a *National Geographic* article. That's an American journal.' He paused, stood up and leaned against the rail. 'No, that's the excuse for me being in India. Why I really came was to try to forget something I did that caused great pain.'

'And have you forgotten?'

'No, but at least now I understand enough to accept my actions for what they were.'

Rinzen waited.

'Look, Rinzen, you had the decency to trust me; the least I can do is to return the favour. It's all to do with a musician – the daughter of my friend Grace – a classical harpist ... Do you know that instrument?'

'I know that a harp has many strings that, when struck, produce haunting sounds through a soundbox.'

'Correct, and the classical version stands as high as a man and has forty-seven strings.' Lawrence hesitated. 'Look, thinking about it, it would probably be a good idea if you heard Clara playing the harp before I say anything else. Is that OK with you?'

'Of course.'

'Tomorrow, after lunch when the mess is empty, I'll play you her CD.'

23

London

'Please just take the money, Clara.'

'No, darling Gail, I told you I can't take your money. It would ruin our friendship.'

'But you could pay me back sometime. See it as a loan. Besides, it's not just my money.'

'I can't see how I could ever pay you back. No, I'll be fine. My mother sends me food parcels, that's all I need.'

'I know how you could repay us,' Gail said.

Clara waited for her to continue, but Gail was now in the kitchen, looking inside the empty cupboards. Cunning girl, wants to be asked how. Cunning but kind, thoughtful. 'All right. How?'

Gail's eyes sparkled. 'You must promise me you won't say no straight off. That you'll think about it.'

'Think about what?'

'Promise?'

'Exasperating girl! All right, I promise. Now tell me.'

'You could do one concert, just you, playing your composition. At the Wigmore Hall. We'll help you get your harp there. My friend has a high van, you could stand—'

'OK, stop. My concert days are—'

Gail pressed her finger to Clara's lips. 'No, no, you promised to think about it. I'm going now, I'll come back next Saturday.'

After she left, Clara looked in the fridge and found the food Gail had somehow sneaked past her.

~

On Monday morning, Clara telephoned Keaton's Estate Agency and said she wanted to sell her flat and buy a smaller one, a studio perhaps. A young man in a shiny silver suit with matching tie came round that afternoon and walked around and talked into his phone about her home.

Pleased with her own decisiveness, she played her composition joyfully and let herself drift within the sounds. She floated through a dark blue sky like the Chagall bride in *La Mariée*, except with her harp rather than a fiddle-playing goat serenading her. Funny to think of Matthew's favourite artist.

Her hands flew across the strings as though they were independent of her, fingering incredibly complex chord combinations she'd never used before, while her feet darted about the pedals, adding unexpected key changes. The effect was spirals of sound so mesmerising that her head bobbed and swayed with the now slow and soft, now almost deafening music, but without losing the perfection of each note. Underneath, a multitude of rhythms coalesced and intertwined … How was she playing this impossible music? It was as though a whole orchestra inhabited the soundbox, but an orchestra consisting entirely of harps, uncountable harps playing in harmony. She'd never in her life played like this, never imagined such technically difficult music could be played on a harp, her harp, her lovely, cherished, very own, magical Lyon & Healy.

As the room came into focus after the finale, Clara had the strangest feeling that the world had shifted a little on its axis while she played, and that things would never be the same again. Her heartbeat quickened, her feet tingled, and before she knew, it she was dancing around the bare room in her bare feet. Her laughter rebounded off the glass doors and clattered into the kitchen. She swirled and pirouetted in complex patterns, controlled by an invisible puppet-master who brushed her against walls but never smashed her into them, who made her jump with ease onto the table and across the kitchen counter then landed her in the splits on the warm oak floor.

When at last the improvised ballet ended, Clara took a moment to regain her breath, then telephoned the estate agent to tell him she had changed her mind about selling the flat. She then called Roland Peach. They had never bothered with pleasantries, and within seconds she'd told him she had composed a piece for solo harp that she wanted him to hear, and that it lasted exactly three hours.

'Is eight tomorrow morning too early?' Roland said, and of course it was neither too early nor too late, time being irrelevant these days.

~

If Roland was surprised at the sparseness of Clara's apartment, or her simple peasant dress and bare feet, or the way the light seemed to shine through her as though she were semi-transparent, he didn't say so. He kissed her, hugged her for a full minute, and took a seat in the only easy chair available.

As for Clara, she didn't feel nervous, or vulnerable or even self-conscious, which was unusual, given that this was not only a public performance of her work but one solely for the ears of a leading conductor.

Three hours later, she opened her eyes and saw that Roland's grey marl polo-neck was damp and that tears were still flowing freely down his cheeks. But Roland never wept! Roland was always in complete control of himself and his musicians. She watched, waited, let her arms hang loose at her side, and took ten deep breaths.

'There are no words,' Roland said. 'At least none worth speaking.' He wiped his face with a lilac handkerchief but did not take his eyes off her. 'I think the Albert Hall, in the round. We'll have to book several nights, because after the first night the whole world will want to listen. And we'll do a DVD. They'll want to see you as well as hear you.' He stood and paced up and down, but his eyes did not leave her face for a moment.

'Naturally, there will be a CD ... And the very best-quality vinyl. I can arrange that. In fact, dammit, I'll arrange everything.' He stopped, stared at her, put on that serious face he used when something either wasn't quite right or was absolute perfection. 'I dare not risk anyone else having anything to do with this music.'

'No, Roland.' Her voice came out as a whisper, unintentionally. 'One night at the Wigmore Hall, no CD, certainly no DVD.'

His mouth dropped open, but only for the count of three, and then he was on the floor, kneeling beside her. He held her right hand in his palm as if it were the most delicate orchid, the last of the most prized species in the world. 'Clara, Clara, the Wigmore, yes of course, your second home or perhaps even your first home, but ... but, don't you realise what you have created? I do. Once in a lifetime, if that. We are artists; what we create must be shared or it is useless. We were born to expose ourselves, to appear naked before the public, to risk everything. Otherwise we are nothing.'

'I could just ask the Wigmore myself.' Clara did not remove her hand from its safe resting place in his palm.

Roland's head dropped and she thought he might start to weep again. What would she do then? Give in, bare herself night after night when all she really desired was this solitude, this simple existence, just her and her music?

He slowly lifted his head. 'All right, the Wigmore, one night only. I will arrange it, but I ask you to do one thing in return: think about what I've said, about why you should share the beauty you've created and bring joy into many, many lives. Will you do that, Clara?'

'Yes, Roland, I promise I will think about it after you've gone. And thank you. Without you ...' Thank God he hadn't said that it was her 'duty', her mother's tired old platitude.

Roland held her close. Was that his heartbeat, or hers? She squeezed him closer, rested her head on his shoulder; she craved this warmth, this affection, wanted it to last forever.

Eventually Roland gasped, untangled himself and hobbled about the room to ease the cramp in his right foot. 'That will teach me to kneel before a harpist!' And with that he was gone.

Clara was left alone to stare at the only photograph on the bare wall, the one of her as a toddler seated on her papa's knee. 'So you see, Papa, I'm still playing the harp after all these years. You will hardly believe it, but I love playing now more than ever, and yes, I do still get goosebumps when I play certain notes.'

She leaned closer to the photograph. 'But I have to tell you that I am not looking forward to this concert, and that surely will come as a surprise to you; you always said I only practised so I could show off on stage. I have no choice. I need to buy food and pay the mortgage and the bills so that I can keep playing and keep Mother, your beloved, alive. I know it is what you want from me, what you expect me to do.'

Clara plucked the strings in the third and fourth octave, didn't damp the sounds, and fell into a simple melody. 'No, I'm worried because this composition – which reminds me, I should think of a name for it – is so personal, so intimate, that I will be baring my soul to the whole audience, and I don't know how that will feel.' The late-afternoon light fluttered over the spruce soundboard. 'Roland will be there in the dark watching over me. And so will you, as you always are, just as you promised.' She found that if she squinted her eyes in a particular way, only her father's face was in focus. It appeared to glow in the dim winter light.

She must have stared at the photograph for a long time, because when the phone rang it was Roland to say that the Wigmore Hall had a cancelled concert on Saturday 25 January and would be delighted to host the world premier of … 'What's the title of your composition?'

'*The Harp Awakening.*'

'*The Harp Awakening.*' Roland tried the words aloud. 'Yes, perfect. It does feel as though you have woken the harp from a long slumber. And our audience will also be awakened by what they hear. Of course, I mean that in more than the literal—'

'Roland, please don't try to define it.'

'Yes, of course. We don't want to spook it. Listen, the Wigmore need a photograph for their website and for the poster. Shall I use an archive photo, perhaps one with that lovely black silk gown?'

'But that was from before.'

'I could come round tomorrow with a photographer?'

Clara didn't say anything for a minute. She would have preferred a photograph of her harp on its own, but if the Wigmore had agreed to put on the concert so soon …

~

When the doorbell rang at nine o'clock the following morning it was not Roland arriving early but Gail with another bag of food. With her acorn-shaped fake-fur hat, her crimson cheeks and emerald-green boots, she could easily have been mistaken for an elf running a couple of weeks late with her Christmas deliveries.

'I hope you're not busy on Saturday 25 January,' Clara said before Gail had even closed the front door, 'because

I've got you a front-row ticket to a concert at the Wigmore Hall.'

Gail dropped the bag and enveloped Clara in a hug that smelled of pine forests and fresh air.

Still in the bear hug, Clara said, 'The director has arranged for a van, but I think I'll need your help. If you don't mind?'

'Mind?' Gail said. 'Mind! I can't think of anything I'd rather do.'

'Do you think I look all right? The photographer will be here in about half an hour.'

Gail agreed that Clara should be barefoot and wear the simple white dress. 'But your hair's not right, it's too shaggy, it should be simpler, don't you think? It should still be long, but trimmed and brushed so it falls straight onto your shoulders. We'll never manage to make you look pale and interesting though – even after all these months inside, your skin is still brown.'

'Cheeky girl. It's olive actually.'

'Whatever. You'll need to wash it first. I'll do it for you over the kitchen sink if you like – save you moving the harp into the bathroom and sticking your arm through the wall.'

Clara smiled at Gail's new familiarity.

It was only after Gail had finished cutting her hair that Clara remembered she'd sold the hairdryer along with almost everything else, so it was still wet – rat's tails, Gail said – when the doorbell rang.

Gail buzzed Roland and the photographer in, opened the flat door, then dashed back to Clara and rubbed her hair in a towel.

'Ouch, you'll pull it out!'

'Pussy.'

'I think I preferred you when you were a well-behaved middle-class girl from the suburbs.'

Gail rubbed harder.

'No need for that,' a woman's voice said, 'I brought a hairdryer with me.'

'Pity, I was enjoying myself.' Gail laughed, blushed, stood with the towel in her hand and her own hair a complete mess after all that tussling.

'Roland,' Clara said, 'this terrible girl is Gail – she's the one to blame for the concert idea.'

Roland's frown turned into a wide smile as he marched across the room to Gail and took both her hands. 'Thank you, Gail. Front row, middle seat, I promise. Sorry if I frowned at you – I thought you were attacking our maestro.'

'Don't, Roland!' Clara turned to the photographer. 'I'm so glad you're a woman. I mean …'

'So am I.' She laughed. 'I'm Frances. Shall I dry your hair?'

'And I'll make coffee,' Gail said.

'Clara,' Roland said, 'why don't you leave your precious harp so Frances can get at you?'

'Can't. Don't let it bother you.'

'And I don't mind,' Frances said.

'Mr Peach, could I have a quiet word?' Gail said in a loud whisper.

She led the way into the hall. Clara heard an 'I see, interesting' from Roland, and smiled at Gail's sensitivity.

Roland did not try to talk Clara into wearing the long black gown he'd brought with him, didn't even insist on the flat black shoes.

Huh, he's worried I'll change my mind.

'Oh, by the way,' she said, 'Gail thinks I should play naked, and I'm inclined to agree.'

'Yes, the purity of the music really demands nudity,' Gail said.

Roland's eyebrows popped into arches; his mouth fell open. 'But, but …'

'I think they're kidding you, Roland,' Frances said.

'You women are ganging up on me, aren't you? I'm going to sit over there and sulk.'

'Just seeing how far you'd go. I think you'd have let me, too.' Clara grabbed his hand as he walked past and squeezed it. 'Thanks, really.'

'How about a splash of scarlet lipstick?' Frances said. 'I want to draw people into the photograph.'

They set up the shot against the bare brick wall with the photograph of her papa visible next to the harp's golden column. Frances took a couple of black and white Polaroids and gave one each to Clara and Gail.

Once they'd all left, Clara wheeled the harp over to the wall and balanced the Polaroid on top of the framed photograph of her papa.

24

At sea

After lunch, Lawrence and Rinzen stayed in the officer's mess and listened to the CD of Clara playing the harp. Rinzen was immediately absorbed in the lovely music and closed his eyes to enhance the experience. Halfway through the third track, his eyes snapped open and he leaned towards the loudspeaker, listening intently to every note. He knew this music, or something very like it. How could that be – he had never heard concert harp music in his life. When the track finished, he asked Lawrence to play it again.

'I know this music,' he said.

'Really?'

'Or something very like it. A few times since Elder Kwato's passing, I've heard strange sounds, like a delicate waterfall, or a stream splashing over rocks. I thought it must be some trick of the wind or that I was dreaming it.'

Lawrence looked at the CD cover. 'Mmm, it's one of Clara's own compositions. She's called it "Waterfall".'

'Perhaps that's it. I'm so used to the sound of mountain water. It's wonderful music, Lawrence. Thank you.'

'Well, she is a virtuoso …'

'Afternoon, gents.' The steward entered, carrying a tray of crockery. 'Don't mind me, just setting up for the new passengers.'

The other passengers arrived during the afternoon and gathered in the officers' mess at 7pm, where a uniformed steward served them drinks at the bar. Rinzen declined, but Lawrence ordered himself a whisky with ice and soda, then turned to the other three passengers and introduced himself and Arnesh Shrestha.

'Major Clutterbuck.' The man's back was so buckled that he looked at them along his forehead, over the top of his spectacles. 'May I introduce Mrs Paula Davis, my companion on this voyage?'

'Mrs Davis.' Lawrence nodded. 'Major.'

'Please call me Paula.' Mrs Davis, like her companion, looked to be in her early seventies. She wore a long cotton dress belted at the waist, straw-coloured hair swept back, face lightly powdered, lips glossed a pale pink. She bestowed a broad smile on Lawrence and shook his hand. Hers looked like they had seen plenty of outdoor work, and Rinzen wondered whether she might be a farmer.

'And I'm Gavin Williams.' Unlike the major, who was smartly dressed in a navy blazer and tie, this man wore a crumpled linen suit and a faded green and white check shirt. He stuck out his hand, first to Lawrence, and then to Rinzen. It felt damp, limpid, and Rinzen noticed his jacket was frayed and stained at the cuff.

'Shall we agree first-name terms?' the major said. 'But if you don't mind, I'll opt for plain "Major".'

'Sorry not to be here to make the introductions.' Captain Patera strode towards them. 'Everyone got a drink?'

Before they could answer, the last two passengers entered behind the captain. 'Good evening, Captain … everyone.' The newcomer's fleshy red face floated on a pink scarf tucked into a lilac shirt.

'Mr Ward-Jones, welcome, and Mr Campbell, do join us. Frank, a gin and tonic for Mr Ward-Jones. And for you, Mr Campbell?'

The latter opened his mouth to speak, but Ward-Jones cut across him. 'George will have the same, thank you, Frank.'

The already meek George deflated even further. Rinzen watched the blood rise from his neck up to the edge of his tightly trimmed white-blonde hair.

During dinner most of the conversation revolved around the occupations of the passengers. Afterwards, Captain Patera gave a brief outline of the voyage, where the ship would stop and for how many hours, and asked everyone to set aside half an hour after breakfast for a safety drill on the cargo deck. He concluded by wishing everyone a pleasant voyage, and warned that they might be in for stormy weather as the ship approached the Gulf of Aden.

Lawrence and Rinzen circled the cargo deck before going up to Lawrence's cabin to continue the story of Clara Martinelli. Lawrence told Rinzen about Clara's precocious genius, the death of her father, her mother's devotion to her career, and Clara's single-minded focus on perfecting her art. 'I've never seen such a close mother–daughter relationship,' he said. 'They depend utterly on each another.' He paused and corrected himself. 'Or at least they did, until …'

Lawrence filled him in on Clara's dream and Grace's reaction. Rinzen empathised with Clara, remembered how distraught he'd felt when Elder Kwato had died. No wonder she was desperate not to lose her mother.

When Lawrence got to the disastrous episode at the Swiss hotel, he placed both hands flat on the table and fixed his eyes on Rinzen. 'You're the first person I've told about this, so bear with me.'

Another sip of whisky.

'About six months ago, Grace decided to do something drastic, reckless … Looking back, I truly believe she was temporarily insane, or at least had lost all reason, because Grace is wonderful, caring, kind …'

Rinzen made to stand to comfort him, but Lawrence raised his hand and continued. He cupped the whisky tumbler and stared at it as he finished the sorry story. 'And to my everlasting shame, I helped Grace execute the plan.'

The sickly wash cast by the green glass wall-light deepened the worry lines on his face, his features etched like a woodcut print of a weatherbeaten farmer in a hostile landscape.

'And it is this shame that brought you to India?'

Lawrence sighed. 'Yes. You see, I knew from the start that Clara had to keep playing, that she was right to do so, and when I saw her face on that hotel terrace, her shock at the betrayal, I knew I had disrupted something momentous, something that was beyond the personal explanation Clara gave, something much more fundamental.'

He stood, pushed back the chair with the backs of his legs, and leaned over, arms locked straight. 'Even now, I can't explain why I did it, why I didn't foresee the consequences. It was so unlike me to be that reckless. It's true that I'd become very fond of Grace, perhaps I even loved her, but I wasn't exactly an infatuated youth! You must understand that Grace is devoted to Clara, would never do anything to harm her, and I suppose that might explain why I was persuaded to help with her plan. But, afterwards, I confess that I ...'

Rinzen could see how important it was for Lawrence to express all this, to share it. 'More whisky?'

Lawrence shook his head. Rinzen averted his eyes, inhaled the man's sour sweat.

'I no longer knew who I was. That's all I can say tonight.' He put his right hand on Rinzen's shoulder, but Rinzen did not lift his head. 'Thank you for listening, Rinzen.' A slight squeeze, a beckoning, to which Rinzen responded by placing his hand over Lawrence's.

~

After breakfast and the safety briefing, Rinzen excused himself to meditate. Two hours later, Lawrence came to tell him that the ship was about to leave the dock. The treads of the iron staircase vibrated as the engines started, and by the time they walked out on deck, the *Oracle* had already moved a couple of metres from the quay. They didn't join the other passengers on the dock side of the ship, in case there was someone checking who was on board.

'Finally!' Gavin Williams said.

'You sound happy to be leaving India, Mr Williams.' Clearly, Mrs Davis was not a person who kept her thoughts to herself.

'Damn right I am. Not a moment too soon.'

'A fine day for it, I must say.' Major Clutterbuck changed the subject. 'Not a cloud in the sky, and no wind.'

The *Oracle* ploughed through the light waves towards the open sea. Rinzen walked towards the bow, leaned out over the port railings and stared into the depths as they left the harbour. Cooling seaspray landed as mist on his face. He emptied his mind, surrendered to sensory experiences, cut off thoughts as they fought for his attention: he tasted salt, smelled diesel mixed with a hint of dead fish; he heard gulls call behind him, and the blast of the ship's horn; the dull rumble of the engines trembled deep beneath his feet, and all the while his eyes sought infinity at the edge of the world that never came any closer. A smile bloomed from his lips and he longed to howl.

If Lawrence hadn't come to get him at lunchtime, he would have stayed in that place, in that experience, until nightfall. He didn't say much during lunch, content to let the holiday-mood chatter waft around him. As soon as he could, he resumed his watch over the vast ocean, under a high sun and clear skies.

~

After three days of calm weather and steady, rolling waves, the wind from the south brought heavy black clouds that billowed across the blue sky before finally obliterating the sun. When the rain started, heavy droplets – some fist-sized – landed in discrete splats on the painted steel deck, but minutes later the water became continuous and its mighty drumming drowned out the warning horn and the distant engine noise. Rinzen, who couldn't see more than a few centimetres in front of him, leaned against a great coil of rope next to the accommodation block and endured the full force of the storm.

Half an hour later the storm passed, flying to the horizon as though God had shaken out a blue sheet over the sky. To stay upright, Rinzen shifted his weight from one foot to the other as the ship heaved and rolled in the churning ocean.

A few of the other passengers, including George Campbell, appeared on deck. He moved unsteadily along the rail, and Rinzen watched him retch over the side. His whole body shook with the effort; he straightened up then doubled over and squatted down, but still gripped the rail with one hand while he wiped his face with the other. No sooner had he recovered than he once again lurched over the rail, misjudged its position and tumbled over the side.

Rinzen watched in alarm as George's fingers slid off the rail. Someone shouted, 'Man overboard!' but Rinzen was already leaping through the air, one hand holding the end of the rope.

A second before he hit the water, he saw George's flailing arms ten metres away; he tried not to think about what would happen if he ran out of rope. He heard the ship's horn blast three times, then he disappeared feet first beneath the waves. The rope slowed him down and the huge waves disoriented him. He lost sight of George. Quickly, he tied the rope around his waist, dived under the water, swam six strong stokes straight down, turned and propelled himself upwards with the full force of his leg muscles, arms stretched in front of him to minimise drag. In the second or two he was airborne he spun round, spotted George, twisted his body to point straight at him and plunged once again into the violent sea, determined that this time he would stay on the surface. Three hard strokes and powerful kicks brought him to George's sinking head. As he grabbed him under his arms, he yelled at the top of his voice, 'Pull! Pull now!' and felt an immediate tug on the rope.

George's body was limp in his grasp. He must have swallowed water. Rinzen thought about upending him then and there but couldn't while they were both flying through the air with a rope around them. As soon as they landed on the deck, he thumped his back with both palms. Nothing. He turned him over, pinched his nose and breathed four long, strong breaths into his mouth. George's chest heaved, he coughed, and Rinzen gently turned his head so the water could splutter from his mouth.

It was only then that he noticed figures crouching all around him and felt Lawrence's familiar hand on his shoulder before he draped a blanket over him. He fell backwards into his friend's arms and let out the breath he'd been holding since he'd given George mouth-to-mouth. 'That was close,' he said.

'My God Almighty,' Christos said. 'Humorous as well as heroic.'

'There may be more water,' Rinzen said. 'Someone will need to watch over him.'

Theo Ward-Jones cradled George's head in his lap, tears streaming down his cheeks from startled eyes. 'I won't leave his side,' he whispered. 'Thank you, Arnesh. Thank you with all my heart.' As he looked down, his floppy brown hair fell in a curtain over his face.

'Who saved me?' George's voice was hoarse, barely audible.

'Arnesh jumped in after you, George,' Theo said. 'Now don't try to speak.'

'But I must thank him. Where is he?'

'We must get them warm,' Captain Patera said. 'Theo, let these men carry George to the sick bay. Christos, heat water for the bottles. Carlo, get blankets.'

'I'll lie with him, warm him with my body,' Theo said.

'What about Arnesh?' Paula Davis said, but Rinzen had already walked towards the cabins, Lawrence's arm around his shoulder.

At dinner, the Captain reported that George was recovering well and praised Arnesh's quick thinking and selfless bravery. 'In all my years at sea I have never witnessed such an outstanding display of man's ability to perform superhuman feats when disaster strikes. I have heard of women lifting the wheel of a bus off a crushed infant, of soldiers carrying several comrades at once from the field of battle, but I have not seen such things until today.'

The next morning, George and Theo had breakfast in their cabin. Lawrence didn't appear in the dining room either, so as soon as he'd eaten, Rinzen went to check on him. He found him with a high fever, shivering in his bed. Rinzen had seen that before, when a visitor had come to Sarmand. Malaria. He went to get medicine from Christos.

For the following four days, Rinzen rarely left Lawrence's bedside. Edmundo the chef knew all about treating malaria, and sent in citrus fruits, raw vegetables and occasional bowls of plain boiled vegetables. Rinzen prepared a lime and lemon drink to control the fever, and every morning Edmundo brought in a glass of hot water laced with cinnamon, pepper powder and honey. During particularly severe fever attacks, Rinzen wrapped Lawrence's body first in linen soaked in cold water and then in a warm blanket for half an hour.

Whenever Lawrence was in a deep sleep, Rinzen meditated. One time, as he focused, wisps of sound floated about him, becoming clearer and louder until he recognised it as harp music. But this was not like the music on the CD, this was layers of music all around him, as though countless harps were playing together in harmony. How could imagined music be so sublime? It felt as though his own sinews were being plucked. Then came silence, as he entered the trance.

When, on the third day of Lawrence's fever, the ship stopped to refuel at Djibouti, Rinzen did not go ashore with the other passengers but instead took the opportunity to stroll around on deck while no one was around. Unobserved, he practised Standing in the Sky on a steel stanchion attached to the superstructure, and realised it was the first time he'd done that since leaving Sarmand all those weeks before. He thought about his brothers quarantined for no reason in the monastery. What was he doing on the ship? He should be where he belonged, meditating with them, not out here in the middle of the ocean on his way to the other side of the world.

He dropped to the deck and walked around to the entrance to the accommodation decks.

'That was quite a thing you did the other day.' Gavin Williams was leaning against the steel wall, smoking. 'You are quite some athlete, aren't you, Arnesh.' The man raised one eyebrow, perhaps because the smoke was getting in his eyes, perhaps not. He wasn't smiling, but his lips were twisted as if to mimic a smile.

'As the captain said—'

'Yes, I heard what our captain said.' He stubbed out the cigarette on the deck, didn't bother to pick up the butt and throw it over the side. 'But I'm not convinced. Convince me, Arnesh.'

'You are welcome to your opinions. I have no desire to convince you of anything.' Rinzen continued towards the door, but Williams grabbed his arm.

'I thought so,' he said. 'Muscles like a boxer. Who are you, Arnesh?'

He lifted Williams's hand off his arm, taking care not to squeeze the limpid thing, went inside and didn't leave Lawrence's cabin for the rest of the day.

Next morning, he went out on deck before dawn, to breathe the fresh air and gaze at the galaxy. There was a cigarette end glowing beside one of the cranes.

'Hello again,' Williams said. 'Sorry about grabbing hold of you yesterday. Dodgy gut, made me bad-tempered.'

'Please, it is not a problem.' Perhaps he had worried unnecessarily?

'I must say, though, you are a remarkable young man.' As Williams sucked on his cigarette, his scowl was clearly visible. 'Even acrobats can't suspend themselves horizontally from one outstretched arm.'

So he had seen him.

'Oh, that's just something we learn at school in my part of India. If you start very young, it's easy. Everyone can do it. Excuse me, I only came out for a minute. I must go and check on Lawrence.'

In the dark, Williams would not see that he was lying.

25

London

Clara had no need to practise *The Harp Awakening*, but she played it anyway. After the first few bars, the walls of her flat melted away and the sky lightened and took on delicate tones: shades of blue from a tropical horizon at noon, pink from the first spring orchids in a pristine Somerset field, a yellow flickering at the edge of an unobservable sun, and beneath this palette a white so pure she felt it through her skin. She inhabited this sky, a bodyless presence with an all-seeing eye and an all-hearing ear. The music played of its own accord: from the first trickle of a mountain spring, down steep ravines into the wide river, out to sea through tidal waves and into the deepest ocean, then on to the horizon, where the sound rose unimpeded into the ether and attained an echo-less purity that she experienced as perfect harmony.

Sometimes, from this great height, she saw the mountain range, the ice caps giving way to deeply fissured ravines, the solitary figure running and leaping along the ridge.

The real world of eating and drinking, pissing and shitting, electricity and thermostatic showers, gas hobs and underwear, plastered walls and coat hangers, was so bland in comparison that when she'd played the last chord, all she wanted to do was start again. Sometimes she did just that. Sometimes she really did need to pee, or eat or drink, and the spell was broken, enabling her to think about what needed to be done to prepare for the concert.

Her mother would be there, Julia too; even Henry might come. When she thought about greeting them, she wasn't able to think of them as connected to the Clara she was now. They belonged in the world of the other Clara. Even her mother, on whom she had relied for everything, now felt remote, barely a silhouette in a landscape glimpsed through a slowly misting winter window. Though she tried to picture her mother walking towards her, she never managed to bring her close; it was as if she was walking on the spot, a flick cartoon in an endless loop. Yes, that was it, the past was populated by cartoons, two-dimensional characters without substance.

Those who had stayed with her, who had travelled with her, like Roland, Gail and Matthew, accepted her changing self, even embraced it. Roland thought that her prolonged solitude had been key to *The Harp Awakening*; he couldn't imagine anyone composing such music while distracted by mundane daily concerns. Gail – generous, giving-of-herself Gail – had never questioned Clara's peculiar habits, had never once asked why she wouldn't let go of the harp. And Matthew had committed the therapist's cardinal sin: he had colluded with his patient's delusion and even encouraged it.

Clara had started out by attaching herself to the harp in order to keep her mother alive, but was that still the reason? Over the past months she had lost interest in judging herself, and in so doing had lost interest in judging others. She had been deeply wounded by Grace's stunt in Switzerland, but that felt like a long time ago now, a different life, almost. Now that she was no longer interested in blame or retribution, why was it she still didn't want to see her mother, or Julia, for that matter?

She strummed the strings with the backs of her fingers, so lightly she had to press her ear to the soundbox to hear it, and tried to concentrate on her mother. She still loved

Grace and was certain that Grace loved her. None of her mother's letters had shown the slightest sign that she accepted Clara's behaviour, but she was nevertheless still firmly preoccupied with her daughter, still unable to move on. It wasn't up to Clara how her mother behaved, but it was pretty clear that she still intended to get Clara to snap out of it and resume normal service, and as long as she thought like that, Clara wouldn't see her. For both their sakes.

Life and music were too important to waste on battles that one could not win, on problems without a solution.

26

At sea

When the *Oracle* left Djibouti, Captain Patera advised his passengers to only go on deck when a member of the crew was present. Although piracy incidents in the Red Sea were infrequent these days, it was still wise to be cautious.

By the evening of the following day, Lawrence had recovered enough to join the others for dinner. Afterwards, he and Rinzen sought the privacy of Lawrence's cabin. 'I thought this article might interest you.' He handed Rinzen a copy of the *New Scientist* dated 13 December 2013. 'I bought it in Mumbai last week.'

Rinzen read:

Climate change is causing the North Pole's location to drift, owing to subtle changes in the earth's rotation that result from the melting of glaciers and ice sheets. The finding suggests that monitoring the position of the pole could become a new tool for tracking global warming …

… This southwards drift is due to the changes in the distribution of earth's mass as the crust slowly rebounds after the end of the last ice age. But Chen's team found something surprising. In 2005, this southward drift changed abruptly. The pole began moving eastwards and continues to do so, a shift that has amounted to about 1.2 metres since 2005 …

... 'Ice melting and sea level change can explain 90 per cent of the [eastward shift],' says Chen. 'The driving force for the sudden change is climate change.'

'So, Elder Kwato's sense that the earth had shifted on its axis is confirmed by these scientists?'

'It seems so,' Lawrence said. 'He must have been a remarkable man. I imagine you were deeply affected by his death.'

Rinzen pretended to read the rest of the article, but the words appeared as a meaningless pattern before his eyes. His temples pounded; his teeth clenched together as he fought to keep the tears inside. 'Yes, I confess I still find it hard to accept.'

They were silent for a few minutes until Lawrence said, 'The other thing I wanted to talk to you about was the Kogi. How much do you know about them?'

'Almost nothing. I only know that they, like the Samudrans, are devoted to protecting the earth. Elder Kwato said they live on a tall mountain that rises from the seashore and disappears into the clouds.'

'Yes, that's right, it is the highest coastal mountain on earth, called the Sierra Nevada de Santa Marta.' Lawrence said. 'I've read about the Kogi, although I've never been to Columbia. They are the ancestors of the Tairona people, from the world of the Inca and Aztec, and the Spanish conquistadors never managed to conquer them. The mountain is so tall that every ecological zone is represented.'

'Like Herr Humboldt's Chimborazo,' Rinzen said.

'Good God, you've read Humboldt?'

'We have some of his books in the library. I particularly like *Views of Nature*. The way he writes about the natural world is like poetry mixed with scientific observations.' Rinzen gave a rueful smile. 'And his "Web of Life", his belief in the interconnectedness of nature, is what we too believe.'

'Yes, Humboldt used that to persuade mankind to refrain from inflicting permanent damage on the earth, unfortunately with little success in the long term.' Lawrence shook his head. 'But thank goodness for you Samudrans, and the Kogi, still flying the flag.'

'Are the Kogi very like us?'

'It does seem that you share a lot. They too believe that they exist in order to care for the world. Some years ago they realised that mining, industrialisation and deforestation was inflicting so much damage on the earth that their task was almost impossible. So they decided to give the world a message, a warning that it needed to change, that we all had to care for the earth, not destroy it.'

'And that's how you know so much about them?'

'Yes, that's right. In 1990 they invited a documentary filmmaker, Alan Ereira from the BBC, to record their warning. The message went unheeded, so the Kogi were forced to issue a second warning, to make us understand that there are critical interconnections within the natural world. As Humboldt observed, it is a subtle and hidden network, and interfering in one part has a major impact on other specific parts. They asked Alan Ereira back, this time to take the audience on a journey into the mysteries of their sacred places and change our understanding of reality.'

Rinzen leaned forward, eyes wide. 'And has that message been heeded?' He held his breath, sensed a tingling in his fingers and clenched his fists.

'Only by those who were ready to hear it. But the Kogi understand that the whole world will not suddenly change to live like them. What they want us to do is care for the rivers, protect them, as it is through the river systems that all life flows. And in this there are signs that their message has had some impact.'

'Water!' Rinzen said, forming the shape of a bowl with his hands. 'So this is the link between the Kogi and the

Samudrans. But I think you already know that "Samudra" means "gathering together of waters"?'

'Yes. The Kogi say that in the beginning was the sea; the sea was the mother, part of a sort of spiritual, foundational intelligence they call *aluna*. Water is the essence of life.'

'Exactly. The essence of life.' Rinzen's face split into a huge grin. 'That must be why the elders want me to go there. Do the Kogi hold continuous meditation like us?'

'For the Kogi *mamas* – the equivalent of your elders – everything they do is born from concentration. They say that without thought, nothing could exist.' Lawrence stopped to drink some water. His eyes, still bloodshot, had deep shadows beneath them.

'I'm keen to hear more about the Kogi, Lawrence, but you look all in.'

'I am tired, but I want to tell you. It won't take too long.' He wiped his hand across his face. 'Correct use of "all in", by the way.'

They both laughed, and Lawrence continued. 'They can maintain this concentration – meditation, if you like – for several days without sleeping. With proper concentration they can pass beyond the material world and work in the world of *aluna*, which binds all things together.'

~

Back in his cabin, Rinzen sat on the floor and gazed at his bowl of water. When he emerged from the trance several hours later, he realised that although he had felt the presence of his brothers, they were faceless, shadowy forms in the inner temple, and he had been with them but set apart as though behind an invisible barrier. He undressed and lay in his bed to consider the significance of this separation, but the rumble of the ship's engines lulled him to sleep.

When he awoke, the porthole glowed orange with the first rays of the sun rising over the Arabian Desert. He hurried out on deck to feel the new day shine upon his face, walking straight past Major Clutterbuck and Gavin Williams. The latter called after him.

'Good morning, Arnesh. I see the lord of the ocean has come to inspect his domain.'

'I have never seen the sun rise over a desert,' Rinzen said. 'The colours are beautiful.'

'Indeed they are.' He fixed Rinzen with a penetrating stare. 'I asked the major here if he knew where you did your teacher training, but he said you hadn't mentioned it.'

Why were they talking about him? 'I did not think it would interest him. Or you.'

'But of course we're interested.'

Did Williams know who he was? A memory of somewhere he'd walked past in Darbhanga presented itself. 'I studied for my diploma at the Primary Teachers Education College, Madhopatti, Darbhanga.'

'There we are. Mystery solved. I have one more question.' He paused to light a cigarette. 'If you don't mind? Why would a primary-school teacher who already speaks very good English want to go all the way to England?'

Rinzen looked unsmilingly at Williams. Within the confines of the ship, it was impossible to avoid contact with this suspicious man. 'I decided to train as a secondary-school English teacher. Lawrence offered to help me.'

'So ...' Williams let a smoke ring billow forth. 'You will study in England?'

'Yes.' He thought about walking away, but both men were staring at him.

'At which college?'

'What?'

'Simple question. Where will you study?'

'I'm not sure ... I mean, I don't know its name. I have it written down in my book. In the cabin.'

'I see.' Williams turned his head and winked at the major.

The major frowned, seemed confused by this signal.

'If you really want to know, I'll look it up and tell you later.'

'Thank you. It is odd, though. I'd have thought you'd know exactly where you were going. I mean, it's not every day that an Indian primary-school teacher goes all the way to England.' He dropped the cigarette butt, looked down at it and rubbed it into the painted deck with the sole of his shoe. It left a brown stain on the otherwise impeccable surface. 'Anyway, see you at breakfast.'

The same false smile appeared like a mask on the man's unshaven face.

By the time Rinzen reached the side rail, the lovely blend of rusts, oranges, purples and reds had given way to dazzling sunshine in a cloudless, pearl-blue sky. How had he let himself get drawn into Williams's web?

Two hours later, Lawrence took some bread and jam and a mug of hot water to Rinzen's cabin. Rinzen told him about Williams's probing questions.

'I get the impression that the man feels he's lost out in life,' Lawrence said. 'And his profession as a journalist has made him mistrustful.'

'It's clear that he hates India. Perhaps he hates Indians as well?'

'Whatever his motive, he takes his questions too far. Where you're from and what you're going to do is not his concern. When he asked me why I was in India, I told him to mind his own business, and now he leaves me alone. We have to stop him interrogating you.' Lawrence drummed his fingers on the desk for a minute or two. 'As you've offered to tell him where you'll be studying in England, you'll have to come up with something, but after that I see no reason why you shouldn't just answer him as I did. I'm sure he's used to being told to bugger off.'

271

Rinzen understood what he meant, even though the phrase was not familiar.

'I could say that I am simply improving my English in England. A short course, perhaps, while staying with you?'

'Good idea. Say you will be studying English at ... let's see ...'

~

After breakfast the following morning, Rinzen went to the front of the ship with the others and looked at the canal slicing through the desert until it became a single point at the end of an enormous arrow. He heard someone say it was 160 kilometres long and would take them all day to reach Port Said at the other end. Mrs Davis and Theo Ward-Jones leaned over the rail and photographed the convoy of ships in front of the *Oracle*, but Rinzen heard the click of a camera shutter off to the side and knew someone had taken a photograph of him. He spun round, but none of the others had a camera. Perhaps he'd imagined it?

He walked across to where Lawrence was standing with George and the major.

'Excuse me, did someone take a photograph of me?'

'Not me, old boy,' the major said.

The others shook their heads.

Williams was further along, leaning back against the rail. 'As you can see, I don't have a camera.'

'Please, I wish not to have my photograph taken.'

'Understood,' the major said.

As Rinzen walked away, he heard someone, he wasn't sure who, mutter, 'Touchy, isn't he?'

Once in his cabin, he put the incident out of his mind. After all, the important thing was to get to Columbia. Everything else was irrelevant. Everything, that was, except meditating to keep the planet turning. He sat on the floor, legs crossed, and only emerged from the meditation as the ship approached Port Said. He found George Campbell in the corridor.

'I wanted to catch you alone, Arnesh.' He sounded breathless. 'To thank you properly for saving my life.'

Rinzen smiled.

'I made this drawing for you, to commemorate your bravery.' He handed Rinzen a handmade yellow folder tied with an emerald-green ribbon.

'Thank you, George. Shall I look now?'

'Yes, why not.' A pink blush rose up George's face like a glass slowly filling with raspberry juice.

On one side of the drawing a huge ship, filling a third of the sheet, crashed through deep-blue waves that curled and splashed against its bright red hull. Parts of its silver deck rail sparkled in the sun. To the left of the ship, the straw-coloured head of a man, his mouth open, arms stretched upwards, was about to sink into the boiling sea. At the centre, suspended against the alabaster sky and appearing to fly over the sea, was a figure dressed in a light tan tunic bound with a black sash; he wore matching baggy pants tucked into white cotton knee-length gaiters crisscrossed with black ribbons to the ankles of bare feet. The man had very short hair and gripped the end of a rope attached to the ship's deck.

Rinzen beckoned to George to follow him into his cabin. Although the door was closed, he whispered. 'George, this drawing is the work of an artist, not an artist's assistant. The colours and textures, the life, the sense of danger and action are all so beautifully realised. Thank you for such a magnificent gift, but ...'

'But what, Arnesh? Is it not what happened?'

'Why have you shown me in the robes of a monk, when I wear trousers and a shirt like you?'

George looked at the drawing, pushed the fingers of his right hand through his hair, glanced up at Rinzen. 'I really don't know. That's just the way I saw it in my mind. Sorry ...

Now I look at the drawing I can see it doesn't resemble you.' He dropped his head. 'God, what a disaster. It was meant to be—'

'No, it's not that. I love your drawing, and that really is me. To the last detail.' Rinzen put his hand on George's shoulder, who raised his head and looked adoringly at Rinzen. 'Have you shown the drawing to anyone else? Perhaps to Theo?'

'God, no. Theo would find some criticism, tell me I was being sentimental or something.'

'And no one else?'

'No, why?'

'The drawing is already precious to me, but I will not show it to anyone on the ship.'

'It's yours, so you can do whatever you wish.'

'Do you understand why?'

'I think so.' George lowered his voice. 'Are you in disguise?'

'Yes.'

'I swear on my dear sister's grave that I will not tell a soul. You saved my life; I will never betray you.' He frowned to show his sincerity. 'And if I can help you in any way, here or in England, please call upon me.'

Rinzen put his muscular arms around the man and pulled him close. He let go after a couple of seconds, stood back, placed his hands together, and bowed. George reciprocated.

Before dinner, Rinzen approached Williams in the officers' mess and handed him a piece of paper. 'This is the name of the college where I will study Advanced English for three months. How is this word pronounced, please?' He pointed to 'Haringey'.

'Ha-rin-gay.' Williams seemed disinterested. 'Good luck with your studies.' He did not sound sincere, but he left Rinzen alone for the remainder of the voyage.

~

When the ship docked in Gibraltar, the major went ashore and returned with a copy of *The Times* newspaper, which he passed on to Lawrence.

'My God!' Lawrence said, pointing excitedly at the arts page. 'Arnesh, look at this.' He gestured to a short piece announcing a solo concert by the harpist Clara Martinelli on 25 January.

'How auspicious! When is that? Will we be there in time for you to go?' Rinzen said.

'Yes, yes, we dock on the twenty-second, but—'

'My, you're both very excited,' Paula said. 'I've never seen you so animated, Lawrence.'

Lawrence stood and made for the door. 'You're right, Paula. I haven't heard such good news in a very long time. Here's your paper, Major. Thanks.'

Rinzen followed him, almost running to keep up.

'You must come too, Rinzen. Of course you must. I'll see if Milos can book us tickets.'

'No, Lawrence. I would love to hear Clara play, but I must continue on my way to the Kogi.'

Lawrence stopped in his tracks, hit his forehead with the flat of his hand. 'Idiot! Why haven't I asked Milos about that? He might be able to find you a ship, although ...'

'Yes?'

He turned to face Rinzen. 'It will be hard saying goodbye to you.'

The night before they were due to arrive in Southampton, Captain Patera knocked on Lawrence's cabin door. On a map of the area around Southampton docks he showed Rinzen and Lawrence the quietest, darkest part of the perimeter fence, well away from the dock gates and immigration control. 'I checked departures to Barranquilla from the main UK ports – Tilbury, Liverpool, Southampton and others – and the first suitable ship, if you can find a way

275

on board, leaves Southampton on 14 February and takes fifteen days.'

'Another month until I get there.' Rinzen dropped his head, sighed. 'And then I still have to find the Kogi.' He snapped his head up. 'Forgive me, Captain, how rude. I … of course I am most grateful for everything you have done for me, and for finding this ship.' He took the captain's hand and shook it, bowed as he did so. 'Thank you.'

'No need, Rinzen. Remember, you are still my hero!' The captain grinned, covered Rinzen's hand with his free one. 'I will see what can be done about the next ship.' He tapped his nose, looked to Lawrence.

'And the upside is that you'll be able to come to Clara's concert after all,' Lawrence said. 'I confess I asked Milos to get me two tickets … just in case.'

In the late afternoon of 22 January, the *Oracle* docked at Southampton Harbour's Western Docks Bulk Cargo quay. Rinzen and Lawrence bade farewell to the other passengers and watched them go ashore from inside the accommodation block. As he stepped off the deck and onto the steel stairs down to the quay, Gavin Williams turned, winked and tapped the camera slung over his shoulder.

Rinzen kept out of sight when customs and immigration officers came aboard to inspect the cargo and check the crew's documents. As the ship had stopped in East Africa, they also checked that no illegal immigrants had hidden in the holds or elsewhere on the ship. Rinzen had secreted his few possessions in Lawrence's baggage and was well into his second hour of performing Man Standing Still at the end of the bed in his cabin when the search party walked in through the open door. They looked under the bed and in the wardrobe, and opened a couple of the boxes, then moved on to the next cabin.

After dark, Rinzen jumped from the bow, ran along the quay and leapt over the fence where Captain Patera had suggested. Lawrence was waiting for him, and together they boarded a train bound for Victoria Station in London.

27

London

Clara stood with the Lyon & Healy behind the door at the back of the Wigmore Hall's semi-circular stage and listened to Roland Peach introduce her and *The Harp Awakening*. She closed her eyes, tried to steady her heartbeat. In a few minutes she would begin laying bare her most private emotions in front of all those people. They'd look, they'd listen, they'd judge. And all because they'd paid the ticket price: a ticket to her innermost self. She'd never thought about it like that before, had always been so pleased that people wanted to listen to live music, but this time—

'And now, ladies and gentlemen, please welcome Clara Martinelli.'

The house lights dimmed, someone opened the door, and Clara wheeled the harp into the pool of light around the harp stool. She bowed her head to acknowledge the extended applause, sat on the stool and waited for silence. She counted to ten, then played middle C, just once. It flew as if from a longbow, true and clear, in a perfect arc. The first note. The rest would follow. The tautness left her shoulders, her jaw unclenched, and the harp awakened.

She'd done a soundcheck earlier, but she knew the acoustics would be affected by the full house. It didn't matter. Those in the back row were probably worried they'd have to strain to hear a solo harp, but Clara knew they would hear every note as if she were sitting next to them.

The music filled the hall, reached the highest, furthest corners. Before she disappeared into its waves and whispers, Clara was gratified that it transposed so well from the confines of her small apartment to the volume of the Wigmore. The acoustics, enhanced by the concave wall behind her, and by the dome above the stage, allowed her melodies full rein, but the overwhelming sensation was one of freedom, music untrammelled by low ceilings or masonry walls, a symphony of sound from just one unamplified string instrument.

After she'd played the last note, she let her arms drop away from the strings and felt the blood flow into her hands. She stretched her fingers, shook them a little, and looked into the dim hall for some reaction from the silent audience. After a long pause, a voice from the back called 'Bravo!' and in an instant the entire audience stood, clapped, cheered and shouted 'Maestro!', 'Bravo!' and other less distinct words of adulation. In their excitement, one or two even called for an encore.

Clara stood, rested her right hand on the harp's neck and bowed. The house lights came up and still they cheered. She bowed again and again, and then looked stage left and with her eyes implored Roland to come and rescue her. He disappeared through the backstage door and appeared moments later beside her. By this time many people had left their seats and were pouring down the aisles towards her; others joined the press between the front seats and the low stage rail. Roland stretched out his arms and made the usual quieting gestures, but no one took any notice; if anything, the cheers got louder, the foot-stamping more insistent. Clara backed away. Roland gestured to Gail and pulled her onto the stage, shouted something in her ear and resumed his attempts to pacify the exultant audience.

Gail rushed over to Clara and helped her manoeuvre the harp through the rear door to the safety of the backstage area, but even this haven had been breached by eager fans. The backstage crew eventually managed to secure the double door that led into the hall and held the line.

~

Rinzen was probably the only one not to applaud. Even self-controlled Lawrence shouted and clapped, with tears running down both cheeks. Rinzen simply stood and stared at the stage, at the place where Clara Martinelli had been, and allowed the vibrations of her music to subside of their own accord. The nearest he'd ever come to feeling like this was the first time he'd mastered the trance with his brothers, when doors in his mind had opened to allow him to pass into other realms. But this was altogether different. That first note had entered his ears and reverberated throughout his body, preparing the way for his mind to float on a swirl of interlocking notes over a wide, meandering river as it nourished many lands on its passage to a vast ocean. He was part of the waves but not in the sea, travelled as fast as light but also in a state of suspended bliss. And then he was back at the waterfall near Sarmand, down the ravine and into the valley, where the sound changed again, quieter, slower, encircling the monastery like a spring breeze laden with cherry blossom.

The man on the stage raised his voice. 'I'm sorry, ladies and gentlemen, but on this occasion audience members will not be permitted into the Green Room. And I'm afraid Miss Martinelli will not be signing autographs, but she hopes you enjoyed the concert.'

'Enjoyed? I've never experienced anything like it,' a tall thin man said. He, like most of the audience, had tear-stained cheeks and startled eyes.

The man on stage called out over the strangers. 'Hello, Grace. I'm so sorry, but as you will appreciate, Clara is exhausted after that performance and has asked me to apologise for not letting anyone backstage; even you, I'm afraid.'

So that was Clara's mother, and Clara still wouldn't see her.

Rinzen waited for her to turn round, but Lawrence spoke. 'Come on, Rinzen, let's get into the shadows at the back of the hall.'

Now almost empty, the hall looked even more magnificent than when they'd taken their seats. He gazed again at the central figure painted on the half dome over the stage, which Lawrence told him represented the Soul of Music holding the Genius of Harmony, a ball of eternal fire radiating across the world. In truth, though, it didn't matter anymore where he was. Meeting Clara was all that mattered.

After a few minutes, both stage and hall had cleared, and the man who had introduced Clara strode past them into the foyer.

'There goes Roland, Clara's boss at the orchestra – now's our chance.' Lawrence dashed down the aisle with Rinzen at his side. They leapt onto the stage and tried the left-hand door. Locked. But the right-hand door was open and they slipped through it. 'If I remember rightly, the Green Room is just up there.'

'Can I help you, gentlemen?' said a voice behind them.

They turned to face a woman in a long black shiny dress. Her black hair was cut like a helmet, not a single stray wisp against her pale, slender neck.

'Harp transport.' Lawrence smiled at the woman. 'I thought it was this way. Perhaps you can help?'

'I thought David was driving tonight. It was David who collected Miss Martinelli.'

'Yes, poor old Dave, dreadful case of food-poisoning. He asked me and my assistant to step in.'

'I see.' The woman didn't look convinced. 'Please wait here. I'll just check with Mr Peach.'

'No problem.' Lawrence smiled again.

They watched her go through the double doors into the hall.

'This way,' Lawrence said. 'You're very quiet, Rinzen.' But he didn't wait for a reply, just took the three steps in one bound and knocked on the door.

'Who is it?'

'That's Clara,' he whispered, nudging Rinzen ahead of him. And then, 'Transport, miss.'

~

The door opened and Clara found herself looking into the eyes of a man who was so familiar to her, he could have been her twin. She felt an immediate and direct connection with him, as though he was inside her mind already. My God, she thought, it's him! The man from her visions, her dreams, the man she'd seen racing along the mountain ridge.

She ignored Lawrence's chatter, registered it as distant noise, and stared at the other man. He held her gaze, and his silence was so much deeper than a simple absence of noise. She felt no need to greet him, or ask his name or how he came to be there.

'Excuse me, gentlemen.' Roland's voice betrayed frustration, a man about to lose control. 'Oh, it's Lawrence Greene, isn't it? Grace's friend?'

'Yes.'

'Well, Mr Greene, I'm sorry, but Clara is not receiving visitors.' He pointed at Rinzen. 'And who is this man?'

'It's all right, Roland,' Clara said, not moving her eyes. 'Lawrence can stay if he's with this man.'

'I suppose we could do with some extra help getting Clara and the harp into the van,' Roland said. 'Welbeck

Way is crammed with people, so it might be a bit of a scrum.'

The man's eyes did not leave hers.

'His name is Rinzen,' Lawrence said.

They fought their way into the van and slowly drove through the crowd. When they got clear, Clara said, 'What's happened?' and felt as though she'd woken from sleepwalking to find herself in an unfamiliar landscape.

'I think they rather liked *The Harp Awakening*.' Roland's eyes were so wide, they appeared as shining discs in his flushed face.

'From the moment your music started,' Lawrence said, staring out of the van window as if replaying the experience, 'my heart was pounding and I couldn't catch my breath. At first, I was in a panic, how I imagine I'd feel if I were on a plane that was about to crash.' His voice wavered. 'But then I relaxed, opened myself to the sublimity of your music. You took me to a place where there was nothing but … harmony, the sort of utopia I used to imagine being inhabited by tribal communities isolated from the rest of the world, communities untainted by envy, greed or personal ambition. God, Clara, your music made me feel at one with everything, as if there was no Lawrence Greene, no self-conscious being puffed up with pride, no has-been anthropologist wracked with guilt about what happened in Switzerland. You ironed everything out, and for the whole three hours this "I" that is me wasn't there at all!'

He's changed, Clara thought. She'd never heard him say anything as personal as that, let alone in front of so many other people. 'Wow,' she managed.

'Blimey, that was embarrassing,' Lawrence said, returning his gaze to the inside of the van.

Roland, Gail and Rinzen all laughed.

'Well said, Lawrence.' Roland grabbed his shoulder.

Lawrence dropped his eyes, then looked at her again. 'I came tonight in the hope that I'd get the chance to apologise for what I did in Switzerland, and to ask your forgiveness, Clara. I have no excuse for what I did.'

'Lawrence has suffered for his mistake.' Rinzen spoke for the first time, a soft, steady, deep voice with a lovely lilting accent.

She turned to Rinzen, and their eyes locked again. 'And it's brave of him to apologise in front of strangers, to expose himself.' Clara's words came out in a monotone, as though she weren't quite conscious.

'I know his words are truly meant,' Rinzen said. 'Lawrence came to realise that he had interrupted something of great importance. And he was right: your music arises from the depths of the earth and issues forth like the very first spring.'

His eyes smiled in the half light.

The rest of the journey was made in comfortable silence.

After they had escorted Clara and the harp up to her flat, she apologised for not inviting them to stay. 'I think I should sleep now.' She reached for Gail's hand. 'Darling Gail, thank you for persuading me to do the concert.'

'God, yes, thank you, Gail.' Roland was breathless. 'I can still hear the harp.'

They all looked at the magnificent instrument, which seemed to glow and shimmer beside its mistress.

'Goodbye, Lawrence.' Seeing him again had brought on a rush of feelings about her mother. Was she right to continue refusing to see her? She'd think about that later, when they'd all gone. 'I forgive you. You've always been so kind to me. And thank you for ...' She looked at Rinzen. At last he smiled, didn't look quite as stunned.

As Rinzen followed the others out of the flat door, Clara touched his arm with the tips of her fingers. 'Would you come and see me in the morning? I am always here.'

'Of course I will. But as you know, we had already decided that.'

~

When Rinzen walked into the courtyard of Clara's building the following morning, the place was crammed with film crews, men with long-lens cameras and others wrapped up in heavy coats, scarves and gloves to withstand many hours spent outside in the cold. He pushed his way through them and saw Roland guarding the main entrance.

The door into the flat was half open, and Rinzen found Clara in the hall, dressed in a simple white dress similar to the one she'd worn for the concert. She was barefoot, with one arm resting on the curved neck of the harp.

He took two steps forward and held out his right hand. She dropped her left hand into it and it felt like the fresh petal of a mountain rose had fallen into his palm. It tingled on his skin. All his senses were alert to her: the pulse at the tips of her fingers slipped into time with his; her natural scent, untainted by manufactured perfumes, soaked into him; he could even hear the strings of her harp vibrate.

He really did want to say something, so he could hear her voice when she replied, but her eyes forbade it, so he gazed openly at her, completely uninhibited. She let go of the harp, slowly stretched her right hand towards his face and held it there, curved like a raven's wing, a few molecules away from his cheek.

When she touched his face a wing-shaped wave of warm energy flowed down his neck, across his heart, down his right arm and into the hand that held hers. She closed her eyes, releasing his to look at the curve of her lips, the indent below them, the smooth sculpting of her neck. He had never looked so closely at anyone, and now he watched her breasts rise and fall with her shallow breaths. His eyes, as sensitised as his other organs, saw the shape of her nipples through the thin cotton, which set off a new wave of feelings, an ache of longing, a feeling that he was already bound to her and would not survive without her. He closed his own eyes to let the experience run through him, every particle of his being connected to hers.

They stayed like that, suspended and speechless, until Roland rang the entryphone and entered the flat an hour later.

'Ready, Clara?' he said.

'I suppose so.' She turned to Rinzen. 'Will you stay with me?'

'Of course, but stay for what?'

'Someone made a recording of *The Harp Awakening* last night,' Roland said. 'And it's gone viral.'

'What does this "viral" mean?'

'It means whoever recorded it has put it on the internet, and so far, six hundred thousand people have listened to it. We want to make a professional version so people can hear it properly. I've arranged for recording equipment to be brought here, so Clara doesn't have to fight through that lot outside.' He opened his iPad. 'Look, you're the top story on the *Guardian* online. It's the same for all the others.' The banner headline read: 'Harp Sensation'.

A few minutes later, two men brought a portable recording studio up in the lift. It took three trips to bring all the components, which included a three-sided enclosure – half a hexagon – of acoustic panels. They set up two microphones about a metre from the harp, asked Clara to play through all the octaves at varying volumes, adjusted the angle and distance and repeated the test. Moments after the first test began, the noise from the crowd in the yard ceased. The acoustic panels cut out the more distant traffic noise.

Rinzen and Roland sat on the sofa and let themselves disappear into *The Harp Awakening* for the second time in as many days. Close up, the experience was even more intense. Rinzen found himself in the inner temple at Sarmand, with Keung on his left and Amdong on his right. He inhaled the familiar waxy aroma from the lamps mixed with the mustiness that pervaded through winter; the light playing on the temple dome's uneven render created patterns, billowing shapes like clouds rising to the heavens through the hole at its apex. They entered the trance, and the music carried them deeper into the meditation, further from consciousness and more spiritually focused than they had ever been. He travelled with certainty, alone but with his brothers, but this time, without elders, he was the one who led the work on the earth's sinews.

When Clara finished playing, the recording engineer removed his glasses and wiped the tears from his face. His assistant stood motionless, legs apart, mouth open, eyes closed. Roland's hands still rested on his knees, palms up, the forefinger and thumb of each hand forming perfect circles.

Clara's eyes found Rinzen's and sparkled in the winter light.

After some time thus suspended, a great cheer rose from the courtyard, and Roland opened his eyes.

Before he left, the sound engineer promised to have the final mix ready later that day, which would mean they'd be able to start pressing CDs on Monday morning. There was a brief discussion about the cover – it would be the Wigmore poster photograph – and it was agreed that instead of the usual album notes there would just be a back-cover photograph of the harp, the title of the piece, Clara's name, and the make and manufacture date of the Lyon & Healy. It was a great shame that *The Harp Awakening* would have to go on three CDs, but Clara identified two places where the recording could be split.

'I'll bring the final mix round later, as soon as it's done,' Roland said.

'No need,' Clara said. 'I trust you completely when it comes to how it should sound. Anyway, I'm not sure I'd be able to listen to it when I'm not actually playing it.'

~

After Roland and the others left, Clara made ginger tea, wheeled the harp towards Rinzen, and sat next to him on the sofa.

He resisted looking at her eyes and said, 'I live in the Himalaya, in Sarmand monastery with the other brothers. I am a Samudran, and we spend our lives maintaining the rotation of the earth through continuous group meditation. A terrible disease has killed the elders of the three Samudran monasteries, and I have been sent to seek help from a Columbian tribe who also work in the spirit world to maintain the health of the planet. On the way I met Lawrence Greene, who offered his help and brought me to you.'

He felt her eyes on the side of his face and wanted, more than he had ever wanted anything in his life, even more than he wanted the honour of becoming a Samudran elder, to turn and gaze at her. 'Last night, when I heard you play, I was transported back to the land around Sarmand, but today you took me into the inner temple and added a new dimension to our meditation. I felt powerful, in total control, capable of … of anything. And I believe my brothers sensed you there, feeding them, energising them …'

He took a sip of ginger tea and turned towards her. 'Can you hear my heart beating? I can hear yours.'

She leaned towards him and kissed him. He parted his lips to let their tongues touch. An arrow of heat shot through his chest and deep into his stomach. Her lips were a perfect fit. He'd never kissed a woman and wondered if all lips fitted perfectly.

She slowly pulled away, her eyes a few centimetres from his. 'Yes, I can hear your heart beating in time with mine. And no, not all lips fit as perfectly as ours.'

She looked away, down at the floor. 'I shouldn't have kissed you, should I? You're a celibate monk … I'm sorry.'

'And you wish it were not so. And now, in this moment, it is not so.' He put his left arm around her and drew her close, cupped her cheek in his right hand and kissed her. In her embrace he felt fragile, his heart vulnerable and his mind empty.

They lay awake all night in her wide bed, talking and kissing, their naked bodies barely touching, as sensitive and tender as if they were sunburned. His Samudran training had included ways to deal with spontaneous erections, had taught him how to channel sexual desire into the pursuit of the one aim. At first that had been difficult; his whole body had screamed for release and there had been several wet dreams. But sometime in his late teens he had mastered the denial of his body's impulses. Yet here, with Clara in his arms, he did not even try to put his training into practice; he surrendered himself to the full force of sexual desire, a natural extension of the intimacy he'd felt the moment she walked onto the stage of the Wigmore Hall.

As the first light of dawn cast shadows from the harp across Clara's body, they gazed into each other's eyes and made love slowly, with a tenderness that was gentle and revealing. She fell asleep lying across his body, so closely entwined they may have dreamed the same dream.

When they woke, she said, 'Would you hold my harp while I go and shower? It no longer matters whether it is you or I who holds her.'

28

London

'Clara, your eyes are sparkling!' Gail said before she'd even taken off her coat. Then she put her hand to her mouth and blushed. 'I thought you might need some food,' she muttered, and hurried past into the kitchen.

She'd brought the Monday-morning newspapers, all of which had pictures of Clara on their front pages along with comparisons with other instant musical hits: the number of times the pirate recording had been played; the fastest a CD had come out after a recording session; volume and speed of sales. On the inside pages of the broadsheets, critics sought new superlatives to describe and praise the music itself. Clara glanced at the review in the *Financial Times*: 'firm musical articulation ... propulsive and intense rhythms ... phrases multi-dimensional yet precisely shaped ... such rippling beauty'.

'Listen to this, Clara.' Gail read from the *Guardian*. '"Her playing has striking freedom and an appealing spontaneity, and her technique is dazzling." And then, "has all the magic of a whole orchestra, especially in the haunting middle section".'

'Enough!' Clara said, and glanced through the tabloids. They all carried photos of Rinzen, asking, 'Who is this man?' The *Independent* had an exclusive interview with Grace Martinelli, but Clara stopped reading after the first sentence: *I always knew my daughter would be world famous.* 'My mother would never have said that!' The *Express* had cornered Henry, and they too must have made up their copy. The only correctly reported interview seemed to be in the *Times*, in which Julia spoke of her long friendship with Clara, saying that even before *The Harp Awakening* she would have named Clara as one of the best harpists of her generation, but now she wished to revise her opinion and say she was one of the greatest composers and musicians of all time. 'A complete exaggeration,' Clara said. 'But it sounds like Julia.'

Gail made them breakfast and left, and Clara apologised to Rinzen for all the unwanted publicity. While she played, Rinzen meditated. This time he saw, or rather he sensed, that all was not right in Sarmand. He felt Keung's exhaustion, and as he focused on others in the circle, he sensed fragmentation, a lack of unified effort.

When she finished playing, she said, 'You're worried about something, aren't you? You don't have to tell me about it, but I am always here.'

He held the harp while she did her exercises and danced around the room. She twirled and swirled, leapt and rolled, moved with a freedom that mesmerised him. He laughed and drummed softly on the harp's soundboard.

'This is my happiness dancing.' She reached for his hand and pulled him away from the harp; his natural agility made it easy to mesh with her spontaneous movements.

'What about the harp?' he said.

'She'll be OK for a while.' She pulled him close and kissed him on the lips before leading him in an arcing spin to the corner of the room; he lifted her high, leapt several metres, landed with a twist and leapt back. 'You're a dancer, too! Do that again.'

'Not a dancer.' He took off once more. 'Just a simple leaping brother.'

'How far can you jump?'

291

They sat on the floor by the harp, and he told her that mastery of the eighty steps enabled Samudrans to leap deep into the trance.

~

When Rinzen meditated that evening, Clara's harp guided him into the inner temple once again. There were only five brothers present, and three of them were juniors who had only recently been elected as seniors. The meditation would be too weak to have any effect, and he began to wonder whether the wasting disease had returned to claim more lives. Then Keung and Amal joined the circle. Before Keung closed his eyes, Rinzen saw that his light-hearted friend had worry lines on his forehead, dark sacks beneath dull eyes, and was too exhausted to feel Rinzen's presence. But something else was happening – Clara's music was in the temple. The notes swirled around the brothers and he sensed their heartbeats steady, then strengthen; their blood flowed freely – lubricating, rejuvenating, healing – as they succumbed to the chords and cadences, let the music lead the way out of consciousness into pure spirit. Soon, the last remnant of fragmentation evaporated into harmony.

When Rinzen emerged from the trance six hours later, Clara was seated on the floor in front of him, looking at his face and smiling.

'You came with me into the inner temple, your awakening harp awakened my brothers and restored harmony. Could you feel that you were there?'

'I was following, not leading.' Clara caressed the harp strings.

He watched her hands flow through the octaves, barely touching the strings, occasionally alighting on particular notes that pierced him first in his chest, then in his feet, next in his stomach, his thighs, his lips, his buttocks, his balls. He tried to stop the erection, but on she played, the almost inaudible notes overwhelming his will, forcing him to let go, to follow not lead. He lay on his back on the bare wood floor, and every muscle tingled.

She undressed him slowly, and covered his body with the lightest kisses, soft as the harp notes. By the time she guided him inside her, every atom of his being was so sensitised that he had no thoughts, and there was nothing to impede the feeling of pure joy. Deep in her eyes he saw lights shining in a clear night sky and knew he was looking at the universe. At infinity.

He fell into a deep sleep and woke unable to recall his dreams. There was a pillow under his head, a blanket over his body, and Clara was draped over the harp as though she were carved of the same wood. He thought, 'She is as one with her harp,' and knew that they had made love for the last time.

He thought about what Keung would say when he told him he had made love to a woman, wondered how he would explain that it was nothing to do with animal lust, that as soon as he heard Clara playing the first note of *The Harp Awakening* he knew she had achieved purity. He would try to tell Keung what it had felt like to look into her eyes in the doorway of her Wigmore Hall dressing room; how they were bodyless spirits who intermingled, shared emotions, explored each other's being without the need for words or even thoughts; how it had become inevitable for them to share every intimacy – mental, spiritual and physical.

A thought struck him with such force that his whole body jolted. Would Clara have the same overwhelming effect on other Samudrans? Would Keung and Clara experience the same bond and also make love? Would he be jealous, or would his training allow him to overcome such possessive sentiments?

But what was he thinking? Keung would never even meet Clara. It would be against all Samudran tradition to allow a woman into the monastery, let alone allow her to play her harp there ... But she was already there in some form, wasn't she? She had come with him to the inner temple when he meditated and ... and she hadn't seemed to find that strange, had seen it as perfectly natural.

He couldn't ask her, could he?

He sprang to his feet from his prone position, walked towards the dawn light that was shining through the linen curtains across the balcony doors, and stepped outside. The unfamiliar sounds of a city waking up – intermittent traffic, the artificial chirps of a reversing truck, the scrape and rasp of metal shutters rolling up – clanged in his ears. He closed his eyes on the grey sky and breathed in the icy air, stretched his toes on the rough stone floor, then flipped into a headstand with arms outstretched.

As the blood flowed around his skull, the noise subsided and his thoughts became coherent. The bond between him and Clara was unique, but he was a Samudran destined for a life of meditation with his brothers. What was the future for Clara, who could never experience such cohesion again? Although she was perfectly content to play her harp in solitude, had he, by going to her after her concert, condemned her to a lifetime of longing? Unless ...

'Hello, man on the balcony, what's your name?'

One of the journalists must have arrived early.

'I can see your feet, so I know you're there.'

He flipped onto his feet and retreated into the flat.

'Who was that shouting?' Clara stretched her arms above her head.

'One of the newspaper men, I think.' He held her hands above her head to aid her stretch.

'That feels good,' she said.

He guided her arms in an arc to her sides, ran his hands up them, massaged the muscles as he went, then massaged her shoulders, her neck and finally her head. She moaned and sighed, and he sensed she wanted him to explore other parts of her body.

'I'll make tea,' he said, but did not stop pressing points on her head with the tips of his fingers.

'I know that was the last time we will make love, Rinzen. Please don't worry about me – you have become part of me and I part of you, and this will be how it is for eternity. It doesn't matter if you are here or in Sarmand, we will be together, and I – like you – do not ask for anything more.'

'Can you see all my thoughts?'

'Oh, that feels so good. My whole head is shivering.' She closed her eyes and released a long breath. 'No, not everything. Hardly anything really.'

~

Lawrence telephoned with news about Sarmand. The army was still blocking access to all the monasteries; every third day all the brothers were required to stand on the monastery walls to be counted, and so far, there had been no more deaths from the wasting disease.

'I sense all is not right with the meditation,' Rinzen said. 'And I fear it was the wrong decision to promote the juniors before they were ready. If it is the same with the other monasteries …'

'Being confined to the monastery must be very difficult, especially as there is no support allowed from the community,' Lawrence said. 'Things are bound to be difficult until the blockade is lifted, but there is talk of that day coming very soon. After all, it's over two months since the last elder at Sarmand died.'

'Elder Kwato.' Rinzen saw an image of Kwato laughing at the sight of Keung standing on his head while Rinzen balanced one-handed on Keung's foot, the other waving at his mentor.

'Now, do you need anything? I have to come over anyway – I'd prefer to speak to you about your travel arrangements face to face.'

Clara suggested he come the next day.

~

Clara watched Rinzen meditate. She played softly, carefully avoided rhythms from *The Harp Awakening*, knowing that she would also go into a trance. She seemed to be able to follow him into his temple and add her music to the energy those remarkable brothers generated. That she could somehow join in must have something to do with what had passed between her and Rinzen, the like of which she had never even glimpsed, let alone experienced with such force, such intimacy, a union without inhibitions in what they said, or thought or did with their bodies. There were instantly no secrets, no deceptions; she would for example, happily let him watch her shit, or menstruate, or … or anything. As she'd lain next to him that first night, not touching, she'd sensed every inch of his beautiful body and had been so exhilarated that when they rolled together in the morning it was if there had already been hours and hours of foreplay.

This time she wanted to look at him while he was in his mountains with his brothers. She had felt the ache of his longing but also knew she'd helped him overcome the obstacles of time and distance to enter his temple unimpeded. She took it slowly, let her eyes linger on his physique, each toe, each muscular finger. She looked at her own muscular fingers and smiled. Even their bodies were a similar colour, a light tan that never darkened in the sun and certainly never blistered. He was immensely strong, but his body was lean, not musclebound like a weightlifter's. She spent the longest time looking at his unblemished face. With every muscle at rest, he exuded peace.

Her skin tingled as she stared at his face, felt her own expression loosen, and let her accepting eyes travel over his forehead and into the gaps between strands of his soft hazelnut hair. She wandered across his skull, around his ears and focused on the pulse in his neck – blip, blip, blip. Why did she need to move her head to stay focused on the pulse? She blinked, looked at his cross-legged body and noticed his bottom was twenty centimetres off the floor. It didn't surprise her.

Sometime later, while she was conducting an in-depth inspection of his stomach – with particular attention on the navel – his eyes snapped open and a smile spread across his face like a spring crocus opening in the morning sun.

~

Lawrence had asked a few of his less salubrious contacts about obtaining a false passport for Rinzen, but none of them could help him. 'It would be difficult, though not impossible, to board that ship to Columbia without papers,' he told Rinzen the following morning, 'but a passport would make things a lot easier.'

'What about all this publicity, Lawrence?' Clara said. 'Roland says that Rinzen's photo is in every paper. Do you think the police might want to know who he is?'

'Well, obviously it would be better if there weren't any photos, but the police are unlikely to look into it off their own bat.' Lawrence stared at the closed curtains and frowned.

'Camera drones,' Clara said.

'For God's sake!' Lawrence sighed. 'At least they haven't got hold of your telephone number. But we really do need to get him some convincing identity papers.'

Clara hoped Lawrence would come up with another option, but when he fell silent, she had no choice. 'I may know someone who could help.' She would have to speak to

Henry after all, and in person. And then, if Rinzen got a passport, he would be free to leave. And he did need to leave; he was a Samudran, after all, and nothing was more important than that. She had told him that they would be together even if they were continents apart, but what would it really be like when he'd gone, when she could no longer touch him, look at him, smell him, when all that was left were images conjured while she played her harp like a mermaid isolated on the last crag in a vast ocean?

'I'll call Henry now, ask him to come round.' Assuming, of course, that he would agree to see her after all these months.

She wheeled the harp into the bedroom and rang his number.

'Clara! God, Clara, thank you,' Henry said, which made no sense to her. 'I've never had so many customers, I mean actual paying customers. How are you, Clara? Ever since that *Evening Standard* article and their bloody misquoting. Did you see it? Anyway, enough of that, how are you? Stupid question, you must be—'

'Henry, you're not making any sense. Please just slow down.'

'Right, yes. Sorry about the article. You know I would never say anything like that, don't you?'

'Yes, I guessed. Henry, I need a favour.'

'Anything, name it.'

She put the phone down and almost ran with the harp into the other room. 'He's coming over right now. I think it would be best if I saw him alone. Let's assume he can help, Lawrence, so maybe you could show Rinzen where to get passport photos done?'

'Old Street Underground has a booth, I think. Is there a back way out? For Rinzen, I mean.'

Clara showed them the fire escape into the yard of the building behind. She pointed at the alleyway that led to the street. 'Wait, look, there's someone there.'

'And he has a camera.' Rinzen turned to Lawrence. 'I'll go over that roof and see you in the next street.'

He climbed onto the fire-escape handrail and Clara watched open-mouthed as he leapt twenty metres onto the first roof and immediately sprang onto the next. He stopped four roofs away, turned and pointed down. Lawrence nodded, dashed down the fire escape, shoved past the photographer and disappeared into the alley.

Henry arrived a few minutes later, carrying a bag of food, which he dropped on the floor so he could hug her with both arms. He held her for a full minute without saying anything, then pulled half away and looked at her face.

'Thanks for coming over. Coffee?'

'I'll make it ... Sorry, you must be an expert in one-handed living by now.'

Good, she wouldn't know how to handle a sentimental Henry.

'I'm sure everyone's saying it to you, but that concert was so powerful, so emotional, so ... I don't know ... bloody mind-blowing. This is going to sound strange, but when I heard you play at the Wigmore, I went into a sort of dream – hah, you know all about dreams! Sorry. Anyway, I was back in my dad's repro-furniture factory. I mean really there.'

'You mean that narrow warehouse on Leonard Street?'

'Yeah, so narrow we had to do each process on a different floor. Anyway, first the bandsaw started up on the ground floor – you know, the one with the high-pitched tone that changes with each different type of wood. In the dream, the saw was in harmony with your ... would you call it multifaceted? ... music, and as I moved up the building the same thing happened with the spindle-moulder, the thicknesser, the circular saw, the linisher, even the bloody lathe was at it. When you finished, I was crying my eyes out.' He was wearing his serious Henry look. 'Thank you, Clara, for taking me back to my childhood.'

'I'm pleased you liked it, Henry.'

'Liked it! I've been listening to it all the time.'

'There's a proper recording coming out tomorrow.'

'I know, I've secured ten copies – all for me. Now, what's this favour? Did you want me to see if I can get rid of those vultures outside? I know some lads who—'

'No, thanks, it's not that, but it is illegal.' She paused, wondered how to explain Rinzen.

'Interesting. Unexpected, but interesting.'

'Lawrence came back from India with a Himalayan monk who doesn't have any identity papers. He needs—'

'The question-mark man in the papers?'

'Yes.' Her head felt suddenly hot. Did it show, this blushing? 'He needs to go to Columbia, on a sort of mission, and ...'

'He needs a passport.'

She nodded, looked into his eyes for the first time. He stayed silent, looked back, didn't seem to know what to do with his eyes. 'You've changed, Clara. I mean that nicely. You are so calm, in control.'

She smiled at him. He reached for her hands and smiled back.

'I only play the one thing these days. I've been playing it for six months or more.'

'Right.' He turned away, pretended to look at her harp. He was either trying not to get wound-up that she was still holding onto the harp or he felt vulnerable under her gaze. It didn't matter which. Henry belonged in her past, to the old Clara, the uncertain, neurotic Clara. He scanned the room. 'I see you got shot of the furniture. Along with almost everything else, it seems.'

'Yes, sorry, I needed some money. Do you mind?'

'No, not at all. It was yours to do with as you pleased.' He looked back at her. 'I do know someone who might be able to help. I haven't seen him for ages, but I think I know where to find him. Can't promise, but I will try. Tonight.'

'Thanks.' She squeezed his hands. 'How's my mother? Have you seen her?'

'Grace gave me this bag of food. She couldn't face that mob down there. She wants to see you, seemed a bit desperate. Heartbroken about pulling that stunt.' He shook both her hands, as if he were trying to jolt them back to how it used to be. 'And she lost Lawrence.'

Clara nodded. She would think what to do about her mother later. 'Thanks for coming.' She let go of him, started to wheel the harp into the hall.

'Right, yes, best be going. Sure you don't want rid of those parasites downstairs?'

'If you mean heavy stuff, then no thanks, Henry.'

He kissed her on the cheek and turned towards the stairs.

She went over to the balcony curtains to listen, couldn't help but smile as Henry let fly at the paparazzi.

'Why don't you lot just bugger off and leave the maestro alone. You should be ashamed of yourselves, harassing her like this. What's that, a fucking drone? Give me that controller, you arsehole. That's right, run, you bastard, and don't come back. I'll be watching you lot. Don't point that camera at me! I said no pictures. Jesus, you're a bunch of leeches. If Clara Martinelli wasn't so nice, I'd have the lot of you. Now just fuck off.'

She heard the journalists and photographers shuffle out of the courtyard, but she knew they'd be back.

The bell sounded with the correct code, and to her joy she heard Gail's lovely lilting on the entryphone. She hardly had time to greet her before Lawrence returned and let Rinzen in through the fire-escape door.

Clara accepted Gail's offer to cook dinner, and for a few wonderful hours they were just four good friends laughing and eating, talking about art and literature, about ancient gods and what it was like to be a student, about anything and everything that had nothing to do with *The Harp Awakening* sensation or Rinzen's quest. Lawrence had delivered the passport photographs to Henry as agreed, so even that issue needed no further discussion. Clara managed to resist slipping into her composition to play requests from Gail and Lawrence, and Rinzen – after much begging and pleading – entertained them with his impossible acrobatics.

When the others left, Rinzen and Clara showered together and then lay naked in the bed, fingers touching as they slept.

29

London

Early on Thursday, release day for the CD, Clara glimpsed the clear blue morning through a small gap in the curtains. She longed to go outside and gaze at the sky, but, even though it was only eight o'clock, she could hear the leeches grumbling in the courtyard.

Roland came at 9am, hugged her, handed over a copy of the CD, and then paced back and forth across the living room. 'Brace yourself, Clara.' He had dark shadows below his eyes and his hair was uncombed, which wasn't like him at all. Either he'd drunk too much coffee or he was beyond exhaustion. 'The record company has received five hundred thousand pre-orders for *The Harp Awakening*. They're producing two million and expect to sell out within two weeks. It might even outsell Band Aid's 'Do They Know It's Christmas', which sold three million copies in five weeks.'

Clara could see that this statement was designed to impress and shock, but she wasn't sure what to make of it. She had only played the concert to get enough money to pay her debts and have a little left to live on, and she'd hoped that people with a specialist interest in the harp might enjoy it. But these numbers meant that all sorts of people, many of whom never listened to instrumental music, liked *The Harp Awakening* enough to pay £10 for a CD. Who were they? Did they even know what instrument they were listening to? Something nagged at the edge of her mind, just out of reach. She smiled at Rinzen, who seemed content to stand against the brick wall and watch Roland pace the room.

'Radio 3 will play all three CDs tomorrow night without a break.'

'That's good,' Clara said.

'Good? It's unbelievable, Clara. Has never happened before.' Roland was clearly frustrated by her lack of enthusiasm. 'You are a worldwide sensation and will soon be a very wealthy woman.'

She wasn't at all sure she wanted to be a worldwide sensation. She already felt that she no longer owned her own life. Press, fans, and no doubt some fanatics filled the streets around her flat; miniature drones, some no bigger than a fifty-pence piece, tried to spy on her through the windows; people constantly rang the bell; and every time she was shown a newspaper, there was another story about her. Her refusal to do any interviews meant that journalists resorted to dredging through her past, harassed her few friends, and then penned outrageous, invented stories. They wrote profiles of her mother, her father, even her teachers at the Royal College of Music.

'I know you've never played just for the money, but you do realise that for each CD sale you get £1?'

What did she need so much money for? Her requirements were simple now: to keep her flat going and maintain her basic diet, that was all.

'Did you hear what I said, Clara?'

'Sorry, I was just thinking …'

'I said that the Albert Hall want you to do some concerts. What do you think?'

She looked at him, hoped her expression was blank. 'Can I think about it?' She would not do any more concerts, but if she said that to Roland, he would spend all morning trying to persuade her, when all she wanted was to be alone with Rinzen.

Roland gave Rinzen a copy of the CD, promised to keep Clara closely informed about sales figures, and – finally – left the flat.

'This is a very good photograph of you.' Rinzen held the CD up to the light above the dining table. 'I think the photographer liked you very much.'

'She is a lovely person – she even dried my hair.' Clara moved close to him and looked at the CD cover.

'Although we do not have a device for playing compact discs at Sarmand, I will cherish this gift.'

'Will you go to Sarmand straight from Columbia?' She hadn't intended to bring up the topic of his departure, but whatever was nagging at her seemed to demand it.

'All is not well in Sarmand. I feel it when I meditate. I feel my brothers calling to me. I should go to them, but I was instructed to go and see the Kogi, to ask for their help.' He looked up from the CD. 'Do you think there is any point in my going to see the Kogi?'

Surely, he was thinking out loud? 'Do you really want my opinion?'

'Yes, please. You have attained purity – the clarity of your name. What you think is very important to me.'

She linked her arm into his, held his hand and guided him to the sofa. 'I think you already know the answer. Perhaps you just can't see it clearly because your discipline, your obedience, won't let you.'

'Are you reading my mind again?'

'Maybe!' She laughed, plucked a few notes with her free hand. 'You wanted to do what the elders told you to do, but then you met Lawrence, who knows so much more about the Kogi. Lawrence told you that the Samudrans do similar work to the Kogi, but go about it in a different way.' She tried to recall exactly what Lawrence had said. 'Didn't he say that the Kogi *mamas* work in the spirit world when they go into their periodic extended trances together, but the Samudrans use focused group meditation all day, every day, without stopping?' Rinzen nodded. 'Then I can't see how a Kogi *mama* could take over from a Samudran elder in the inner temple.'

'So, you are reading my mind! And it would take me many months to go to Columbia and then all the way back to Sarmand. I fear that in that time the meditation cycle at Sarmand will be broken beyond repair.'

'You know, Rinzen, maybe we both need to have more confidence in our own decisions.' Clara smiled at him. 'I used to make hardly any decisions without my mother's approval – especially about my career. But since ... since Switzerland, I've been forced to make my own choices. And that has to be a good thing, right? Even if I sometimes get it wrong.'

Rinzen eyes widened. 'I see what you're saying. On my travels, I've been forced to act without an elder's guidance – and I've made plenty of wrong judgements – but I no longer immediately think "What would Kwato do?" when something presents itself. Like ...'

'Like what happened between us?'

Rinzen smiled, nodded.

They sat in silence for minutes, maybe longer. She thought again about what life would be like without Rinzen by her side. She would be like a moth trapped in a lampshade, circling round her harp, prevented by her fame from going anywhere, even onto her own balcony. Fame, the curse her father warned her about, had come to her when she least wanted it.

'Will you play for me?' Rinzen unlocked their hands and put his at his heart centre. 'As long as you play and I meditate, we will keep the cycle going.'

Clara stood, bowed to him and wheeled the harp towards the stool in the centre of the room.

~

Over the next few days, while they waited for the passport, they fell into an easy rhythm: Clara played the harp while Rinzen meditated; they slept and ate when they were tired or hungry; and the only interruptions were the occasional visit from Gail bringing food or from Roland to report on sales and ask about the Albert Hall concerts.

About a week passed before Lawrence rang the bell and delivered the British passport.

'I have decided to return to Sarmand, Lawrence,' Rinzen said. 'I must go and help my brothers maintain the meditation.'

God, he's decided, thought Clara. I hope I didn't push him too hard.

'But you've come such a long way, overcome so many obstacles …'

'Yes, and without your help I would have stowed away on a ship bound for Columbia, been caught and thrown off in Djibouti, and then who knows what would have become of me.'

'You would have found a way.'

'My time has not been wasted, quite the reverse. I have seen what is happening in the world, and the challenge we face to correct it; I have met many remarkable people, and been humbled by their generosity and kindness; of these, my chance meeting with you was the most fortunate. Your honesty and openness, your willingness to share your knowledge and wisdom, let me see things differently. And then you introduced me to Clara—'

She willed him not to say any more, butted in with 'I'll make some tea,' and walked towards the kitchen.

Rinzen ignored her silent plea. 'Clara and her music have shown me the way. *The Harp Awakening* has a profound effect on my meditation and lets me think clearly. And now I know for sure that I must return to Sarmand.'

'And the Kogi?' Lawrence said.

'It is good to know they toil without rest, but although they are kindred spirits, they travel a different road to the Samudrans.' When Lawrence, typically, asked for no further explanation, Rinzen continued. 'Once more I find myself asking for your help. Do you think there is a ship going back to Mumbai?'

'I can find that out very easily, especially as you have a passport now.'

'Couldn't he just fly back? I have some money now, and—'

Lawrence interrupted her. 'The problem would be at the other end. We must assume Rinzen is still a wanted man. If he goes by ship, he can sneak ashore in Mumbai.'

'I suppose it might be more difficult to find out who those men in black were who chased me from Barnang to Igatpuri?'

Clara looked up from making the tea. Why hadn't he mentioned these men in black to her?

'As it happens, I did look into that,' Lawrence said. 'They were almost certainly Indian Special Forces, occasionally requested by the Nepalese Army to carry out covert operations. I would hazard a guess that they were asked to eliminate anyone who broke the army cordon.'

'What – kill them?' Clara shouted the words.

'I'm afraid so,' Lawrence said. 'We will have to be careful.'

'What is this "we", Lawrence?' Rinzen said. 'You must stay here, make things right with Grace.'

Clara couldn't recall seeing Lawrence blush before.

'Sorry, I shouldn't have spoken.' Rinzen bowed to Lawrence and walked across to Clara to carry the tea tray.

They sat in a row on the sofa and drank the tea in silence, but Clara could feel the room filling with questions, tangled thoughts, high and low emotions. She finished her tea, set up her harp in front of them, and played Vivaldi's

'Spring'. Both men rested their heads against the wall and closed their eyes.

When she finished, Rinzen went to the bathroom and Lawrence said, 'That is my second favourite piece of music. Thank you. My friendship with your mother will have to wait until Rinzen is safely back in Sarmand. There is nothing more important than that. Without the Samudrans, where would we be?'

In that instant, Clara knew she would be going to Sarmand with them.

30

London

A few days after he'd delivered the passport, Lawrence phoned Clara to say that there was a cargo ship bound for Mumbai departing in two weeks and that he had reserved cabins for himself and Rinzen.

'What about me?' Clara said. She had spent many hours thinking about the implications of her decision to go to Sarmand, but it was only now, at the mention of an actual departure date, that she realised she hadn't asked Rinzen if she could go with him.

'With your harp, I assume?' Lawrence said.

'Naturally. But I'd better talk to Rinzen first.'

A frown had spread across Rinzen's brow like desert sand rippled by the wind, and she hoped this was a sign of confusion rather than disapproval. She replaced the handset, and faced him.

'I do not want to leave you, Clara, but I have no choice.' The frown now seemed permanently engraved. 'I know you would like me to stay, so you have asked Lawrence not to make my reservation. But—'

'No, wait, that wasn't what we were talking about. I fell into the trap of thinking too much. I've been projecting myself into the future after all this time living in the present, even though I know it's pointless to worry about what is yet to happen.'

'I don't understand.'

She took a deep breath, said, 'Will you let me come with you to Sarmand?' and wondered what she would do if he said it was impossible for a woman to enter the temple, especially a foreign woman. She hadn't even considered that until now, but the longer he remained silent, the more inevitable it seemed. The frown unravelling into his hair was a sign, but of what?

Finally, frownless, he spoke. 'I have dreamed of you playing your harp in the inner temple while I meditate with my brothers, but I dared not ask you to make such a sacrifice.' His eyes widened, he jumped up and rushed towards her. 'Will you really come? Really?'

'Yes! Yes! Yes!'

He leapt in the air, did three backward flips, then in one bound landed on his knees before her and bowed his head. 'Thank you, maestro.'

'Don't do that, Rinzen!' She laughed, knelt in front of him, pressed her head against his, unclasped his praying hands and kissed his fingertips. 'We're not ready to say goodbye just yet.'

'You're right, of course you are right. You're really going to come to Sarmand, to play in the inner temple? I can't quite—'

'Neither can I.' His forehead seemed to be melting into hers. 'But what will your brothers say?'

'I'm certain they have already heard your harp in the temple, even though they can have no idea where such music is coming from. But I suppose …'

'Yes?"

'It is possible there will be some resistance – after all, not even the Mothers are allowed inside – but we face disaster if something is not done, and if that means breaking some traditions, then I'm sure my fellow seniors will agree that we will lose nothing by trying.'

Clara cupped his head with her hands, buried her fingers in his short hair. 'Promise me that if your brothers do not want me to stay, you will let me leave immediately.'

'I'll show you the wonders of the mountains: we'll bathe in clear water pools where the rocks shine in all the colours of the rainbow; we'll climb to the high mountains and breathe the clean air while eagles circle around us; we'll lie on the soft earth and gaze at a million stars.'

'Promise me, Rinzen.'

'I promise, Clara.'

~

Two days later, Gail handed Clara an envelope. 'A man outside handed it to me, and as it had a photograph of that ship Lawrence talked about, the *Oracle*, on the outside, I thought I'd better take it.'

Clara read it aloud.

Dear Ms Martinelli,

We have a mutual acquaintance, the man whom the tabloid press are keen to identify. Since meeting him on board the Oracle, I have discovered his true identity, but I do not wish to be the one to give the tabloids the information they so desperately desire.

I hope you will agree to meet me to discuss what can be done to maintain secrecy. I look forward to receiving your telephone call.

Yours sincerely,
Gavin Williams

She looked up from the letter, and said, at the same moment as Gail, 'Blackmail.'

'That man was on the ship,' Rinzen said. 'He asked many questions and was not friendly.'

Lawrence came straight over and telephoned Williams. He agreed that he and Rinzen would meet him at an address in Bethnal Green the following morning.

When Williams answered the door of the small house, he looked, if anything, even more untidy than he had on the *Oracle*: a baggy grey sweatshirt hung around his scrawny neck, and his navy trousers sagged at the knees and rippled over dirty, worn-out slippers.

'Hello, Lawrence, so glad you could come. And Arnesh, or should I say Rinzen? Well, this is almost a reunion, is it not?' Williams's mouth twisted into a forced grin. 'If you wouldn't mind removing your shoes – my sister is a bit fussy about shoes in her house. She's out, by the way.'

He led them down the narrow hall and into a small living room. 'Please wait here while I make us some coffee.'

He returned a few minutes later and handed them mugs of instant coffee. He didn't ask if they wanted milk or sugar.

'What is it you want, Mr Williams?' Lawrence said.

'It seems to me that the *Sun* – or the *Express* or *Mail* for that matter – would pay a goodly sum to learn the truth about our fugitive monk here, the fact that he might be carrying a deadly disease and is wanted in both Nepal and India. And I can't see the Metropolitan Police ignoring such a report, can you?'

'Rinzen did not leave his monastery to avoid the disease that killed all the elders.' Lawrence approached to within a foot of Williams and stared him in the eyes. 'He is a highly trained Samudran brother whose lifelong task is to maintain the stability of the earth for the benefit of all, including leeches like you. He does not carry the wasting disease, as the Indian authorities well know. Following the death of all the elders, he was despatched to seek help from others who share the Samudran calling. If you report his presence here, you will jeopardise his mission and in so doing will be

313

directly responsible for causing irreparable harm to the planet.'

He stepped back a pace, as though to avoid a bad smell. 'Are you prepared to take on that responsibility, *Mr* Williams?'

'What a load of spiritual gobbledygook.' Williams bared his nicotine-stained teeth as he faced Rinzen. 'Maintaining the stability of the earth, my arse. These monks are the leeches, not me. They take food, clothing, money and anything else they want from the peasants, making the poor even poorer, all on spurious spiritual grounds. I can't stand such parasites.' He turned back to Lawrence, his mouth in a grimace.

Williams continued to speak, but Rinzen didn't listen. He would not waste his breath explaining to this real parasite how the Samudrans worked with all the villages around them, how they helped with medical matters, taught the illiterate to read and write, ran courses in building and engineering, and so much more. He felt the man's hatred as a physical sensation in his stomach, a burning lump that gained intensity with each second.

'Stop!' he said. 'Stop speaking now.' Both men turned towards him. 'He's not worth talking to, Lawrence. Ask him what he wants, so we can decide whether to give it to him. But as you know, I would prefer to let him do what he likes with his information, rather than give him anything. I have evaded capture before and will do so again.'

'Oh, he speaks, does—'

'Didn't you hear Rinzen?' Lawrence squeezed Williams's jaw with his right hand. 'Stop ranting and answer the question.'

'OK, OK. But don't think of harming me. I've lodged the information with my solicitor, with instructions to publish if anything happens to me.'

'What – do – you – want?' Lawrence squeezed a little harder with each word.

'I need money. I don't own a house or a car, all I have is a crummy little rented flat off Roman Road.'

Lawrence released him. Williams rubbed his jaw.

'I don't want much, just one day's worth of Clara Martinelli's royalties from the sale of her CD. I calculate that to be two hundred thousand pounds.'

'That's ridiculous. The *Sun* wouldn't pay anything like that, and you know it.'

'By this time next week,' Williams said.

'Impossible. Royalties take at least three weeks to be processed.'

'Nonsense. I checked. Payments will start on Monday.'

'And what's to stop you taking Clara's money and then selling the story anyway?' Lawrence said.

'You'll just have to take my word for it, won't you?'

'No, we won't have to.' Rinzen picked up a thick log from the fire basket, gripped it with both hands and snapped it in two. He strode from the room, with Lawrence close behind, retrieved his shoes from the mat and left the house, preferring to replace his shoes on the street rather than spend another second in Williams's company.

'Shall we walk, Lawrence? I need to walk.'

~

'You two seem unusually cheerful considering you've just come from dealing with a blackmailer,' Clara said as she and Gail welcomed Lawrence and Rinzen back into the flat.

'That's because we've thought of a way to stop him,' Rinzen said.

Clara raised a quizzical eyebrow.

Lawrence took over. 'We will simply take an earlier ship – from Rotterdam. We can drive through the Channel Tunnel, then on to Rotterdam, and take the next ship going east. If we —'

'Isn't that a bit risky?' Gail said. 'Someone might see Clara's name on the passenger list and alert the press. What about flying?'

'Even riskier to show up at an airport pushing a bloody great harp,' Lawrence said.

'Not if you go by private jet.' Gail pulled a brochure from JBL Airlines out of her bag. 'Eighty thousand pounds. Gulfstream GV. Take off from Biggin Hill, land at a place called Muzaffarpur in northern India, quite near the Nepalese border. Small airports, all very low-key. Look, it says here: "Discretion assured" – that's code for "no leaks to the press". It gives rock stars and politicians privacy to go where they like without being hounded by the paparazzi.'

'But eighty thousand pounds?' Clara said.

'Well,' Lawrence said, 'Williams is right about one thing: the CD is selling at the rate of two hundred thousand a day, and you get a pound for every one.'

'God, we are rich, aren't we?'

'No, Clara, you're rich,' Gail said.

'I won't touch a penny unless you all agree to share it with me. Without you, all of you, and Roland of course, none of this would be happening.'

No one spoke.

'Well, unless you all agree to share the royalties equally, I won't have the pleasure of flying by private jet to Muzzawhatever.'

'If you put it like that.' Gail laughed, hugged Clara, whispered, 'You are the kindest best friend ever.'

Lawrence grumbled his agreement, and Rinzen nodded, his eyes bright, no doubt anticipating his return to Sarmand. Clara noticed a smile slowly spreading across Lawrence's face. 'You're thinking something sly, aren't you?'

'It just occurred to me that if we can get to India before Williams realises we've gone, Roland could announce Rinzen's identity to the press before that slimy little sod has a chance to sell his story to the tabloids.'

~

Two days later, Roland had two boxed harp trolleys delivered to Clara's flat. In the afternoon he placed an anonymous call to the *Daily Mail* saying that Miss Martinelli was fed up with all the media attention and would be leaving the flat to go somewhere more private. He hung up without telling them where. A black van with no side windows pulled into the courtyard at 5pm. A woman dressed in a navy overcoat, headscarf and sunglasses got into the van with the Salvi Diana harp. The van drove off, followed by some of the paparazzi on scooters. An hour later, another van arrived and the same thing happened, this time with the second Salvi. Those journalists who'd remained behind, having figured that the first van had been a decoy, now assumed that this one had to be Clara Martinelli and duly chased after the second van.

Roland, Lawrence, Clara and Rinzen waited in the darkened flat until 4am, when a third van reversed quietly into the yard and drove them and Clara's harp to Biggin Hill Airport. Lawrence regularly checked the rear window to see if they were being followed, but once they were past the Isle of Dogs and had crossed the river, he let out a long breath and announced that he was satisfied they were in the clear. 'That was a bloody good ruse with the two harps, Roland.'

'Thanks, but it's Gail and Frances we really need to thank, for agreeing to drive around all night in the back of those vans.'

'And I hardly know Frances,' Clara said. 'Oh hell, Roland, I haven't told my mother I'm going to Sarmand. Would you ...?'

'Of course. Without the exact details, naturally.' Roland grinned at her.

Clara wondered why Rinzen was so quiet, so serious. Perhaps he was worried about flying? With Lawrence and

Roland close by, she couldn't ask him, but she shifted her position holding the harp and rested her head on his shoulder.

He put his arm around her, pulled her close, and whispered, 'Until we're in the air, we must be very careful.'

She squeezed his leg. If Rinzen sensed danger, you took notice.

Biggin Hill was empty save for one man standing ten metres from the entrance. A couple of airport staff sat at desks across the hall.

'What are you doing here?' Lawrence asked the slim man with short, white-blonde hair.

'Thanks for coming, George.' Rinzen shook the man's hand.

His tan leather jacket was so tight, Clara wondered he could move his arms.

He grinned, blushed, didn't seem to know where to look. 'Of course, Rinzen. Anything. And my friend is outside, as you asked.'

'May I introduce you to Clara Martinelli and Roland Peach?' Rinzen said.

'Miss Martinelli, what an honour. I can't stop listening to *The Harp Awakening*, it's so enchanting.'

'Thank you, Mr ...?'

'George Campbell. I met Rinzen and Lawrence on the ship.'

'What's all this about, Rinzen?' Lawrence said.

'I think you call it an insurance policy.'

'Against what, exactly?'

Rinzen, who was looking over Lawrence's shoulder, said, 'Against him.' He grabbed Lawrence's arm and whispered. 'Leave him to me.'

'Who? Oh!'

'Mr Williams, I see you found us. Very clever. How did you do it?' Rinzen walked towards the scowling man.

'Easy. I put a little tracer bug in Lawrence's shoe when I went to make coffee at my sister's house. You won't get far, you know. I'll call the police and the airline will have to tell them your destination, client privacy or not.' The scowl had turned into a sort of leer.

'That's against the law, isn't it? To place a bug in Lawrence's shoe?' Rinzen was perfectly calm.

'So what? No one can prove it was me. You are all fools.'

Rinzen grabbed Williams's right hand and shook it as though he were a friend. 'It's so good of you to come and see us off, Gavin, but there was really no need.' He put his other hand on the man's neck, and George caught him as his legs crumpled. At that moment, another, much taller, leather-jacketed man strode into the terminal. Unlike George, he had the chest and biceps of a weightlifter.

George pulled out his phone, touched the screen, and held it up so they could all hear: '... Easy. I put a little tracer bug in Lawrence's shoe ...' He turned it off, nodded to the others. 'That should do it. Come on, Gavin, I told you you shouldn't have had that last bottle of champers. Dear me, what a state.'

'Shall we go to our plane?' Rinzen said to his open-mouthed audience.

31

India

As the plane taxied down the runway, Rinzen gripped the armrests, thankful that Clara and Lawrence were bound up in their own thoughts. Leaving the land by sea had been thrilling enough, but this, this he had never imagined he would do. The jet took off as the sun rose in a cloudless sky. After a few minutes, Rinzen opened his eyes and breathed out. He had a god's eye view of the fields, towns and villages below. He was flying! It wasn't quite like floating on the waves of sound from Clara's harp, but this was flying while seated in a comfortable chair. He could get up and walk around if he wished, talk to Clara, even use the toilet. Wait until he told Keung!

He gazed at the early-morning traffic on a wide road that swept around south London. From this silent distance everything looked ordered, clean and simple after the crowded confusion of Shoreditch with its prying eyes and threatening blackmailers.

He turned to look at Clara. Her eyes were closed but her lips showed the hint of a smile. She had left behind loving friends and family and chosen to come with him to his foreign land, to a mountain monastery peopled only by male brothers. She had turned her back on fame, and the wealth that came with it, to be with him, and to help the Samudrans when they most needed it.

The plane landed in Muzaffarpur at 10.30 that night and, just as the brochure had promised, their arrival was kept very discreet, with minimal staff in attendance and even a seemingly affable immigration officer. Even so, they knew they had to get away as fast as possible. They bundled into the rental van, with the harp, decided not to risk going to the hotel Roland had booked, and continued north up the NH22. The roads were deserted and in the dark Clara found it hard to accept that she was actually in rural India.

Lawrence drove past Sitamarhi and on for another two hours until they were a few miles from Sonbarsa, where he turned left along a dirt track that led to the Nepalese border. He pulled in and parked outside a ruined barn, out of sight of passing traffic. They dozed in the van for the rest of the night, and just before dawn Rinzen set off to see if there was actually a border post on the tiny road. He returned an hour later, laughing so much it was hard to understand what he said.

'Please, Rinzen, say it again.' Clara held onto him as he jumped up and down.

'The army have gone. They left Sarmand two days ago.'

'Which means,' Lawrence said, 'that they will not be looking for you anymore!'

'Yes, and my brothers will be able to run in the mountains, the Mothers will come back to look after the novices. Life will return to Sarmand.' Tears streamed down his face and dripped off his chin. 'I want to dance, Clara, and I want to hear your harp in the temple.' He pulled her close and kissed her on her mouth.

Lawrence cleared his throat. 'Excuse me, I thought you Samudrans were celibate.'

'So we are, so we are, but I also love Clara like I love you, Lawrence, my dear, dear friend. Shall I kiss you too?'

'No, thanks, but I do love both of you.'

Rinzen pulled Lawrence close and the three of them – the Samudran, the anthropologist and the harpist – held each other tight and laughed until the air was full of laughter.

Lawrence's stomach rumbled as they drove north in jubilant mood. 'You see, I was right to fill up with that delicious food on the plane. But now I'm starving.'

'Did you see the border post this morning?' Clara asked.

'I saw the border – it's marked with a concrete pyramid – but there's no building. I went all the way into Malangawa to check. Nothing.' They drove on for a few minutes, the state of the track deteriorating every minute. 'There, see, over there.' He pointed at the insignificant little pyramid in a field near the road.

The sun was now well above the horizon, and people were already out in the rice fields; others walked along the track laden with sacks, tools and barrows. Clara stared out of the side window at the wide plain. A few children, dressed in no more than rags, waved at her; she waved back. As they neared Malangawa, the number of people increased. Most looked terribly poor, but some were smarter – men in ironed shirts and smart trousers, women in pink and emerald saris – though only a few of the children wore shoes.

They stopped in Malangawa to look for a restaurant, but everyone they asked said they should go to the main highway, about half an hour's drive away, and then continue east to Gautam Hotel.

Lawrence tried to avoid the worst of the potholes, but it took both Clara and Rinzen to stop the harp bouncing around in the back of the van. As they turned onto the relatively smooth highway, Clara suddenly realised that what she had thought were low clouds on the horizon were the snowcaps of the Himalaya.

She was in Nepal.

With Rinzen.

Six weeks ago, she was penniless and on the verge of selling her flat, and now she was heading into the Himalaya, to an isolated monastery where the brothers spent their lives maintaining the earth's rotation. It seemed like a fantasy, but the smiling, beautiful Rinzen was certainly real. She watched him as he looked north towards Sarmand.

Gautam Hotel was on the East–West Highway near a major crossroads – the mountains to the north, the main road to India to the south – and the road was busy with pedestrians, cyclists, trucks, taxis and cars of all ages. Most of the roadside buildings were either dilapidated or neglected, but the people were more prosperous: children in smart uniforms with neat little rucksacks walked or cycled to school; well-dressed men sauntered along the roadside, presumably on their way to work; and everywhere the startling colours of saris bestowed an elegance on the women.

After breakfast, they headed north towards the mountains. The road climbed, wound along the side of the valley and offered more spectacular views at every turn. Lawrence reckoned it was about two hundred kilometres to Sarmand and that they should be there by nightfall. The hairpin bends made it almost impossible to control the harp, so Lawrence strapped it to one of the seats using some rope he found in the toolbox. He carefully protected the woodwork with items of clothing, and Clara thanked him for treating her instrument like a delicate old lady.

They stopped to stretch their legs a few times, and once they bought fruit from a roadside stall, but otherwise they pressed on.

It was mid afternoon when they drove into Sunkhani, the village where Rinzen had stopped on the first day he left Sarmand on his way to Qo. His eyes had become wider and brighter now they were so near his home. He climbed into the front seat and looked all around. 'Stop!' he said. 'I saw one of my brothers down that lane.'

Lawrence braked immediately and pulled into the side. There was no one about; the place felt deserted.

Rinzen threw open the door and jumped down. 'He looked like Keung. It feels like Keung.'

Lawrence opened the side door and Clara jumped down, without her harp. They both chased after the sprinting Rinzen, across the road and down the lane. He disappeared round a bend, and when they eventually caught up again, they saw that he was crouching down and surveying the surrounding buildings. Just ahead of him stood a Samudran brother: he was holding a rifle and had his boot firmly planted on the chest of a man sprawled on the ground and dressed in black.

'Keung!' Rinzen called.

Keung turned, shouted something, and gestured behind them. He raised the rifle and they all turned to see that he was pointing at another man in black, about thirty metres away. The man in black had a rifle raised to his shoulder.

Rinzen leapt towards Clara, but Lawrence had already pushed her into a doorway. The single shot caught Lawrence in the back and spun him to the ground. To Clara, everything moved in slow motion: she watched Lawrence fall to the ground, then saw Rinzen take off and leap at the gunman as he let off another shot; she saw Rinzen land with both feet on the man at the same moment that the bullet left his rifle and travelled over the houses towards the distant trees; she watched the bullet from Keung's rifle hit the man's body a split second before Rinzen smashed into him; and she felt the agonising milliseconds tick by as she tried to go to Lawrence. The other man in black had wriggled free of Keung's boot and was attacking him with a long, serrated knife, but Keung sprang vertically in the air, landed behind the assassin and slammed his head to the ground with a sickening crunch.

Finally, time returned to normal and Clara knelt beside Lawrence and cradled his head in her lap. Rinzen was by her side in an instant and carefully opened Lawrence's shirt.

Lawrence opened his eyes, looked at Clara's tear-drenched face, and closed them again. She said something about it being all right, but it wasn't at all all right. Her dress was covered in blood. Lawrence's blood.

32

Nepal

Rinzen felt the life ebbing from Lawrence's body. He heard a nearby door creak open and called to the woman who peeped out. She flung the door wide, called out behind her and raced over to them. A young boy ran after her but carried on down the lane, shouting that the Samudrans needed help. Within seconds the previously deserted village came to life. Two men hurried up to Keung and sat on the semi-conscious man in black; two more pinned the wounded one to the ground. A man in a thick apron lifted a house door off its hinges and he and three others carefully laid Lawrence onto it and carried him into the woman's house, with Clara and Rinzen right behind them.

Rinzen put his mouth to Lawrence's and tried to breathe life into him. He massaged his heart, blew some more and felt a hand on his shoulder.

'Let me see,' the old man said, and Rinzen stepped aside.

The old man leaned over Lawrence, placed his hand on his chest, closed his own eyes and said, 'The bullet is inside his heart.' He looked up at Rinzen. 'We cannot revive him.'

'What did he say, Rinzen?' Clara asked, but the tears that flowed from Rinzen's eyes were answer enough.

Everyone in the room was silent, and Rinzen heard no sound from the street or the hills or the sky. Lawrence's spirit was waiting in his body, and the world seemed to wait with him. Everything, even his own tears, had stopped. He took Clara's hand, led her to Lawrence's side and placed her hand on his; he held Lawrence's other hand.

~

Sometime later, Keung and a village man lifted the door and, with Rinzen and Clara still holding Lawrence's hands, carried it out to the van. Keung thanked the villagers, said he would return the door the following day, and climbed into the passenger seat. The village man drove them slowly out of the village, followed by a procession of villagers, old and young, all hatless and with their heads bowed.

They continued to as close to Sarmand as possible and pulled over where a trail joined the dirt track. Amdong and Amal were waiting for them. Keung explained what had happened and Amal turned and sprinted up the trail, returning an hour later with four juniors, all running at full Samudran speed.

The brothers lined the eighty steps in the gloom. Some held lamps to light the way, others had their hands crossed over their chests. Rinzen's return was supposed to have been a joyful occasion, but here he was carrying another dead elder to Kwato's cell so that he could sit vigil one more time. As he climbed the steps, he nodded to the others, their empathy a warm physical sensation in his gut. Some of them switched their attention to Clara, but none openly questioned why this young woman was permitted to enter the inner courtyard. All the brothers looked gaunt, pale-skinned and with shadows below their eyes; while some made an effort to stand erect, others weren't able to hold their shoulders straight and slumped like famine victims. That was what he'd seen when he meditated, but he'd never imagined they would be in such terrible condition. He wanted to turn away but made sure he looked them straight in the eye.

From the top of the steps he watched Keung and Amdong carrying Clara's harp as though it were a sacred object. Other brothers carried the luggage. They brought everything to Kwato's cell, where candles had already been lit and the bed prepared for cleaning the body.

'I need to speak with Keung for a few minutes. I'll be right outside if you need me,' Rinzen said.

Clara nodded.

Before they spoke a word, the brothers embraced with the intensity of family members reunited after years of enforced separation, and stayed that way for several minutes.

When they broke apart, Rinzen said, 'The murderers?'

'Locked up in the village and well guarded. They called a doctor for the injured one.'

'Thank you for preparing Kwato's cell. Lawrence Greene was an elder in his own way.' His voice broke, he waited for it to pass. 'Without him, I would ...' But he couldn't continue.

'We will give him an elder's funeral,' Keung said. 'If Clara Martinelli so desires.'

'What? How did you know?' It was good to see the old quizzical look on Keung's face, but even he had sallow cheeks, hollow eyes.

'Amdong seems to have an ear to the outside world.'

'We always said that one was destined for something special.' Rinzen clasped Keung's shoulder. 'Clara is strong, but this will be very hard for her. Will you ask Amdong to take her and her luggage to one of the empty cells, so she can wash and change? And she should eat something before she joins the vigil.'

'Of course. A room is already prepared. What about the harp?'

'It must stay with her at all times. Will you help me clean Lawrence?'

'Two juniors are bringing everything we need.' He covered Rinzen's hand with his. 'I've missed you, Rinzen.'

'I've watched the meditation.'

'Ah.' Keung lowered his head a little. 'Well, the army has left now. And I noticed you and Clara helping us. But some brothers can barely keep awake during the meditation, and I fear it is the same at Barnang and Qo.' He gripped Rinzen's hand. 'We will think of a solution later. First, we must attend to Mr Greene.'

At first Clara refused to leave Lawrence's side, but when Rinzen said that she needed to be clean and not hungry or thirsty before she joined the vigil she relented and followed the polite and awestruck Amdong to her room.

Rinzen and Keung undressed Lawrence, washed him with flannels dipped in herb-scented water and dried him with soft towels. They selected clothes from his holdall, dressed him, and cleared away everything except the holdall and his battered old briefcase.

'He called this his life-support bag.' Rinzen showed it to Keung. 'I'll wait until Clara returns before opening it.'

'So you don't know what it contains?'

'It was one of his few secrets.'

'I'll wait with the elder. Go and wash, and please eat something.'

He met Clara and Amdong as he turned the corner, manoeuvring the harp along the stone path. Her pale face shone in the light of Amdong's lamp, and the Samudran saffron cloak over her simple white dress gave her the appearance of a nun amongst brothers, which seemed appropriate for the only woman inside the inner walls of Sarmand.

'What would Kwato say?' The words appeared in the air before he realised he was speaking his thoughts. 'Sorry, I didn't mean to speak. Have you eaten, Clara?'

'Yes, Amdong is very kind.'

The self-controlled senior blushed and shifted on his heels.

'I'll be a few minutes,' Rinzen said. 'You can wait or ...'

'I'll go to Lawrence.'

He longed to put his arms around her, to find and give comfort, but that wouldn't have been the right thing to do in front of a new senior, so he walked away at speed, had a quick wash, changed, and quickly ate the bowl of rice and vegetables he was offered in the kitchen. He carried a pitcher of water back to Kwato's cell, where he found Clara seated next to Lawrence, holding his hand and gazing at his face.

She didn't look up as he entered. 'Thank you for attending so lovingly to him. He looks as though he belongs here, and we are both here with him.'

He put his hand on her shoulder and she unfolded like a dancer into his arms. Her body shuddered against his, but she no longer wept. He closed his eyes and stilled his thoughts, intent on bringing calm, peace, to the cell, to let Clara accept Lawrence's death and allow his spirit to slowly be released. They remained like that until he felt her body soften, warm against his chest.

Once more they took their places on either side of the bed and watched over their departed friend. He recited Ryōkan and held images of his valiant, trusted friend in his heart and mind.

A little while later, Amdong knocked and entered with a brazier full of charcoal, which was topped up by various seniors and juniors throughout the night. At dawn, Keung appeared and told them to go for a walk around the cloisters while he sat with the elder.

'So you are the brother I feel I already know,' Clara said.

'Sorry, I should have introduced you.' Rinzen frowned. 'Clara Martinelli, may I introduce Keung, the best friend a brother could have. Keung, I am pleased to present Ms Clara Martinelli, who has enriched my life in so many ways.'

'I see you have learned some manners on your travels.' Keung bowed to Clara and offered his hand. 'I think the correct polite reply is "My Pleasure", but in this case I mean it sincerely.'

Rinzen picked up Lawrence's satchel and led the way to the cloisters. Weeds had sprouted in the gaps on the stone path. They went to the bench at the far side, where they would soon feel the sun on their faces.

As he was about to sit, Clara gripped his sleeve. 'Lawrence saved my life, didn't he? If he'd stayed where he was, the bullet would have hit me.'

Her lips were bloodless, her eyes red with tears and exhaustion.

'Lawrence's instinct was to save you, yes, but that man was aiming at me. He saw me leap, calculated where I would land and aimed the bullet there.' He dropped his head; waves of despair pulsed in his temples. How had he let that happen? 'I miscalculated. I should have leapt straight at the gunman.'

'If I hadn't been there, that's what you would have done.' She frowned, refusing to have the blame lifted from her.

For a few moments he thought about those crucial microseconds. 'No, I would have tried to protect you and Lawrence. That would always be my instinctive reaction – to protect those I put in danger, then deal with the attacker direct.'

She turned away from him, looked at the sky above the inner walls, where sparks of the dawn sun flickered on the uneven parapets. She was angry with him, and rightly so. He'd recognised the men in black – they were the same two who'd stalked him on his return from Barnang and whom he'd humiliated on his departure from Sarmand. He needed to ask Keung why he'd been fighting them in the village, but the answer didn't really matter – it was he who had nourished their thirst for revenge.

'I'm not angry with you,' Clara said. 'But I can't help being angry with myself. I took Lawrence for granted – I should have talked to him about Mum, about Switzerland.'

She moved her hand towards him but quickly withdrew it. Despite her grief, she remembered where they were. 'And now it's too late.'

He could not think of any words to comfort her. 'Let's sit and wait for the sun.'

'You brought his bag. I think it's time to open it.'

Rinzen placed the bag between them and unbuckled the straps. Clara folded back the flap and looked inside, then removed the contents one at a time and placed them on the bench. A hardback copy of Herodotus's *The Histories*, its spine creased and split by many openings; *Selected Poems of TS Eliot*, its covers held together with black tape; *The Epic of Gilgamesh*, battered but in one piece; an ancient copy of *Views of Nature* by Alexander von Humboldt; a black card-covered journal as thick as her wrist, kept closed with red elastic; a pocket knife with a walnut handle, silk-smooth from decades of use; and a small felt drawstring bag. Clara placed the little bag in Rinzen's palm and he opened it to reveal a conical amethyst pendulum attached to a delicate silver chain. She held it aloft between thumb and forefinger and let it hang motionless between them, sparkling in the sunshine.

'Used for divining, I think,' she said.

'Like the Kogi?'

'I thought you said they used bubbles in bowls of water for that.'

He nodded, wondered what Lawrence divined for.

Clara returned the pendulum to its pouch, put it on the bench and reached into a smaller compartment inside the briefcase. An orienteering compass, quite new; a compact telescope in a soft protective case; two ballpoint pens and a couple of pencils.

Finally, she withdrew three envelopes. 'What? Rinzen, this is addressed to you.'

'But—'

'And this one is to me. Why did he … Wait, this is to …'
Her body jolted as she looked at the third envelope; her
mouth fell open and a single tear traced a course down her
cheek.

Rinzen took the envelope, read the words *Grace
Martinelli* and immediately put his arm around Clara's
shoulders and pulled her towards him. They sat in silence
for several minutes. A small bird sang in the bare branches
of the cloisters' solitary cherry tree. He recognised the song
but did not look at the wren.

'That's a lovely song,' Clara said. She wiped away the
tears, then opened her letter.

He did the same.

My dear Rinzen,

*You'll probably never get to read this, as I have no
intention of checking out any time soon, but I suddenly
felt the need to write to you. I can't explain it, but
spending time with you has taught me not to ignore such
impulses.*

*I fear Clara will need comforting as she feels
everything so deeply, so acutely. But then you know her
better than anyone, and who better to leave her with than
you.*

*She told me you are her kindred spirit, that meeting
you has completed her, and she knows that you will
never be apart, even when you are physically parted. I'm
only saying this to you because we men are pretty useless
at gauging these things, and, yes, I know you're a
Samudran brother with heightened sensibilities and
extraordinary insight … but you are also a man, and
therefore prone to emotional stupidity.*

*I did so want to see Sarmand, Rinzen, to meet Keung
and Amdong and the others, to watch the rock eagles you
love so much soar over the mountains, to observe the*

novices perform their meditation and learn how to leap the eighty steps, and to sit beside the Well of Life and feel the wisdom of ages radiate out into the world.

I am not an enlightened man, but I do have one insight I wish to share with you, and it is this. For generations the Samudrans have looked after the earth, and will continue to do so for generations to come. Your ancestors suffered famine and war, landslides and earthquakes, and winters so harsh that even the wells froze. For all this time the continuous meditation was maintained, as it be will under your stewardship and those who come after you. Your work is too important to fail – there are those in the world who know this and who will help you.

My spirit will leave you soon, content that the world is in your safe hands. If it is permitted, I would like to remain in the mountains, to be cremated on a simple pyre and for my ashes to be disposed of as you see fit.

I would like you to accept my Gilgamesh and Humboldt, and my knife, as mementoes of our time together. I would have liked to have been able to finish our talk about Humboldt, but you will just have to imagine the conversation!

I leave you with one last observation, and after our conversations on the subject it will surprise you. Notwithstanding the many chance encounters that led you to her, it was your destiny to meet Clara.

Your comrade, fellow traveller and dear friend,
Lawrence

He reread the letter. Another elder had died before his time. And yet, Elder Kwato would have corrected him for thinking this way, and this letter showed that Lawrence had anticipated his own death and had been ready to accept it. Despite his assertions to the contrary, Lawrence had in his

334

own way been enlightened. Perhaps that was why Keung had so readily suggested an elder's funeral?

While he waited for Clara to finish her letter, he smiled at the sentence about emotional stupidity, and opened the Humboldt. He read the inscription – *To Rinzen, my dear friend, wise beyond his years.* To think he now had his own copy of *Views of Nature*, a book he had read and reread so many times in the library at Sarmand.

He let Clara dry her tears, then silently passed her his letter. She did the same.

My dear Clara,

You'll probably never get to read this, as I have no intention of checking out any time soon, but I suddenly felt the need to write to you. I can't explain it, but spending time with Rinzen has taught me not to ignore such impulses.

These last months with you and Rinzen have been some of the happiest in my life. Whether it was luck or destiny that brought Rinzen and me together does not matter* – it's what we made of the encounter that's important. I'm sure he has a positive effect on everyone he meets, but for me it has been rare to find someone I immediately trust and to be fundamentally changed by the experience. I know you don't think me sentimental, so when I say I love Rinzen, you know I mean it sincerely.

I don't suppose you ever thought you'd hear me expose my feelings like this either. Well, prepare yourself for more of it.

After that day when Grace and I had lunch with you, I sensed you were doing something really important, and yet I went ahead and colluded in that dreadful deception. Afterwards, I couldn't understand why I'd done it, so I went travelling, hoping that distance and time would give me some clarity. I confess I never really worked out why I did it, but I learned something very important – even at my advanced age. I learned not to meddle in other people's affairs, to try not to judge others, to accept everyone at face value. Spending time talking with Rinzen on board the Oracle was also a great help. He helped me realise that I could not undo what I'd done but that I could ask for your forgiveness without expectation of receiving it. But you did forgive me and have not borne a grudge against me.

When I saw you at the concert, I knew you had grown in strength and focus, that you had achieved a state of simplicity – Rinzen calls it purity – that enabled you to compose and play music so sublime that no one who listens to it remains unaffected. It is, of course, a mystery to me.

You forgave my terrible behaviour and I now want to ask you to forgive your mother, my saving Grace. Please give her my journal – she will tell you why.

I would like you to have my TS Eliot volume and the divining crystal. Wash it in spring water so that it will forget its previous owner, and use it whenever doubt visits. I also bequeath you my Herodotus, which you can open anywhere and find something of interest – perhaps you could start with Passage 23, the story of Arion the harpist ...

I depart happy that you are helping the Samudrans in their hour of need. Live your life to the full, and do share your music! As for me, I look forward to further adventures in the next life.

Your loving friend,
Lawrence

PS. On second thoughts, I am convinced that it was definitely my destiny to meet Rinzen and introduce him to you. Now your life begins a new chapter.

When he had folded her letter, Clara faced him and said, 'Oh, Rinzen, how can he be dead?' She stood up and walked across to the Well of Life, her shoulders slumped, her head bent. She went to touch the stones but hesitated.

'It's fine to touch. I like to run my palms over the old stones and think of all the love and wisdom contained in there.' He stayed on the bench to give her room.

She walked around the well, eyes closed, her hands stroking the stones, worn smooth as polished walnut by countless brothers. The sun was now high enough to have some warmth in it, and he leaned back, closed his eyes and welcomed its healing rays.

After a while they returned to Elder Kwato's cell to find Amdong setting out breakfast on a table outside the door. He relieved Keung inside so he could join them for breakfast. They sat in silence for a few minutes, then Rinzen said, 'Clara, will we grant Lawrence's wishes and cremate him here at Sarmand?'

She didn't hesitate. 'Definitely.'

'He will join the other elders in the Well of Life, if my brothers agree.'

'He was too modest to ask, but I am certain he would feel honoured.'

'It is the brothers who would be honoured.' Keung shifted on his seat, couldn't seem to manage to eat anything.

'Ask your question, please,' Clara said.

'That's what I was about to say.' Rinzen laughed, put his hand on Keung's wrist, and grinned at him.

'I wanted to ask if you would play your famous composition for all the brothers to hear? Not now, of course. Afterwards.' Keung adopted his usual stance – eyes downcast to allow others the freedom to answer without scrutiny.

'Yes, of course, but ... no, it's OK, another time.'

Rinzen glanced at Clara, then turned to Keung. 'We should also ask the others if they agree that Clara should play in the inner temple,' Rinzen said, knowing that this was what Clara had wanted to ask.

'Agreed. But I have my reasons for asking you to play to all of us together. First, it will lift our spirits, and second, there are grumblings from some of the younger ones that Rinzen returned to Sarmand without any Kogi and accompanied only by one English musician.'

'And a woman at that,' Clara said.

33

Nepal

For two more days and nights, Rinzen and Clara sat vigil with Lawrence; Rinzen often chanted while Clara played the harp. They had short periods of respite when Keung or Amdong came to relieve them, but neither of them slept much and it was with heavy heads that they walked to their cells on the fourth day.

Rinzen and Keung had decided to properly introduce Clara the next morning, when she would play *The Harp Awakening* in the dining hall an hour after breakfast. When the brothers returned from their tasks at the appointed time, they found Rinzen holding the neck of Clara's harp at the front of the hall.

He waited until everyone, including the novices, the Mothers, and those who were on meditation duty, was seated. 'It is good to be back at Sarmand.' He looked at the faces, which were all focused on his. 'I—'

'Welcome, brother!' The cry went up and soon everyone was shouting it.

He swallowed, waited for silence. 'Thank you, my brothers. I travelled halfway across the world to England, but when I heard the spirit of Sarmand calling me back, I knew I must answer. As you know, my companion for much of my journey, Lawrence Greene, was shot and killed, and tomorrow we will conduct the funeral rites. My other companion was Clara Martinelli, a harpist.' He stood aside from the harp and looked at it. 'This is her harp, and she will now play *The Harp Awakening*, her own composition.'

Keung led Clara from the kitchen to join Rinzen.

She stood next to him and looked out, hands in prayer position. 'Namaste.'

'*Swagatam*,' the brothers chorused.

Rinzen and Keung took their seats in front of her; she bowed, then sat on the stool and began to play.

Exactly three hours later, she played the last note, dropped her hands by her sides, and let her head bend forward, eyes closed. For three hours, no one had moved, no one had made a sound, not even the youngest novices. Another full minute passed in silence, and suddenly, without any prompting from Rinzen, everyone stood and clapped their hands politely. Then, as one, they cheered and stamped their feet.

Clara bowed and stared out at the joyful faces. Whether it was the perfect audience, the ideal location or the fact that she had silently dedicated her performance to Lawrence, she knew that her delivery had been better than ever. She didn't feel at all embarrassed by the close scrutiny, even when the younger ones at the front – presumably the novices – giggled and pointed at her. All she felt were waves of goodwill. She smiled for the first time in days.

Rinzen came and stood beside her. Dried rivulets of tears stained his cheeks. The room fell quiet as he held his hands in the air. He turned to her and bowed. 'Thank you for playing such beautiful music for us, Clara.'

He turned back to face his brothers and said, first in Nepali, then in English, 'I have invited Clara to stay with us for a while. I know it's unusual to have a person who is not a Samudran brother staying in Sarmand, but these are unusual times. Not only have you endured the death of our elders, but you have persevered through many months of quarantine imposed by the army. When I first heard Clara

Martinelli play that piece of music, I knew that every Samudran would feel what I felt, and your response tells me I was right.'

Clara tugged his sleeve, whispered, 'Please thank everyone for listening so patiently.'

He nodded and translated her words. Another cheer went up, and then all the younger ones filed out, the smallest shepherded by two women, no doubt the Mothers Rinzen had mentioned. The remaining group sat down. Keung helped Clara wheel the harp out of the hall into the kitchen, where they waited with the door slightly ajar so they could listen to Rinzen. Keung whispered the English translation to Clara.

'My brothers, I want to ask you something. While I was away, I know some of you felt my presence in the inner temple.'

Clara peeped around the door – many of the brothers nodded.

'A few weeks ago, I was somewhere I could meditate for many hours a day, and as I meditated, so Clara Martinelli played her harp.'

'That's what I heard,' someone said.

'And me,' said another.

'Me, too,' several more said.

'You heard her because I invited her to play,' Rinzen said. 'I know that during these last months it has been difficult to sustain the meditation. There are too few in the circle and so each of you has had to meditate for longer. Fatigue takes its toll, and the trance is weak.' He looked at the tired, silent faces. His sympathy for the exhausted brothers seemed to be palpable, as though it was a wound on his own body. 'We need to think about how to overcome this problem, but while we do that, I want to ask you to agree to something that goes against Samudran tradition. I would not ask if I did not consider it a necessity…'

A silence that felt like a cold draught was broken by someone out of her line of sight. 'Ask us, Brother Rinzen.'

'I seek your permission to have Clara play in the inner temple while we meditate.'

A few brothers turned to each other and whispered; the whispers soon became a general rumble.

Rinzen raised his hand. 'For centuries the only people allowed inside the inner temple were elders and experienced seniors. Out of necessity, we broke that tradition and included juniors and new seniors. It is out of the same necessity that I ask for Clara to be allowed to play. I do believe that her music will enhance the meditation and help us deepen our trance.'

The rumble died down, and Clara saw a hand go up.

'I say we should try it for six days and then discuss it again.'

'Good idea. Does anyone object?'

No one answered.

'All are free to speak.'

'Of course they want you to play,' Keung whispered. 'Why must he make such a fuss!'

'Because ...' Clara raised an eyebrow to Keung.

Keung snapped his eyes back to Rinzen, and his mouth dropped open. 'You're right, Clara! That's what it is. That's how he's changed. He's using his own judgement, isn't he? He's no longer blindly following the elders or constantly referring to what Kwato would have done ... He has become an elder, hasn't he! But a new type of elder, one who has seen that the state of our planet needs the Samudrans to do more than simply continue with our traditional ways.'

The creases on Keung's brow became more pronounced, as though he were forcing his thoughts to make sense. Clara willed him on.

'I mean to say, which of our revered elders would have even considered inviting you to Sarmand?' He had a look of awe on his face as he turned back to watch Rinzen. 'I wonder what he'll think of next?' He whistled.

Rinzen pressed on. 'Then I will ask Clara if she will play with us the day after tomorrow, after we've performed the funeral rites.' He walked into their midst and hugged those he hadn't greeted since his return, smiled at others, put his hand on the shoulders of the younger ones.

As the brothers filed out of the dining hall, Clara asked Keung where she could find the nearest telephone. He said it was at least two days' walk away but that a man in Sunkhani carried letters down to Gongabu once a week.

Clara didn't want Rinzen to feel he had to look after her, so after a brief exchange, she said she wanted to rest in her room until nightfall. Her cell was small and sparsely furnished with a narrow bed, a small table and chair, and a niche for an oil lamp beside the bed. The bed had been pushed against the side wall to make room for her harp. A tiny window overlooked the thickly wooded valley.

She wrote to her mother about Lawrence's death, then screwed up the paper and started again. After three attempts she decided her final version would have to do. She stood at the window for a long time, gazing out at the multitude of greens rising up the valley and the long scree slope that reached to the snowline. The mountains were tantalisingly out of sight, veiled in a mist so fine it was almost as white as the snow. Out of nowhere a huge bird glided close to the window and soared heavenwards.

When Rinzen came to get her for supper, she asked him to bring her something in her room, saying that she would feel uncomfortable about pushing the harp into the dining hall until the other brothers had got used to her and her peculiar behaviour.

~

At noon the following day, all the brothers assembled in the courtyard beside the outer temple. Clara had no choice and left the harp in her room. Rinzen, Keung, Amdong and Dachen carried the litter from Elder Kwato's cell into the courtyard and led the procession out through the inner gates, down the eighty steps to the outer gates, and on into the forest, where they were met by the villagers who'd helped Rinzen and Keung on the night of Lawrence's murder. They sang a song – Amal whispered that it was about those about to embark on a long journey – and walked behind the brothers to the appointed place.

The bearers placed the litter on the ring of stones and joined the circle around the pyre.

Rinzen stepped forward and stared at Lawrence's body. 'Death is the only certainty; it comes when it will and we welcome it. Lawrence Greene spent his life learning about the peoples of the world, from whom he gained wisdom and tolerance. His courage knew no bounds, his love showed in practical acts. As we do for our elders, we have built a pyre from fallen trees. Lawrence Greene's ashes will nurture the roots of the living trees and make their flowers brighter. His spirit has flown above the mountain and shines down upon us.'

The sixteen seniors lit their torches, approached the pyre together and set it alight. Without further ceremony, without a tear being shed, Keung led the procession back to the monastery, leaving Clara and Rinzen to watch over the cremation until late at night, until the last ember had lost its heat. She gazed into the fire, mesmerised by the flames, then the embers, and finally the ashes. Time passed unnoticed.

Rinzen collected the ashes into a simple clay pot.

The sky was already lightening as they entered the cloisters.

'Let's pour his ashes together.' These were the first words Rinzen had spoken since the pyre had been lit. He lifted her hand to hold the urn with his. He didn't say any special words or do any chanting, he simply smiled at her, nodded and slowly tilted the urn over the well's mouth.

As they walked to their rooms, one of the juniors approached with two earthenware mugs of tea. He passed one to each of them, bowed, and walked away without speaking.

When she awoke sometime in the afternoon, she donned the Samudran cloak and explored the monastery. She stopped in the archway that led to the juniors' courtyard and took in the sight of six brothers balanced on their heads with eyes closed and arms folded on their chests. They looked like inverted statues. She inspected each brother in turn but failed to detect a leg sway, or a muscle twitch or even a pulse behind an eyelid. She moved on to the seniors' garden, where things got even stranger: one senior's arm was raised straight up above his head while the second senior was suspended in mid air, right arm in line with his shoulder and gripping the first one's raised wrist. Again, no muscle shuddered, no leg vibrated. She closed her gaping mouth and focused on a third senior – stripped to the waist – on the other side of the garden. He hung upside-down from a wooden pole; next to him was a large urn on a stone column and on the ground below him was another large urn. In his right hand he held a small cup the size of a shot glass, which he filled with water from the urn on the ground, then swung his body up and emptied it into the urn above. She watched his abdominal muscles tighten into steel cables as he propelled himself up and down in a continuous movement.

'It will take him several hours to fill the vessel.'

She jumped at the interruption. 'Keung! Sorry, I didn't see you there.'

'That's the general idea.'

Clara felt the blood rise up her neck, suddenly aware she was intruding on the brothers' private domain. 'I'm so sorry

... I'll go.' She turned, lowered her head, and almost ran from the garden. Her heart thumped. The shame of it!

A laugh and footsteps followed her. 'No need, Clara. They're not even aware that you're here.' Keung gently touched her arm. 'It is I who am sorry for startling you. I confess, I couldn't resist.'

She stopped and slowly raised her head to look at his smiling eyes. He definitely hadn't been in the garden, she would have noticed, but then how ...? Lawrence had told her that Samudrans could do impossible things – was becoming invisible one of them? It seemed idiotic to ask, so she just grinned at him inanely, made an excuse and hurried away towards the cloisters.

A flight of stone steps led up to the inner wall of the monastery, and she went up them to look at the sky colouring in the west. She watched the sky darken and floated off into a daydream of half-thoughts and images of Lawrence and Rinzen. Lawrence would have loved Sarmand – there was plenty there to interest an inquisitive anthropologist – and the brothers would have been impressed with his tales of places he'd visited and the strange things he'd seen. Rinzen would have stood beside him and laughed at his terrible jokes, and all three of them would have explored the mountains and been at ease at last.

There was a Lawrence-sized hole in her chest, but she didn't feel sorrow, only loss. As she'd watched over his funeral pyre, the grief had diminished and she'd come to accept that Lawrence would indeed be reborn. Was she already under the Samudran spell?

The atmosphere here was definitely intoxicating, but she was an outsider, untrained, foreign and female. She couldn't stay long, she knew that. It wouldn't work – for the Samudrans or for her.

She shook her head, brought herself back to reality, didn't want to dwell on thoughts of leaving Rinzen. In any case, she'd been separated from her harp for well over an hour. She descended the steps and returned to her room, where she noticed the book of TS Eliot poetry Lawrence had left her, lying on the small table that must have supported the writings of generations of elders. Up to now she hadn't felt ready for whatever inscription he'd written in it. She picked it up and was about to open it when she remembered the pendulum. She withdrew it from its pouch, took it outside with the jug of water and gave it all her attention as she washed it. The moon was full, which was surely auspicious.

Back inside, she tested which way the pendulum moved when she asked a question to which she knew the answer. Am I a harpist? The pendulum swung in a circle. Am I a man? The pendulum swung back and forth. Is it time to open Lawrence's book? The pendulum swung in a circle. She opened the book and read Lawrence's forward-slanting script:

To my dear Clara,
If you asked the pendulum whether it was time to open this book, then it is meant for you. If you didn't, then leave it in the library at Sarmand!
Either way, I hope you find solace in these beautiful words.
Your number-one fan,
Lawrence

These men and their intuition. She flipped through the book to *The Wasteland*, sat on the bed and stroked the harp strings while she read 'The Burial of the Dead'.

~

She was awake when Rinzen came to her room the following morning. He had brought a bowl of rice porridge and a beaker of sweet tea, and he sat with her while she ate.

The lamp lit his face from underneath and made him look stern.

'There's a short ritual when the meditators change. The signal for you to start playing will be when we fresh meditators sit in the circle and ring the handbell. The only light will be from small oil lamps on the floor, the only heat will come from our bodies. We meditate continuously for eight hours, and we do not chant.'

She took a sip of the sweet tea. 'Are you worried for me, Rinzen?'

'As far as any of us know, this will be the first time in Samudran history that anyone but a trained Samudran has entered the inner temple.' Now that she had finished eating, he took her hand in his and looked into her eyes. 'We who are not properly confirmed elders took the decision to ask you to play because we truly believe you will help Sarmand through this hardship. But ... we feel the weight of our predecessors on our shoulders and, while we are sure of our decision, we are also anxious about it.'

She wanted to say that she thought Samudrans never got anxious, but she thought better of it. She tried not to dwell on the fact that she was about to do something no outsider, and certainly no woman, had ever done before. 'I may need to stop playing from time to time, to retune the harp or just to rest my arms. If I remain quiet, do you think that would be all right?'

'Of course, Clara, stop whenever you wish. We do not expect you to play all the time.'

With her eyes still locked on his, she said, 'It is a great honour, Rinzen. My harp and I are ready.'

He squeezed her hand and stood up.

They wheeled the harp along the path to a tall door that looked like the entrance to a medieval castle, with great iron nailheads evenly spaced across the rough-grained nut-brown wood. Rinzen opened the door and they entered a lobby. Its stucco walls were tinted terracotta red, the floor tiled with hexagonal stones of a similar hue. Moments later they were joined by Keung, Amdong, Fulong, Dachen and one other brother whose name she didn't know. She and the brothers bowed to each other, Keung nodded, and Amdong opened the door to the inner temple. Keung and Rinzen lifted the harp and carried it inside. They carefully set it down in front of a stool in the corner, waited until she had made herself comfortable, then took their positions behind the meditating brothers.

Apart from the six oil lamps set around a wide bowl in the centre of the circle, the only light was a similar lamp in a niche behind her, which cast a silhouette of the harp upon the cool, seamless floor. As she waited for the bell, her eyes grew accustomed to the dark. The temple was square, high-walled and with a tall dome at its centre. Impossible to control the echoes, she thought, but she would see what could be managed.

The single ring of the handbell sounded ageless and elongated in that hall of spirits. Clara gently plucked middle C, let the note carry, added two more notes, then played a short glissando that seemed to spiral round the dome before expiring at its apex. She watched where the notes travelled. Now she knew how to play in that space. She moved seamlessly into the opening phrases of *The Harp Awakening* but deliberately slowed its pace by a quarter and played softly so as to complement and not overwhelm the brothers.

Eight hours later, when they'd gathered outside after the changeover, the brothers all spoke at once.

'The colours, did you see them?'

'See them? I was riding on them.'

'Yes, on the layers of sound.'

'I've never been there before, have you?'

'How can one person create such music? It sounded like many harps all playing at once. Or an orchestra?

'How do you know – you've never heard an orchestra.'

'At one point I was certain I was under water.'

349

'Clara,' Rinzen said, and suddenly all the chatter stopped. Six faces stared at her, then six brothers bowed deeply and stayed bowed.

'Was it OK?' She looked first at Rinzen, then at Keung. 'Does it work – my playing in the temple, I mean?'

Keung approached her. 'This day will go down in Samudran history as the day that Clara Martinelli opened new doors of perception for the brothers of Sarmand. A simple thank you is not enough, but we are so overwhelmed, we ask you to give us time to properly express ourselves.' Another deep bow.

'Oh,' Clara said, and laughed her high laugh.

When she entered the dining hall for supper that night, everyone stood and bowed, and then, as if to spare her embarrassment, immediately sat down again. After they'd finished eating, a tall thin youngster came and stood beside her.

'He wants to ask you something.' Rinzen said. 'You may speak, Dawa.'

'Madam, a pleasing it would be to have you in the other place. They ask me. Will you please?'

A laugh burst from her mouth before she could stop it. 'Sorry.'

'He wants to know if you will visit the novices.' Rinzen grinned and put his hand on Dawa's arm to calm him. 'I think you made a few fans there.'

~

Over the following days, Clara's life settled into a pattern: she played in the inner temple from dawn until early afternoon, ate a modest meal, rested for an hour, then walked around the cloisters and other parts of the monastery for an hour, before two brothers came to carry her harp down the eighty steps to the novices' dining room.

The first time she went, they crowded around and called her name. The smallest ones wanted to hug her, the older boys tried to resist her, but not one of them showed anything but utter fascination with her. They sang their favourite songs and she accompanied them on the harp; she played old English folk songs and lullabies and they were so bright, so eager to learn, that they mastered several of them despite the language barrier. When it was time to go, the ever-patient Mothers had their work cut out to stop them mobbing her again. She left to cries of "Morrow, 'morrow' and wished she had the ability to leap the eighty steps with joy.

After six days, Rinzen told her she had to have a day off and took her into the mountains without the harp. He presented her with a thick wool coat and wool-lined boots, and they set off under a windless blue sky, heading towards the snowline.

They stopped to eat their picnic at one of his favourite lookout points, seated beneath a leafless tree twisted by winds and stunted by storms, with Sarmand far below.

'Thank you, Clara. You have restored harmony to Sarmand.'

'But the brothers all look exhausted, Rinzen.'

'I know. There are not enough of us to sustain the meditation and everyone is doing too much. We're neglecting our studies and our training, and we're getting very tired. Many now find it difficult to enter the trance, and that weakens our effectiveness. And there are only six of us in the circle, instead of ten.' He stood and walked to the edge. She joined him. 'I had to come back, but what can I do, even with your help?'

This was the first time she'd heard despair in his voice. At Sarmand he was always positive, smiled at everyone, encouraged the juniors, instructed the seniors late into the night, and regularly did two eight-hour meditations in one day.

'Perhaps it would have been better to go to the Kogi after all,' he said.

He didn't turn to her, just stared into the distance. Her heart ached for him. 'Do you think the other brother, the one from Barnang, made it?'

His head snapped round. 'How could I have forgotten about Lobsang? You're right, he might have made it. We should send someone to Barnang to find out if they've heard from him.' But his voice sounded flat, as though he'd given up hope.

'And if not, we could fly to Columbia. I have the money, and you are no longer a wanted man.'

He sighed. 'Perhaps.'

34

Nepal

As agreed, after Clara had played in the inner temple for six days, the seniors met again to decide whether she should continue. It took less than five seconds to agree unanimously that she should, and another ten minutes for those who wished to speak to relate with enthusiasm their experiences of meditating in her presence.

'But it's not enough, is it?' Keung said. 'We are very fortunate to have Clara Martinelli's help. She has restored harmony to Sarmand. I even heard a lark sing in the garden yesterday, and the old oak has sprouted new buds, but things cannot go on with so few of us in the circle.'

'What about the brothers from Qo?' Dachen said. 'They were prevented from coming by the quarantine, but now that the army's gone, we could join with them.'

'But wouldn't we be even more vulnerable to things outside our control if there were only two centres?' Amdong said.

'I agree,' Rinzen said. 'Another disease, or some natural disaster.'

'Since when have we worried about what might or might not happen?' Dachen said.

'Exactly,' Choden said.

'Wait,' Keung said. 'We may all have our opinions, but Rinzen should decide what we will do. After all, he is the only Samudran elder still alive.'

'What do you mean?' Rinzen glowered at Keung.

The others fell silent and looked at Rinzen. As one, they bowed their heads and pressed their palms together.

'What are you doing? I am the same as you, a senior.'

'But we can tell an elder when we see one.'

If Rinzen hadn't known him better, he'd have said that Keung's serious expression was reverent.

'I refuse to discuss this,' Rinzen said. 'We all agree anyway: we'll ask a villager to go to Barnang for news of Lobsang's quest to the Kogi. After that, we'll decide whether to ask the Qo brothers to join us here.'

Before anyone could answer, he turned and strode from the cloisters, took the steps up to the top of Sarmand's inner wall and looked towards Sunkhani, the village where Lawrence had died. The trees lining the rough track that wound down the valley cast long shadows in the late-afternoon sun.

They think I'm an elder, but I am no more an elder than Keung or Amal.

Keung mounted the wall. 'Please listen to me, brother.'

'No, you listen to me. How can you even think that I'm an elder? There's been no examination, and in any case, as I said, I am no different to you. I mean—'

'Who saw that Clara Martinelli could help us in our hour of need? Who persuaded all of us to let her inside the inner temple, where no outsider has ever been? Who convinced us to allow her music to play there, where only a solitary bell had sounded before? Who is not afraid of trying new ways to hold together our sick planet, not afraid to acknowledge that the old need to give way to the young?'

'So what? You would have done the same if you had travelled as I have.'

'Naturally. And I'd probably have been quicker about it, certainly more decisive.'

'Huh. Have you finished?'

'No. You no longer say, "What would Kwato do?" You had the bravery, the confidence, to decide that Kwato and the Barnang elders were wrong to send you to Columbia; you made your own judgement. Well?'

'Well what?'

'It wasn't one of us who did all these things, it was you, my dear friend. You are the first of the new Samudran elders.'

'Who's that?' Rinzen pointed to the track below. There was something familiar about the solitary figure striding towards Sarmand. He definitely had a monk's silhouette, but where had he seen that particular monk before? Words sounded in his head – 'a problem for the Samudrans is a problem for all'– and he said aloud, 'Of course, it's Kunchen.'

'Who's Kunchen?' Keung asked, but Rinzen didn't answer.

His mind flew back to the day he'd collapsed on his way from Barnang to Sarmand, to the beautiful woman who'd washed his hands and face, to the kind Kunchen who'd also said, 'Perhaps I can help you?', an offer he had refused, unwilling to trust even a Buddhist monk after Chodak's betrayal at Barnang.

As he watched Kunchen's rapid progress up the track, his chest tightened, his constricted throat seemed full of hot sharp rocks. He choked, tried to cough, bent double and felt the full force of the shame he should have felt at the time but had, he now realised, banished to some dark corner of his mind.

'What's the matter, brother? Are you ill?'

'No,' he spluttered. 'Sick at heart. I refused his help. The shame of it.'

'And yet here he is, nearly at the gates of Sarmand.' Keung put his hand on Rinzen's shoulder. 'I wonder what he wants?'

'Let's find out.' Rinzen jumped down from the wall into the outer monastery and leapt down the eighty steps in one bound, to be ready to meet Kunchen at the outer gate. The sudden action cleared the burning from his throat but failed to calm his thumping heart. Why was it beating so fast? He wasn't anxious about meeting Kunchen; on the contrary, he welcomed the opportunity to apologise. There was something else, something just out of reach of his consciousness.

Keung landed just as the knocker sounded three times, and Rinzen opened the gate.

As soon as he was face to face with Kunchen, his mind filled with fleeting thoughts, images that flashed before his eyes. It was all he could do to smile at the visitor, and he did manage to join his hands and bow; speaking, however, was impossible. He saw Kunchen's lips move, heard sounds from his mouth, but couldn't make sense of them ... But ... Kunchen's arrival at this exact moment was crucially important. Why?

A sentence from Lawrence's letter flashed: *Your work is too important to fail – there are those in the world who know this and who will help you.* That was also what Adil had said an hour before they boarded the train to Mumbai: 'We will do anything, anything at all, for the Samudran brothers. I mean to say, where would we be without your devotions?' Then an image of Angyo, the monk who'd helped him on the Pawan Express: 'It's more sensible to spend your energy focusing on the solution than worrying about the problem.' No sooner had he taken this in than a clearer, more detailed vision appeared – of Clara playing in Shoreditch; in the background he saw himself and the others in the inner temple, and he could hear clearly *The Harp Awakening.* She had woken him up, helped him to see that he must return to Sarmand, so that he would be here to welcome Kunchen.

Keung was saying something, he couldn't tell what.

Kunchen, the real, present Kunchen, swam into focus before him. He wanted to apologise for his rudeness in not speaking, needed to apologise for his rude response at their first meeting as well, but his mind had taken over from his instincts. It was as if he were underwater or in a cloud as he recalled what he'd said to the young brother at Qo who'd been so envious of his travels: 'It is true that I saw the vastness of the world from the high peaks ... but I realised there is no need to travel to experience the wonders of the world ... we are among the few who can fully experience what it is to be alive, and during our lives there is more to discover within the realm of our sanctuaries than we can ever hope to know.'

The first words he spoke to Kunchen were: 'I did not need to leave Sarmand to find the solution.'

'But if you had not left, would you have become the elder I see before me?'

35

Nepal

Some days later, while Clara was reading in the cloisters, Keung entered and sat next to her.

'Big news. Happy news, I hope,' he said.

Clara grinned at him, expecting some Keung-style trick or joke.

'Your mother has just arrived in Sarmand.'

'What? No, impossible!' She leapt up, heart thumping, and stared at the entrance to the cloisters, expecting to see her, her mind a chaos of images of her mother trekking in the mountains. She ... Impossible. She spun round, glared at Keung. He grinned like an idiot. 'Wait, this is one of your mind games, isn't it?'

He jumped up and bowed, his expression suddenly serious, the pious brother. 'No, Clara, not a joke. She is drinking tea in the dining hall.'

'Are you sure it's her?' Stupid question, which he didn't answer.

'Aren't you happy?'

'Happy?' Was she happy? 'I don't know, it's too surreal to even think about.'

'Perhaps when you see her?'

'Yes, yes, of course, let's go.'

With Keung's help, she manoeuvred the harp along the cobbled paths, nearly toppling it as they hurried along. As soon as she saw Grace, she let go and ran to her, put both arms around her, nestled head to head as she had as a child. 'Hello, Mum. Thanks for coming.' She felt a jolt in Grace's chest and pulled away to check if she was really crying. She wasn't, but her eyes did look red.

'Oh, Clara, how I've missed you.'

'Are those the tears of happiness that Papa never understood?'

'Yes, I suppose they are.' Grace laughed between her sobs, pulled one hand away and wiped her face.

They sat opposite each other at the end of the long middle table, and Clara looked at her. Forgive her! Forgive her! Why won't I forgive her?

All she could think to say was, 'Why did you come, Mum?'

'Your letter was such a shock, I … I straightaway thought I must come, and before I knew it, I'd booked a flight.' Her face looked older, lined, her cheeks and mouth drawn. 'I nearly didn't get on the plane, and then when I got to Kathmandu I almost turned back, but I needed to see you, now that Lawrence is …'

'They gave him an elder's funeral. A great honour.'

'You said. Is there a …'

'Yes, the Well of Life, where all the Samudran ashes reside. I'll ask the brothers if I can take you there.'

'Please forgive me, Clara, even though what I did is unforgivable.'

Clara saw her eyes flick towards the harp. Was that disappointment on her face? After all this time?

All Clara's old anger came surging back in a great whoosh. So much for the weeks and months of calm, so much for the tranquillity of Sarmand and the influence of the brothers' meditative approach to life – all it took was a single look from her mother …

She fetched the harp and pulled it close enough to hold. 'As you see, I'm still holding onto the Lyon & Healy.'

'Yes, I do see. And it's all my fault—'

'I know, that's what you said before.' Clara spat out the words.

'What I mean is, if I hadn't put so much pressure on you when you were young, if I'd encouraged you to do other things besides playing the harp, you'd have other interests, more friends—'

'Is that what you think?' Clara hissed, the anger a hard knot in her stomach, getting tighter. 'You think it was all your doing? Hasn't it occurred to you that I'm the one actually playing the harp, professionally, and quite well, if you haven't noticed. For God's sake, listen for once: *I didn't want to do anything else!*'

'Oh, Clara.' Grace's pale face whitened.

'Why can't you accept that I'm a grown woman, Mum! I'm not *your* little girl any longer. Why can't you trust my judgement and accept that what I do with my life is up to *me – my* decision!'

She had to get away, think about all this. For months she'd convinced herself that she wasn't angry with her mother, that even though she couldn't forgive her, she understood that she'd faked her own death out of love – a moment of insanity, now regretted. But seeing her there, in her beloved Sarmand …

Clara wished she could talk it over with Rinzen, but he'd been called away from Sarmand a couple of days earlier. He'd assured her he'd be back very soon and that Keung would look after her meanwhile. Which he had. But she couldn't talk to Keung about her mum; she needed Rinzen for that.

She stood and looked past Grace. 'I play my harp while the Samudrans meditate. It is why I am here, and I need to start my session in ten minutes. I'll ask Keung to prepare a room for you.'

'Please don't go, Clara.'

Grace stood, and made to hold her hand, but she pulled away.

'I need to think, Mum. Please let me think. It will be late when I finish, so I'll see you in the morning.'

~

Each time Clara played in the inner temple, she was drawn deeper into the brothers' meditation. She had always entered a trance when she played *The Harp Awakening*, but now, instead of floating above a vast, calm ocean as she had when she'd played in her London flat, she entered an unfamiliar world, an immense jungle of tangled sinews that twanged like hyper-sensitive nerves. Above her, below her, all around her, there were streams, oceans, thunderstorms and torrents, sunshine and moonlight, and every imaginable shade of colour floated and trailed in another dimension.

Somewhere in the distance the harp played on.

That night, after playing her allotted eight hours, she lay on her narrow bed with eyes closed and tried not to think about her mother. It would only keep her awake and destroy her sublime mood; she focused on the sound of her own heartbeat and fell into a deep sleep.

It really did feel like she was falling backwards through her eyes. The lamplight that filtered through her eyelids diminished to a dot then vanished to a point before it opened up as a spotlight on the stage of the Wigmore Hall. In all the many variants of the dream, this was the first time she'd seen herself and not just the harp in the spotlight as she played her final solo. There were concentration lines on her forehead, but otherwise her face looked almost ecstatic – was that really what she looked like when she played? Her expression was almost erotic. Perhaps watching her play was an erotic experience. Henry used to say he was turned on by her playing, but she'd taken that with a pinch of salt: he was always saying rude things. God, how embarrassing. What must the rest of the orchestra think of her? She watched herself play the last bars, drop her arms to her sides and then stand to acknowledge the applause.

She let go of the harp to join the conductor at the front of the stage, and in that instant she was inside herself looking out, not watching herself on the screen in her mind. She took another bow, invited the audience to applaud first the conductor, then the orchestra, walked straight through the open door at the back of the stage and into Rinzen's arms. There was no mother in a hospital bed, no throat gurgling as Clara walked away.

When she awoke, she didn't need Matthew Cleary's help to analyse the dream. Its meaning was so obvious, she couldn't believe she hadn't seen it until now. Her mother's death at the moment she left the Wigmore stage symbolised her own inability to let go of her mother, to allow her mother to put herself first after so many years of making Clara her priority. It was not, as she had so stubbornly insisted for almost a year, that her mother would die if she let go of the harp; rather, her mother's dream-death symbolised the death of Clara's reliance on her mother, which was to be welcomed and embraced, not feared and prevented at all costs. What the dream showed was that it was time to let go of her mother – symbolised by letting go of the dream-harp – and free them both from their mutual dependency.

She sat up in bed, swung her legs over the side and looked at the Lyon & Healy. She knew every centimetre of it, every subtle variation in its patina, the idiosyncrasies of each tuning nut, the slight differences in the weight and shape of each pedal. She felt each string's vibration like the synapse of a nerve, each sound as an echo of her heartbeat, and was sure she felt the warmth of the soundbox as though it was one of her own limbs. Yes, the harp was as intimate to her as a limb, or a muscle, and as sensitive – as sensitised – as an erect nipple. She would find it hard to say where she ended and the harp began. In the subdued light from the one small window the harp rested at last, no longer anticipating the call to service by its demanding owner.

The room narrowed to a tunnel as her mind raced through the mad scenes of the past months: the lengths she'd gone to to cling on to the harp; the friends and lover lost; how she had embroiled Gail, Rinzen, Lawrence and Roland in her madness; the pain she had caused her mother, and what it had driven her to do.

The irony was that her actions over the past months had made it impossible for her mother to start having more of her own life. By attaching herself to the harp and withdrawing from the world, she had actually forced her mother to become even more involved – keeping vigil in Fulbright's flat, pulling the Switzerland stunt and embroiling Lawrence in it, leaving food parcels and notes.

And yet... Her mother was not blameless. Far from it. Clara stiffened and stared unblinking at the harp as realisation hit. For a long while she'd convinced herself – and Matthew, for that matter – that she understood her mother's motives for faking her own death. She'd convinced herself that she was keeping her mother out of her life in order to spare her mother the pain of seeing her still attached to the harp. But the truth was, she'd locked her mother out because she was furious with her. Furious with her for having pretended to die. Clara could not forgive her that.

She was seasick at the recollection; each thought brought a new wave of remorse. She grabbed her head with both hands, tried to contain the speeded-up rollercoaster tour of the last turbulent, hysterical year.

All from a dream.

That she thought was an omen.

Thoughts crackled in her swollen head: what if she hadn't met Rinzen, hadn't come to Sarmand? Her mother wouldn't have been able to live freely until she died of old age. She stood up and leaned her back against the cool stone, gazed without focusing at the blank wall opposite. It was such a twisted reality: if she hadn't played in the inner temple, she wouldn't have had the insight to see the dream for what it was; she only played in the temple because she'd met Rinzen; she'd only met Rinzen because she'd reached inside him when she played *The Harp Awakening* at the Wigmore Hall; she'd only played *The Harp Awakening* because she'd had all those months of solitude to compose it; she was only isolated because she'd had a dream that if she let go of the harp her mother would die. And now it turned out that wasn't what the dream meant after all …

She found her mother staring down the Well of Life.

She didn't say hello, just launched straight in. 'I dreamed the dream again. I got its meaning wrong the first – and the second – time.' There, she'd said it. Just like that.

Grace's face lifted; life sparked in her eyes. 'Really? I wondered why the harp wasn't with you but didn't dare ask …' The frown reappeared. 'Or isn't that what you mean?'

'No, you're right. No longer attached.'

As she looked at her mother, then reached for her hands, there was no knot of anger, no resentment. There was just tenderness. How cruel she'd been yesterday, when her mother had travelled across the world to find her. A trickle of sweat shivered down her spine: it was her she'd come for, not Lawrence. God, she hadn't asked her about … Her heart raced, the sweat now itched in her hair. Oh God, oh God, deep breath.

'Tell me, Mum.' She gripped her mother's hands, closed her eyes. 'Any more … health issues?'

When no answer came, she felt the tears start. She opened her eyes and saw Grace smiling at her. Why? Why didn't she just tell her?

'I've had two scans since last April. The first showed the thing had shrunk, and by the second it had disappeared altogether.'

Clara almost fainted on top of her, as if a plug had been pulled from her feet to let all her blood pour out. Grace held her tight, stroked her back, her hair, and said nothing.

Clara led her mum to her and Rinzen's favourite bench. She told her about the Samudran mission, the inner temple, and how they liked her to play *The Harp Awakening* while they meditated.

'Well, *The Harp Awakening* certainly woke me up!' Grace said. 'I've listened to it countless times and many passages still feel fresh, new, as though some magician changes the CD when I'm not looking.' She took a sip of water, seemed to be considering whether to continue. 'That section, after the first adagio, has a very strange effect on me. I don't really know how to put this without sounding daft, but your father actually materialises in the music room, and I ... I talk to him.' She looked at Clara to gauge her reaction, and saw a goofy girl with her mouth hanging open. Grace bowed her head and mumbled.

'What was that, Mum?'

She looked up, straight into Clara's eyes, and Clara saw a look of pure love, unquestioning, non-judgemental love. A mother's love that knew no bounds, had no conditions attached.

'And he talks to me,' Grace said, loud and clear.

'And I forgive you.'

Grace didn't react; it was as though she hadn't heard. 'Sorry, you said something – I was miles away, thinking of your papa.'

'I forgive you. And I'm so sorry I caused you such anguish.'

Tears poured from Grace's eyes and she made no attempt to wipe them away. She reached across, took her daughter's hands, and peered inside her.

There was a light rustle. 'Hello,' Amdong said. Then, 'Forgive me, I have interrupted.'

He made to turn away, but Clara said it wasn't a problem, and introduced him.

'Keung asked me to come, said you would want to see something from the wall.'

~

The brothers had lined up along the top of the monastery wall to welcome Rinzen home. They waved at him and cheered loudly when they saw the thirty Buddhist monks he'd brought back to Sarmand with him. The monks were dressed in their saffron robes and although they were all older than him, and had already walked thirty miles that day, they marched alongside him as though they had just started out. The Samudrans continued cheering and calling out their welcome as the monks passed through the outer gates. The monks had such poise, they seemed to float up the eighty steps, but they still had time to bow and smile at the novices, all of whom were open-mouthed at the sight.

Rinzen caught Clara's eye and his whole body filled with joy; his face broke into a huge grin. With Keung beside him, he stood on the plinth that supported the inner temple building. Keung rang a bell, and the chatter in the courtyard stopped abruptly.

'My brothers, today is a day of joy. These monks, all elders from Budhisera Monastery, have offered to help us with our work. They are already adept at meditation, but they have come to learn the Samudran way, so that together we can keep the earth correctly balanced on its axis, and ensure the health and clarity of her rivers.'

A cheer started from a group of seniors and soon spread to the others.

Keung rang the bell.

'Ten monks will remain with us, while ten will travel with one of us to Barnang, and ten more to Qo.' Rinzen looked up as the sun appeared from behind a cloud. 'Out of disaster, hope is born. The helping hands of our brother monks herald a new era for the Samudrans.'

Another cheer, another short ring of the bell.

'Please welcome Brother Kunchen, who helped me when I most needed it on my way home from Barnang.'

This time Keung allowed the cries of welcome to die down naturally.

'A problem for the Samudrans is a problem for all,' Kunchen said. 'You probably do not realise how much your work is valued by the wider community of brothers and monks, but I can tell you we hold you all in the highest regard, and each one of us would gladly drop whatever it is he is doing to help a Samudran in trouble. And I know the same applies to the laity, to the farmers, the bakers, the teachers, to everyone in your community. Budhisera Monastery is, I am sure, only the first of many monasteries who will switch their priorities to help with your momentous task, and they, like us, will consider it a great honour.

'Rinzen has been kind enough to ask me to be one of the ten to remain in Sarmand, so I hope to get to know you all better and to learn from you over the coming months.'

Kunchen placed his hands together and bowed deeply. After a few moments of silence, he looked up to see every Samudran returning his bow. A broad smile lit his kind face.

~

Before dinner, Rinzen knocked on Clara's door. He had so much to tell her about his journey to Kunchen's monastery, but as soon as he saw her, he opened his arms to her and buried his face in her midnight hair. Mixed with the fragrance of her skin was another aroma; he inhaled deeply and detected tears. So, she had wept profusely, but now her warm breath was even, her heartbeat steady against his chest. They could just stay like this until someone came to tell them it was time to let go, and even then, they could pretend not to hear them. And now that the Buddhists had joined them, he could go with her, travel the world, watch and listen to her play the harp ...

'I dreamed my dream again.' She did not pull away.

'Was it the same?'

'You were in it.'

She held him even closer, shifted her head slightly to fit more perfectly into the crook between his chest and his neck. His shoulder muscles released the last of their tension; he didn't feel inclined to say or do anything but knew she needed to tell him about the dream. Perhaps this time he would be bold enough to tell her his own interpretation. 'Please tell me.'

She pulled back so they were face to face and told him.

When she came to a halt, he nodded but didn't say anything.

'Did you want to say something, Rinzen? I can feel you holding back.'

'Your intuition?'

'I know everything.' Clara's eyes sparkled in the evening light.

'On 1 April last year, the first elder was afflicted by the wasting disease. That was also the day you awoke from your second dream convinced that your mother would die if you let go of your harp.' He saw the surprised look on her face and smiled. 'Ah, so there are some parts of my mind that are still private.'

They both half laughed: he with nervousness about whether he should be telling her this, she probably anxious about where it was going.

'When you first told me about your dream, I thought: she dreamed that Mother Earth was dying, and she has been playing the harp to keep the earth alive ever since, culminating in the creation of *The Harp Awakening* – music that has the power to change everything.'

'But—'

'There's more.'

'OK.'

'Perhaps your dream has more than one meaning? First, to free your own mother, and by so doing, free yourself; second, to ignore everything except your harp, for only by doing that, by deep, sustained concentration, were you able to bring into being music with the power to awaken everyone who hears it.'

'And this new dream, where you are there waiting for me?'

'You love me, as I love you.'

A sound, like a breath held too long then suddenly exhaled, puffed from Clara's mouth. Hadn't he told her that before?

'You love me, the Samudran brother who is destined to spend his life looking after the earth. That is why you found me waiting behind the stage.'

'Waiting to invite me into the inner temple at Sarmand,' she said, vaguely, and tried to grasp what he'd said about the power to awaken everyone who heard *The Harp Awakening*. She focused on his serious face – he really meant it. And the other brothers seemed to be convinced about the value of her music in the inner temple. Maybe ... 'You mean, I should play to anyone who will listen so that they too will find you?'

'To join us in spirit, help us look after the planet.'

She spun round and looked at the harp. 'I no longer need to hold the harp all the time, but I don't want to leave you, Rinzen. I want to hold you forever.'

~

Later, after Clara had introduced Rinzen to Grace, Clara and Rinzen walked away from Sarmand into the hills. They walked upwards for about an hour. The mountain they topped was below the snowline but above the trees; from its summit they could see Sarmand on one side and the string of high white peaks on the other. The wind was cool and constant, blowing hard. They held hands and watched a flight of starlings swoop and dive and finally reunite as one graceful squadron at the edge of their vision, soaring to a speck against the bleached Himalayan sky.

Rinzen turned to face her. 'I did not need to travel across the world to find the solution to our problem, but if I had not done so, had not made the wrong decision, I would never have met you and heard *The Harp Awakening*, never have loved you, never have had you with me to open my eyes to the fact that the solution was right here.'

That 'love' word again. It stunned her for a few moments. She looked at him and wondered if the dreams about making love with him would ever stop.

ACKNOWLEDGEMENTS

My thanks to harpists Audrey Douglas and Hailey Wild, who patiently answered my naive questions and shared what life is like as a professional harpist. I bow down before Catrin Finch, whose transporting music has been the inspiration for all my descriptions of Clara composing and playing: I can't thank her enough. I'm grateful to my writing group, fellow alumni of the Faber Academy – Lesley Kara, Hannah Cox, Susan de Villiers, Richard O'Halloran and Brandon Cheevers – for their encouragement and feedback on early drafts. Thanks also to author Gail Levy for her boundless patience and incisive comments and, together with Andrew Levy, for helping me get the manuscript ready for publication. Special thanks to my editor, Lucy Ridout, without whom I would not have had the courage to publish.

And I'd like to thank my wife Caroline for encouraging and supporting me and, along with Allison Scott-Allan, David Irwin, Robin Cook, Sandy Brownlee, Clive Mills, Lizzie Haylock, Julian Paine, Mike Abrahams and my daughter Alice Howard, for giving me thoughtful feedback on the penultimate draft.

ABOUT THE AUTHOR

Peter Howard is an alumnus of the Faber Academy 'Writing a Novel' course. He lives in Hertfordshire and spends as much time as possible in his writing shed.

Other books include *The Certain Guilt of an Innocent Man*, a political thriller set in West Africa and London, and *The Best Guitarist in the World and Other Tales of the Unexpected*, a short story collection.

To find out more about Peter, to sign-up to his newsletter or order his books, please visit www.peterxhoward.com.

You can connect with Peter on www.facebook.com/peterhowardauthor.

He would be delighted if you sent him an email to peterxhoward@gmail.com